The Wayward Eight:
A Contract to Die For

Robert E. Waters

Zmok Books

For my wife, Elizabeth Kelly Waters. You read everything I write, and you're my first line of defense.

Zmok Books is an imprint of Winged Hussar Publishing, LLC
1525 Hulse Road Unit 1
Point Pleasant, NJ 08742

www.WingedHussarPublishing.com
Twitter: WingHusPubLLC

www.Wildwestexodus.com

Cover by Michael Nigro

ISBN: 978-0-9896926-4-9
LCN: 2014947205

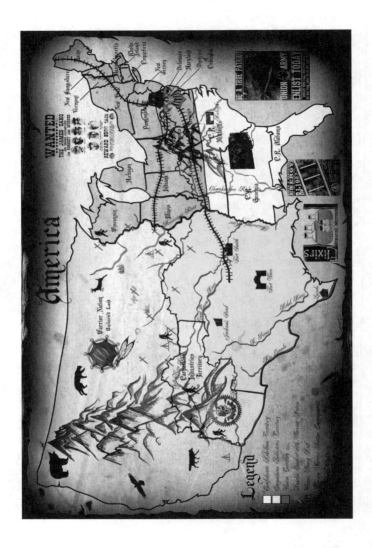

Something Wicked is Coming

Blood drenches the sands of the Wild West as the promise of a new age dies, screaming its last breathe into an uncaring night. An ancient evil has arisen in the western territories, calling countless people with a siren song of technology and promises of power and glory the likes of which the world has never known. Forces move into the deserts, some answering the call, others desperate to destroy the evil before it can end all life on Earth.

Legions of reanimated dead rise to serve the greatest scientific minds of the age, while the native tribes of the plains, now united in desperate self-defense, conjure the powers of the Great Spirit to twist their very flesh into ferocious combat forms to match the terrible new technologies. The armies of the victorious Union rumble into these territories heedless of the destruction they may cause in pursuit of their own purposes, while the legendary outlaws of the old west, now armed with stolen weapons and equipment of their own, seek to carve their names into the tortured flesh of the age. Amidst all this conflict, the long-suffering Lawmen, outgunned and undermanned, stand alone, fighting to protect the innocent men and women caught in the middle . . . or so it appears.

Within these pages you will find information on wild skirmishes and desperate battles in this alternative Wild West world, now ravaged with futuristic weapons and technology. Choose the methodical Enlightened, the savage Warrior Nation, the brutal Union, the deceitful Outlaws, or the enigmatic Lawmen, and lead them into the Wild West to earn your glory.

As you struggle across the deserts and mountains, through the forests and cities of the wildest frontier in history, a hidden power will whisper in your ear at every move. Will your spirit be strong enough to prevail, or will the insidious forces of the Dark Council eventually bend you to their will? Be prepared, for truly, something wicked is coming!

Learn more about the world of the Jesse James Chronicles at:

www.wildwestexodus.com

Prologue

The Ironhide strained under excessive speed. Its heavy bolts and rivets ripped and wrenched against its armored plates as the driver – a half-man half-machine abomination – tried desperately to keep its wheels in the worn ruts of the curving path. The two constructs that guarded eight bound Warrior Nation women in its metal truck bed took rifle shots at the warriors that had given chase. Their energy beasts, aglow with blue spirit energy, kept stride alongside the Enlightened vehicle, and they rammed their thick muscular necks and heads into its sides to set it off balance. Already the iron canopy protecting the cab of the vehicle had been ripped open, exposing the driver to further assault.

Twenty paces ahead rolled another Ironhide, laden with ten young male and female warriors; a few as young as ten years, bound in similar fashion, being guarded by a winged beast of metal and patch-work flesh, human sinew, and strips of black corduroy that hung from its sharp, fibrous arms like flails of burnt fat. Iron Horses and other wheeled, horrible constructs supported this rolling horror.

Walks Looking rode her beast along the left side of the Ironhide that carried the women. She prayed.

She prayed for strength, for speed. She prayed for the women and for the young ones. She prayed that the blue glowing spirit blade in her hand would strike true and deep and let the foul red liquid that fueled these creatures spill forth. She prayed, spurred her horse forward to the Ironhide's cab, and then struck out at the driver through the wrenched visor.

Her blade pierced its chest and red liquid spurted out. She pulled her blade free quickly to keep it and her hands from being sprayed by the burning, acidic fuel. She then punched with the blade again, this time through its throat. The Ironhide lurched forward as if it had hit a stone, its forward firing mini-guns blasting away uncontrollably, its driver convulsing as it bled crimson RJ-1027 across its seat. Walks Looking reached into the cab, grabbed the animation by its shoulder, pulled it through the broken canopy, and let it fall to the ground. The Ironhide's steel-banded wheels ended its convulsions.

She tried jumping into the cab, but her horse was struck by a bullet from one of the constructs in the truck bed. She reached out and grabbed the side of the vehicle before her horse dropped. She dangled against the side as the Ironhide skipped the trail and rolled uncontrollably down the bank and into the valley floor toward the river.

The construct took another shot, but Walks Looking lashed out with her blade and cut its arm in two. She pulled herself up and into the bed. At her feet, eight terrified women lay, their faces bruised and bloody from the construct's attack against their encampment. Walks Looking dodged a shot from one of the monsters, lashed out again with her blade, and took off its head. The headless body lolled in place for a few seconds, then dropped over the side.

That left only one, which she hit with her shoulder and pushed over the side before it could take a clear shot at her head with a Walker Colt bolted into its arm. She kept her balance and turned toward the women.

Their hands and legs were bound. They could not jump to safety without her cutting their restraints, but there was no time for that. So she grabbed one up and hoisted the screaming lady over the side. A tribesman rode up and grabbed the woman. Then another and another, until all but two were removed from the vehicle. Walks Looking then turned toward the cab and peered down the slope. The river was coming on fast. There was no time to flee. She braced herself against the last two women and waited.

The Ironhide hit the river square, tossing her and the women against the back of the cab. Walks Looking groaned as she felt her ribs give under the pressure. Three cracked, but luckily bone did not pierce the skin or a lung. She gritted her teeth and took the pain, waited until the vehicle settled in the water, then pushed the women away.

The Ironhide tilted to the right in the river's strong current. A warrior brought his mount into the shallow of the water, and Walks Looking cut the bindings of the women and fought the current to hand them over.

"You take them to safety," she said to the one accepting the women and helping them up onto his horse. She then turned and walked back into the deep water.

"Where are you going?" the man asked.

"To the other side," she said, her voice agitated and breaking. "I must save the rest."

"Please," he said, his face red with sweat and concern, "take my horse. You cannot reach the bank by yourself. The current is too strong."

"No. Take them to safety. Do not worry about me. Go now!"

She did not wait for his answer. She dove into the water and began swimming to the other side.

It was a strong current. The spring rains had made it so, but she pushed herself forward, despite the pain in her chest from cracked ribs, which forced her to take shorter, harder breaths than she wanted. At times, she allowed the river to carry her. She knew when to rest and when to swim. She knew where on the opposite bank she needed to go. She knew the road that the villainous raiding party traveled, and she knew where the road turned.

Her blindfold was heavy with water and the burning stink of RJ-1027. In the heat of the fight, she hadn't realized that her blindfold had been sprayed with the fuel; holes were forming everywhere. She ripped it off and let the river take it. Her eyes could not see regardless; she had been born blind. That was just fine, she had come to understand. Eyes only showed you what they wanted you to see. She saw better than most people. She not only saw things as they appeared in the physical world by sending out a pulse that echoed the shape of things back to her, but she saw the truths within them. She saw a lot of truths in the fight that she and her men were having with Carpathian's monsters. She saw the truth that if she failed to save these young boys and girls, if that Ironhide reached Doctor Burson Carpathian's territory before it was stopped...

She let that terrifying thought leave her mind as she pulled herself out of the water. Her white buckskin leggings and brown hide boots were soaked, but she ignored the cold and ran up a gentle slope, through a patch of fresh pine trees, and toward the sound of gunfire.

Her men were still fighting. She was proud of them. She had trained them to press on even if she was not present. They were fighting and *dying* for their people; the united

Warrior Nation. And she would now join them again in glorious battle.

Over the ridge line she ran. In the valley below, the rolling fight had broken into three separate skirmishes. Two warriors battled Iron Horses whose drivers had had their torsos bolted into the seats, their legs clearly removed long ago to serve the foreign devil's amusements. Another skirmish saw three of her men in an almost steeple chase with animation riders whose saw-like limbs tried striking out against horse flesh. The third skirmish was the one that she cared about the most.

Two of her men raced alongside the Ironhide, one stabbing the winged beast perched in the vehicle's bed with a spear, the other trying to get close enough to pull the young ones to safety. Walks Looking fixed her sightless eyes upon this struggle, quickened her pace, put her fingers up to her mouth, and blew a short, sharp note. One of her men riding further behind the Ironhide heard it and turned to her. Mid-run, she grabbed his arm as it was offered, pulled herself up behind him, and spurred the horse to action.

She tucked her blade away and grabbed the rider's spear. It was hot with spirit energy, its blue hue deep and inviting. "Run!" she yelled at the horse, giving it a jab with the shaft of the spear. "Show us your power!"

As if it understood, the horse sped forward; Walks Looking tucked the spear under her arm and stood up on the beast's broad back. She supported her weight against the man's shoulders. He helped by reaching back and grabbing one of her legs. He knew what to do, for she had conducted this move with many of them before. She grabbed the spear with both hands and prayed it would work.

The two warriors which had been fighting the flying creature had fallen back, one due to a deep cut across his face. Now, the beast turned toward Walks Looking and screeched like some mad eagle. From its left arm, it waved a sharp, bloody scythe in the air and prepared to take flight.

Walks Looking aimed the spear at the large, red glowing pulse on its forehead, the source of its RJ-1027 supply. She fixed her sight on that orb, raised the spear high, and then launched herself through the air.

The beast was faster. It struck the spear at the tip with the scythe and broke it clean. Walks Looking slammed into its chest, and both toppled over the side of the Ironhide and into the tall grass at the edge of the road.

Down the bank they rolled, one atop the other. The creature smelled of sweat, ash, RJ-1027, and feces, its human flesh sallow and oily, and tender red and puckered at the places where the mechanics of its wings and iron accoutrements had been affixed. Its sharp edges cut into Walk Looking's arms and shoulders. It tried biting her with a mangle of real and silver teeth, but her blue blade was in her hand and stabbing at each snap of its jaw. It tried several times to sink its teeth into her flesh, but each time her strength and reflexes kept it at bay. Then she drove the knife into its rotten nose. It squealed like a dying rabbit, tucked its powerful steel legs up between them, and then shoved her away.

Walks Looking flew through the air. She hit the ground and felt her ribs give further. The pain was near unbearable, but the beast did not give her time to recover. It was on her again, this time pushing its weight into her, trying to claw away her leather blouse, trying to tear her limbs apart. She freed a hand, drew her blade, and severed its right arm which housed a repeater rifle. It screamed and fell back, waving the stump in the air as RJ-1027 pumped out like blood. It tried to recover, tried coming at her again, but its clawed feet were made for grasping and flying, not walking. It moved awkwardly as if it were on stilts. It unfolded its wings and flapped them in quick bursts, forcing itself toward her. She stumbled away, holding the blade back, waiting for the moment to strike out again and perhaps pierce that red orb in its head.

Three arrows buzzed past her and hit its chest.

The beast howled, raised itself up on the steady and powerful beats of its wings, flapped them harder still, and flew toward the setting sun. In seconds, it was gone, disappearing into the dying sunlight.

Walks Looking held her hand tightly against her sore ribs and forced herself to stand. Over the embankment, she heard cheers and shouts of happiness; enough to give her energy and courage. She scaled the embankment and looked south, where the Ironhide had been forced into the grass, its driver ripped from its wheel and hanging out of the side window like torn leather. Warriors circled the iron wagon and howled their joy and shot their rifles into the darkening sky. Walks Looking forced a smile and limped over to her men.

All ten children were safe. Some had suffered a few cuts and bruises. One had a broken wrist, a bloody nose, but otherwise, they were whole. No long term or severe damage on any of them. She breathed a sigh of relief, thanked the Great Spirit, and stepped up to the back of the Ironhide.

Despite the pain in her chest, she helped them down and cut their bindings. They huddled around her for safety, and she cupped each of their faces in turn, kissed them gently on the head, and said prayers with them.

"Thankfully, you are all safe," she said, giving them encouraging smiles and tiny pats on the shoulder. "It is over. The foreign devil's evil beasts are gone. They will not harm you again today. Let us go home and rest beside the fires and tell stories of your bravery and –"

Before she finished speaking, a large shadow of wings covered the ground. She looked up, and down the beast flew, screeching madly, its large metal claws outstretched and diving. She ducked just in time, and the beast swooped into the huddle of young boys and girls and plucked one off the earth like a flower. It soared back into the sky holding the small boy from his shoulders, its long nails locking into his skin and bone. Walks Looking howled and ran after it. She drew her blade and threw it at them, but it fell harmlessly to the ground. Warriors shot arrows and rifles at the rising beast, but soon it could not even be seen. Then it was gone for good, and so too the boy.

She fell to her knees and howled deep sorrow. She struck the ground with her fists and rocked back and forth as a child might when they've lost. She stayed that way until the sun set and the people of the Nation gathered themselves and turned back up the road to return to their encampment. An encampment that they and their parents had made alongside the river to await Walks Looking's arrival. They had been waiting to join her cause, for they, like her, had been unable to connect with their spirit animal, and had refused to live a life as defined by their chiefs. They wanted her wisdom and guidance. She had been late, and they had been attacked.

All my fault…

Finally, she rose and returned to the ruined Ironhide. She fell to the ground and sat with her back against its broken wheel. A mere foot from her face the mangled, monstrous corpse dangled in the light breeze, RJ-1027 dripping like blood from its destroyed face, burning the grass below it. She wanted to touch it, to see if she could feel the energy contained within it, but that would be foolish. It would burn her skin to the bone, corrupt her flesh, and possibly turn her into a horrid beast like the one dangling in death beside her. Or would it?

Perhaps it wasn't the red fluid that was evil. Perhaps it was the men who used it to destroy, to dominate, to kill indiscriminately. The same RJ-1027 that she had seen light harmless lamps was the very same fluid pumping out of this ghastly creature at her side, and also the very same that had put a bullet into her energy beast just a few moments ago. Perhaps her father Sitting Bull, Geronimo, and the other chiefs of the Nation were too quick to judge the wrong villain. Perhaps in the hands of responsible people, like herself and her men, RJ-1027 could become a strength and give the people back their pride and dignity. It wasn't the red fluid that was evil. No. The real villain was Carpathian.

He had come across the sea from Europe. He had brought the red fluid with him, and he was using it to create an army of so-called 'Enlightened' that would, in time, destroy everything in its path. That's what Geronimo and her father believed, and that is what they had told the Nation. So it was constant war… with everything and everyone that used Carpathian's fuel: outlaws, lawmen, Union soldiers, Southern rebels, Enlightened beasts. And for that, the foreign devil had to die; something that she at least agreed upon with her father. "But how?" She asked the dead face that hovered beside her. It did not answer.

There were rumors of Carpathian's impenetrable fortress lying somewhere south, in Arizona, deep inside the Tonto Forest. But where? And how could one get into such a place? It seemed impossible.

Walks Looking heard the rattle of the snake just before it struck.

She reached out with lightning speed and snatched it within an inch of her throat. She held it tightly below its diamond-shaped head. She pulled it up to face her and squeezed until it opened its mouth to reveal long, white fangs. She smiled back. "Not very nice of you, great snake," she said. "Trying to bite a friend."

She believed her spirit animal was the snake. It came to her in dreams, in visions, and yet, she had never been able to connect to it, no matter how much she tried. And here it was still, trying to reach her, to sink its fangs deep into her neck and kill her. She wondered why. She had tried to find the answer to that question, but the Great Spirit never answered.

She rubbed the rattler's back and let it curl itself around her arm. It felt odd and uncomfortable against her skin, unlike any other snake she had held. Its scales were much more coarse than usual, and they shimmered green and blue. She had never known a diamondback with such thick scales and colors. She squeezed harder, and a small drop of poison hung from the left fang. Using her echo sight, she looked deeply into the white droplet and found a shape there.

She saw eight faded figures, near indiscernible through the haze of her vision. They rode 'Horses with many weapons. She tried making out the riders' faces, tried listening to see if any sounds, any echoes of voices, could be heard. Nothing. Just eight riders, strong, determined, unrelenting. Then the image was broken in half by a red hand, raised into the sky as if in worship or in warning; it was hard to know for sure. Then the vision was gone forever.

Walks Looking shook as if chilled. She gripped the snake with both hands and ripped off its head, tossing its limp body away and standing. She pulled the animation's husk from the cab of the Ironhide and flung it over the embankment. She howled and sang. She thanked the dead snake on the ground at her feet.

She was happy, for the vision had given her hope. The eight riders that she had seen in the rattlesnake's poison would come west… and they would bring death and desolation to that foreign devil Doctor Carpathian.

Chapter 1

Captain Marcus Wayward was annoyed. The early spring Kentucky air had cooled, and he had forgotten to wear his thick duster. Sierra Icarus had offered to lend him her blue-black cotton shawl, but he had refused. He wouldn't be caught dead in it, he told her as she snickered at him behind clenched teeth; and besides, they weren't going to be stuck here in this ramshackle barn for very long. But fifteen minutes had turned into thirty; thirty minutes into an hour, and still the people he had agreed to meet had not arrived. That, perhaps, annoyed him more than the cool air filtering through the weak pine slats of the nearby wall. He paced while the rest of his team kept busy.

A bowie knife struck the post near his head, square in the middle, an inch deep. Marcus halted and leaned away from the post. "Goddammit, Jake! You hit me with that thing, I'll kill you."

Jake Mattia chuckled in his low, gruff voice. He walked over and pulled the knife out and pitched it back and forth between his hands. He smiled broadly and made a motion as if he were going to thrust it into Marcus's stomach. Marcus stood like oak, gritting his teeth and trying to maintain his patience. Jake Mattia was the best fighter in the Wayward Eight; as good, perhaps better, than Marcus himself. But this was no time or place for games. He stared bullets at Jake until the impetuous brute put the knife away.

"Sorry, boss," Jake said, rubbing his goatee and looking embarrassed. "I wouldn't strike ya with it for nothing. Just having some fun is all."

"Find something more constructive to do with your time," Marcus said, trying to control his temper.

Jake sighed. "I might, if I knew how long we were going to be here, and *why* we're here. You ever gonna tell us?"

Marcus shook his head. "Sorry, I can't. Not yet. Not until Sun and River arrive." Marcus was annoyed about that as well; they were later than planned.

Jake rubbed his face, and Marcus could see the anxious southerner growing redder by the minute. He leaned in and whispered, "I don't trust her, Marcus. None of us do."

Marcus nodded and put his hand on Jake's shoulder. "I know that. But you know what? I trust her."

He didn't give Jake time to respond, nor was he going to engage in another stale 'discussion' about what he and the 'others' thought of Sun Totem and his sister, Flowing River. They were from the Warrior Nation, true, and perhaps that made some nervous. So be it. They were an important part of the group, and he would wait until they arrived to say what he needed to tell them all.

He pushed past Jake and went over to inspect the vehicles.

Six Blackhoofs, all lined up along the back wall of the barn. They had had these horse-like vehicles for a long time, and it showed. Scrapes and gashes and dents, bullet holes everywhere, rust spots, weak shock absorbers, tricky struts and springs. His specifically had hoof problems and a nasty gash in the RJ-1027 power supply casing. Marcus shook his head, further annoyed by their dishevelment. How could they possibly get anywhere of any distance on these?

He stepped over Hicks Kincade as the mechanic lay between the hind legs of his wife Zarelda's steed. Marcus chuckled and pushed the Blackhoof's leather tail bundle aside. "I guess you're grateful right now that these things ain't real."

Hicks tossed his wrench aside and wriggled himself out from under the machine. Once he cleared the legs, he sat up and carefully pulled off his reinforced steel and canvas gloves, the ones he wore when working on equipment. The RJ on them smoldered, its light red smoke swirling into the air, dissipating quickly. "Don't let them fool you, Captain. They may be made of metal, but they're as real as any flesh and blood horses I've ever met. Each has its own personality, its own fits and starts, its own way of walking and trotting. No two are alike, and one of these days, I swear, those Union scientists will figure out how to make them crap.

"But I tell you true, Marcus, these steeds aren't fit to travel long distances right now. It'd take me two weeks to get them in shape, and I'd need more assistance than we have, and more equipment and resources. Whatever reason we're here, and whatever mission you got planned for us, it better be damn close."

"Watch ya mouth," Zarelda Kincade said from her perch nearby. "Da good Lawd's gonna tan ya for such a foul tongue. And if he don't, I will."

Zarelda Kincade was as tough as nails. She had come to the Eight from the South Carolina coast, where her Root voodoo mother had taught her a deep connection with the spiritual world. She had never been a slave, but her Creole heritage had brought her in contact with the worst sort of people. She left her home and joined Marcus a few years later, where she had met Hicks. She never looked back.

Hicks blew his wife a raspberry.

"You better listen to her," Marcus said. "She's the one with the gun."

All the guns, in fact. She sat in the middle of a pile of rifles, pistols, and shotguns like she was the queen of the mountain. Marcus had asked her to check all their firearms to ensure they were clean and ready for action. Zarelda was not as mechanically inclined as her husband, but she knew weapons, and if she said they were ready, by-God, they were ready.

Kimberly Ann Free, better known as K-Free, appeared from behind one of the Blackhoofs, all smiles and enthusiasm like always. "I got the reins and handlebars tightened as you asked, Hicks. Wanna see?"

They left Zarelda alone and walked through the Blackhoofs to look at K-Free's work. One of the most common failures with these vehicles was their rein and handlebar assemblies. All the riding, the pushing, the prodding, and the yanking on the bars and the reins caused them to perpetually work loose, and in the heat of a chase or a rolling gun fight, a loose handlebar could be the difference between a steady ride or a toss and a broken neck.

"Nice work." Marcus gripped the bars and pulled as hard as he could. "Hicks, this woman's gonna give you a run for your money some—"

Before he finished his sentence, his left knee gave, despite the brace that held it tightly beneath his canvas legging. Hicks and K-Free caught him before he hit the hard barn floor. "Damn!" He winced at the pain.

"Still bothering you, eh?" Hicks asked.

Marcus nodded. It would bother him for the rest of his life, he figured. An old war wound. Got it at Shiloh, first day; thrown from his horse, a real one this time. The knee had hit the ground square and twisted. Trying to catch his fall, he managed to break his left hand. And since Fate is generous, the concussion from a cannon shell exploding near his head knocked out most of the hearing in his left ear. Now it rang on occasion like a hearing fork. The worst of it, though, was the knee. Someday, he hoped to get it fixed. There were ways to repair it, new methods to explore. There was one person in particular who could fix it, and someday perhaps he would. Someday…

"Captain!" Sierra said, waving them forward. She was peering through a hole in the barn door. "They're here."

Marcus walked carefully to the door on his own, favoring his left leg. He looked through the hole. Sun Totem and Flowing River had arrived.

Their Blackhoofs were adorned with eagle feathers and strips of colorful leather which hung from hooks on their flanks. Their imbedded saddles were covered with red and white quilts. Sun Totem himself rode the front Blackhoof. He sat high and tight in the saddle, his eastern clothing clean and well kept. The golden chain which looped across his chest held a Waltham watch tucked into his velvet vest pocket. He did not wear a hat, but his long dark hair was tied into a pony-tail that hung down his back. Marcus shook his head. Sun Totem was unlike any Indian he had ever met.

Flowing River's clothing was less garish. A simple violet dress crimped at the waist by a metal belt that served as moderate protection for her torso. She wore a necklace of wolf claws around her neck and her brown knee-high boots were reinforced with steel shin guards. She looked anxious.

Sierra opened the door, and the two trotted inside. They climbed down, and Marcus greeted them warmly. He shook Sun Totem's hand. "It's nice to see you both again safely. You were delayed longer than I expected."

Sun lowered his head apologetically. "My sister, she was reluctant to come. She's been having powerful visions of late. She was afraid of what you might say; what this mission might be about."

"Yes," Jake said, impatiently folding his arms, "and now that they have arrived, boss, maybe you can tell us why we're here?"

Marcus waited until K-Free and Hicks secured the new horses with the rest. They then circled around their captain and waited.

Marcus cleared his throat. "We, the Wayward Eight, have been invited to accept an important mission, one with national implications. So said the men that invited us here."

"Who were these men?" Sierra asked.

"Union officials approached me three days ago and made an offer."

"Union?" Jake said, disgust growing in his tone. "You want us to work for the Union?"

Marcus nodded. "We're mercenaries, Jake. That's what we do."

"Not for the Union we don't. Not me. I say to hell with those goddamn Yankees!"

"What do dey want?" Zarelda said.

"I'm not sure. They wouldn't give me details. That's why we are here. But I gathered from the reward that they mentioned, they're dead serious about it."

"How much?" Hicks asked. "Those blue-bellies better have deep pockets to get me to fight for them!

Marcus paused, then through a wry smile, he said, "Two hundred thousand. Split eight ways."

"Lawd Almighty," Zarelda said, lowering her atomic repeater, her mouth agape in shock. "Dat's twenty-five thousand each!"

No one else spoke for a long time, not even the loud mouth Mattia. Marcus eyed them carefully, seeing that they were working it out in their minds, trying to decide *what* to say, how to react. Flowing River had sunk to her knees and was etching out a picture of some sort in the barn floor dirt with her ritual blade, humming something to herself.

Sierra shook her head. "Impossible, Captain. No one, not even the Union, would pony up that much money for anything or anyone. It's too good to be true."

Sierra Icarus was the financial officer of the Eight, and she was always concerned about money. She had learned her knack for coins in a saloon and brothel in Arkansas, her mother having died at an early age, and her cowpoke father landing in jail. Sierra had been on her own since sixteen, when she finally had enough and killed her pimp. Marcus and Jake had freed her from jail before the trial, and she had been in their company ever since. She picked up knife and gun play quickly, but her true skills lay with money, knowing instinctively the exact amount to charge any client for any job. If she had concerns, they were worth considering.

"Maybe." Marcus scratched his chin. "But we're here, and we're going to wait and see what they have to say."

They didn't have to wait long. Ten minutes later, an armored wagon with Iron Horse escort arrived.

The armored wagon resembled a Doomsday but without its Gatling guns. Even its firing nest, which usually sat on the top so rifleman could ride along into battle with protection, had been removed and replaced with additional armor plating. It still had entry hatches on its sides, however, obviously to allow occupants to come and go as they pleased, but it had no discernible offensive weaponry whatsoever. It was a roaming tank, almost like a turtle, and its power supply pulsed with RJ-1027 as its thick armored wheels left deep track marks in the soft ground. It moved quieter than Marcus would have imagined; the Iron Horses on its flanks making more noise and disrupting a flock of jaybirds as the machines came to rest about thirty feet from the barn door. Everything stopped. Marcus opened the door and walked out. The rest followed, save for Flowing River who kept working at her drawing.

"These are Pinkerton-men," Jake hissed in Marcus's ear.

Indeed they were. All four Iron Horse drivers were Union agents, dressed in their fine blue-belly uniforms, with Union blaster rifles slung across their backs and fully loaded pistols on their hips. They did not speak, but instead took guard positions around the wagon and waited.

The side hatch on the Doomsday creaked open and then unfolded out into a set of stairs that touched the ground. One of the men who had met with Marcus a few days ago emerged and stepped out. He walked around the wagon twice, inspecting everything, looking into the cluttered ruins of the rest of the buildings on the farmstead, then returned to the stairs. He looked up the steps into the dark wagon and nodded as if he were conveying a silent message to someone inside. He then walked over to Marcus.

The man tipped his hat in greeting and tried to place a sincere smile on his face. He sported a mustache and a brown bola-style hat with goggles atop the brim. He wore the standard blue Union coat. He wasn't carrying a sidearm, unless something was hidden beneath that coat. Marcus thought that a distinct possibility; all these Union goons were shifty at heart. But this was the man he had personally met with already. There was no need for concern.

"Good evening," the man said. "To those of you who do not know me, I am Robert Pinkerton, head of the Pinkerton Secret Service." He stepped aside and motioned to the steps. "Captain Wayward, if you will accompany me inside, we will…"

"Don't do it, boss," Jake said, moving up to stand next to Marcus. "This is a trick. They're here to collect on our bounties."

That certainly was a possibility. Jake had two Union bounties on his head, and perhaps three with that recent incident in Lexington. Marcus had at least one, and the Wayward Eight itself had one or two. He had lost count. Instinctively, he ran his hand down to his holster, sad to remember that his gun was piled in the barn with the rest of their firearms. The only one standing behind him with a weapon was Zarelda, and she wasn't stupid enough to draw it. Jake was not so smart.

Jake pulled his knife. "We'll settle this right now. Ain't no one gonna take you away."

He took one step toward the secret service agent, and every gun in the entourage turned and leveled itself at the impetuous mercenary.

Pinkerton gnashed his teeth but remained calm. "No need for such an abrupt move, Jake Mattia. We are here on good faith, and I can assure you, no harm or arrests will befall Captain Wayward or anyone else tonight. But my client wishes to maintain a certain level of physical anonymity." He turned back to Marcus. "I think you will understand why once you meet him."

"Put the knife away, Jake," Marcus breathed the words, trying to calm the rising tension. "I think we can trust Mr. Pinkerton, tonight at least. Tomorrow… Well, we'll see."

Marcus went to the Doomsday and climbed aboard. Pinkerton followed.

It was roomier inside than he imagined, but the air was a bit stale and aromatic with RJ from light sources imbedded in the iron walls. Nevertheless, he found a seat across a table from a man covered head to toe in a blue Union great coat. The man hid his face with a broad blue hood. He sat there, solid as stone, unmoving. Then he reached up and pushed his hood back. Marcus immediately knew the revealed face.

"Lincoln," Marcus whispered. He couldn't believe his eyes.

The former president of the United States sat as tall and stiff as Marcus had remembered him before the war. Face still gaunt, shallow, but covered handsomely with well-kept black and grey whiskers. His eyes were still keen and thoughtful, and they blazed out from beneath two bushy eyebrows raised slightly in bemusement. Clearly, ol' Abe Lincoln thought his expressions of shock and surprise amusing. Marcus didn't think it funny at all.

"Begging your pardon, sir," Marcus said. "You're supposed to be dead."

Abe Lincoln offered his hand to Marcus. The captain took it reluctantly. "Some days I feel like the dead. But no, change of plans, Captain Wayward. Such a tragic demise was necessary to fake so that I could live on in secret and help fight the war that's coming. And to that end, Captain, let's talk about the future."

Pinkerton, who was sitting beside Abe Lincoln, produced a map and spread it out across the table. He placed a small red glowing lantern on it to keep it well-lit, and then a

few stones at its corners to keep it smooth. The map depicted
the western United States, highlighting disputed borders
between the Warrior Nation, Contested Territories, and points
south. In the southwestern corner of the map was a hastily
sketched outline of a forest. An arrow had been drawn into the
sketch with a large red circle at its tip. A name had been
scribbled beside the circle.

Where have I seen this map before? Marcus
wondered. Then he remembered: River's scribblings on the
barn floor shortly beforehand when they were discussing the
mission. She had hastily sketched out the map with her blade.
How did she know?

"You recognize that name, Captain Wayward?"
Lincoln asked.

Marcus nodded.

"He is why we've asked you and your Eight to meet
us. We're here to discuss the eradication of Doctor Burson
Carpathian."

Marcus raised an eyebrow. "Come again?"

Pinkerton cleared his throat. "We know that
Carpathian's laboratory is here, somewhere in the Tonto
Forest, and we have tried to penetrate that thicket to ascertain
its exact location. We have been unsuccessful, primarily due to
the iron grip that the doctor keeps on it. His so-called animation
patrols are large and powerful. Every attempt so far to get
beyond the edges of the forest has been thwarted. But we
believe that a small and highly skilled group, such as your
mercenaries, can do the job. Your well-known anti-Union
sentiments, plus your standing with the Confederate Rebellion,
will greatly aide in your cover story as you journey west. These
positions will help you travel deep into the Tonto Forest and
find that foreign devil."

"Not only find him, Captain." Abe Lincoln leaned over
the map. "But find him and kill him. Preferably, remove his
head from his body and deliver it to me personally."

Marcus placed his hand on the map and ran his finger
from the Mississippi River to the Tonto Forest. "With respect,
Mr. President, why us?"

"Because you're the best. Everyone agrees with that. The Wayward Eight is the strongest, most skilled mercenary group in America. Perhaps the world. Your reputation precedes you, Captain."

He could not argue with that. Whether it was actually true or not, the reputation of the Wayward Eight was out there. They were good, very good, and when they rode together, there were few who could stop them. He was proud to be their captain.

"Given the nature of your business," Pinkerton said to Marcus, "I don't have to tell you that Doctor Carpathian is a threat, not only to the Union, but to the Confederate states as well, and to the Warrior Nation."

"What does the Union care about the Nation?" Marcus asked, ignoring protocol and courtesy. "Or the Confederacy for that matter."

"I do not represent the Union," Lincoln said, "not specifically. I represent America, and that does indeed encompass the Union, and you're welcome to be unhappy about that if you like. My job is to the country, to its citizenry. A war is coming with Doctor Carpathian and with his Enlightened allies. He's creating an army that will sweep over this land, and no one, not you or me or Robert Pinkerton, or anyone else, will be safe. I'm asking for your help, Captain Marcus Wayward. I'm asking you to set aside your antagonisms toward the Union, toward Washington, and put your country's interests before all else. I'm *asking* for your help."

Marcus had to hand it to the president – or ex-president – or whatever the living dead man was: the old coot still had a flare for drama. There was truth in Lincoln's words. Marcus could not deny that. Dr. Carpathian was a threat, plain and simple. But Lincoln's viewpoint on the matter was clearly his own, concocted from his own perspective, his own personal experiences. What about Marcus's truth? Or Jake's? Or Sun Totem's for that matter? Where did *their* interests lie? Perhaps in time, the Confederate states still in rebellion could work with Carpathian and destroy the Union. Marcus could not deny that that thought was comforting in a way. Jake certainly wouldn't have a problem with that either. And yet, once again, Lincoln had spoken the truth. That 'foreign devil' was a threat, in the here and now, and no amount of 'what if' could change that. If there was one thing that Marcus had learned in all his years, it was this: madmen never change. They stayed mad all their lives.

Pinkerton produced the contract and spread it out on the map. He held it flat with an inkwell and quill at one end and a stack of money at the other. "This is the contract. We ask that you read it and sign it, every one of you. If so, we agree to the sum that we discussed the other day. Two hundred thousand paid in full at the completion of your assignment, that is, the killing of Doctor Burson Carpathian and providing proof of said death, and a pardon of any and all bounties on the Wayward Eight up to the date indicated on the contract. And as a gesture of President Lincoln's goodwill, you may accept this money as a down payment. It is yours, whether you sign the contract or not."

It was clear from his expression that Pinkerton did not like making that last statement, but there was nothing he could do about it. His president was sitting beside him, and it was clear who was in charge of this matter.

"Thank you, sir." Marcus examined the contract and ran a thumb over the money. At least five thousand in cash. "This is a nice gesture. But, before this gets any further, I have to say this. Our rides aren't capable of making that distance. If we're to get all the way to the Industrial Territories, we'll need those refitted in full or new transportation provided. In writing."
Lincoln and Pinkerton discussed the matter across the table. Marcus watched their animated discussion. In the end, Pinkerton scribbled an addendum onto the contract. "Very well," he said, "we will offer you eight new Iron Horses, which will be delivered to you in the morning, assuming all of you sign the contract, and we'll also provide a few additional blasters to supplement your already impressive firepower. Is that acceptable?"

"Yes, that's acceptable. But... I want to discuss this with my team, if you don't mind, before we sign anything. They're putting their lives on the line for you, Mr. Lincoln, a ghost if you'll pardon the expression, and it's something we'll need to discuss together."

"There is no time to waste, Captain." Pinkerton's patience was running out. "We've given you everything you've asked for and more. It was my understanding that you had already accepted –"

Lincoln put his hand on Pinkerton's who promptly shut his mouth. "That will be fine, Captain. You may have an hour to decide. I'll leave one man behind to deliver your decision to me. We will await your word at the train station in Roscoe. Oh, and one more thing, Captain."

Lincoln motioned to Pinkerton who pulled a small square object from beneath his seat. To Marcus, it looked like a red cedar music box, with tiny gears and cranks, push pins and sliders around its body. On the top it had a circular pad, like thin paper. Lincoln accepted it and turned a few cranks, touched a few gears. The box sprang to life in glowing RJ red, and it made a funny buzzing sound.

"Have you seen one of these before?" Lincoln asked. Marcus shook his head. "Not that I recollect."

"It's a vocal reiterator. It's one of a few prototype models that we're testing in the field right now. We'll be using these more and more in the future to communicate with our men across far distances. You will take this one with you, if you decide to accept the mission, and when you find Carpathian's hideout, you will use it to speak to my men and let them know. It's very easy to use. Just turn it on like I did, and talk into the augmenter." He pointed to the circular spot of paper on the top. Lincoln pushed the box over to rest beside the stack of money. Marcus nodded and then grabbed up the map, the money, the contract, and the box. Pinkerton opened the door and gave Marcus room to leave.

Marcus paused at the door. "Sirs, I must apologize for Jake, pulling that knife and all. He's very excitable, and—"

"No need for apologies, Captain." Lincoln was as cool and calm as the moment he had arrived. "That's why I picked you... you and your team. Jake had the courage to pull a knife on a secret service agent, despite insurmountable odds. Foolish, perhaps, but that's the kind of courage I need out there in the west. That's the kind of courage that will bring that European bastard to heel. You have great potential, Captain Wayward. I can see it in your eyes. The question is... do you

have the courage to rise to this great moment in history, to put away your partisan tendencies, and serve the greater good?"
Lincoln winked, nodded, then put his hood back over his head. "Goodbye, Captain Wayward. I look forward to hearing from you soon."

Marcus climbed from the wagon and watched them leave.

"What the hell was that all about, boss?" Jake asked, running a thumb across the blade of his knife.

Marcus handed the money to Sierra. "They want to hire us for a job."

"What job?" Jake asked.

"He wants us to kill Doctor Burson Carpathian."

"Who wants us to kill him?"

Marcus turned to face them all, a calm yet serious expression on his face. "The President Abraham Lincoln."

****

"I don't trust them," Pinkerton said as he rode the Doomsday with Abe Lincoln toward Roscoe in the dark of night.

"They seem like a decent sort." Lincoln was flipping through the pages of a hardback of Greek tragedies.

"Decent? That Mattia fellow pulled a knife on me, sir. And judging from Wayward's hostile response when you stated in truth that you serve the entire country, including the Warrior Nation, I wouldn't turn my back on him."

Abe shook his head. "I'm certain Captain Wayward will keep them all in line and focused on the mission, including himself."

"I'm not so sure. They'll steal that money, sir, plain as day. We shouldn't have given it to them."

"Perhaps, but it's a small price to pay for their attention, wouldn't you say? And I think they *will* accept. Marcus Wayward is an ambitious man. He wants to make a name for himself before he dies."

Pinkerton seemed to grow frustrated. He leaned forward to try to catch all of Lincoln's attention. "Sir, with respect. It's too big a job for such a small team. It's been tried before – *we've* tried before – with larger forces. Carpathian will not fall at the hands of eight simple mercenaries."

Lincoln closed his book. Oh, if only this move against the doctor could unfold as a Greek tragedy, as Aristotle had defined in his three unities: of action, of place, and of time. There should be one action that the play should follow. The play should cover only one physical space. The play should encompass no more than twenty-four hours, one single day. None of these unifying factors would be part of this mission against the Enlightened. It would certainly take more than twenty-four hours. It would encompass many, many spaces. And there would be multiple sub-plots and twists and turns along the way. That's how real life evolved. Lincoln was not stupid. He knew all this. And just like a good card player, he always had an ace up the sleeve. "Get out the chess board."

"Sir?"

"The board. Get it out, and set up the white pieces."

Pinkerton did as he was told, put the chess board between them, and set it up as directed. When finished, Lincoln turned the board until the white pieces were on his side.

"Sixteen pieces comprise an army, correct? The front eight are pawns." He moved a few of them forward. "Their job is to ensure that lanes are opened for the pieces behind them to conduct deep strikes. Their job is also to block the movement of their opponent's pieces. But," he said, moving one of the pawns to the last row across the board, "if lucky, one or more pawns can get through the opponent's defenses and become a queen, with all the power and privileges entailed to that piece. Understand?"

Pinkerton looked at the board and nodded. "So, you are hoping that at least one of the Wayward Eight will finish the job."

"No, Robert. I'm saying that in the game of chess, I never rely entirely on my pawns. Their responsibility is to create opportunities for the *other* pieces. And die if necessary for their player to ensure that his other pieces catch the king."

Pinkerton had nothing further to say. Lincoln tipped over the eight pawns one by one, leaned back in his seat, and opened his book once again. "We'll be meeting some of those other pieces in Roscoe, two in fact. And they, my friend, will ensure that this tragedy that we have put into motion plays out the way that I want it to."

Chapter 2

Sun Totem stood beside his sister and listened to the arguments, silently weighing the options of Abe Lincoln's offer. He eyed the contract that lay on the makeshift table they had constructed in the middle of the barn. He eyed the large map lying beneath it. He studied carefully the expressions on everyone's faces. There was no consensus in the room, and his heart was heavy.

"I don't trust him." Sierra accepted her checked and cleaned atomic pistol from Zarelda. "If he's willing to deceive the entire country with his death, what will keep him from deceiving us?"

"Not a damn thing," Jake said, pulling his rifle from Zarelda's hands, perhaps a little too forcefully. It was clear to Sun Totem that the brawler's blood was up, as was often the case. Sun Totem also saw fear behind those dark eyes. Being told that Abe Lincoln was still alive had spooked Jake beyond what he was willing to admit, and he was covering that fear with anger. "I say we take the money and go. That's a lot of loot, Marcus. We can live high on the hog, at least for a little while. Ain't no reason to put our necks out for a damn Yankee president who's supposed to be dead."

Marcus cleared his throat. "I don't know all the particulars behind why Lincoln faked his death, but it's pretty clear to me that he is providing a service vital to the country. I trust the Union about as much as you do, Jake, but remember, Lincoln told me himself that he does not serve the Union specifically. I take that to mean that he serves a higher cause."

"Shoot, boss," Jake kicked a wooden barrel angrily as he balled hands on hips. "He was probably lying to you. Like Sierra said, he can't be trusted. I don't care what he says with his Pinkerton boys around him, he works for the Union plain and simple."

Marcus let an exasperated sigh flair out his nostrils as he tried to work through Jake's anger. "Alright, what's your opinion on this, Hicks?"

Sun Totem liked Hicks Kincade. A fine mechanic and a great shot. Hicks was from Boston, born from sophistication and finery, though he had found that lifestyle a little too clutched and suffocating for his own aspirations, which is what compelled him to leave and join the Eight. He also lacked that large chip on his shoulder for the Union that Jake carried on his all the time. One could have a conversation with Hicks that did not boil down to a rant against the 'blue-bellies', or the 'damn Yankees', or whatever other obscenities Jake or Sierra or even Marcus himself were prone to use.

"It would be a dangerous mission," Hicks said, rubbing his hands with a dirty brown rag and giving Zarelda a metal spring to take back to where the Blackhoofs were stationed. "Zarelda and I are for it. The reward money is too great to refuse, plus acquiring new 'Horses? The prestige of such a job, if we can pull it off, would be tremendous as well. We say go."

"I'll say again, Marcus, the money is what concerns me the most." Sierra pointed to Lincoln's advance payment she had set before them on the map. "This advance plus two hundred thousand on completion? That's a fortune. They could raise an entire army with that amount and attack Carpathian on their own."

Marcus nodded. "Yes, they could, but then they'd have to get it west. Heavy rail goes only so far into the Contested Territories, Sierra, and then they'd have to disembark and march the rest of the way, with a vulnerable wagon-train miles long behind it. They wouldn't be able to take one step without the Warrior Nation on their heels; outlaws, banditos, not to mention Carpathian's living dead things. If they're lucky, they'd lose only a quarter of their men from death and desertion by the time they reached the Tonto Forest. And then they'd have to find it. After all that, they'd probably break against whatever defenses Carpathian has in store for them, since such a large force moving in strength would undoubtedly alert him far in advance. It would be a disaster. But," he said, taking out his own knife and stabbing it into the map where the forest lay, "like Pinkerton said, a small group like us, with the resources and firepower and reputation that we have, *could* get in there and kill him. We could cut the head off that snake. We cut off the head… and the body dies."

Sun Totem felt Flowing River shiver beneath his hand. He rubbed her back warmly, trying to help keep up her strength and spirit. She had been having visions of late, and nightmares, strong ones that had kept her awake, tired and unfocused. Ever since Marcus had invited everyone to this barn, she had been inconstant and anxious.

"Kimberly, what's your opinion?"

K-Free holstered her pistol and stepped up next to Marcus, where she glanced at the map. "It's a risk, Marcus, but I'm in. If you think that we have a good chance to succeed, then I say we go."

Sun Totem didn't know much about Kimberly Free. She was the newest member of the Eight, and he had only gone on one mission with her. She was competent, no doubt about that; a good mechanic herself and a decent shot. She had served them well in Lexington, but she still had that sense of wonder about being a member, what one of Sun Totem's teachers would have called, 'her blissful awe of the new.' She was still ingratiating herself to Marcus. If he asked her to jump off a cliff, she would do it just for the honor of having followed his order.

Sun Totem felt the captain's eyes fall upon him next. "And what's your opinion, my friend?"

Sun Totem took his hand off Flowing River's back and walked around the table. He eyed the map carefully, following the outline of the Tonto Forest, remembering that same outline that Flowing River had carved into the barn floor when they had arrived. How she had known what the map would reveal, he did not know. Perhaps her spirit animal told her. What nonsense! There was no such thing as spirit animals, or the Great Spirit for that matter.

"I say we go." He leaned over the map and let his hand brush over its coarse fabric. "I do not trust the Union, or Lincoln. I do not think that they have anyone's best interests in mind, except their own. However, the threat that that foreign devil poses to the Nation is too great to deny. My people are in grave danger because of this man. His death will bring them comfort."

"You told us many times, Sun Totem," Zarelda said, returning to the group from the steeds and carrying more weapons to hand out, "dat you hate the Nation."

Besides Jake, Zarelda Kincade was the best shot in the Eight, but her religious fervor sometimes got the best of her. Many a times had she given Sun Totem an earful for his heathen lack of faith in the creator and in his own people.

"No, that is not true." Sun Totem shook his head. "I do not hate the Nation. I hate those that lead it. Geronimo, Sitting Bull, White Tail, Spirit Walker... all the rest. Liars and witch doctors, controlling the people by telling them of the Great Spirit. There is no such thing, nor are there spirit animals. All lies. These witch doctors use RJ to do their transformations, and they hide this truth by publically railing against it. But I know their game, their agenda. I would be happy to see all of them go the same way Carpathian must go. But the people, the innocent women and children, the tribesman that toil sun to sun making a life for their families and neighbors, they have suffered tremendously under this perpetual war that the chiefs have declared against everyone. It cannot be sustained, and it must end. And the first step toward that will be Carpathian's death. I say we go. We go now, and we strike him hard."

"Well," Jake said, eyeing Flowing River across the table, "what does your sister have to say about it?"

"Shut up, Jake." Marcus's brows dipped heavily in annoyance. "That's a low blow. You know she can't talk."

"No, but she can make that sign language that she does, and her book-learned brother can translate for us. You've asked everyone else their opinion, boss. It's only fair that we hear from River as well."

"Yes," Sun Totem said before Marcus had a chance to respond. "You should ask her personally, Jake. Speak to her like a human being and ask for her opinion."

All eyes fell on Jake Mattia, whose smug attempt at causing trouble had been thrown back into his face. He cleared his throat, and said, "Fine." He looked straight at Flowing River. "What's your opinion, River, of this fool's errand? Do you want to have us traipsing all over creation and get us all killed, including your brother, or do you think we should just snatch up that money right there and leave?"

Sun Totem wished that his sister could speak. That would have made their lives easier over the many long years they had lived on their own outside the Nation. But she had been born without a tongue, and many in the Nation were afraid of her; marked, they said, by evil. Even their parents had believed it. So she had created a kind of sign language that only Sun Totem and scarce others could understand. It was relatively easy to grasp once you got the hang of it, but speech was ideal. There was nothing he could do about it. She was who she was, and he loved her. She was the only family he had left.

Her answer to Jake was simple. She smiled at him, despite his hostile question. She moved slowly and sleekly around the table, undulating like a snake, humming a gentle song that she had learned as a child. Walks Looking had told Sun Totem once that Flowing River's spirit animal was the snake, just like her own. Ridiculous, of course, but River seemed intent on trying to free that spirit, to bring it forward and let it thrive. She moved and turned and twisted, keeping her eyes on Jake all the while, until she reached the contract. She took the quill in her hand, dipped it into the ink, and wrote her name in big flowing letters across the bottom. She then returned to her side of the table and continued humming.

In a show of support, Sun Totem followed her and signed his name below. He handed the quill to Marcus.

"Who's next?" Marcus asked, holding it up and waiting.

Hicks and Zarelda came up and signed quickly, followed by K-Free. Sierra hesitated, gnashed her teeth, shook her head, but signed it in the end.

"Jake?"

Jake stood there like stone, arms folded across his chest. "It's a mistake, boss. A big one."

"We're mercenaries, Jake." Marcus held the quill out to him. "This is our business. And as mercenaries, we always have the option to switch sides if things go south. We've done it before; we can do it again. We're the Wayward Eight. We're the best. Or are you no longer a member? Should we be known as the Wayward Seven instead, Jake?"

Sun Totem watched the two men as they stared nails at each other. He wondered how long they could go on like that, neither one wanting to give ground. Jake was the first to blink.

"Whatever you say, boss." He took the quill, dipped it, and scribbled his name across the paper. He held the quill at the end of his name and let the ink soak through the paper, leaving a large black spot on the map below. He threw the quill down, grunted, and stalked out of the barn.

Everyone else went back to what they were doing, and Marcus took the quill and signed his own name last. Then he motioned Sun over to him and they had a brief, quiet conversation alone.

"Did you bring your new ion pistol?"

"Yes, Captain." Sun nodded. He drew it from inside his vest, and handed it to Marcus who hefted it in his hand as if it were a toy. It wasn't by a stretch, but it certainly was smaller than other pistols, and far lighter.

"Did you test it?"

"Oh, yes. It works very nicely. It should come in handy during the mission—"

"No, I don't want you using it on the mission, understood? We'll give you one of the blasters that I negotiated for instead for the day-to-day work."

"Very well. But why?"

Marcus leaned in and whispered, "Because I don't want anyone knowing you have it. It's relatively new technology, and it won't hurt for us to have a few secrets as we go forward. So, keep it secure for the trip, and don't take it out. Don't show it to anyone; we won't use it, until we *must* use it. And if and when I ask you for it, give it to me. Understood?"

Sun accepted the pistol back and nodded. Marcus turned to the contract, but Sun grabbed the sleeve of his coat. "Marcus, I'm worried about Jake. He's not himself."

Marcus shook his head. "He's always ornery like that."

"Yes, but there's something more. He's afraid. I've never seen him like this."

"Well." Marcus slid the money aside to pick up the contract. "Whatever's ailing him, he better get over it quick. This is gonna to be a tough mission. We're gonna need everyone at their best, and we'll definitely need his unique spirit and skills to prevail."

Jake Mattia walked out into the cool Kentucky air and cursed. He cursed himself, cursed Marcus, Sun Totem, and even Flowing River. He breathed deeply and rubbed his face to try to calm down. It wasn't working.

Why am I so unsettled?

The mission was certainly dangerous, but they had gone on dangerous missions before. Perhaps not quite this deadly, but nobody could tell him that the mission into Virginia six months back, or the most recent one in Lexington, had been easy. Not a bit. So why was this mission giving him fits?

"Lincoln." He didn't realize that he had said the name out loud until he said it twice. That traitorous swine, showing up alive, then not having the courage to prove it by revealing himself to everyone. Only Marcus was worthy to see him. Who the hell does Lincoln think he is? "I should have gone on that wagon myself," he whispered, walking up to the fence that lined the road to the barn. "I would have sunk my blade right into his throat."

Another thing that upset him was Marcus's quick agreement to the deal, taking ol' Abe at his word without a second thought. The ex-president was a lying sot. He wasn't working for no higher purpose, nor was there any big war in the future, unless it was the Confederacy knocking the tar out of the Yankees. He was working for the Union, undercover maybe, but they were all the same. The Pinkertons, their president Andy Johnson, the Union army, General Grant, Sherman, Tesla... all blue-bellies. So if the Eight took this job, they were working for the Union, plain and simple. And Jake had vowed never, ever to work for the Union.

And Flowing River plain scared him. She was a hell of a fighter, he couldn't deny that, but she was 'touched' as her people might say; born without a tongue. Prone to fits, always lurching around, huddling, humming. She'd be an impediment on such a long and difficult trail. And that northern educated brother of hers. *I'd like to put my hands around that chicken neck and...*

"Nice evening, isn't it?"

Jake turned and drew one of his Grandfather pistols. Behind him stood the agent that Lincoln had left behind for the signed contract. "Damn, son." Jake breathed deeply, uncocking his pistol, and tucking it away. "You near got your head shot off."

The man put up his hands and smiled. "My apologies. Just thought I'd come over and chat. It's a nice night, don't you think? A little cold, but a clear sky. Got a light?"

Jake shook his head as he watched the man draw a cigar from his pocket. "Sorry, I don't smoke."

The man shrugged and tucked the cigar away. "A bad habit anyway." He gestured to the barn. "Tough decision, eh?"

Jake didn't understand what he meant at first, then said, "Yeah, I guess so."

"You going to accept Mr. Lincoln's offer?"

"Looks like it." Jake turned and put his arms over the fence, letting it support his weight on the snake railing.

"Don't you worry none. Abe's an honest broker. He'll keep his word."

Jake huffed and spit into the knee-high weeds at the base of the fence. "No offense to you, *sir*, but I don't hold much stock in anything a Union official says."

The man chuckled and leaned into the fence beside Jake. "Well, it's good to know that the Wayward Eight will be riding west to take out that son of a bitch. And it's good that you will be riding with them, keeping your captain protected."

Jake was about to nod agreement, when the weight of the words hit him. "Wait, what? What are you talking about? The boss is the best fighter we got. He don't need my protection."

"Oh, I think he does." The man touched Jake's arm, and Jake turned to look at him.

His eyes were dark with a tinge of blood red. They did not seem real. Jake was about to pull back, but he felt a sharp pain behind his forehead. The man kept a strong grip on Jake's arm. "Didn't you see how quick that Injin girl and her brother signed that contract?"

"How… How the hell'd you know they—"

"And why were they late arriving? Hmm? They got someplace better to be than where their captain tells them to be? They were planning their move, that's what they were doing. Shoot, I'm figuring that they'll strike somewhere across the Mississippi. Fort Smith, perhaps."

The pain in his head grew sharper, more acute. Jake rubbed his temple. "What are you talking about?"

"They ain't nothing but no good Injins, Jake. And they mean to kill your boss and take over the group. Don't you see it?"

He did indeed see it, in those dark red eyes, the whole thing unfolding before him. His heart raced. His breath short and harsh. His temples pounded. "Yes, I... do see it..."

"But you can save him, Jake. All you got to do is watch his back, and yours, and when the moment comes, you strike them first. Kill those snakes before they kill your boss."

The barn door opened, and Marcus stepped out, the contract in his hand, rolled up and tied with leather cord. Jake turned abruptly and greeted him. "Boss, what you doing out here?"

"Giving him the contract," Marcus said. "What do you think?"

His headache gone, Jake turned back to the Pinkerton man. His eyes were normal again, white and pleasant. He was smiling. He took the contract and nodded politely. "Thank you, sir. I will hand this to Mr. Lincoln personally."

"You do that. And tell him that we will wait here till dawn for a certified copy, and for our new 'Horses. We don't move until they're delivered. Understand?"

"I understand, sir." The man nodded again, turned, and mounted his Iron Horse. He disappeared quickly down the road.

Jake stood there, his heart still racing, his face wet with sweat and white as a sheet. "Are you okay, Jake?" It took Jake a few moments before the words sunk in and he realized it was Marcus speaking to him. "You look like you've seen a ghost."

Had he seen a ghost? What *had* he actually seen in those eyes? Was it real or had he imagined it? He shook his head clear. "I'm fine. No problem. Let's get to it."

Marcus seemed relieved at the change in attitude. "So it looks like being outside here did you some good. You okay with it all now?"

Jake smiled and nodded. "Absolutely, boss. I'm ready to go. Let them blue-bellies and their dead president try to double cross us. I'll see them in the ground before that."

As they headed back to the barn, Jake paused, pulled his pistol and shot a barrel near the door. It shattered and spilled its rancid corn mash across the ground. "And boss, that's what's going to happen to anyone who tries to harm you on this ride. I swear it to the Almighty."

Chapter 3

They rode south on the eastern side of the Mississippi River. They had crossed the Kentucky border and were now in the Midlands, just north of Jackson in the county of Madison. They rode their new Iron Horses, keeping to main roads and trails whenever possible. They had little to fear in this lightly hilled and wooded country. This was Confederate Rebellion territory, and the Eight were well-regarded and respected in these parts.

Marcus knew the country well. Early in the war, he had been part of the Confederate's Army of the West, had fought at Pea Ridge, Shiloh, and Corinth. His wounds at Shiloh had taken him out of action for a while, and due to those injuries, his return saw him billeted to cavalry. He fought bravely at Corinth, and then served under the command of Nathan Bedford Forrest, and then under Sterling Price during his raids into Missouri. Marcus had been born in North Carolina, but Tennessee, Mississippi, Missouri: those states made up his true home. With the war over, the Confederate Rebellion had reshaped the South, and many of the states he remembered, no longer existed. They had simply been absorbed into new and larger states known as C.R. Georgia and the Midlands. He knew the land well, but had never traveled it on Iron Horse.

The powerful machine took a little getting used to. It was like riding a big sled with an iron cow-catcher on the front, but he could appreciate the need for such a weapon moving west. Its speed could not be matched, and its double forward-mounted Gatling guns would serve him well, as would the mini-cannons and rocket pods on the others. Lincoln had given them a nice variety of weapon types to handle any contingency. Tactics would have to be discussed and perfected, but they had plenty of time for that. They would be riding this road for quite a while.

His plan was simple. They would keep to the eastern side of the river and follow it down into C.R. Georgia, then cross the river along the border with the former state of Louisiana, far south of Warrior Nation territory and, quite frankly, from the Union as well. If they tried crossing the river in the C.R. Midlands, they would have had to deal with both right quick. Now, perhaps they would only have to tussle with outlaws and banditos up from Mexico. Marcus was not concerned about either. With the firepower they had, very little could stand in their way.

"I'm not so sure about this plan, Captain," Sun Totem said as they reached Jackson and slowed their Iron Horses at the city limits. "Warrior raiding parties have been known to strike as far south as the Mexican border."

"That's in Contested Territory. C.R. Georgia isn't Contested Territory."

"They've been known to strike there too, Captain. I would not let our guard down."

"We never do, fancy boy," Jake said in jest. He winked as he pulled his Iron Horse up between Marcus and Sun Totem. "Any raiding party that hits the Eight will find my rifle in their gullet."

Jake had warmed up quickly to the mission, once everything had been signed and settled, but had become particularly curt and disrespectful to Sun Totem and Flowing River over the past few days. Marcus had warned him a couple times about it. Jake had shrugged off the warnings and went about his business. It looked as if he was trying to provoke Sun Totem on purpose, and that was not something that Jake wanted to do. Sun Totem might be thinner and physically weaker, he might be east coast educated and intellectual, but no one should ever doubt his fighting skills. Sun Totem was showing great restraint under Jake's goading. Marcus figured it was his sister. Flowing River had a knack for keeping her brother's temper under control.

"Are we stopping here in Jackson for the night?" Hicks asked as they rolled through the town.

Marcus shook his head and spoke loudly over the roar of his engine. "No. I want to get at least another hour toward Memphis before we stop. I know of a good hotel that'll put us up."

"I'd like some time to inspect these 'Horses a little better." Hicks did his best to raise his voice over his own vehicle. "I didn't get a chance to do that in Kentucky. I need to make sure their RJ supply will last us awhile. I'd also like to take a look at that communication box Lincoln stuck us with a little closer and figure it all out."

"Not much further."

Hicks had been put in charge of Lincoln's reiterator for obvious reasons. That seemed to upset K-Free. Marcus could not quite figure out why. Perhaps she was finally coming out of her shell and wanted to take on more responsibility for the team. He made a mental note to think about what that responsibility could be. Everyone in the Eight had their specialty.

What were Sun Totem's and Flowing River's specialties? That was a legitimate question. Certainly, they had firepower and combat experience. They also worked well at night, which would most certainly come into play. Marcus's biggest concern about the strategy that he had devised was their travel time in the south. Southerners didn't take kindly to Yankees on their soil, like K-Free and Hicks. Many of them did not like members of the Warrior Nation either, especially ones educated in New York like Sun Totem. Raiding parties had been known to cross the river and strike into Confederate territory. Not recently, but it had happened in the past. How would they take Sun and River in their midst? So far, at least, everything was working out.

The people of Jackson were friendly, and as the Eight drove by on their Iron Horses, they waved and some even cheered. Just a year ago, they had conducted a mission in Nashville, where a gang of thugs had rode into town and had taken over a bank. The Eight had been hired to root them out. Not a single bandit survived. It had been a thoroughly successful mission, and Sun and River had been a part of that. Apparently, word of that mission had reached all the way to Jackson.

Marcus was glad that no towns this far south employed UR-30 Enforcers for their law duties. A few towns along the Kentucky and C.R. Midlands border used them, but not here, which was a great relief. He didn't want Jake to try to take a pot shot at one in his infinite ability to get into mischief. They could ill afford the delay. The key was to have their travel through this country as quiet and as uneventful as possible.

They passed through Jackson quickly and proceeded toward Memphis. While they had the time, Jake wanted to talk tactics.

"I ain't never been in a fight on one of these things," he said, "but I'm figuring that we go in like a wedge, you know, like we seen them used in other fights during the war. "

Marcus nodded and sidled up next to Jake so they could communicate better. "Yeah, I figure that'll work when we're talking about flat open country, I'm not so sure that'll play well in more hilly terrain, or woodland like we got around here. Do you think it'd be best to put the Gatling guns up front, with the rockets and cannons in support?"

"That's what I'm suggesting, though I don't like the idea of you being in the front, boss. Maybe you should swap 'Horses with Sierra."

Marcus laughed. "I'm not going to swap now. I just got used to this one. I wouldn't worry about it much, Jake. With the kind of firepower this thing's gonna put out, I'd be able to pin any enemy down before I broke off to allow the rest of you to come through."

"A frontal shot ain't what I'm worried about." Jake drifted back a few feet to let Zarelda and K-Free come closer for the conversation. "It's the side shot that worries me. These things ain't protected much on the flank. You could get tore up pretty quick with counter fire."

"Well, dey ain't heavy support, Jake," Zarelda said, in her finest Creole accent, revving her engine and pushing a little ahead. "Dey for fast moving, see? Maybe da best tactic in more difficult terrain is to ride up and dismount, like cavalry does normally. We's got enough weapons on ourselves to do da job on foot anyway."

"But we should use all the firepower we have," K-Free added, anxious to join in. "Isn't that right, Captain?"

Marcus nodded. "Yes, but it all depends upon the situation. Jake's right. On a straight assault, a wedge formation is the best. Strike the target fast and with as much fire as you can. But in this kind of terrain, I think Zarelda has the right of it. Move up and dismount, then use the terrain to provide support. Don't run the risk of having your 'Horse getting bogged down in ditches or streams or on rocks. These things are pretty maneuverable looks like, but not invulnerable."

The conversation on tactics stopped, and there was silence for a long while. Then K-Free asked a question. "What do you think it's going to be like when we get there?"

"Carpathian's?" Marcus shook his head. "I don't have a clue, and frankly, it's a waste of time to speculate. If there's anything I learned in the war, it's not to worry about ground you don't know. The walls of his hideout could be a hundred feet high. They could be made of pure iron. We'll find out when we get there. Too much speculation now might hamper our ability to adjust tactics later. I've seen it happen before."

An hour later, the sun was setting, and a light wind was blowing from the west. An uncomfortable growl ran across Marcus's stomach. Luckily, about a mile ahead lay a small town. He could see the rusty tin roof of the hotel he had mentioned earlier.

"Okay, ladies and gentlemen," he said, bringing his Iron Horse to a stop. The rest pulled up behind him. "There she sits." He pointed to the town. "First person through the gate gets the finest room available and doesn't have to pull guard duty for the 'Horses tonight. Go!"

He punched his wrist into the throttle before he even got the word out. Behind him, Jake was cussing, and he could have sworn Sierra pulled her pistol to fire at his engine, but he didn't care. He was exhausted, and by-God, he was going to sleep all night through.

Before he knew it, however, K-Free and Zarelda were at his sides, bumping his skids and pulling ahead. He bumped back, careful not to get his Iron Horse caught up in theirs. That might cause a wreck, and he could almost hear Hicks giving him an ear full about that. He could be assured that Hicks would cuss him out anyway at the end of the race for pushing their 'Horses too hard before he had had a chance to look them over properly. But it didn't matter. A feather bed was calling his name.

Jake came up to his left and took the lead momentarily as Zarelda, her Iron Horse a little wobbly at full speed, had to fall back. She was out of the running, but K-Free was holding her own well, smiling and laughing, gunning her engines and letting them roar. Marcus pushed the throttle down and focused his attention toward the town square which was coming on fast.

At his right, K-Free inexplicably fell back, replaced by Sun and River on the same horse. *Amazing*, Marcus thought, *the ingenuity of those two*. River had apparently jumped from her 'Horse onto her brother's as soon as the race began. Sun was in the seat; River was draped over the rocket pods, extending her arms forward as if she were diving into a lake. Marcus could hear Jake scream foul from behind, but there was nothing either of them could do. Sun pushed his 'Horse forward, bumping Marcus out of the way and taking the lead. To keep from hitting the white picket fence that surrounded the hotel, Marcus pulled back and let Sun fly though the gate.

The rest slowed their 'Horses and gathered in front of the hotel. Jake was piping mad.

"Bullshit! Total Damn Bullshit!" he said, moving toward Sun, his hands gripped into fists. "You cheated!"

"I did not cheat," Sun said, turning off his 'Horse and climbing down. "The first person through the gate would win. That was the only rule given. We played within the rules. We won."

"You didn't win," Marcus said, putting himself between Jake and Sun. "River won. She was the first person through the gate. A good tactic, my friend, but you came in second. River gets the best bed and the best sleep. You," he said, putting his hand on Sun's shoulder and winking, "get first watch."

Jake began laughing, and Marcus turned to collect his saddle bag and weapons from his Iron Horse. Hicks pulled up behind him and killed his engine. "Ah, Captain," the mechanic said calmly, trying to contain his rage, "may I have a word?" *Here it comes.*

*****

Nikola Tesla loved the practical application of science, and although he was not a violent man by nature, the manner in which his genius had been employed by the Union made him very, very happy. War! That's what General Grant loved;

that's what his superiors desired, and that's what he, a Serbian scientist, had come to America for: to make weapons of war for a federal government being pressured from all over the continent. Just recently he had been holed up at Fort Frederick, under the watchful though burdensome eye of General Custer, helping to stem the incessant wave after wave of warriors from the Nation. Now he stood in the ever-growing heat of a Tennessee spring, ordered here by Grant himself, to once again utilize his scientific prowess, and this time, on a field of battle. Tesla wiped sweat from his brow and smiled as his newest Construct of war was uncrated and readied for action.

"Isn't he marvelous?" Tesla asked Captain Wade, who stood nearby. The Union officer leaned away from the robot as if it was invading his personal space. Tesla ran his hands over the machine's duel lightning repeaters that served as its arms, and gloried in its vibrant blue glow indicting the electrical charge pulsing through its frame. "An absolute wonder of modern science… and it's all mine.

"These repeaters deliver a bolt of fully powered electricity that cooks whatever it strikes; its nose cannon can do the same. And its legs—" he tapped the Construct's iron-pistoned feet, "—can crush a 'Horse. I'll sit right up there in the chassis. I'll be all nice and snug in its electrical tubes and wiring, and I'll have full control of its every move. And tomorrow morning, we will attack those traitors and bring them to heel."

Tesla moved around the Construct, checking gears, pistons, tubes, ensuring that everything was in place, that nothing had been broken or shaken loose from its travel south. Everything seemed in order. "Have the new Shredders been assigned drivers yet?"

Captain Wade nodded. "Yes, sir. They're being tested right now."

Tesla nodded. "Good. Everything is coming together."

General Grant had sent him and a full company of Union soldiers, supported with Rolling Thunders, Iron Horses, Shredders, and Tesla's new Construct, to face an apparent growing threat within the rebellious Confederate territories, and although they were quite a ways from Kentucky, the Union army was concerned that a border crossing in force was imminent. Their orders were simple: crush the threat now before it materialized; and, while they were at it, field test a few new weapons. Tesla was almost giddy with excitement. Rarely, did the Union allow their top scientist to test his own equipment in the field. He was too valuable an asset to risk getting shot, they said. Not this time; this time, General Grant had finally given in.

"I think we're ready to go, Captain," Tesla said, pulling out a handkerchief and rubbing the nose cannon clean. "We'll move at dawn."

Captain Wade cleared his throat. "Sorry, sir, but I'm afraid I have new orders from central command." He produced a piece of paper and read it aloud. "By order of General Grant, we are to hold in place until Captain Freemont arrives with his reserve company. And you, Mr. Tesla, are specifically instructed to stand down and serve as an observer behind the lines, and therefore appoint an officer, or competent soldier within the ranks, to test your Construct."

Tesla snatched the letter from the captain's hands. He read the words twice to ensure he wasn't missing something, or that perhaps the words could be interpreted in another way. But they were as the young officer had read them.

He tore the order to shreds and let the pieces flutter to the ground. This was Tumblety's doing, most certainly. That damned butcher had gotten to someone on Grant's staff and had turned them against this venture. Well, he wasn't going to stand for it. Not this time. No one would test this new creation of his. Only he would sit in its cockpit.

"Garbled in transmission, Captain Wade. We did not receive General Grant's new order properly."

The captain raised an eyebrow. "Sir, you do not have the authority to render such a judgment."

"Look around you, Captain. I *am* this army. Every weapon held by your soldiers. Every wheel and skid beneath your vehicles is mine. Mine! I made them all. You would not be here if it wasn't for me, Captain Wade. I have the authority and the ability to shut it all down. And there's nothing you can do to stop me."

Under the scientist's furious glare, Captain Wade tried to make one final move of regaining control of the situation. "I—I could have you clapped in irons."

Tesla walked forward calmly. With his face mere inches from the captain's wiry beard, he said, "You know that I have very powerful friends in the capital, sir, and those friends will take great offense if I'm harmed or imprisoned in any way. So please don't put yourself into a position where a man like Tumblety, for instance, would be given the opportunity to add you to his planned butcher army for the Union."

Tesla watched Captain Wade work that last statement through his mind. Tesla wondered if the man knew Tumblety and his ruthless, unorthodox scientific methods. Then the captain's eye grew to the size of eagle eggs as enlightenment came.

"No, sir. I wouldn't like that at all."

Tesla nodded and placed his hand on the captain's shoulder. "Wonderful. So I will ask you again, sir. Was General Grant's order garbled in transmission or not?"

"It most certainly was, sir."

"Then get your men prepared. We attack at dawn."

The captain stumbled away to make plans. Tesla watched him leave. Then he turned again to his Construct. He smiled at it as if it were alive. "Well, my friend, tomorrow will be the test. And we'll show them all, Grant, Johnson, all of them, that Nikola Tesla will not be denied his science. This is my army, and I will prove its worth myself."

The faceless Construct stared back at him with flat, unfeeling iron.

*****

Marcus was awakened the next morning by Sierra pounding on his door.

"Captain," she said, "wake up. There's trouble."

The trouble she was referring to was the sound of battle, far in the distance, but clear to Marcus. He had been in enough scraps to recognize the familiar tones and hymns of war.

He threw on his clothes. He buckled on his saber and pistol and opened the door. Sierra was already dressed and ready to ride. "Where's it coming from?" he asked, putting on his steel reinforced boots and dark brown duster.

"Toward the east," she said. "Maybe a mile."

"Any idea what it's about?"

She shook her head. "No, but it's got to be the Union, Marcus. Listen to that electricity."

Through the normal din of muffled gun and cannon fire, he could hear that popping, buzzing sound of electrical current arcing through the air. There was no mistaking it. His heart sank.

"Okay. Gather everyone at the 'Horses."

Sierra went from room to room waking everyone up, rousing them to the distant battle sounds. On her way out, she paid for their stay and for the food they had eaten the night before. The owner of the hotel took her money gladly, then grabbed his hat and let out on foot, fearful of the ruckus that seemed to creep ever closer to the town. Marcus followed her to the Iron Horses that had been placed in stables near the hotel to keep them hidden. There were no civilians in sight.

The Eight gathered around their 'Horses, sleep still present on all of their faces. Marcus fought the down-pull of his eyelids. He forced himself to speak. "Sounds like we've got a skirmish going on."

Through a yawn, Hicks asked, "Who is it?"

Marcus shook his head. "Don't know, but it's modern weaponry."

"Then it's the Union," Jake said, hefting his fire rifle. "We've got to go have a look."

"I agree. We need to see what this is, measure the threat. But let's just have a quick peek. No commitment. We've got our own troubles to treat with. Follow me in single file, low throttle. Understood?"

They mounted their Iron Horses and followed him as directed. About a mile up the road east and through a fallowed cornfield, they parked behind a line of pines and then moved slowly up a ridge line to look down upon the skirmish.

"Holy hell!"

Marcus agreed with Jake's assessment. A small, but powerful Union force of infantry, supported by Shredders, Iron

Horses, and Rolling Thunder heavy tanks, were moving in strength against a Confederate defensive line that had been established along a sunken road. The Confederates had, perhaps, a company-sized unit, a hundred men at best, lined up shoulder to shoulder, using a mix of old Civil War rifles, carbines, and Union blasters that they had obviously poached off dead blue-bellies. In the center of their line, they had a wrecked Iron Horse, clearly incapable of movement, but its mini-cannon could still fire. It was anchored to the ground by heavy oak logs and dried brush that had been piled on top to give it some protection from barrage. The soldier sitting in the seat beneath it all lobbed shells into the oncoming Shredders as best it could, but it did little damage; the narrow vehicle was too slick on the skis that hovered just off the ground.

"They've got a good defensive position and more men," Marcus said, "but they ain't gonna hold for long, especially if that 'Horse gets hit."

"And it will," Jake grit his teeth, his hatred for the Union overbearing. "Ain't nothing gonna hold back those tanks."

"Or dat."

Marcus looked to where Zarelda was pointing. Behind the Union line was a short, squat Construct with bulky arms and legs. Electricity popped across its iron torso. It moved slowly, but deliberately, lifting one mighty foot then another, moving forward like some robotic behemoth. From its arms arched blue current that reached out against the Confederate line and tore away the thin piles of wood slats and logs that had been placed there for protection.

"Is there somebody sitting in it?" K-Free asked, mouth agape.

Marcus pulled his binoculars from their carrying case on his belt and focused in on the electrified blue giant. In its cockpit, he could see coiled tubing that held a passenger firmly in place. He squinted to see if he could make out who it was exactly, but range and static electricity shimmering across the man's face obscured his features. All Marcus could discern was that the man had on a metal skull cap with an attached ocular piece covering his right eye, just above his dark mustache.

From the right flank came a Rebel yell. Marcus turned and saw a small squadron of Blackhoofs charging the front Rolling Thunder, their riders screaming at the top of their lungs. The Rolling Thunder tried to turn its Gatling gun in time, but failed. The front rider threw a sticky, ball-like mass that he held in his hand into the barrels of the Gatling gun. A few seconds later, the substance ignited and exploded, shattering the barrels and forcing the tank to pause momentarily. This victory was short-lived, as the walking beast behind it lashed out with two ropes of electricity and tore the riders from their steeds and left their burnt husks scattered across the battlefield. A minute later, the Rolling Thunder turned its main cannon toward the Confederate line and blew their Iron Horse off the ground.

Marcus and the rest had to duck behind the ridgeline to keep from being showered with shrapnel, broken wood, and dirt that flew nearly a hundred feet into the air.

"They're gonna rout, boss." Jake looked pleadingly at Marcus, hurt and guilt burning through his eyes. "We got to help them."

"We ain't *got* to do anything, Jake," Marcus said, collecting himself from the powerful blast. "We're on our own mission. We don't have time for this."

"If we don't go down there," Sierra said, raising her voice, not caring who heard, "they will sweep up this ridge and enter the town and destroy it. Is that the kind of hospitality we want to leave behind? These are our people, Marcus. They deserve our help."

They were right. He couldn't deny it. It boiled his blood to look at it all, and yet, to go down there, to get involved, meant a delay that they could ill afford. It could also mean death, and *that* they could afford even less. It was one thing to lose a member of the Eight while doing the activities they were hired to do; it was another thing entirely to lose one in a sideshow. But they were right. He could not allow the Union bastards, no matter what their mission was, to come down here and test out new technology on the bodies of his brethren.

"Okay." He sighed reluctantly. "We'll go down there. But we do this my way. You follow my orders to the letter, every one of you. Are we clear?"

They nodded agreement. "Very well." He smiled and put his hand on Jake's shoulder. "Let's go try out those tactics we discussed."

Chapter 4

They rode in wedge formation into the Union right flank, hunched low in their seats as instructed by Marcus to keep their faces protected behind the armored crest jutting up between the handlebars. Jake was in the lead, his Gatling guns whirling madly, followed by K-Free and Marcus himself on the flanks and back slightly. Behind them the rest settled in formation, with Sun and River in the rear, ready to unleash their rockets when given the word.

Marcus laid on the triggers of his twin Gatling guns, with an echoing cry from K-Free's vehicle. Although the Union forces were comprised primarily of vehicles, the infantry dispersed between them began hitting the ground for protection. The Union light support, the Shredders and Iron Horses, tried shifting their focus toward this new threat, but their exposed drivers fell violently to the hail of withering Gatling fire. One Shredder and two Iron Horses smashed to the ground, their drivers ripped from their controls.

Then just like they discussed, Marcus, K-Free, and Jake peeled away and allowed the mini-cannons to move forward and pound the tanks. Powerful shots from Sierra, Hicks, and Zarelda broke the stride of one of the behemoths, but its side Gatling gun returned fire, peppering the ground in front of Hicks and ricocheting off Zarelda's front armor, forcing her to break formation before they had gotten close enough for the kill shot. Sierra kept her focus and put several rounds into the tank's large iron-banded tire. The shot rocked the tank and nearly knocked it over on its left side, but it stopped tilting just in time and came crashing back down. The force of the hit, however, mired it in the soft ground, and it couldn't move; the driver's frantic spinning of its tires only caused it to dig deeper in.

Marcus saw this and raised his hand into the air, shouted, "fire," then pointed at the tank. Together, Sun and River unleashed their rockets. The missiles swirled off their racks, making a long, ear-piercing, banshee-like whistle as they found their mark and exploded. The side of the tank erupted in a cloud of wrenched iron, rivets, bolts, and fire. The passenger was blasted out, his twisted body left smoldering on the ground, after it landed with a sickening squish. The rest of its crew tried desperately to scramble out before being burned to death, only to be gunned down by Sierra as she put rounds from her atomic pistol into their chests.

The sight of the tank burning gave the Confederate troops in their weakened trench line reason to return and pour fire upon the stalled Union advance. The Union troopers who had been pinned from the initial flank assault now tried to return fire, all the while falling slowly back toward the road and trails that they had used to enter the clearing and begin their assault. They were still firmly supported by a Shredder and two Rolling Thunders that were trying to keep the rest of the Eight occupied. Marcus unsheathed his electrical, shimmering sword and swung it to the sides of his Iron Horse, slashing at any blue-belly that tried to turn his gun to shoot. Soldier after bloody soldier fell as the blade of his energized saber cut and electrocuted men where they stood.

Jake swooped in between the two remaining Rolling Thunders to try to steer away from the Shredder that was trying to ram him. Gatling fire from the tanks cut a swath of dirt behind his Iron Horse. Jake didn't seem to mind the danger, as he stood on the sidesteps of his vehicle, one hand on the handlebar, the other working his blazing rifle, setting fire to any blue soldier that came near. There was almost a maniacal madness to Jake's face, a twisted joy that came from seeing flesh peel from skulls as the searing heat from his weapon torched man after man in the Union blue.

K-Free and Sierra were going toe to toe with one of the Union Iron Horses. One soldier from another 'Horse had abandoned his own vehicle and had jumped on Sierra's. She tried to react quickly, realizing the soldier was trying to steer her 'Horse into a tree. Sierra beat him in the head with the butt of her atomic pistol while K-Free ran alongside them, trying to find a chance to shoot the bastard before he could take Sierra down. The active Union Iron Horse was giving her fits, however, bumping her side and attempting shots at her chest. One of the shots must have grazed her, as the front of her orange jump suit was suddenly torn and covered in blood. The wound didn't seem too deep, thankfully; she kept control of her 'Horse and looked for an opportunity to fire.

The Kincades were holding against a group of Union soldiers who had overrun Zarelda's 'Horse. She had been able to get free of their assault with the help of Hicks, who came in and put several down with his blazing shotgun. The husband and wife team were now holding a defensive position behind their stalled vehicles, Zarelda aiming slow and true to put radiated rounds into their assailants with her mini-atomic repeater rifle. The Union bodies literally fell apart against her assault, and those that managed to stay alive were now corrupted with radioactive material and would affect any that they touched.

With all their rockets fired, Sun and River had stopped their 'Horses, dismounted, and were attacking the walker Construct. In the chaos of battle, Marcus had nearly forgotten about it. It had not fired on any of the Eight as they had started their assault, intent on keeping its attention on the Confederate line. Whoever was piloting it had a singularly focused mind Now that it was being attacked, however, it turned and faced its new threat.

Sun was holding back, keeping his 'Horse between him and the arcing electrical current that shot out from the Construct's barrel arms. He had positioned his 'Horse just far enough away to receive minimal scorch damage from the blue current, but still be able to shoot a Union blaster at the driver. The Construct could have moved forward and gotten into range, but River was moving against it — fast. She seemed to be able to anticipate where the electrical shots would hit, jumping from place to place, holding her ritual blade and tomahawk before her as if they were shields. But the arcing light never found her as she moved, step by step, until she rolled across the ground and put herself beneath the legs of the Construct. The man made an angry, barking sound. "Stand still, you savage. Show yourself. Fight like a man!"

Marcus whipped his 'Horse around to try to give her assistance, to pour Gatling fire into the Construct, but a Shredder came beside him and bumped him out of the way. Its driver tried to use its deadly blades to tear a hole into the side of his Iron Horse, but Marcus swerved just in time; a move that almost threw him from his seat. He tried to recover and bumped the Shredder again, taking a long scrape across the right side of his hull. Marcus kept his balance, rose up on determined legs, turned his Iron Horse once again toward his assailant, and lashed out with his saber. The long electrified blade caught the driver by the cuff of his glove and sliced his left hand clean off. The man screamed, jerked the Shredder to the right, and plowed into the Rolling Thunder, exploding on impact and showering the Union troops nearby with lethal RJ-1027. Marcus gunned his engine to try to miss the spray, but caught some of it on his back. He grit his teeth against the pain as tiny droplets of the red fluid burned straight through his duster and scorched his skin. He considered himself lucky though: only a flesh wound and not enough to cause any serious, long term problems.

River had managed to climb atop the Construct and was slashing at the man in its cab. There was an electrical shield around him, and every time she swung her tomahawk, it was repelled with a shower of blue sparks that nearly pushed her off. The man in the Construct had freed his arms and was striking out against her, but he was having difficulty finding purchase. Her body was so fast, so agile that he couldn't put his hands around her in any meaningful way. "Stand still, you slimy cretin!" He said, growing angrier by the minute.

Then River made a mistake. She hesitated a little too long as a spray of blue sparks blinded her for a moment. The Construct was able to get one of its barrel arms underneath her and propel her through the air like a stone from a catapult. River came down hard on the ground twenty feet away.

"River!" Marcus laid on his Gatling triggers, putting every bullet he had left into the Construct. The shield blocked most of it, but the torrent of firepower made the machine fall back, turn, and run.

Seeing their leader bolt, the rest of the Union forces routed. They dispersed immediately, running in all different directions as they were shocked by the crushing defeat.

Invigorated by the Eight's actions, it was now the Confederate forces' turn to give pursuit as they stormed after the remaining Union troopers. Marcus ignored them and rode to River's side, where he found Sun holding her in his arms.

"She's okay, she's okay," Sun said, waving Marcus and Sierra back. "She just got the wind knocked out of her. She'll be fine."

Marcus called everyone in, and they crowded around River and Sun. "Okay," he said, taking a deep, calming breath. "We've given them a chance to retake ground. They should be able to take care of it themselves. Now, let's collect ourselves and get back on the…" He looked around. "Where's Jake? Where's K-Free?"

They all looked around, and then Hicks pointed down the road where the Union soldiers were fleeing. Marcus turned and saw Jake far ahead of the advancing Confederate line. K-Free was close in pursuit.

"Damn!" Marcus spit as he leapt upon his 'Horse.

"We better go after them," Sierra said, "before they get killed."

*****

Jake pulled his goggles from his eyes so that he could better ignore his blinding headache and focus on the Union Construct bounding down the road in front of him. Moving like a giant, the thing didn't seem to care about its own soldiers as it plowed through them, smashing heads and bodies as it ran. Jake fired his Gatlings, cutting a swath through the panicked blue-bellies as they tried jumping out of his way. Some tried firing back, but his Iron Horse was too swift for them to get a good shot.

The Construct was hit by the gunfire. It stopped, turned and fired with both arms and its nose gun. The three lines of deadly electricity shocked the air, and Jake's hair stood on end like a puff ball. It was hard to breathe and he swerved his Iron Horse off the road to dodge the attack. Two arcing shots missed him; the third hit his Iron Horse square in the engine.

The front of his vehicle ripped apart. The rest of it tumbled into the light woods along the road and hit a tree. Jake watched the whole thing occur as he flew through the air in slow motion, having been tossed up and high from his seat. He hit the ground hard and slid beneath dead leaves. When he came up, he felt around for his rifle, but it was gone. He drew both Grandfather pistols and fired them together, popping off shots with each footstep.

"You ain't never gonna come down here and hurt my people again," he spat, accentuating words with each shot. "Never again!"

The Construct's shields had apparently been damaged, for it didn't try to shoot again. Instead, its driver used its arms to block Jake's gunfire. Jake kept himself steady and calm, aiming true to try to find a crease between those brutal guns. He moved closer and closer, until he was close enough to see who the driver was.

"Tesla!"

He gasped and paused in pursuit as he gazed upon the man with black hair and matching mustache and goatee. He had never seen the Union's pet Serbian scientist before, but everyone had heard of the man who had been using electricity for weaponry. He matched the description perfectly, and the Construct he rode only helped to further that. Tesla had removed his skull cap and was working desperately to stay alive.

Click! Click! Jake's pistols were out of ammunition. He cursed, holstered them, and drew his knife. He charged Tesla, giving the Rebel yell, his face wild with sweat and rage. He got five feet from the Construct. Tesla turned the torso, then struck out with a cannon arm, picking Jake off his feet and tossing him through the woods like he had thrown River.

Jake hit the ground and winced at the pain in his back. He tried recovering, but Tesla moved against him, the ground shaking with impact tremors from his Construct's massive feet. Jake scampered back, clawing the ground, pulling himself away. Tesla came up on him quickly, raised a mighty foot, and then brought it down toward Jake's head.

K-Free's 'Horse slammed into Tesla's side.

Both went flying, the 'Horse's skids impaled into the Construct's armor. The ground where they hit was scooped away as if stone claws had scraped the earth. K-Free went over her handlebars and hit Tesla in the shoulder. The Union scientist yelped and tried grabbing her hand as she pointed her blaster toward his forehead. Tesla was too strong for her, however. He batted her arm away, then regained control of his machine and brought it back to its feet. K-Free held onto the Construct's shoulder and took shots as the machine righted itself, but the blaster rounds ricocheted harmlessly away.

Tesla drove the barrel arms of his Construct underneath the impaled 'Horse. He let out two long streams of electricity, which knocked the 'Horse to the ground. The residual shock from the electricity knocked K-Free off as well. She recovered, tried answering with another shot, but had to roll out of the way as her 'Horse erupted into three large pieces while the blue current raced through it and ignited its RJ-1027 supply.

Through the roiling red heat and smoke from the Iron Horse's explosion, Jake regained his feet and tried to join the fight, but it was too late. Tesla had recovered, turned, and let out. He was already fifty yards down the road before Jake could do anything about it.

Marcus and the rest arrived shortly thereafter.

"I had him, boss!" Jake screamed, his face still flush with anger. "I had that bastard right where I wanted—"

Marcus drove a fist across Jake's face, cutting his nose, busting his lip, and knocking him down. "You son of a bitch! I gave you strict instructions not to pursue. Now look what you've done. Two ruined 'Horses and K-Free injured!"

"I'm okay, Captain," K-Free said, standing with Sierra's help.

"I should smack you too, K-Free," he said. "You could have been killed."

"I was trying to save Jake," she said defiantly. "I saw him let out, and I figured he'd get killed if I didn't pursue. No time to discuss it with you."

Marcus shook his head. "You two should know better. I don't give orders to hear myself talk. We've got our own problems to deal with. And now we have injured and two fewer 'Horses. What the hell has gotten into you, Jake?"

Jake stood carefully and accepted a kerchief from Zarelda. He patted the blood below his nose. "I'm sorry, boss. I don't know what happened. Just seeing that monster do all that damage to our people... I just went crazy. Had to kill it. I'm sorry."

Marcus grit his teeth. Jake could see that the boss wanted to say more, but he calmed himself, and said instead, "Can't know for sure if that force was their entire unit or just the vanguard. Can't wait around here to see. We'll let our boys take care of the rest. We need to head out. K-Free, you ride with Sierra. Jake, you're with me."

"I'd rather ride with Hicks," Jake crossed his arms and looked away.

"I don't give a damn what you'd rather do. You're riding with me until we find new 'Horses. Maybe we'll find some in Memphis, but I doubt it. And by the way," he said, climbing into his seat and waiting for Jake to take his position behind him, "I've changed my mind. We're crossing the river in Memphis. We can't afford to ride through C.R. Georgia with the threat of Union soldiers out to get us. I'd rather we cross now and deal with outlaws and whatever else awaits us over there. We ain't losing one more 'Horse to bull-headed behavior. You got any objection to that?"

Marcus looked right at Jake. Jake took his spot behind the captain. "No, Captain. No objection."

"Good, and if I hear one peep out of you before we cross the river, I'm gonna drown you in the Mississippi myself. You hear?"

Jake heard, but said nothing.

*****

Robert 'The Wraith' Gunter held the half-naked, sniveling little cow patty over the balcony of the whorehouse. The man yelped and pleaded for mercy, while the simple folk in the street shuffled away quickly, pretending not to notice.

"I'm giving you mercy," The Wraith said through a half-smoked cigar clenched in his teeth. "I'm giving you an opportunity to fess up and come clean."

"C-come clean about what?" The man's voice wavered as a piece of chipped tooth mixed with gum and blood slipped out of his broken mouth and ran down past his blackened eye.

"I have it on *real* good intelligence that you have been to the Tonto Forest," The Wraith said. "And that you have seen Doctor Carpathian's lair. Is that so?"

The man cackled nervously as if he had heard a dirty joke. "N-no, that ain't true one bit. I ain't never been there in my life."

The Wraith let the man's sweaty wool sock slip a little further, then he clutched the heel and gave it a small twist. The man howled. "Wait! I-I remember now. It kinda went down like this. My family and I, we was in a wagon train heading, you know, to the ocean out west, for gold and such. For a better life."

The Wraith dropped him further. "You fools know that's Warrior Nation territory, don't ya?"

The man quickly replied in hopes of stopping the pain. "Ya-yes, we knew, but had to risk it for the gold. Then one night these monsters came out of the woods and attacked us."

"Monsters?"

The man wiggled as he nodded. "Y-Yes, sir, the most foul things I-I ever did see. Creatures with pale and green sunken faces and eyes – s-so empty – and hollow! Definitely hollow! Hollow as if the devil himself had reached in and ripped out their souls. Half flesh, half machine, guns and saws sticking out of their arm bones and glowing, always glowing with that red stuff. You know the stuff, like you got in your s-shotgun."

The Wraith let him slip a little further. "Go on."

"Well, they kilt most of us, but me and my boy and my wife. This two-headed demon-looking thing grabbed us up and threw us in the back of some wagon, took us south. We rode like that for days, got deep into the forest, and then I had a chance to escape. I took it, promising my wife and son I'd come back for them. That was a long time ago. So, you see, I never did get all the way there."

"Tell me by your best recollection where exactly you were when you escaped. Be specific now."

The man struggled to remember, but he laid it out for The Wraith as best he could. The Wraith finished his cigar while he listened, and then spit it out over the balcony.

"That all?"

The man wiggled. "Yessir, that's all I remember. Honest to God. Say, why don't you let me down from here, and

I can help you find the place? I can take you back to where I was. I'll be your partner. What do you say? No hard feelings on the broken nose and teeth either. It was my fault. I put my face too close to your fist." He cackled again.

"Let you be my partner, eh?" The Wraith considered it, spit out a few flakes of tobacco, and then shook his head. "No thanks. I can handle this one alone."

He let the man fall and listened to him scream all the way down, until his head hit the slats below and cracked like an October pumpkin. The Wraith looked over the balcony and spit again. "And that's for abandoning your wife and child, you sorry son of a bitch."

He straightened his black duster, adjusted his dark colored, broad-brimmed hat, rubbed the stink of the man's feet off his gloves, and then re-entered the room. The buxom lady was still lying on the bed. She had done her job well.

"He won't be returning tonight." The Wraith thumbed back to the balcony. He pulled a few coins from his coat pocket and flipped them onto the mattress. "For your troubles, my dear. Don't spend it all in one place."

She rolled over and rose up on all fours, arching her back invitingly. "What's your hurry, mister? I got all night."

He nodded, smiled, and said, "Good for you, but I don't."

He walked out and took to the stairs and passed a few other ladies who were too afraid to look him in the eye, to which the metal skulls adorning his shoulders, knees, and chest piece probably did not help with. He paid them no mind and walked to the bar.

"You got a bottle of whiskey in this place?"

The bartender produced one quickly, uncorked it and set it on the bar without saying a word. The Wraith took a big swig, then found a table near the stairs leading up to the brothel. He fell into the chair and leaned back until he settled comfortably against the wall, took another big swig, and then started thinking.

He thought about his mission, what Abe Lincoln had said and the money he had offered, what the squirrely little man had told him upstairs. He thought about Doctor Carpathian and his growing army of constructs. Just like the man had said, these so-called 'animated' monsters were the talk everywhere. More rumor and hearsay than anything else, especially here in the Contested Territories where few of these abominations had actually been seen. That didn't mean that the mad European's touch had not extended this far north. Hell, it extended even further, with RJ-1027 being used in nearly every modern technology out there, in weapons and whatnot. Why, the Union itself could barely function without the fuel. They should be *praising* the good doctor instead of wanting his head on a plate. The Wraith didn't care about the politics of the situation, nor any perceived threat from Carpathian as defined by Lincoln and the Pinkertons. He cared about the money, and oh, there was so much of it! So he had accepted the mission gladly. Why wouldn't he? He was The Wraith.

He had gotten his moniker because he was the fastest, meanest mercenary on take. The only one that might even come close was Marcus Wayward, but that ex-Confederate soldier relied on others to do his work. The Wraith relied on nobody but himself. He was the best. The ex-president had been wise to pick him for the job, just as he had been wise to hire him to put down Jesse James. One man with his skills could easily sneak into the Tonto Forest, find that bastard, and cut off his head. That's what The Wraith intended to do.

He took another swig of whiskey and promptly spit it out. He looked into the bottle. The alcohol had turned green, like a swirl of algae on the top of an overgrown watering hole. He started to feel light-headed, nauseous. He blinked and looked deeply into the liquid, and could not believe what he saw.

An image of a barn, Lincoln and his men meeting with a person, many people. Agreements made, contracts signed. And then a blur of Iron Horses riding south, then turning west crossing the Mississippi.

The faces of the blurry images came into view. The Wraith stared at those faces, blinked to make sure he wasn't dreaming. They were as plain as the rising sun.

"Well, what do you know! Looks like I've got some competition."

He grabbed the bottle and took another swig. The whiskey inside was back to normal, no longer green. He took a third and final drink, then set the bottle down gently, got up, tossed a coin to the bartender, then pushed his way through the batwing doors and into the cool night air.

He stopped and reconsidered what he had saw. He wondered if he was dreaming. He shook his head, took his hat off and rubbed his brow. It was nonsense thinking; had to be. He was imagining it, surely he was. A bad bottle. Nothing more. And yet, if what he saw was correct, then Abe Lincoln had tricked him, deceived him. There was nothing he could do about that old man, and it was folly to even consider revenge. No. The contract was signed, the mission had begun. He had to see it through.

But first he had to know if what he saw in the middle of that bottle was true. If so, he would be hard-pressed to finish the job without meeting the Wayward Eight somewhere along the way, and then all hell would break loose. If they were heading, like him, to Carpathian's territory to find and kill him, well then, they had to be stopped. From the image, it was hard to know exactly where they were right now, and the exact route that they would take, but The Wraith knew someone that could help him find them.

He put his hat back on and crossed the street toward his Iron Horse. "I'll learn the truth," he said to himself, lighting up another cigar. "And *if* it's true, I'll kill them sons of bitches before I let them win. *I'm* the only one that's gonna put a bullet in Carpathian's head."

He climbed onto his Iron Horse, gunned the powerful engines, hit the throttle, and shot out of town toward Fort Smith, toward the Medicine Man.

Chapter 5

Sasha Tanner didn't bother letting the ink on the contract dry. He folded it up and tucked it into the pocket of his brand new, silk stitched black duster. The sickly sweet smell of RJ-1027 burning off the waiting train in Richmond Station made his head hurt, and he pulled back from the track and rubbed his nose. The Union official that had brought him the contract from President Johnson thought it funny.

"No need to worry about the smell, Mr. Tanner," he said, smiling as if he had just eaten a canary. "It isn't gonna hurt you."

Sasha pulled his 1860 model Colt Army revolver, opened the cylinder and checked bullets. "I got this off a Union soldier after he forgot to show courtesy." He snapped the cylinder back in place and cocked the hammer. "Haven't used it since, but I'd like to."

The man suddenly got serious. He backed off and put up his hands. "My apologies, Mr. Tanner. Didn't mean any disrespect."

"That's the problem with you Union boys," Sasha said, un-cocking the hammer and putting the gun back in its holster. "You never mean disrespect, but you always give it, especially to us Europeans. As if you're better than we are."

Sasha had come to America many years ago as a journeyman. He had come for the technology, but had stayed for the money and the killing. He found out that he was good at killing, but unfortunately not with a gun. The pistol was just for show. The real lethal weapons lay in his satchel on his back, the blades that he attached to his arms when real fighting needed to be done.

"Now, are you certain that this man you speak of will be at Fort Smith?" Sasha asked.

The Union man nodded. "Yes, sir, guaranteed. The garrison in the fort is watching over him until you get there. He's afraid to speak to us, doesn't trust us. But he has agreed to speak to you if you pay him the money that we've discussed. He claims to know where inside the Tonto Forest Carpathian can be found. If what he says is true, you should be able to locate the bastard and kill him."

Sasha nodded. "I have every intention of doing that."

"Yes, and the president is expecting proof of this, of course. You must present his head, if not his entire corpse, to President Johnson. It's all defined in the contract."

Sasha had read the contract word for word. He never signed anything that he didn't fully understand, and he understood his responsibilities well for this mission. "Sir, with the money the Union is paying me, I'll bring back Carpathian's corpse, his assistant's, any sons and daughters and wives that he may have as well. I'll fill a whole damned boxcar with Enlightened dead."

"That's impressive, sir, but just his corpse will suffice." The man saluted. "Good luck, Mr. Tanner. The president prays for your safety, success, and speedy return."

Sasha half-heartedly saluted back, then pushed past the man and boarded the train. It was a heavy roller, whose final destination was Fort Smith. It would be a long journey, but one Sasha Tanner was looking forward to. At least the first leg of it anyway. A passenger car had been attached to it, and there were a number of lovely high-society ladies in it heading to Kentucky. Sasha entered the car and took a seat near them. The fresh scent of aftershave and witch hazel was still on his smooth face. He tipped his neatly buffed silver-studded *gaucho* toward them, cleared his throat, and said, "Good morning, ladies. I'm Sasha Tanner. Would you like to see my blades?"

*****

Zarelda Kincade took off her riding goggles and rubbed away the grit and grime of the trail from her face. They had crossed the Mississippi in Memphis, as Marcus had decided, having found no new Iron Horses for sale in the city. They could have stolen one, but that wasn't the captain's style. Besides, that would have probably gotten them into another scrape, and he wasn't having any of that. Zarelda wasn't excited about another fight so soon either. They needed a rest and refit already, and Hicks needed time to assess damage and make repairs.

"What is da damage, lover?" she asked Hicks, who was buried underneath Marcus's Iron Horse, trying to dislodge a piece of shrapnel that had gotten wedged between the underbelly and the skid.

"Not too bad," he said, grunting as he struck the wedged piece with a hammer. "If I can just get this thing…"

Three more strikes and it popped out. Hicks breathed a sigh of relief and chucked the piece out for Zarelda to see. "Lawd have mercy," she said, whistling. "I thank God dat didn't hit none of us."

"Indeed." Hicks pushed himself out and stood, wiping dirt from his leggings and removing his gloves. He ran a bare finger across the gash in the Iron Horse's side. "This isn't going to be fixed till I can find some soldering tools and a good piece of iron. And I doubt that little town over there has either."

They had decided to stop for the night outside a small Arkansas town just east of Crowley's Ridge. Most of the land in this area of the state was flat, good for large crops like corn, rice, and wheat. It was early spring, and so all the land lay fallow and soft from winter snow and rain. Marcus liked it that way. Tonight, they would sleep under the stars and be able to see any danger coming toward them and be able to respond quicker than being holed up in a stable or in a hotel, and run the risk of damaging property if such a danger were to occur. Plus, the small town nearby had no hotel or saloon with rooms. It was really nothing more than a few buildings, a livery, a stable, a dry goods store, a church, and a few residentia homes. Nice, but small. There was no reason to disrupt their lives with eight unwelcome mercenaries.

Hicks motioned Zarelda to follow him. "Come," he said in a whisper, "let's check out this communication box."

Sun and River were over by their encampment getting some rest. Marcus, Jake, Sierra, and K-Free had walked to town to see if they could find food, water, information, and hopefully transportation of some kind. One of the fellows that had greeted them as they had passed through the town suggested that he had an old Iron Horse for sale. Hicks had begged off going to see it, not convinced in the least that the trip would prove fruitful. Zarelda could tell that he had refused to go because there was something on his mind, and it wasn't just about a funny-looking box.

She followed him to his 'Horse and he pulled the box free from beneath his bedroll. He placed it on his seat, and they looked at it. A simple cedar box, with a few gears, cranks, gyros, and that funny-looking round spot on the top that Abe Lincoln had said to talk into. Hicks turned it up and down, left and right, moved a couple cranks, pushed a button. It lit up bright red, RJ-1027 pumping through its innards like a glowing jellyfish.

"Come closer," Hicks said, putting his ear up to the round spot. "Take a listen."

Zarelda didn't want to put her head anywhere near it, but she leaned in as far as she was comfortable and listened. Through the odd buzzing sound that the contraption made, she heard a faint voice. Her eyes lit up. "Lawd Almighty, can you hear dat? Somebody be talking on da other end."

She couldn't make out the words, but it was someone. She concentrated harder, covered her right ear so that she could pick up the voice better in her left. It was a man's voice, for sure. But what was he saying?

Hicks turned it off and let the box grow cold and dark. "If we can hear a voice at this end, they can hear ours, can't they?"

Zarelda shrugged. "Sure, but Lincoln did say dat we is supposed to use it to contact him once we find da doctor."
"Yes, but give another listen."

She put her ear to it again. The voice was still there, fainter for sure, but clear enough. "I thought you turned it off."

"I did," he said, tucking it under his bedroll. "But it doesn't turn off. Turning it on just boosts the signal. It's on day and night. What does that tell you?"

"I don't rightly know."

"It tells you that everything we say can be heard by someone on the other end, and I don't trust that it's Lincoln. I'm keeping it tight beneath by bedroll to hopefully muffle our conversations. Marcus made a mistake, Z. He shouldn't have accepted it."

Zarelda put her hands on her hips. "It was part of da contract, and I don't recall you objectin' to it at da meeting."

Hicks shook his head. "I didn't know what it was. Hell, I'm still not too sure, but I know it's not anything good. We should destroy it."

"You do dat, and Marcus will put a boot in your ass." Hicks couldn't help but chuckle at that. "And that's another thing I want to talk to you about, love." He took her hands and guided her over to a quiet, dark place beneath a patch of trees, away from the encampment so that no one could hear. "Marcus isn't running this mission very well. He accepted that box, he's letting Jake act like some wild beast, and we got two Iron Horses destroyed because he couldn't leave well enough alone."

"You agreed to attack dem blue-bellies, same as da rest of us."

Hicks nodded. "Yes, because everyone else was so raring to go, including you. My vote against wouldn't have mattered either way. But we're not even five days out of Kentucky, and already we're limping." He clutched her arms firmly, looked around as if he were worried someone was listening. "It's time, love, for you and me to set a new mission for ourselves."

She pulled back a little, raised her brow. "What you talking about?"

"We've discussed it before, setting out on our own. I'm a mechanic, Z, and there just isn't enough for me to do with this group; fixing an Iron Horse here and there... shoot! It isn't enough. I need to expand my knowledge, you know? Move forward with my skills just like every other professional I've ever met. You too. You want to discover the medicinal purposes of RJ, don't you? And the only way to do that is to get whatever knowledge we can once we get there, assuming we get there. The only person who knows all of this is Doctor Carpathian."

He was right about RJ. They had discussed it before, and she was convinced, like many of the voodoo ladies she had grown up around, that there was medicine in that hot red liquid. The problem was its heat and energy release. How could they get around that and make it consumable or pliable to the skin without burning the patient to death? There was a way, she was certain of it. And the most knowledgeable person in the world that would know how to do it was Carpathian.

"What do you want us to do?"

"Let Marcus and Jake and Sierra and whoever the hell else wants to try to kill that bastard, try and kill him," he said. "That is not our concern. I doubt this mission will succeed. Lord knows what awaits us in that forest. You've heard the rumors like I have. One hundred foot walls of solid rock, a legion of undead soldiers, metal beasts flying through the sky. It's suicide. We'll play along and do what we can to get there, but once we're there, I say we break and go our own way, find things we can steal, blueprints, maps, diagrams. And if we're lucky, we'll find Carpathian before they do, and we can switch sides. Marcus said as much already: if things get too tough, we switch sides. We have an interest in seeing the doctor live, Z, and I don't believe half of what people say about him. He's just a man trying to survive in a crazy world. Just like us. What do you say?"

Zarelda pulled away. She shook her head. "I don't know, Hicks. It don't seem right to turn on Marcus like dat."

"He's already turned on me."

"What you mean?"

"Didn't you hear what he said to me in the barn? He insulted me right in front of K-Free, suggesting that *her* work on the steeds was superior to mine, and right after I had told him it would take me weeks to fix them. I looked like an incompetent fool. He's going to replace me with K-Free, and soon I bet."

"Dat's silly, lover. Marcus has been good to you, to us."

"Come on, Z. I'm your husband. Haven't I also been good to you?"

He had. Hicks Kincade had been the only white man in her entire life to show real desire for her. He did not care about her skin color, or her accent, or her background. He had accepted her for who she was, her skills, her abilities.

But Marcus had as well, though without desire. He had found her in the Midlands shortly after General Sherman had driven his army through the state, raping and burning and pillaging. A squad of his men rushed her grandmother's house. When the first man slammed through the door, Zarelda had grabbed her grandfather's tiny little derringer, aimed carefully, and put a ball right through the man's eye. That was the first time she had ever fired a gun; it was the first time she had ever killed a man. She liked it. Not killing per se, but shooting. She found she was good at it, and she tucked that little pea-shooter away and ran and ran and ran, until she crossed the border. That's when Marcus found her, riding on a mission with Jake and Sierra and Hicks. Marcus saved her, fed her, gave her new clothes and made her a member of the Eight. And now here she was, one of the most feared and respected women in America, and respect was a hard thing for a woman to earn these days.

"Okay, Hicks." She shook her head, admitting defeat. "I'll go along with you. On one condition." She gave him a gentle smack across the face. "You stop all dat cussin'."

Then she looked up in the trees.

There they were, the shape of two black crows in the moonlight, their eyes beaming blood red. Her heart sank as she stared into those eyes. It seemed as if she were being pulled away, her soul ripped from her body, like some voodoo trance. She had been in some of those trances in her days, but this was a different kind of feeling, more sinister, foul. Fear struck her chest and she pulled away, drew one of her atomic pistols and snapped off two quick shots.

The birds squawked loudly and flew away, unhurt.

Hicks dropped to his knees, holding his ears. "Jesus Christ, Z. What the hell are you doing?"

She paused a moment, then holstered her pistol. "Crows, I guess. Nasty looking creatures. Devil eyes. Odd, though. I missed dem. I had dem dead cold, and I never miss at dis range."

****

Marcus sighed when he heard the shots. He shook his head and rubbed his face. "Sierra, go see why Zarelda is shooting in the dark. I can't have five minutes rest without someone causing me grief."

Sierra nodded and let out.

He didn't mean it to refer to Jake, but the impetuous man took it as such. "Hell, boss, how many times have I got to say I'm sorry?"

He waved a hand and said, "No problem, Jake. Let's just see what this fellow has, okay?"

They had found some food and had filled their canteens with water. Now they were waiting at the stables for a man who claimed to have an Iron Horse. When he arrived, Marcus greeted him politely, trying to seem as hospitable as possible. He didn't want the old man to have a spell at the sight of three heavily armed mercenaries outside his place of business.

The man took Marcus's hand wearily. "Name's Pritchard, Seamus Pritchard. You wanna take a look at my Iron Horse?"

"If you got one."

"That I do. Come on."

He guided them into the stable, past a couple real horses. "I only bought this stable a year ago, so I wasn't around when it happened. But the townspeople tell me this band of outlaws come through a few years ago and hit our stores and church, looking for food, collection money, whatnot. They said it was Billy the Kid's men, but who knows for sure? One outlaw don't look much different than another I reckon. Anyway, we got lucky and knocked one from his ride, and they were so anxious to be done and gone, they left it behind. The fellow who owned this place before me hid it back here, afraid I guess that they would come back. They never did. Here it is." He pulled off the gray canvas that covered it.

It was an Iron Horse all right. "It's pretty banged up as you can see, and it leaks RJ."

Marcus could smell it. He walked around, checking its skids, the dry rot of its seat, the rust along its entire frame, the pipes running off its mini-cannon where mice had gnawed through. "Well, what do you think, Kimberly?"

The junior mechanic checked the damage. She shook her head. "Don't know, Captain. She's in rough shape. The biggest problem is the leak. If Hicks and I can get that stopped, we should be able to get her going again, and then get her to a charging station for a full juicing. The rust and the dry rot isn't much of a problem. The cannon, though, might be dangerous."

She looked at its trigger and followed the line of heavy rounds that fed into the weapon from its underbelly. "Looks like it jammed at one point, and the driver never tried fixing it. Probably didn't know how. It's been sitting like that for a long time, Captain. It could blow at any time, and I don't want to be around when it does. If we take it, we're gonna have to remove the gun before we even move it out of this stable."

"How long would that take?" Marcus asked.

K-Free shook her head. "Hicks might be able to tell you."

Hicks *would* know, and why he had begged off coming to see the Iron Horse, Marcus couldn't say. He'd been acting strange all day.

"But like I said, it'll run if we can stop that leak."

Marcus nodded. "Okay, Mr. Pritchard. How much you want for it?"

The old man considered. "Oh, I don't know. It's causing me more trouble than it's worth. I just assume you drag it out of here than pay for it. How about fifty dollars?"

That was a steal, and Marcus could see that the man was afraid of them, wanting them long and gone. He shook his head. "Too low. How about a hundred fifty?"

Pritchard perked right up. "Oh, yes, that'll be just fine, mister. Take it away."

"We'll come back in the morning." Marcus turned to leave.

"Fine, fine." Pritchard led them out of the stable. "And come early enough, I'll have my wife fix you up some biscuts and gravy. Maybe some chicken too."

"That'll be fine. Thank you sir," Marcus said, shaking the man's hand and nodding.

They left the town and returned to the encampment. Sierra and Zarelda were in a shouting match.

"If it had been me," Sierra said, waving her pistol in Zarelda's face. "I'd have hit them."

"You didn't see dem, girl," Zarelda said, pushing the pistol away. "You ain't half da shot I am."

"You care to make a wager?"

"What's going on?" Marcus said, stepping between the two ladies.

Sierra chuckled. "Z here thinks she's a better shot than me. She was shooting at birds, Marcus, and she wasn't much further away from them than you from me. She missed them both. That sounds like pretty bad shooting."

"Dem birds weren't natural, I tell ya," Zarelda said, and Marcus could see the apprehension in her eyes. She was spooked. "Dey had red eyes and dey was as black as black can be. Devil birds."

"You're just mad because you missed them," Sierra said again.

"Okay, you want a wager? I'll give you one. Pick a target," Zarelda said, pulling her pistol. "Here in da dark. I'll hit it before you do."

"Ladies," Marcus said, trying to settle things down. "I don't think this is the time or place to—"

"Here," Sierra said, picking up a canteen from the ground. "We'll shoot at this. Jake, go put this up on that post we passed thirty yards yonder. We'll see who's the best."

Hicks tried to intervene, but Zarelda would have none of it. Jake grabbed up the canteen and headed out into the dark. "Okay," he yelled back. "It's set."

"Back away some," Sierra said. "I'll shoot first."

She waited a minute before raising her pistol. She held it out at arm's length, both hands wrapped around the handle. She aimed slow and steady, then fired. The sound of the round echoed across the flat land. A few seconds later, Jake called, "Miss!"

"Damn!" she spit and stepped back. "Thought I had it."

Zarelda pushed her aside and took her place. "Tough luck, girlie. Now watch dis."

She aimed as well, her arms longer than Sierra's and even steadier. She pulled the trigger, her shot ringing out like the other.

Jake called, "Hit! Right in the middle!"

Zarelda yelped in joy. "I told you I'm da better shot!"

Jake came out of the dark and handed her the canteen. She looked at the massive hole in its center. "See, look here. I—" She paused, flipped the canteen over and over. "Wait… dis is my canteen!"

Everyone, including Hicks, broke out laughing. "Yep, sure is!" Sierra was bent over laughing, "You're the better shot!"

Zarelda wasn't amused, and she balled up her fist, but Marcus came up and grabbed her arm before she had a chance to throw a punch.

"Now, now," he said, "let's not get violent. It's just a bit of fun."

Sierra offered a hand of apology. "That's right, Z. I'm just playing with you. And you proved it: you're the better shot. You can have my canteen if you want."

Zarelda settled down. Marcus let her go. She smiled, though he could tell there was still bitterness behind her dark eyes. "Okay, Sierra," she said, accepted the hand and winking. "Good joke. But I get you back someday, girlie. You wait and see."

Marcus was about to close out the night when Sun appeared. He was sweating, out of breath, his eyes filled with fear, desperation. "What's the matter, Sun?"

"It's River," he said through gasps of air. "She's... She's gone."

Chapter 6

She had a dream, and the dream became real. Or so it felt, calling to her through the hazy uncertainty of sleep. It was her spirit animal, its body undulating across the ground toward her, seemingly unmoving as its cold, smooth scales shifted back and forth to propel it through grass and soft dirt. It came to her and told her to awake, and she did. Then she followed it into the darkness, her arm outstretched and reaching for it. She tried to shift into it, as she had tried hundreds of times in her life. Her hand was just above its tail. She grabbed for it and imagined herself a snake, coiled up beneath a rock, ready to strike. It slipped away, as it always did, and she kept chasing it.

Follow me, it hissed, deep within the recesses of her mind, and she did so, across the cold, wet Arkansas field, away from her brother, away from the camp. *Let me show you something.*

But it had already shown her things that she did not want to see, like the tall man with a beard, the one they called Lincoln. It showed her the Tonto Forest days before they had met the ex-president of the white nation, who was now himself a ghost, dead and yet not dead. And now it wanted to show her something else, and she feared the worst: an image of a death, perhaps, one of her family, her brother maybe or Marcus at the end of this mission that they had agreed to take. Showing her such terrifying images would be punishment for not being good enough, brave or strong enough, to shift. Sun did not believe in the spirits, but she knew the truth. Those worthy were allowed to shift, and Flowing River had not shown her worthiness.

Show me, she said in her mind, and it did.

A large building with concrete walls. A fort with guards in blue, walking the ramparts. Large piles of steel track lay near a train that stood waiting to unload the terrible weapons and soldiers of the Union army. Around the fort were tiny white tents, hundreds of them, all mixed together, some bigger, some smaller. And people, scores of white people, living in those tents, taking comfort and security from the large walls nearby, but scared too, she could see it on their faces. Everything aglow with the red fluid, weapons and lanterns and batteries, vehicles and mighty iron trains. It terrified her, and she tried to turn away.

What is this place? She asked, for the image, though clear and precise, seemed distant, almost foreign. She did not recognize it, did not remember ever seeing it before.

The snake changed the image again, of terrible men waiting for them there at the fort, mindless killers, and she saw her friends, her family, fall, one after the other, in fires ablaze and red acidic bursts. Her heart raced and she stopped following her spirit.

Do not go there, the words flowed numbly through her mind. *Do not go there.*

The snake spirit faded away, and Flowing River stood alone in the middle of a dark field, light from the moon shining down, casting her faint shadow across the fallow rows. She turned left, right, trying to see the light from their camp, the light from the small town they had passed through. Nothing. Just darkness.

Which way should I go? Which way back to camp? She asked these questions but received no response.

She smelled them before she heard them. A deep musky scent of sweat and male stench, the sickly sweet pungent odor of wet fur and unclean, sweaty skin. Then they shuffled into view, each distinct and threatening, with war paint masking their faces, and hands holding knives and sharp hatchets. She counted them: one, two, three… eight. Seven scalpers and a half man, half wolf creature that towered over her like a giant, a seven foot mass of muscle, teeth, claws, and greasy black fur. Not an uncommon sight in the Warrior Nation: a master shifter with a pack of younger, less experienced scalpers learning the ways of the people. And here they stood, far away from home, circling her, waiting, watching to see what she might do.

She pulled her weapons.

The man-beast bared its fangs, snarled, and motioned its followers forward while it fell back to observe. The seven killers closed in, like a noose, moving cautiously, but determined.

Am I dreaming? She bent her knees and waited. *If I am dreaming, let me wake.*

The first one attacked, leaping at her through the darkness. River ducked and slashed up with her ritual blade, catching the man in the chest and opening tough skin to the ribs; he stumbled away in pain. Another came at her and knocked her down, swatting her arm and nearly knocking her tomahawk away. She recovered and rolled, came up swinging, and caught another scalper across the throat, spilling the man's blood. She punched him in the back of the neck with her blade and let the steel cut through his spine. He dropped flat to the ground and stopped moving.

A fourth reached out and yanked her hair, pulling out a handful and tossing her onto the ground. She recovered quickly, swung her tomahawk against his face and split open his eye. Blood poured from the wound and spattered across her face. The man howled in agony and lashed out with his blade, cutting through the thin fabric of her dress and puncturing her shoulder muscle. She screamed and sliced off his ear. He howled again, letting go and falling out of her reach.

More came at her, over and over, slashing at her dress, cutting her arms, legs, nicking the soft skin at her neck, but never finishing the job. They were playing with her, like a cat with a mouse, counting coup, marking their prey before the end. Again and again, they attacked, and she twirled and twirled, like a ballerina in a New York play, cutting their muscled arms and haunches, splitting their noses and breaking teeth. But she could not end their assault. In time, she slowed and fell into the mud, her lungs in pain, her arms and legs weak and shaking. She reached out one last time with her knife. One of the scalpers caught her arm, held it tight, and then clutched her throat.

He lifted her off the ground and brought her face up to his. The man's breath was rancid, his teeth sharp like his master's, but smaller; some were missing.

"Now, you die," he growled, trying to mimic the snarl of a wolf, while pushing his blade into her tender throat and cutting her skin. "Now you die."

A loud shot rang out. The right side of the scalper that held her exploded as the bullet ripped through his ribs and lungs, passing clear through and striking the chest of another scalper that stood nearby. His back was blasted out in a shower of flesh, lung, and bone, as the same bullet passed through his body and brought them both down.

River hit the ground and lay there, gasping for air and rubbing her throat. She looked up and saw the dizzying shape of the man who had fired the shot. He was tall, burly, a pistol glowing red in one hand and a thick glove covering the other. In the center of the glove was a red glow, and it pulsed like ripples on a lake. It took a moment for the scalpers to realize what had happened, but once they did, they were on this new threat instantly, two and three at a time. They threw themselves at the man as River sat and watched.

The man fell to one knee as a savage jumped on his back, ripping and tearing at his dark blue duster with two knives. The man reached up and pulled his attacker to the ground, balled up his glove, and then smashed the scalper's head with a punishing fist. The strike was so strong that the man's gloved fist went down the neck and into the native's chest, where the man grabbed the still-beating heart and ripped it out. He tossed the heart into the face of another scalper trying to cut his throat. He opened his fist, let the pulsing RJ-1027 build with heat, and then he flicked the glove. A bright white portal opened in front of him, and he stepped through and was gone.

He reappeared behind River, and she moved quickly to look at him.

The master scalper, clearly despondent and shocked at the appearance of this powerful stranger, leapt toward River to finish the job. The man, coming through his oval doorway, stepped into the path of the charging beast and blew its head off with another round from his gun. He caught the headless shifter just before it plowed into River. He tossed the bloody corpse aside and said, "You're one lucky girl, River."

Another scalper, seeing the headless corpse of his master, gave a mindless howl and charged the man. A second scalper from behind charged as well, as both tried to strike the stranger from opposite sides. The man stood his ground, opened his glove wide and let the red liquid course up into it through the tubes running across his chest and into the backpack on his shoulders. "Roll out of the way, girl."

She did, just before the savage in front of the man leapt toward his throat. The man flicked his glove and another portal opened. The scalper disappeared into it. The man turned quickly and reopened the portal behind him. The scalper reappeared and leapt into the face of his charging partner. Before he realized what had happened, the scalper struck out with his tomahawk and ripped his partner's head clean off. Their bodies struck one another in a massive crunch of bone and muscle. Both were down and dead.

"Ooo whee!" The man yelled, quite happy with himself. "I've always wanted to do that! Come on, you sons of bitches. Give me more corpses!"

But the fight was over. The last remaining scalper bounded off into the night and was gone.

River lay on the ground, bleeding. She closed her eyes. Perhaps she slept. She did not know for sure, but when she opened them, the man stood over her, his non-gloved hand offered to lift her up. She took it and stood.

He smiled and pushed a strand of hair out of her eyes and adjusted her dress on her shoulders. "Excellent fight, River. You do your Nation proud." He turned at the roar of Iron Horses approaching. He holstered his pistol and bid her farewell. "Good night, River. It's been a pleasure. We'll meet again soon."

Before she blinked, he disappeared through a portal.
She turned, stared into the light of her brother's Iron Horse, and then passed out.

*****

Sun Totem held his sister in his arms while she lay near the campfire. Sierra and Zarelda were helping him clean River's wounds, while Marcus and Hicks stood nearby on guard, their weapons drawn. Jake and K-Free had gone scouting, looking to see if they could find out who had attacked her, and if they were still nearby. The seven mutilated bodies that they had found lying around River were the most disgusting, terrible killings Sun had ever seen. And no way could River have killed them all, and in the manner that they had died.

"Who was it, River?" Marcus asked her as he stood nearby, but she was drifting in and out of consciousness, and her sign language was weak and chaotic. "Who killed those scalpers and that shifter?"

It was clear to Sun who had made the attack; their bodies had littered the ground around her. River had given her sign for eight, which if true, meant that one had gotten away. But why were there a shifter and his followers this far east, and why had they attacked her? He could not get any answers.

"Leave her be," Zarelda said, trying to stitch up the deepest wound on River's shoulder. "You keep asking her questions, and she be moving around too much. I can't get da wound closed."

"We need answers, Z," Marcus said. "We need to know for sure how many there were, and we need to know how they died like that. There ain't many weapons in all the world that can do that to a body, especially men as tough as scalpers and shifters. Was it more than one person that did all that damage? A whole gang? We could be in big trouble, Z, out here in the open, if we're being followed for some reason by the Nation. We got to have answers."

"Well, let me finish dis stitch first," she snapped back. "And den you can ask all da questions you want."

"Maybe there's a doctor in town." Sierra was rubbing River's face clean with a wet bandana. "She needs more help than we can give her."

Sun nodded. "Yes, that would be a good idea."

Sierra got up to go, but was stopped my Marcus. "I don't want you going by yourself. Take Hicks with you, and don't be long."

They jumped on their Iron Horses and headed toward the town.

As Marcus stepped closer to the fire to get a better look, Sun stroked River's hair and stared deeply into her eyes. They were half closed, which meant she was sleeping and dreaming. Dreaming good things, he hoped. She had been so lucky... so lucky to have survived. He should never have taken his eyes off of her. But he was so tired after their fight with the Union, and then a non-stop push to get across the Mississippi. He had dozed for just a second, and when he awoke, she was gone.

If she dies because of me, I'll...

"Done," Zarelda said, making the last stitch and covering it with a bandage.

"How is she?" Marcus asked.

"She's fortunate, I tell you true. She got cuts everywhere, da worst being her shoulder and back, but I think we got da bleeding stopped pretty much, and da bigger cuts are stitched. She good for now, but I can't say for how long. I need more medicine. She needs those wounds cleaned proper. We need to get her to as."

They waited a while and let her rest. Sun held her the entire time, watching her face, looking for signs of improvement. She woke up not long afterward and began to move.

"Maybe she wants to speak." Marcus perked as he rose to his feet. "Ask her again, Sun."

"Sister... how many were in the pack?" River signed back the confirmation. "Eight, like she said before."

"River," Marcus said, bending down next to her. "Who killed them?"

River responded by pulling herself away from Sun and sitting upright, letting the skids of her Iron Horse support her back. Her hands and arms moved fast. Sun tried discerning her words. She mixed them up, and sometimes she repeated herself, starting over from the beginning. He did not try to interrupt. He let her work it out, and when she was finished, he said, "It was a man. Tall. She said he had a pistol so powerful that it killed two with one shot. And he had a red hand... no, he wore a glove. It was powered with RJ. It glowed red. She said he punched one of the scalpers in the face and ripped its head right off." She signed more, but he couldn't quite make everything out. "She also said he could disappear and reappear, through some kind of doorway. He used that to kill two others. He spoke to her. He had a soft, pleasant voice. Then he was gone."

"Lawd Almighty," Zarelda said, shaking her head. "What kind of man could do all dat?"

Sun had heard of a lot of warriors in the Nation who could attack so savagely. They claimed to use some sort of natural energy of the land to change into wolves or bears or mountain lions, but Sun knew that RJ had to be behind their strength, and the chiefs were lying to the people about it to maintain their control. One among the fallen had been one of those shifters; it was evident that the headless body was not all wolf, but part human as well. What kind of *man* wielded weaponry that could literally rip a heart from a chest? He had never heard of anyone, outlaw, mercenary, or lawman, who possessed such a weapon. Could it be one of Carpathian's constructs? So far east? Then again, what was a shifter doing in eastern Arkansas? None of it made sense.

"What did he say to you, River?" he asked her.

She signed it.

"What did he say?" Marcus repeated.

Sun swallowed, cleared his throat. "He said, 'We'll meet again soon'."

Marcus held his gaze on River, puzzling through it all, as they heard the crunching boots of Jake and K-Free returning. "Find anything?" Marcus asked as he finally turned away.

Jake shook his head. "Not a thing, boss. No trace of anyone. Whoever they was, they long gone now."

K-Free went to River's side. Sun pulled back to let her in, and they enjoyed a tender moment as K-Free gently rubbed River's head. "Are you okay?"

River nodded and laid back, letting Kimberly's soft touch comfort her.

"What she needs is a good night's sleep." Zarelda grabbed River's bedroll and laid it out beside the fire. "Then maybe she'll be strong enough to travel by morning, and we can find a doctor."

"We ain't taking her, are we boss?" Jake came into the firelight. "I mean, look at her. She ain't in no shape to travel, and she sure as hell ain't gonna make it to Fort Waco. She's an impede—" he stopped as Marcus glared at him. "—I mean, she's hurt too badly. Don't you think so, Sun?"

Truthfully, he wasn't sure. He had seen people of the Nation with worse injuries, near death, recover and come back even stronger. But he had never seen River beat up so badly, and he wasn't sure how her body would respond, especially with her mind in so much turmoil. She did not appear to be in any immediate danger, and yet, Jake was right. No way could they make it to Fort Waco without her first seeing a real doctor. And where was one of those? If the town nearby didn't have one, what would they do then?

"She'll be fine," he said. "She needs rest. That's all."

"Rest, hell," Jake said, spitting into the flames. "I say Sun and River stay behind. Perhaps they can catch up later, once she's better. But it's crazy to try to move her in her condition."

"We're the Wayward Eight, Jake." Marcus said with anger in his inflection. "None of us move unless we all move."
It looked as if they would argue the point further, but the roar of Iron Horses broke into their discussion. Sierra and Hicks slid into view, killed their engines, and walked to the fire. Sierra was the first to speak.

"Well, they have a doc, but he said he won't treat no member of the Warrior Nation, and then he locked himself in his office. I had a good mind to break down the door and drag him out here, but I thought I'd let you make that call, Marcus. You want I should go back and fetch him?"

Marcus looked at Zarelda. "What do you think, Z?"

She shook her head. "Ain't no cause to go getting da townsfolk in a tizzy with violence. Not yet, anyway. As long as she don't develop a fever, she'll keep till morning. We can wait and see how it goes during da night. You comfortable with dat, Sun?"

Sun nodded. "She's strong. She'll keep."

"Then where do we go in the morning?" K-Free asked. "Jake's right. She isn't going to make it all the way to Fort Waco, and there may not be anyone there qualified to look at her anyway."

"We could go back to Memphis," Jake said, spitting into the fire with a cynical sneer.

Everyone fell silent, but Sun could tell by their expressions that no one wanted to do that. Regardless of the situation, Marcus didn't like crossing the same ground twice. Their mission lay west, and west they would go. But where?

"Is there another town or fort nearby?" Sun asked.

River sat up quickly as if she had been stung by a bee, groped around the campfire until she found a stick. Then she rubbed out a clear patch of dirt near the fire, and began drawing.

"What the hell she up to now?" Jake stared angrily at her scratches.

"Shh!" Sun said, putting his hand up for silence. "Let her draw."

She drew a line and then crossed it with smaller lines, like a railroad. Then she placed a large box near the railroad with towers on each end, and then drew small teepee-like shapes... no, tents, all around the base of the square.

"I've seen that before." Hicks said, rubbing his face. "Yeah, that's Fort Smith. It's not too far from here, in fact, due west if I recall correctly. It's here in Arkansas. A hard ride in the morning will get us there by noon I think."

River began to moan and thrash around, waving her arms and running the stick through her picture. She started signing, and Sun tried to interpret.

"What is she saying now?" Marcus asked.

Sun shook his head. "Not sure. She's saying something about a snake, about a vision. Something about Fort Smith, but it's hard to say." He grabbed her and hugged her tight, trying to calm her down. Zarelda helped, and they got her to relax and lay on the bedroll near the fire. "If she's drawing pictures of Fort Smith, however, then I say we go there. She needs to be seen by a real doctor."

"That's a Union fort, boss." Jake's dissatisfaction with the idea rang clear. "We just got finished beating the tar out of them, and you want to jump back into the lion's mouth?"

"I know, Jake. It's not the best thing to do. But I don't see as how we have a choice. We're not back-tracking, and I'm not leaving them behind. River is a valuable member of the Eight, and we'll get her to a doctor, even if it's a Union one. We'll go in as cautiously as we can, stick to the tents, stay for a day at the most. We'll be okay."

"How the hell do you think we can go in cautiously, being who we are, and riding Iron Horses?" Jake asked the question, but no one answered. The conversation was over, and everyone drifted away from the fire, letting River and Sun have their space. Everyone except Jake.

He stood there, his arms folded across his chest, staring down at River, a nasty scowl on his face. Sun stood up and caught his attention. "Is there something you want to say to me, Jake?"

Jake turned and looked straight into his eyes. They were blood red and dry from the smoke. It seemed as if he were staring past Sun, his expression cold and disconnected. "Me? Yeah. I got plenty to say, but now's not the time or the place. I know exactly what you're up to." He leaned in and smiled darkly. "I'll be watching you — both of you. You can count on that."

He walked away, and Sun watched until he disappeared in the darkness. He scratched his head over what crazy Jake had just said, wondering what in the hell it all meant.

Chapter 7

By the time they arrived at Fort Smith, it had stopped raining. Marcus was glad of that, because his duster, as thick as it was, felt heavy and uncomfortable on his shoulders with all the water that had soaked down to his skin. He needed to stop, take a breath, and grab a bite to eat. They all did, and so reaching the edge of the sprawling refugee camp encircled around the fort made him happy. And despite her wounds, River had held up well. He was glad of that the most.

Fort Smith itself towered in the distance, a veritable fortress of grey concrete brick, its four walls at least thirty feet high and guarded around the clock by Union soldiers carrying blaster rifles and pistols. At each corner rested a heavy gun pulsating with RJ-1027 and manned by crews of three men. Beyond the fort lay the heavy rail of the Union army, with all the equipment needed to continue building those tracks deep into Contested Territory. A train lay at the station, and mighty cranes moved equipment and supplies to pallets and platforms. A Doomsday heavy support vehicle was being unloaded, and Marcus stopped his Iron Horse to observe. Its massive twin cannons and thick forward cow-catcher seemed to twinkle in the noon sunlight that had finally peeked out from behind storm clouds. Other vehicles and weapons were being unloaded as well, and it was clear that Fort Smith represented the full strength of the Union army in the Contested Territories. Marcus shook his head. Jake was right: they should not have come here.

The tent city that lay before him would provide them the needed buffer from the fort. The city, affectionately called Burlapville, or more often Canvastown, housed many of the families and proprietors of prairie towns who felt threatened by the constant pressures placed upon them by outlaws, corrupt government officials, the Warrior Nation, the Enlightened, and even mercenaries. They had come in droves to live under the protection of Fort Smith. The Union allowed it because it provided them cheap labor and recruits for the armies that they were building to send west. Everything that could be found in a normal town was here: banks, hotels, print shops, dry goods, restaurants, tobacconists, whorehouses, saloons, laundry services, gambling… you name it. All housed under an elaborate texture of tents and makeshift shanties.

"Let's find a place nearby to fix camp," Marcus said when everyone had come up. "Then Sun, you find a doctor for River. The rest of us will get some food, and Hicks and K-Free can look over the 'Horses. Let's try to keep a low profile here. I'm sure there'll be Union patrols through the tents. We're not staying for long, just enough time for River to get looked at and for us to refit. We'll need to head out by morning at the latest."

They followed Marcus to a quiet patch of grass right on the edge of the town. They circled the patch like a wagon train, killed their engines, and dismounted. They had opted not to take the time to buy that seventh Iron Horse, much to the disappointment of the stable owner, but they had no time to worry about it at this point. Once River was better and when another opportunity presented itself, they would seek extra Iron Horses. For now, they remained doubled up; and for the ride to Fort Smith, River doubled with her brother and Jake drove her 'Horse instead. K-Free stayed with Sierra. Their six 'Horses were now set in a circle and would serve as protection from anyone foolish enough to try to enter their camp at night.

Jake dismounted and stretched his back. "*Phew!* That was a long haul. I need a drink."

He started off toward the tents, and Marcus stopped him. "Now, what did I tell you, Jake? Low profile."

"Oh, hell, boss. I'll be fine, I promise. I just need a little juice is all. I ain't had a sip of anything hard since Kentucky. I need to relax, shake the ride and the rain off."

Marcus nodded, but grabbed Jake's rifle which he had bow-slung across his back. "Okay, but you ain't going to fight, so no rifle. Just pistols for personal protection. Understood?"

Jake huffed, but let Marcus take the gun and place it back on his 'Horse. "You're a hard man, boss."

Marcus nodded and smiled. "Just trying to keep your sorry hide alive. Now get, but remember what I said."

When Jake was gone, Marcus helped River to her feet. "Can you take her by yourself?"

Sun nodded. "Yes, we will be fine. She can walk."

He helped them to the edge of the tents and then let them go. River was walking, but slowly. The cuts on her legs were red and swollen, but she had not come down with a fever and that was good. All she needed was some medicine, some food, another good night's sleep, and she'd be fine. He hoped so, anyway.

As he turned back to camp, he saw a little boy standing beside a tent, ragged and thin, dressed in a dirty white shirt, suspenders, brown shoes, and grey woolen trousers. The boy had bright blonde hair and deep black eyes. He smiled, and his eyes flashed blood red.

Marcus stepped back and blinked, shook his head. He looked again. The boy was gone. "Where'd he go?" he wondered aloud. He looked through the crowd of passers-by, and there he was again, now ten feet away, the same disheveled boy. He smiled and red flashed in his dark eyes again. The boy put up his hand and motioned for Marcus to follow.

Marcus took a step toward the boy but stopped. The brace on his left knee bent, and he nearly fell down. Zarelda was there to catch him. "Whoa, there, Captain. Keep it steady now."

He clutched her shoulder and looked at the boy again. The little tyke still stood there, defiant, smiling and waving. "Do you see that boy?"

Zarelda strained to see. "Sure do. Who is he?"

"Don't know, but we need to find out."

As if the boy heard them, he turned and ran.

"Sierra, come here!" As she approached him, Marcus continued. "You and Zarelda go follow that boy yonder, and don't be seen. Just follow, don't talk to him or try to grab him. Just see where he goes. Then come back and let me know. And take your rifle, Z, just in case."

"You didn't let Jake take his." She raised her eyebrow in suspicion.

Marcus smiled. "You ain't Jake."

"Why do you want us to follow him?" Sierra asked.

"I don't know, but there's something strange about him. I got this odd feeling when he looked at me. I want to know where he goes, to make sure we ain't falling into some kind of trap. So follow him, and be extra careful with it."

The two ladies gathered up their weapons and headed out into the crowd toward the boy.

Marcus turned slowly on his sore left knee and returned to the 'Horses. Hicks was already working on River's, and K-Free was fiddling with the ammunition chamber of her own Gatling gun.

"Why don't you take a nap, Marcus," she said, "and rest that knee? I'll go get us some food shortly."

It was a good idea, but no. They hadn't had any time yet to get information on the whereabouts of Carpathian's hideout. This was a great place to interview, what with so many people there from the Contested Territories. If anyone knew anything about the doctor, it would be here. He couldn't pass that up. "Thank you, Kimberly," he said, removing his wet, heavy duster and placing it on the seat of his 'Horse, "but I'm going to poke around, ask some questions. You and Hicks get some work done. I'll be back directly."

She nodded and went back to work. Marcus turned and limped into Canvastown.

*****

The ugliest man The Wraith had ever seen stood in front of him. He was known as Medicine Man, and the patch over his left eye covered a hollow socket that had been mutilated with a fork. Both of his front teeth had been chipped in a saloon brawl, and his hair was pure white, long and stringy, which he held in a ponytail at the back of his neck with a large turquoise bead. He was short and hunched over like a man twice his age, holding a cane of elk bone and Canyon live oak. He smelled of stale whiskey and half-rotten meat. He was grotesque, but the Warrior Nation loved him.

He was the half-breed son of an old chief, his mother having been captured and kept as breeding property until her death. He carried strong medicine, and he was treated like a son by Geronimo. He was the only man with white blood that the chiefs would accept into their communities.

"It is true," he said to The Wraith as they stood in Medicine Man's tent near the south-facing wall of Fort Smith.

"Just like your vision revealed. The Wayward Eight are on the move."

The Wraith nodded, forcing himself to ignore the stale air of the dank space. "Did your scalpers kill any of them?"

Medicine Man looked down at his worn moccasins, his one good eye blinking. "No. They caught the Indian girl alone. She was chasing her spirit animal. They attacked her, but she survived."

The Wraith shook his head in amazement. "Eight born and bred killers could not take out one tiny little girl?"

"She killed one, but they had her dead to right, and then this man came out of the dark, as if from fog. He killed two with one shot of his pistol, smashed another's head with a golden glove that had a red glow in its center, and then used a magical doorway to kill two more. He killed their master as well."

"A magical doorway?" The Wraith was more impressed with the strange term the man used, as opposed to the death of a shifter – something that no ordinary man could accomplish on his own.

Medicine Man nodded. "A doorway into time. He could disappear into it and reappear somewhere else. He forced one of my scalpers into it and then had him reappear and attack one of his brothers by accident. Only one escaped. I've never heard of anything like it."

"Was this mystery man riding with the Eight?"
Medicine Man shrugged his withered shoulders. "I do not know for sure, but my survivor did not think so. He and the others had been tracking Marcus and his people for a couple days. They never saw this man until he attacked. Do you know him?"

Yes, The Wraith did, but he did not answer. No cause to tell this scrawny shrew everything. His service to The Wraith was up, and he had not performed it to satisfaction. Best thing to do was kill him and rid the world of his ugly face and stench. But not yet. He might have use later.

So his vision was correct. The Eight were heading west, and most assuredly, they were heading to the Tonto Forest to find Carpathian, just like he was. That's what the vision had shown him, and that's what was proving true. Who had hired them? Abe Lincoln? Surely Abe wouldn't be so stupid as to pull the rug right out from under the best mercenary in America, especially since they had worked so well in the past. Would he? Perhaps; politicians were snakes, every last one of them, and no telling what craziness lay in the mind of a man who was supposed to be dead. The Union? He could not imagine Marcus accepting a job from President Johnson, no matter the reward. Then who?

He shrugged off the question. Did it really matter? What mattered was that he, The Wraith, be the one to find that foreign peckerwood, that it be his shotgun to shoot a slug into the madman's pompous chest, that it be his knife to cut off Carpathian's head and be placed next to Abe's if that tall stick of knotty oak thought about double-crossing him. It didn't matter if the Eight were trying to elbow into his score. They would not make it to Arizona alive.

Just then a small boy appeared at the open flap of the tent, frail and meek, wearing a dirty white shirt and grey woolen trousers. He tried to knock on the flap as if it were a door, realized his error, and tried to hide. "Come in, boy," Medicine Man said, raising his voice above a whisper. "Don't waste our time."

The boy came in. "Begging your pardons, sirs, but I thought you'd like to know that they are here."

"All of them?" Medicine Man asked.

The boy nodded. "Yes, sir. I did as you instructed. I waited at the edge of the tents, and like you said, here they come, all eight, riding 'Horses as pretty as you please." He pointed out the tent. "They are about a mile that way, on a nice patch of grass."

"The Eight are here?" The Wraith raised an eyebrow.

Medicine Man nodded. "I thought they might come, since my men had wounded the girl so badly. No other place to go but here, unless they turned back to Memphis, and they obviously didn't do that."

"And begging your pardon again, sirs," the boy said, "but two of 'em are out there right now."

The Wraith pushed Medicine Man out of the way and went to the flap and peeked out cautiously to see two women standing about fifty yards away. They were trying to seem inconspicuous, but he could tell that they were casing the tent, waiting for the boy to come out. He recognized them immediately.

His hand grabbed for the shotgun on his back. "You did good, boy," he said, reaching for coins in his pocket. He gave the boy two and tossed a third to Medicine Man.

The one-eyed old man groaned. "This isn't even half of what we discussed."

"I'm withholding payment on account that I have to go out there now and do what your scalpers should have done last night."

The nasty scowl on The Wraith's face kept Medicine Man from arguing. The Wraith checked the multiple chambers of his shotgun and motioned to the back of the tent. "You go over yonder, boy, and sit in the corner. Don't come out until the bullets stop flying." He drew his knife and handed it to the boy. "And keep an eye on this old coot, will you? If he leaves the tent, stab him in the balls."

*****

Walking away from their campsite to find a drink was foolish, Jake finally admitted to himself, but so necessary. They had been going virtually nonstop since Kentucky, and too much had already happened. He just needed to kick up his boots and unwind a little, take a moment for himself. So why not find a saloon in this sea of tents and knock back one, or two, or three? And as long as Marcus was not alone with Sun and River, there was little to worry about. He was on his third whiskey by the time he realized his mistake, but it was too late by then; he was enjoying himself far too much to stop.

A group of fellows had invited him to a game of five card stud with no bring-in. He accepted. It was on an improvised table of barrels and crates, but the cards weren't that worn and the fellows seemed nice enough. They didn't appear to be in cahoots with trying to bilk him out of his money; he didn't have much anyway since it was Marcus and Sierra who had held on to the lion's share of Lincoln's advance. But the cool breeze flowing through the tent, and the pleasant music coming from an automated organ thrown up in the corner, made the game fun and relaxing. The fourth whiskey didn't hurt either.

They were on the fourth hand, and he was dealt his third card face up. He looked at his down card again and grimaced. "What's a-matter there, slick," one of the men sitting at the table said, "gonna have to fold?"

Jake had never been good at a poker face, which was something that had been a problem all his life, even in the early days before the war, when he had been a bare-knuckle boxer in the Smokey's of the East Midlands. His eyes always gave away where he was going to lean, and thus, he'd get punched in the jaw more often than not. The war itself had not given him many opportunities to be subtle, but he had joined late anyway, and by the time he had seen real action, he deserted and joined Marcus as the first member of The Eight. He had never looked back since. Needless to say, subtlety was not Jake Mattia's strong suit.

"Don't you worry about me, friend," Jake said, throwing in his bet. "You keep your eyes on your own cards."

Another round of cards was dealt. Jake's new card didn't improve his odds, and he sighed, trying to catch himself before the fellows noticed. He shook his head. He was going to lose it all this time.

He leaned back and waited for the rest of the bets to come in. That's when he heard the conversation of three men at the table behind him.

"I wouldn't speak to no dandy from Europe," one man said, spitting brown juice into a rusty cuspidor. "They lie like the devil himself."

"Tanner's got money," said another, wearing a weathered red blouse, leather boots and a dusty black bowler. "And I need that. Besides, what I got to tell him is important."

"And what's that?"

"I know where that crazy doctor lives."

"Carpathian? Horse shit!"

"It's true. I seen the walls of the town he lives in. I've been there."

The third man looked him up and down. "Well, you ain't dead. So how'd you see what nobody else ever has? I hear tales."

"What you hear ain't half of it," the man said, clearly growing agitated by his companions' lack of faith in his story. "I seen it, I tell you, and if Tanner wants to pay for that information, he's gonna get it."

They fell silent, then one said, "Well, you better get then. Can't keep a man like that waiting. He'll kill you if you do."

"Friend!"

Jake shook his head and refocused on his card game. Everyone at the table was staring at him. "Are you in or out?" one asked.

Jake looked at his cards again, but his mind was on the talk he had just heard. If what the man had said were true, then Marcus needed to know. Hell, they could grab this man themselves and get him to squeal, and they probably didn't even have to pay him money.

I need to get my hands on this fellow, Jake thought as he looked into his cards. *That'll get me back in Marcus's good graces.*

He stared at his cards and his head began to hurt. As he reached for his bet, another plan emerged from the smeared colors of diamonds and spades, a different plan, but one that made more sense. *Of course*, Jake thought as he watched the new plan unfold on the cards themselves. *This is a much better idea.*

"I fold," he said, pushing the rest of his money forward. He stood. "Thanks kindly, you goggled-eyed sons of bitches, for stealing my money."

The men bid him a fond farewell, and Jake stepped out of the tent. He found the man wearing the red shirt and black bowler walking fast down the worn street between two rows of crowded tents. He put his hand on a pistol at his hip, cocked the hammer, and began following. He smiled through the nagging pain in his head.

Marcus will be pleased with me.

*****

Zarelda had little time to react before she saw the flaps of the tent fly open and a shotgun leveled against her.

She pushed Sierra out of the way, whose attention was elsewhere. "What the—" was all she heard from Sierra before she herself rolled to the right just as the man holding the gun fired his first shot.

A huckster display of sun-dried rabbit and muskrat hides exploded behind her, its operator blown back from the shot. Another slug followed the first, hitting a wagon wheel and shattering its spokes just as Zarelda found protection behind a pile of crates. She rose up and returned fire, letting her mini-atomic repeater unload against the man, who quickly ducked behind a display of Eastern jewelry and buckskin leggings. She was trying to avoid hitting civilians, who were now just coming to realize they were in the middle of a gunfight. Women screamed and grabbed their children and tried ducking into wagons and tents. Men hit the dirt and covered their heads, but that didn't seem to matter to the man who popped back up and sent another slug her way, hitting a woman in the back who was running for safety. Another round destroyed the crate in front of her, and Zarelda jumped out, ripped off another round, which forced the man back into cover. Then she made for Sierra.

Realizing why she had been pushed, Sierra was protecting herself behind a pile of corn sacks, putting shot after shot into the barrels that the man was now hiding behind. Zarelda popped off shots as she moved, trying to ensure that the man would stay put until she reached her friend. The man, having expended his shotgun rounds, now pulled two UR-30 blasters and was firing them in tandem against both positions, seemingly able to keep his right arm still, while tracking Zarelda with the other pistol as she moved. He was skillful, she had to admit, but she wished that she now had some of those voodoo fetishes that her grandmother used to make. She'd shout incantations and wave them at this man to peel his flesh back and burn his face from inside. But she didn't have any of those things, Lord forgive her, so she'd have to do this the modern way, with RJ weapons, and it seemed as if their assailant had better ones.

She dove behind the corn sacks. "Holy Jesus. What have we gotten ourselves into?"

"I don't know," Sierra said, "but that's the last time I follow a child for Marcus."

"Amen to dat." She put her head down as the man moved forward and shot again, ripping massive holes into the sack that was protecting her, showering her with corn dust. She crawled away from the spot and took up behind a post. Sierra moved as well, taking cover behind a pile of buffalo hides. "We gonna have to do something you don't like, Sierra."

"What?" she said, popping up and ripping off another three shots. The man grimaced as if he'd been hit, and dived behind a group of huddled civilians, not caring if they took the rounds. Sierra stopped firing. "Dammit!"

"We gotta back off. Now!"

Sierra shook her head, but didn't put up a fight when Zarelda grabbed the petticoats of her dress and tugged. "You ready?"

Sierra nodded, fell back on her own and took another shot.

"One, two, three… Go!"

They both turned and fled, hearing the buzz and feeling the wind of UR-30 blaster rounds race past their heads.

*****

"You're late!"

Sasha Tanner didn't like to be kept waiting, especially when money and time were of the essence. He especially didn't like to be kept waiting for the kind of two-bit hood that stood before him right now, smelling of stale pretzels, whiskey, and fear.

The man removed his black bowler and held it in sweaty palms. "My apologies, sir, but I was delayed."

"Yes," Sasha said, "I can smell it on your breath." He sat down in his chair and ran a thumb over the steel edge of his hand blade. He'd put them on just for this meeting. He'd learned long ago that when talking to civilians, intimidation was an excellent tool. "So, my Union contacts tell me that you have information on the whereabouts of Doctor Burson Carpathian's hideout. Is that true?"

The man nodded. "Yes, sir. I know right where it's at."

"Why haven't you given this information to the Union?"

The man's expression changed to pure hatred. Sasha had seen that kind of expression before, leveled against him more often than not. He could appreciate it, even coming from a laggard like this man. "Begging your pardon, sir, but those Union bastards can go to hell for all I'm concerned. They can torture me if they like, but I'll never tell them."

Sasha shrugged and put out his hands as if he were begging. "Why tell me, then? I can simply turn around and tell my contacts."

"What you do with the information, sir, is up to you. But this mouth of mine will never tell truths to any Union official for as long as I live. Not after what they did to my family in the war." The man seemed to choke up a little on that. Sasha could see a small line of tears at the bottom of his eyes. "But I have no love for Carpathian, I can tell you that. I've seen what he does to men, to women, children, and so whatever I can do to get that foreign devil in a pine box, I will. Just so long as I don't have to treat with the Union."

Sasha nodded and stood. "I understand." He pulled a stack of coins and twenty dollar bills from his duster pocket. He laid it on the cot near the chair. He pointed to it. "There's your money, and you may have it, so long as you tell *me* truths. But first, tell me… how did you come by finding the place?"

The man rubbed the thick shadow of whiskers on his face and refocused. "Quite by accident to be honest. After my family was killed, I headed west. My plan was to get as far as the Pacific Ocean, you see, and pan for gold. I got there lucky enough, found a few nuggets, but never struck it rich. Almost got myself killed by those goddamn Warrior Nation savages. Most people don't even make it out alive, you know, but anyway, I shacked up with this squaw for a while, and we decided to head into the mountains to stay hidden from the savages. One night, an avalanche took her from me, nearly took my life too. But I clawed out of it and stumbled south, no food, no shelter. I was near death when they got me."

"Who got you?"

"Carpathian's men, I reckon. Nasty-looking creatures, too, one of those scouting parties that he's famous for. Snatched me right up as I was close to dying and took me back to his lair. Got as close as Payson. I even seen the mouth of his canyon. But that's it. Ladue and her lady desperados attacked."

"Desiree Ladue?"

The man nodded. "That's the one. They killed most of the scouting party, but couldn't get inside the canyon, which is what I guess they were trying to do. Anyway, when they saw me still alive, they grabbed me up and retreated. But you know, Miss Ladue don't take too kindly to men. Her ladies treated me worse than Carpathian's monsters. Once they grew tired of beating me to a pulp, they dumped me in the purple sage and let out. By God's grace, I survived and found my way back to civilization. But I remember the ordeal, all of it. I got a good mind, sir. I don't forget much."

"Do you know where Ladue hangs out these days?"

The man considered. "No. They headed south once they left me to die. Could be somewhere in the Contested Territory, I reckon. Ladies like that don't take to polite society. But I'd recommend against finding her, sir. She's a polecat through and through."

Sasha scoffed at the suggestion. There wasn't a woman living that he couldn't tame. "Okay." Sasha pulled out a map and unfolded it on his cot. "Your story seems credible to me. Now's your chance to impress. Show me where it's at, in exact detail."

"No problem." The man got down on his knees and placed his hand on the map to smooth it out further. He then began to point toward what had become known as Carpathian Industries Territory and the Tonto Forest. "It's right here—"

Boom!

Before his finger touched the map, the man's head exploded in a splash of broken skull, hair, blood, and brains. The wall of the tent behind the cot was washed red with blood and gore, and Sasha's face was covered in it too. The man slumped dead over the map.

Sasha fell back, his heart racing. He looked to the opening of the tent. And there he found a long arm sticking through the flap, holding a smoking Grandfather pistol.

Chapter 8

"Desiree Ladue?"

Marcus wanted to be sure that that was the name the old man had said. The sweaty, beefy butcher slurred his words through a row of foul teeth that were best pulled. Marcus would gladly oblige if he didn't have to get so close to the man's mouth to do it.

The man cut off the head of the chicken and began plucking feathers. "That's right, Desiree Ladue. Now I ain't making no guarantees, you understand. But from what I hear tell, she's the one you'd want to talk to. They say her and her crazy ladies have been as far as the most Western parts of Warrior Nation territory. If she been that far, she been through Carpathian's territory I figure."

"You know where she's at?"

"If she's in the Contested Territory, she's probably in Fort Waco. All the crazies go there."

The Eight were headed there anyway, so that was good to know, and all it took was agreeing to buy three chickens from the man. Of course, Marcus was going to lose them in the gutter once he was out of eye and earshot. He wasn't about to eat anything this disgusting cretin had held, nor allow his people to do so. He had picked up some bread, a few dried carrots and peas, and some stew meat anyway. He didn't need the chickens; he needed the information the goon possessed.

"What she look like?"

The man shrugged. "Don't know. Never seen her. They say she was once pretty, then she got shot in the face by Carpathian himself. But you know how rumors start. She could be a darkie for all I know."

He had a name at least. That was good enough for now. He was about to thank the man when a shot rang out. A shotgun. An RJ weapon. Not one of his people's.

The man huffed. "Don't worry about that. Happens all the time around here. People firing in the air. The Union garrison in the fort'll take care of it."

Another shot and then another. He recognized it immediately. "Zarelda!"

Marcus pulled his sword, and then he heard the shot he prayed he wouldn't hear: the long, deep crack of a Grandfather pistol.

"Dammit – Jake!"

He didn't bother paying or bidding the man goodbye. He turned away and ran toward the gunfire.

*****

Jake didn't realize what he had done until a silver blade on a long chain snapped past his face and cut his ear. He dropped his arm and fell back. Sasha Tanner was on him like a mad dog.

They fell into the muddy road, civilians scattering, screaming, shouting to get out of the way, as the two rolled through the mud and horse dung, each gripping the other's coats and trying to bury their faces into the wet gore of the wagon ruts. "I'm sorry." Jake tried to apologize and explain, as if reasoning with Sasha would make a difference. He had met the journeyman twice on other missions, and they had exchanged cordial but curt how-do-you-dos. But no amount of reasoning was going to stop this madman, his eyes glaring with a rage that Jake knew all too well, all too often.

Jake pushed his knee into Sasha's groin, but his metal codpiece prevented any true damage. It was enough of an attack, however, to push Sasha up and off of him. Jake rolled away, jumped to his feet and pulled his pistol. "Hold it right there, hoss," he said, leveling the barrel at Sasha's head. "I ain't against pulling the trigger."

"Pull it then," Sasha said, "if you can."

"I got no beef with you."

"Then you shouldn't have killed my contact, you miserable cretin. He was going to tell me…"

Jake smiled. "What was he going to say, hm? Where Carpathian lives?"

"How do you know about that?"

Jake found himself chuckling, despite the sharp pain in his head. "Why do you think I killed him?"

"Why you son of a—"

Jake pulled the trigger, but the blade on Sasha's left arm shot out so fast that it hit the pistol and pushed Jake's hand up and the round went over his head. Jake tried shooting again, but Sasha charged him, slashing with his arm blades, trying to get at Jake's face.

Jake twisted and turned, using his arms to block Sasha's. The sharp blades cut through Jake's coat, slicing his skin and drawing blood, but he kept blocking, until Sasha let his right arm slip down a bit. Jake balled up his fist and drove it into Sasha's jaw, knocking the journeyman back and giving Jake time to recover. He holstered his pistol and drew his knife.

"Okay, pretty boy," he said, passing the blade back and forth between hands. "You want to play with knives? Then come at me."

Sasha shook off the punch and struck out with his chain blades, throwing one after the other, arching them through the space between them, trying to cut Jake's throat. They were fast, and Jake stumbled a couple times, even taking a strike across his forehead. But he kept dodging and weaving until he found a chance to catch one of the chains and tie it up, throwing it into the other chain and locking them in place. Sasha tried pulling them back to their metal sheaths on his forearm but he couldn't get them untangled.

Jake pounced, driving into Sasha, lifting him off the ground, and body slamming him into a crate piled high with canvas trousers, breaking the crate and scattering the nearby civilians who were huddled around watching the fight. Jake tried stabbing Sasha in the chest, but Sasha's hand came up and held him firm, denying him a good angle for the blade.

Boom-boom-boom!

The sound of rapid fire from Zarelda's rifle stopped Jake cold. He pushed away from the fight and gained his feet. Sasha struggled to climb out from beneath the canvas clothing. Jake didn't give him time to recover. He drove his boot into the man's sternum, knocking the air out of him and throwing him back into the pile. "That's for knickin' my pistol. I'll deal with you later."

Jake turned and ran through the terrified crowd, toward Z's cracking gunfire.

*****

They fired and fired, and still he came on, pushing through the running crowd, killing some, knocking others down. It didn't seem to matter: men, women, dogs, horses. Anyone or anything in the way was a target. They had hit him a few times, praise be, a couple times in the chest, once in the arm, but his steel chest plate and shoulder pads prevented a kill shot. He shrugged them all off and kept coming, tucking away his pistols and reloading his revolving shotgun, pumping slugs into them like they were game in the field. Zarelda was running out of ammunition; Sierra as well.

Civilians were not idly standing by anymore. Some had pulled their own guns and were firing, but they didn't know who to fire at. In this rolling battle, who was the good guy, who was the bad? They were just firing at both sides, whenever it suited them to do so, to defend their wives, children, their possessions, their tents. The man pursuing didn't seem to care about any of it.

"Who the hell is this son of a bitch?" Sierra wondered aloud as she loaded her pistol with her last rounds.

"The Wraith!"

Marcus came up and stood in the center of the road, seemingly oblivious to the shots being fired around him, and stared down the man whom he called The Wraith. The captain's confidence in the face of so many bullets flying around him, or perhaps it was stupidity, that made The Wraith cease firing. He walked up to Marcus as confidently as Marcus had entered the fray, and they stared at each other over a deadly five feet.

"Marcus Wayward," The Wraith said, gnashing his teeth. "I should have killed you in Virginia when I had the chance."

"You were always good at starting fights, Robert," Marcus said, running his thumb over the hilt of the sword in his left hand, letting its electrical charge dance along his hand. "But you were never good at ending them. Just like today. Are you prepared to see this to the end?"

The Wraith chuckled. "The bigger question is why you are interested in Carpathian? Why are you and your little friends en route to the Southwest?"

"You are flying on false information, Robert. We're not here for that."

Zarelda could see that The Wraith was annoyed by Marcus using his real name. *Keep saying it*, Zarelda tried to will into the captain's mind. *Agitate!*

"Oh, come now, Marcus. Let's not play childish games with each other. I know why you are here, for it's the same reason that I am. Who hired you? The Union? Some of your Confederate goons? Lincoln?"

"Lincoln is dead," Zarelda said. She came up to stand beside Marcus. She looked down and noticed blood dripping from inside the man's coat sleeve and splattering on his boot. That was a good sign. It meant that at least he'd been nicked by their gunfire, and with radiated bullets, how much longer would he last?

The Wraith nodded. "So you say, but does it really matter? In the end, it won't be you who finds that European bastard. It'll be me, and you'll be whistling Dixie past the grave."

The Wraith made a move, but Marcus was faster than she had ever seen him. The edge of his sword was against The Wraith's throat before the man had a chance to twitch his fingers. "I'll cut your throat and burn your insides before your corpse hits the ground, Robert. Now back off, nice and slow, and we'll let you live."

"*We* may let you live," Zarelda said, pointing to the fort, "but dose fellows might not."

Coming out of the front gate was a column of Union soldiers, armed with blasters, heading into Canvastown.

"What will it be, Robert?" Marcus said. "We part now and live, or shall we die at the hands of blue-bellies?"

The muscles in The Wraith's jaw worked overtime. Zarelda could see the rage welling up in his eyes, like tears, but there was no sorrow there. Hate and unbridled anger. His face grew red as a beet, but he backed off, nice and slow. "We'll meet again, Marcus. Under less pleasant circumstances."

The Wraith slung his shotgun over his shoulder, turned and disappeared into the gathering crowd.

"What we do now, Marcus?" Zarelda asked.

Marcus tucked away his sword. He took a deep breath, and then said, "Run like hell!"

And they did, he and Sierra and Zarelda, back toward their camp. Jake caught up with them in mid run and asked, "What happened? I heard shots."

"The Wraith is in town," Marcus said. "He's hunting Carpathian as well. That's trouble."

"We got a worse problem than that, boss," Jake said, trying to catch his breath. "Tanner is here as well."

"Lawd Jesus!" Zarelda said. She had met Sasha Tanner before. Good-looking man, but a killer, pure and simple. "What's he doing here?"

Marcus shook his head. "Don't know, but he's been known to work with The Wraith in the past. Holy hell, I hope they ain't working together again." He shook the fearful thought from his mind and glared at Jake. "And why the hell were you firing your gun?"

Jake looked embarrassed. "I'll tell you later. Let's just get."

The Union troops were close behind, fanning out through the various paths around the tents. Zarelda could hear the men shouting, given encouragement by the civilians who were pointing at them as they ran past. She was grateful that no one tried stopping them. Marcus had a policy of never wanting to harm civilians if at all possible, but under the circumstances, he might be willing to drop a few if they got in the way. Luckily none did, and their path was clear.

"Zarelda," Marcus said, "I want you and Sierra and Jake to gather up Hicks and Kimberly and make for Fort Waco. I have to go find Sun and River."

"No, sir," Jake said, shaking his head like a dog. "I ain't leaving you here with them."

What does he mean? Zarelda wondered.

"It's not a suggestion, Jake," Marcus said. "It's an order. We can't afford to have the Union catch us all, and we can't get in a fight with them again, not with their numbers. The mission will be over. I said *go*. We'll catch up."

Zarelda thought about protesting, but thought better of it when she saw his face. The captain was in no mood to discuss it, and besides, he was right: the blue-belies were right on their tails. If they didn't go now, they'd never leave alive.

"We'll leave you two 'Horses!" Sierra said. "I'll double with Jake."

Marcus nodded. "Very well, now go!"

He broke off from them, going deeper into Canvastown. Zarelda tried to keep eye contact for as long as she could, then turned away and headed for their camp.

Lawd, keep Marcus safe, she prayed.

*****

Marcus could almost feel the boots of the Union troops on his back, but he needed to find Sun and River, and somehow, they needed to get away. An impossible task, indeed, but nothing they hadn't done before. The Eight were made for impossible tasks.

He rounded a corner, seeking the tent with a red cross or the word 'doctor' on its side. He found neither. He thought about shouting out, but no. Why draw unwanted attention? But if he didn't find it soon, he'd have to do just that. Time was running out.

He ducked between two large tents, and that's when a coil of chain wrapped around his legs and brought him down into mud.

Pain shot through his knee as he thought back to the war. He was on his face again, in pain, but this time, it was less worrisome. The mud cushioned his fall, and he rolled back over to find a man standing over him, two large, sharp blades tied to his forearms.

"Tanner!"

"I am growing tired of you Eight." Sasha said, winding his chain up his arm. "I can't get rid of you."

"And you won't," Marcus said, drawing his sword. He thrust it toward Sasha's belly. Sasha blocked it with a forearm blade and fell back. A mistake, for it gave Marcus a chance to gain his legs. His knee still hurt, but he fought through the pain and attacked, slashing and stabbing, letting the energy from the sword's edge slash through the air like a whip. Sasha couldn't handle it. He backed away further, lost his footing, and fell into a tent. Marcus raised his sword and moved in to deliver the final blow.

"Halt!"

The voice of the Union officer was shrill and pronounced, echoing through the tents like the booming voice of God. It was quickly followed by the sound of two dozen blasters being raised and leveled at Marcus's chest.

The Union officer pushed through his men. "In the name of President Johnson," he said, walking up to Marcus and snatching the sword from his hands. "You are both under arrest."

Chapter 9

Sun Totem watched from the doctor's tent as Marcus and Sasha were cuffed and taken away by the Union troops. He felt a sickening pang in his gut. He knew he should have gone out there to help, but he could not bring himself to do it. Why not? He looked back into the tent at the reason: River, sleeping soundly on a cot, the doctor having given her some Dover's Powder to help her rest. If he went out there to help Marcus, he'd probably get shackled too, and what would happen to River? No. He needed to stay with her, to see her through this. That mattered more than Marcus, or the Eight.

The doctor had sutured up the deepest cuts on her back and shoulder, replacing the work that Zarelda had done hastily, and was relieved that no infection had set in.

"I'm surprised," the doctor had said. "With cuts like this, it's a wonder she isn't down with fever."

But River was strong. *The strongest of all of us. She always has been. Stronger than me at least.*

He looked through the flap again, at the civilians cleaning up the mess from the fight that had taken place. He hadn't seen the rest of the Eight during the scuffle, and he wondered where they were. Hopefully, they had managed to escape, for if they hadn't, it was over. At least this mission, and who knows, perhaps it would mean the end of the Wayward Eight. No, he couldn't think like that. The others had gotten away, and everything would be okay. He was certain of it, and when the sun fell, he'd go scouting to see what else had happened. He had heard gunfire all across Canvastown. Had anyone else been injured? Sierra? K-Free? Jake? The thought of Jake made him pause. What was the matter with him? Why had he been so off-kilter, so high strung on this mission? Since the beginning of the job he had been nothing but leery and distant to both himself and River. Why? These were questions that needed to be answered, in time, and before they finished the mission… if they finished the mission.

River moaned behind him, and he turned to her. She was sitting up in the cot, straddling it for support. She looked strong, refreshed. "How do you feel?"

She signed the answer. *I am fine. I am ready to leave.*

Sun shook his head. "No, we cannot leave yet. The doctor says that you must rest for the night. Maybe in the morning."

Where are they? Where is our family?

He was dreading having to tell her, but he did; at least, as much as he had seen. In his telling, her face grew pale, distraught.

We should not have come here.

"You drew the fort in the dirt," he said. "You wanted to come here."

River shook her head. *No. I was trying to say 'No'. My spirit told me no, as I chased it across the field.*

Sun grew angry, pointed at her. "Why didn't you shake your head then, just as you did now? Why didn't you tell me 'no' then?"

She was near tears. *I tried. I could not say it, nor shake my head. Something inside me would not let me.* She wiped her eyes. *We must save him, Sun. We must save Marcus. It is our fault that he has been captured. We can't let him stay in the fort.*

Sun placed his hand on the side of her face, rubbed a tear away from her cheek. "No, it is not your fault. It is mine. I have known you all your life, and I should have understood you better; I should have known something was amiss. This is my fault. And I will make it right."

He returned to the tent flap. He looked toward Fort Smith, its mighty concrete walls looming on the horizon. No telling what might happen to Marcus once he was taken into the fort. The Union would certainly not allow him to leave. They might even hang him. All the possibilities were too grave to imagine. River was right. The captain needed to be saved.

"I will go tonight," Sun said, looking across the rows and rows of tents. "And I will get him out."

A hand fell on his shoulder. Sun turned to see his sister standing there, strong, smiling. *Yes, you will go to him, and you will save him. And I will go with you.*

*****

Marcus and Sasha were flung to the ground in the central square of the fort by the captain who had arrested them. Marcus winced when he struck the ground and his left hand turned beneath his weight in the handcuffs and strained the old war wound. Union soldiers encircled them, holding their blasters forward. There was no chance for escape. His weapons had been taken.

"This is your fault," Marcus said, righting himself and trying to find some comfort on the hard dirt.

"On the contrary." Sasha was catching his breath as he sat up. "It's Jake Mattia's fault."

"What did he do?"

"He killed my contact!" Sasha was clearly furious over this. His face grew red, his breath agitated. "He killed the little twit right before he was going to tell me."

"Tell you what?" Marcus asked.

Sasha opened his mouth, about to say, and then closed it. "None of your damned business."

"Was it about Carpathian?" Marcus took a shot with that question. The Wraith had clearly been hired to find him; why hadn't Sasha been as well? All of these mercenaries in one place at the same time? No coincidence. "Don't play stupid with me, Sasha. You don't do it very well."

"Who sent you?" Sasha rose up on his knees. "Tell me. Who sent you here to kill my contact?"

Marcus shook his head. "No one. I don't know anything about that. What I do know is that you are trying to find Carpathian, same as me. Now, who hired *you*?"

"Shut up!" The captain said, walking up and pushing Sasha back down with a boot to the shoulder. "Talk again, and I'll shoot you both!"

Marcus didn't say anything further, but his mind raced with scores of questions. Why had Jake killed that contact? So much about Jake these past several days had been a mystery. He was not himself. Sun had said as much in that Kentucky barn. How did Jake know that this man that Sasha spoke about was a contact? And what was the man going to tell him? And why, if Jake knew this, did he not simply snatch the man up and bring him to the Eight? Whatever the man knew, it must have been something incredible for Sasha to get so angry that he would attack Jake in broad daylight and bring the Union army down on them. So many questions. But the most important one was who had hired Tanner?

Another officer came out of the complex of wooden buildings at the rear of the fort. He carried a blaster on his hip in a worn leather holster and sported a finely polished ceremonial sword clipped to his belt. Marcus admired the sword. *Wish I had mine.*

The officer walked up to them. "I'm Colonel Shamus Thawley, commander of Fort Smith and the Union's Fifth Heavy Cavalry Regiment. I want to know why you have disrupted the peace of my town, killing innocent civilians and damaging property."

"I did nothing of the sort," Sasha said, raising up again on his knees. "Contact Washington, and you'll know why I am here."

Marcus could see by the expression on the journeyman's face that he didn't want to give away that precious piece of information. But it was every man for himself now.

Colonel Thawley looked at him warily. "Who are you, sir?"

"Sasha Tanner. I'm on an important mission for President Johnson, which I am not inclined to speak about, but is nevertheless true."

The colonel motioned for one of his officers and whispered something into his ear. The man saluted and left quickly. "And who are you?" he asked Marcus.

The man who's going to kill you. "Captain Marcus Wayward, ex-Confederate officer. And I did not kill any civilians, nor damage property. That would be Robert "The Wraith" Gunter, another man who was in town, and trying to kill me. Did your soldiers happen to find him?"

The expression on Sasha's face made it clear that he knew nothing of The Wraith's presence. Marcus turned to him and winked. "Something I know that you don't."

"There was no other man out there," the colonel said. "Just you and you. Now, what are you doing in Canvastown?"

Marcus shrugged as best he could. "Just passing through, Colonel."

"Passing through with seven compatriots," Sasha said. "They let out when they saw your men come out of the fort. You should be out there looking for them. They haven't gotten far, I bet. Jake Mattia is the one you want. He's a sorry bastard, that one. Find him and shoot him."

Marcus glared at Sasha. *Shut up, you fool. One more bad word about Jake, and I'll...*

"Don't you concern yourself about what we should do, Mr. Tanner. We are following all leads and interviewing many eyewitnesses. I can assure you, we're on top of it."

The officer that had left returned and handed Colonel Thawley a piece of reiterator paper. The colonel took it and read the message, littered with broken words, quietly. When he was finished, he looked straight at Sasha, his eyes wide like a bug's. "Seems that you were right, Mr. Tanner." He motioned to have Sasha's handcuffs removed. "Please accept my apologies, and I have been ordered to extend to you any courtesy necessary to ensure your safe departure."

Sasha rubbed his wrists and accepted his blades from one of the guards. He buckled them onto his forearms, checked the chains for damage, and locked everything in place. "Thank you kindly, Colonel. All I require is an Iron Horse with as much firepower as you can give me." He pointed to Marcus. "And throw *that* sorry son of a bitch in jail."

Marcus said nothing, not giving Sasha the satisfaction of a response. Sasha fixed his broad-brimmed hat and adjusted his coat until it fit snug and proper on his shoulders. He knelt down and gave Marcus a smile. "See, it's good to have important friends."

"I *have* important friends," Marcus said. "Seven of them."

"Indeed, and where are they now?"

Sasha laughed, bid Colonel Thawley goodbye, and followed another officer out the front gate toward a row of Union vehicles.

The colonel turned his attention back to Marcus. "Now, what to do with you?"

Marcus wriggled in his discomfort. "Best thing to do is let me go, Colonel, give me back my weapons, and let me kill that bastard before he gets away."

"That's not going to happen, Captain Wayward." He looked at the note again. "This here paper also instructs me to detain you until the morning, when you'll be shipped back to Washington to stand trial for many, many crimes against the Union."

"I didn't kill anybody," Marcus said, struggling to get up. Two soldiers held him down. "I was defending myself."

"Oh, they're not just talking about what you've done here, Captain Wayward," the colonel said, "which I will inform them about in detail. You've got crimes stretching back years. They're gonna make you pay for all of them, and I suspect they'll hang you for them."

A soldier came up to the colonel, holding Marcus's weapons. Thawley accepted them as if they were his own, clipping the sword on his belt next to the other. Marcus made fists so hard behind his back that he could feel his fingernails dig into his skin.

"Take this man away," Colonel Thawley said, seemingly growing bored of the situation. "Lock him up!"

*****

It was dark without a moon. That was a blessing and a curse, in Sun's mind, but there wasn't anything he could do about it. At least the Union would have some lanterns burning RJ. Red-tinged light was better than no light at all. They didn't need much; just enough to give them perspective on the layout of the fort grounds.

They had left the doctor's tent near midnight. Parts of Canvastown were still active, a saloon, a gambling hall, a small brothel on the edge of a patch of wood, but they kept to the quiet places, the residential rows. Even there, it would be difficult to sneak past anyone without being seen, and there were still Union patrols out and about. Not many, but enough to give them pause. First, they went to see if their Iron Horses were still where they had left them. Two were, neither of which were River's. They'd have to double up on the escape, which was acceptable so long as things didn't get out of hand. The rest were gone. That was a joyous thing to see, for it probably meant that the others had gotten away. It was unlikely that they had been confiscated and taken into the fort; if so, why leave two? Sun was also thankful that they hadn't been stolen. Given the nature of Canvastown, he was quite surprised. Perhaps it was because the fight which had occurred earlier in the day was still fresh in peoples' minds. The civilians weren't about to get near any weaponry that reminded them of that.

With those burdens removed, they made for the fort, heads down and crouching through the thick array of tents.

We should split up, River signed. *Cover more ground.*

No, Sun signed back, giving no voice to his objection. *Too dangerous. We stick together, we do this together, or we don't do it at all.*

She didn't argue further, though he could see that she was unhappy with the decision. River sometimes took too many risks, relying too heavily on her instincts, her assumed contact with her spirit animal. She was the snake, she had said over and over again. It was all bunk, of course, and she relied on the notion too often. The snake was a deadly creature, no doubt about it, but it often struck out foolishly, getting itself caught and killed. River was brave, the bravest person that he had ever met, but she lacked education, lacked the knowledge of tactics and strategy. There was safety in numbers. On that, Geronimo was right. Perhaps when they got inside the fort, another tactic would reveal itself. But for now, they'd stick together and scale the walls as one.

They passed through an area that had clearly seen fighting during the day. Tents and tables that displayed and held goods were down and broken, still lying about on the ground. A make-shift hospital had been erected for the wounded. There were dozens, and children too, although it appeared as if those wounds were not inflicted by knives or guns, but from panic and stampede; from being caught up in the general scuffle as bullets began to fly. Sun bit back his regret, hoping that these injuries were not due to any of the Eight.

They moved from shadow to shadow, tent to tent, hiding behind barrels and crates, the occasional wagon, and even a line of Blackhoofs that looked in reasonably good shape. He made a mental note of their location and kept going, River close behind.

They reached the very end of Canvastown where it buffered the south wall of the fort, but there were fifty feet at least between the last row of tents and the wall itself. Clear and open ground with no way of hiding themselves as they crossed it. Sun looked up to the parapets. There he could see guards walking lazily up and down the length of the wall. At either end of the wall lay a heavy gun, inactive, humming lightly with RJ, but pointed upright. In the dim light it was hard to tell where their crews were. Perhaps they weren't manned at all, but Sun had to assume that they were. He looked once more at the ground between them and the wall. Making the distance was easy; getting over the wall without being detected was something else entirely.

River came up beside him and pulled her tomahawk. *Find me a long piece of rope.*

Immediately, he knew what she planned to do. He went back into the tents and found one, cut it free from its post, and gave it to her. She tied it around the hilt of the axe, pulled it tight, and handed it to Sun. *I'm not strong enough yet to throw it. You must do it.*

Sun nodded. *I will go up first, then you follow.*

They waited until the guard turned and walked away. Sun checked the cannons again to ensure that he hadn't missed seeing an errant crewman in and around their structures. Then he counted down… *four, three, two, one!*

They ran together, across the space, as fast as they could fly, until they fell against the cold, grey concrete wall of the fort. Sun hefted the tomahawk, let it swing on the rope below his hand. He had no way of knowing if it would find purchase on the other side, but it was time to throw. The guard would turn back very soon.

He swung the tomahawk to give it speed, letting it swing like a fan blade, then let it go. He let the rope slip through his hand. The axe flew through the darkness and over the parapet. It struck. Sun pulled it back. It fell to the ground.

Damn!

He wound it up again, this time taking longer, until the tomahawk was nothing but a blur. He released it and it soared over the parapet. Sun had to grab the rope at the last minute to keep it from slipping out of his reach. The axe snapped back, struck the concrete wall, and stuck. *Click!*

He wasted no time. Up he went, hand over hand, until he was at the top. He paused a moment, looked over the parapet, saw the back of the young guard, waited until he moved further away, then climbed up. Then he turned and motioned River to follow. She was up the rope even faster than he was, up and over the parapet and beside him before the guard started turning back. By then, he was far enough away from the light of the nearby RJ lantern highlighting the cannon that he couldn't see very far in front of him. Sun took advantage of the situation, unhooked the tomahawk, and gave it back to River. He coiled the rope quickly and tucked it under his belt, thinking it might come in handy later.

They dropped down into the yard of the fort. They hid behind a latrine, trying not to grow ill from the foul air around it. Sun looked across the yard. On the far wall was a long, multi-windowed building; clearly the barracks. Beside it lay another clump of buildings; officer quarters probably. What was behind those, he wondered. Surely the jail cells were near there; it made sense to have them clustered close to the soldiers, in case there was a breakout. Sun sighed and wiped sweat from his brow. *Life is never easy.*

He pointed across the yard, in the direction that they should go. There was a small group of soldiers huddled around a heating element powered by RJ near the gate; far enough away that Sun didn't give them much thought at this moment, but perhaps later they might be a concern. He also checked the rest of the guards, one patrolling each wall. And as he surmised, there were no crews manning the guns. A lucky break.

They kept to the edge of the yard, moving left, holding to the shadows and scant cover. There were a few Iron Horses that they could pause behind. Sun was thankful that they were not real horses. Real horses might have given away their position, something that Sitting Bull and the rest of the Nation's leaders could not seem to comprehend. Some modern equipment would be very useful for the Warrior Nation. Imagine a war party of a hundred men, riding Blackhoofs, or even Iron Horses if they were lucky enough, charging a Union position, without fear of real horses bucking them off or being spooked and running away. There was value in some modern technology, but how could he ever convince stubborn minds to change?

They were behind the barracks now, and they paused in the darkness to allow a soldier to finish his smoke. When he went back inside, they crossed the wooden walkway from the barracks to the mess hall.

Behind the barracks, built into the wall of the fort beneath the parapet, was a colonnade of five jail cells. Between each cell was a sconce, holding an RJ torch, lighting the way and revealing each cell and casting a shadow of their long, iron bars. It was gruesome looking, Sun thought, like the maws of beasts, frightening, unsettling in its mix of black and blood-red color. The light from the sconces would make it easy to find which cell the captain was in; it would also make it easier for guards to see them.

There was only one guard in the center of the row, sitting in a chair, leaning back against a post. A lazy half-smoked cigar hung from his mouth. He was flipping through a small picture book, oblivious to what was going on around him. His hat was pulled down over his forehead. His position in the middle of the cells was untenable; he needed to be removed.

I will do it, River signed, pulling her knife and tucking away her tomahawk.

Sun nodded. *Careful going.*

River stepped out into the red light. She moved fast but adroitly, sneaking up on the man before he turned a page. The man removed his hat just in time to see River's blade slice across his neck. He gurgled a little and died on the spot. She held him in the chair, making sure he kept from falling on the floorboards and making noise. When he stilled, she laid the chair down gently, grabbed his leg, and pulled him back to their hiding place. Sun was both impressed and pleased. She was regaining her strength.

He rifled through the guard's pockets and found a ring of keys. Apparently, there was one key per cell. That seemed terribly inefficient to Sun. But then again, if only one key fell into a prisoner's hands, then it only opened one cell; the other four were secure. He just didn't like the idea of having to pause to cycle through them all when he found Marcus. Time was something they did not have in abundance. Every second spent in the fort meant that much more time to get caught.

You stay here, Sun signed. *Watch for movement. Alert me if you see any.*

River nodded and gave her brother a small peck on the cheek. He smiled at her and began searching the cells.

He went to the first one. Empty. The second held an old man, drunk apparently, knocked out and snoozing loudly on a bed of straw. The third was empty. The fourth was not.

"Marcus," Sun hissed through the small barred window of the iron-enforced door. "Marcus."

The man sitting on the bed shot up quickly. His face was revealed in the dim red glow of RJ. "Sun. What the hell are you doing here?"

"Saving your hide, Captain," Sun said, winking and rummaging through the keys on the ring. "Be quiet, and we will have you out of here in a minute."

He tried the first key. The second. The third worked. He slipped it into the keyhole, held it there for a brief moment, then turned slowly, trying to keep the tumblers as quiet as possible. He opened the door slowly as well. It creaked.

"What in hell —"

The voice was behind him, but before Sun could turn and see who it was, the man fell dead with River's tomahawk in his back. She came out of the shadows, straddled the man, and cut his throat for good measure.

"We cannot stay here any longer," Sun said. "We go now."

River firmly agreed as she pulled her axe from the man's mangled back. Marcus shook his head. "No, we can't leave till I get my weapons."

"Where are they?" Sun asked.

"Colonel's quarters."

"Where are those?"

Marcus pointed to a clump of structures down the colonnade. "In there somewhere."

Sun shook his head. "No, we'll be caught."

"I go nowhere without my sword."

The look on the captain's face made it clear to Sun that the debate was over. They could all three be caught and thrown into cells, and it wouldn't matter. They weren't leaving without that sword. Sun had known Marcus Wayward long enough to know that when his blood was up, there was no stopping him. And his blood was up, coloring his face with a bright red heat just at the surface. He was angry, at a lot of things no doubt.

"Follow me."

They followed Marcus to the end of the colonnade, practically crawling below the windows along the back wall of the barracks. When they reached the end, Marcus waved Sun forward. "See that group of blue-bellies around that heater? They might give us trouble. I need you or River to stay here and watch them, and give me the signal if they so much as move to take a piss."

River came up and volunteered. Marcus, seeing her in such good spirits and in better shape, patted her cheek with a tender hand. Some of his pent-up fury subsided. "It's good to see you so well, River. Stop scaring me like that, okay?"

River smiled and nodded. She took up her post at the corner and Sun and Marcus moved ahead.

They slipped behind the officer's building. A narrow walkway was behind it, but there were no RJ torches or lamps along the way. The only light visible was coming through a pair of small windows in the building. Sun followed Marcus as he slowly crept up to the first window on tiptoes and peered inside. He mouthed a curse, and moved on.

The next window was face-high and sitting beside a small door. Marcus looked in the window and smiled. He motioned for Sun to have a look, and he saw a slightly heavy-set man sitting at a table, quill in hand, writing a letter in the light from a normal oil lamp. The man was smoking a cigar and had removed his uniform for the evening.

"That's him," Marcus said. "Son of a bitch clipped my sword to his belt. I'm gonna clip his brains with it when I get it back."

"Keep calm, Captain," Sun said.

"I'll be calm once I get my weapons. Come on."

The door was unlocked. It led to a long hallway that ran the length of the building and ended at another door, which probably led out to the yard. The corridor split into a T-shape at the center point. Marcus walked to that point.

They peeked around the corner. Down this other hall lit faintly by RJ was a line of officers' quarters, their doors closed. The colonel's quarters were right there at the corner, and his door was at arm's length.

"How do we get in?" Sun asked.

Marcus shrugged. "I guess we knock."

He knocked, three quick raps with his left hand. "Yes, who is it?"

"I need to speak with you, Colonel," Marcus said, trying to disguise the southern drawl in his voice.

A pause, then the colonel said, "Who is it?" Marcus fell silent, and they could hear the man push away from the table and walk to the door, his socked feet sliding across the wooden floor. When he opened the door, Marcus pounced.

He lifted the colonel off the ground, his left, weaker hand underneath the man's jowl. He carried him through the room and slammed him onto his cot. Marcus squeezed until the colonel's eye bulged. "I don't like people taking my sword. Where is it?"

Colonel Thawley, his face growing a nasty shade of purple, motioned with a weak finger toward his belt which hung on a peg beside the bed. It held Marcus's sword and pistol. "You'll… You'll hang for this," the man managed to squeak out from between his pursed lips.

Sun grabbed the belt. Marcus holstered his pistol and pulled the sword from the belt hook. "Maybe," he said, "but not tonight, and not by you."

With one elegant motion, Marcus ran the sword across the colonel's neck. His head rolled free to the right like a ripe melon, the energy coursing across the blade, singing the flesh and cauterizing the wound somewhat. Still, blood poured across the white linen sheets.

Sun cringed. "Was that necessary, Captain?"

Marcus nodded. "He'd have barked the minute we let him go, and we ain't got time to tie him up. Besides, *no one* steals my sword."

The faint hoot of an owl came through the still of the room. "River," Sun said. "We have to go."

"Yes," Marcus said, turning away from the headless colonel and making for the door. He looked into the hallway. No one. Their commotion hadn't stirred anyone inside at least. "We need a diversion, and I'm tired of scooting around shadow to shadow."

"What do you propose?"

Marcus looked down the hall to the door leading out to the yard. "Let's go out the front."

Sun was about to object, but Marcus sheathed his sword, drew his pistol, and headed out.

They stopped at the door and saw that there were only three men now around the RJ heating element. Two had moved away, by Sun's recollection of the number that had been there on their arrival, and where they had gone was hard to say. Marcus was right, though; with three kills to their credit, and soldiers moving about the yard and on the walls, continuing to lag around in the dark was an untenable plan. The chances of them being spotted now had grown exponentially. So, how were they going to escape?

Marcus answered the question by opening the door. He stepped out, took three steps toward the men around the heater, smiled, and raised his pistol. "Good evening, boys," he said with a big, boisterous voice. "Happy New Year!"

He pulled the trigger, and the heating unit exploded, throwing flaming RJ everywhere. The men nearby were showered in it, their screams echoing off the walls as they flailed around on the ground, trying to put out the flames.

"Let's go!"

They ran, straight across the yard, guided by the light of the growing fire. This distraction also caused the guards on the wall to pause and reconcile their minds to this sudden threat. Some even jumped straight off, one injuring his leg as he fell. River joined them halfway, her hands going a mile a minute, signing her discontent to this new plan. River was never one for big entrances and exits; subtlety and subterfuge were her ways.

Sun shot the closest guard on the wall and watched him fall into the yard. "We need to jump the wall, and make for our campsite. Our 'Horses are still there."

Marcus said nothing but ran toward the steps leading up to the wall. They followed closely.

A post in front of them disintegrated in a powerful blast of RJ fire.

"*Halt!*" said a tinny, robotic voice behind them. Sun turned and saw the stolid, metallic shape of a UR-30 Enforcer Bot, obviously brought to life by the explosion and gunfire. It held a blaster in its hand. "*Lay down your weapons and surrender!*"

Marcus turned and fired, sending a round into the Enforcer's shoulder. Sun followed, putting one into its leg. The strikes rocked the bot backward, but it kept its balance and fired again, sending a high-velocity round into the wall and showering them with grey dust and concrete shards.

Marcus let River take the stairs. Sun followed. "Let River jump first," Marcus said, firing again into the bot's leg. "Then you go."

"No, sir," Sun said, firing another shot of his own, striking the Enforcer right in the crotch. "You cannot make that jump with your knee. You'll break it. I'll help you down."

Marcus shuffled up the stairs, dodging shot after shot from the Enforcer that struck the stone steps and left deep, hissing craters. When he got to the top, Sun offered his hand. Marcus took it, jumped onto the parapet, and then over the side.

His weight carried Sun forward into the hard concrete, but he held firm, stiffening just in time to lower Marcus down the wall. He could only lower him a few more feet, but that was better than a power jump from the top. With Marcus's own height and the distance afforded Sun's arm, the captain would only have to drop two-thirds the distance, and River was down there to help him land properly. Sun stretched his arm as far as it would go, then released. He looked back once more, took a final shot, sending a round into the Enforcer's head, then swung out over the wall. A shower of UR-30 bullets hit the parapet around him, nicking his hand. Sun grimaced as pain shot down his arm, but he held tightly. He took one last look back into the fort before dropping. He wished he hadn't.

Another Enforcer had joined the first.

Chapter 10

Marcus raised his hand and helped Sun find his feet in the darkness. "We have big trouble," Sun said as he straightened. "There are two of them."

Marcus wagged his head. "Damn! Let's move."

They made the distance between the fort and the first row of tents. Marcus would have preferred that they move around the perimeter of Canvastown, away from civilians, but there was a practical need to go through it. It would be harder for the Enforcers to get a bead on them as they ran. That of course meant that innocent lives would be at stake, but that couldn't be avoided. This was their last chance to escape. Besides, he was hoping that the bots would favor the civilians and temper their shooting.

He was wrong. Blaster rounds shot past them and struck the soft ground with an eruption of mud and grass. Marcus looked back and saw both Enforcers on the wall. One jumped and struck the ground in full run. It held both its pistols forward, ripping off shot after shot, igniting the dark air with each blast. Behind them, in front of them, to their sides, rounds struck. River fell to the ground. Marcus shielded her and yanked her up. "Go!" he said, pushing her forward.

The second bot dropped down and joined the first. They entered the tents in tandem, four pistols firing relentlessly.

Marcus stopped and took shelter behind a wagon. He shot thrice, striking the lead Enforcer in the head and shoulders. "You have to hit them in the chest," Sun said, taking his own shots, and trying to pull Marcus away. "That is where they are vulnerable, or so I have been told."

Marcus huffed. "I don't see how that's the sweet spot. Their armor is thick there."

Sun nodded. "That is probably why. It is hard to penetrate, so naturally that is where its most important parts are located."

Marcus rose up and threw two more shots square into the chest of the lead bot. It fell, wiggled on the ground as if the bullets had struck its RJ supply. Then it stood again, and rejoined its partner. For a second, it seemed as if they had both lost track of their prey.

"Go!" Marcus hissed, and all three ran, around the end of a multi-roomed tent and into the main road that would lead them to their camp.

The Enforcers caught sight of them again and continued their pursuit. Thankfully, it was dark and although the commotion had brought many out of their tents to see what was happening, no one was stepping into the road. All they had to do was keep this line straight on and they'd make it.

Blasters fired again. Sun went down.

"Sun!" Marcus screamed and ran over to him.

Sun rose up on his backside, fired off three shots and said, "I am all right, Captain. They just nicked me... again."

His right arm was bleeding. Marcus helped him up, and they kept running.

The deep, powerful roar of an Iron Horse came up the road, and then headlights appeared. Marcus jumped out of the way just in time to let it pass, moving fast and deliberate toward the Enforcers. The man piloting it stood straight in the seat.

It came to a halt just in front of the bots. The driver swung its tail around and hit one of the Enforcers square in the legs, knocking it down. The man stepped off, balled up his gloved hand and drove it into the neck of the one that was grounded. A flash of sparks and red fluid sprang from its neck as its head popped off. The man then grabbed the head and tossed it to Marcus.

"A souvenir," he said, yanking the bot off the ground and flinging its headless body over his shoulder to protect his back. The other Enforcer put round after round into his partner, while the man, holding the bot tight, climbed back onto his Iron Horse. "Keep running," he said, waving Marcus and the others forward. "I'll cover your retreat."

Marcus did not argue. As they ran, he kept looking behind, and the man was following closely, letting the flailing bot on his back take the blaster rounds of the other. Occasionally, the man would release the handle bar of his 'Horse and shoot a wall of energy out of his glove, and the chasing bot would go down as it struck the invisible shield, cutting a huge swath of mud through the road as it slid. It would eventually find its feet again and keep coming. The one on his back, however, finally ended its struggle as a blaster round found the vulnerable spot on its chest. The man finally tossed it away. He then drew his pistol, turned at the waist, and put a high-velocity round into the charging Enforcer. It went down for the final time, a massive hole ripped through its chest.

They reached the two Iron Horses that were waiting in their old camp. Marcus climbed on one and gunned the engine. Sun and River took the other. They let their engines warm for a few seconds, then headed out, followed by the man.

Behind them, danger sirens blared on the walls of the fort. The fire that Marcus had started was glowing hot and red in the night sky. He looked down at the head of the Enforcer, given to him as a souvenir. *Souvenir?* It was still warm from RJ, yet its eye was dark, empty, lifeless. He gripped the skull tight, and then tossed the head over his shoulder.

He wanted nothing to remind him of Fort Smith.

*****

They rode all night, through a blinding rain that began about an hour after leaving the fort. They paused briefly as the wind whipped up, fearful that a tornado or terrible thunderstorm might pitch up and damage their Iron Horses. None did, but the rain soaked them clean to the bone, just like it had done a day ago. Marcus took it as a sign: never visit Fort Smith again. Words of wisdom, indeed.

The rain ended a few hours later, but that did nothing to soothe their minds, nor give them cause to speak. They said nothing to each other, and that was fine with Marcus. Nothing good or positive could come from talking at this time anyway, still so angry with what had transpired over the past day. He was exhausted and in pain. His hand, his knee, even his weak left ear rang and throbbed. All he wanted to do was find his people. Getting them all back together was paramount, and if they kept to the main road that they were traveling, they should eventually find them. They had had instances in the past where some had been required to flee while others would catch up.

The standing rule was always to keep to main roads and if necessary, find camp near them. That way, those following behind could travel approximately in the right direction and eventually link up. By the time the sun began to rise, that's exactly what happened.

Sierra had posted herself in a tree along the road, and when she saw them, gave a whistle. Marcus recognized it immediately. She motioned for them to follow her as she jumped on her Iron Horse that she had hidden with pine branches and leaves, and led them off the road and down a worn path and up into a patch of evergreens, where needles had fallen over the years and now lay thick on the ground, brown and dry, but soft. A pit for a fire had been dug, and someone had bagged a pheasant. Marcus could smell its remnants as they parked their Iron Horses near the edge of camp. The others roused from their sleep to greet them.

He shook Jake's hand, careful not to further harm the man's forearm which was bandaged up from the cuts he had received from Sasha's blades. He hugged K-Free and Zarelda, nodded to Hicks, and then walked over to the gloved man who was just climbing off his Iron Horse. With one swift move, Marcus swept the man's legs, grabbed the lapels of his coat, and took him to the ground. Seeing their captain move so suddenly and with such determination, Jake and Zarelda drew their guns and pointed them at the man. The others gathered around, taking defensive positions.

"Carl Fredrickson," Marcus said, drawing his pistol and sticking it under the man's chin. "What is a Union toady like you doing following us?"

Carl cleared his throat, but kept still, eyeing wearily the firepower arrayed at his head. "Now this is a fine hello for a man that just saved your life… and Flowing River's."

"You better fess up, son," Jake said, letting a shot of flame leap from his rifle's barrel. "We're likely to get angry."

"My people get *real* angry, Carl, when they feel put upon," Marcus said, "so I recommend you speak, and do it now."

"Let me up, and I will."

Marcus paused then pulled away, holstering his pistol and letting Carl get to his feet. The man straightened his coat, wiped errant pine needles off with his non-gloved hand, and cleared his throat. "Abe Lincoln hired me to follow you."

"Why?" Marcus asked.

"To make sure you did your job. He's got a lot of money riding on you."

"Ain't that something?" Jake shook his head, clearly disgusted with this revelation, just as much as Marcus was. "Son of a bitch don't trust us, boss. Now you see why I didn't want to take this deal?"

Marcus ignored the question, turned his attention back to Carl. "If Lincoln was so concerned with us jumping the agreement, then why didn't he just assign you to us in the first place? Why the shadow work?"

"Because I refused to do so. I'm no mercenary, Marcus, nor do I have any desire to meet Carpathian face to face. I'm no fool, even though I agree with the rationale for wanting that monster dead. I like life too much. Let others find him and kill him if they can. My job was to see you safely to Arizona and then turn around."

"That job's over," Marcus said.

"And what about Tanner?" Jake interrupted again. "How's he fit into this?"

"He's been hired by President Johnson," Marcus said. "They let him go the minute we were taken into the fort. What we have here, ladies and gentlemen, are two people, two groups in fact, working at cross purposes. We got the Union trying to take matters into their own hands by hiring Sasha, and we got Lincoln hiring us to do the very same thing, with bragging rights going to whoever gets that European polecat first. It's all about ego."

Carl shook his head. "No, sir. I can assure you, Lincoln's intentions are sincere."

Perhaps they were at that, Marcus considered. Lincoln had all but stated in the Doomsday in Kentucky that he did not work for the Union, but like Jake, he only gave that notion half a listen. Sasha was the proof that Abe was truly working independently from his old pals. Politicians lied all the time to keep their true feelings, their true intentions, secret. Hell, the fact that Lincoln had hired Carl to track them wasn't all that surprising given a politician who always hedged his bet; there was a lot at stake here. If he hadn't been tracking them, River would have certainly died in that field. But who had sent those beasts against them? That was still a mystery.

Marcus pulled a stern, serious face. "What do you know about The Wraith?"

On that, Carl seemed to blanch. He averted his eyes, clearly not wanting to say. But they would stand there all day if necessary until he spoke. "Lincoln hired him."

"To do the same thing we're doing?"

Carl nodded.

The collective gasp and boiling rage that went up among everyone was shared by Marcus. This angered him, although Robert Gunter had admitted at the fort that he was on the trail to Carpathian. The truth of who had hired him, however, was infuriating.

"Did he send those beasts at us?" Marcus asked.

Carl shook his head. "I don't know, but I doubt the Warrior Nation would deal with Gunter personally. He's everything they despise."

"And a madman," Marcus said. "Your boss made a big mistake, Carl. Hiring The Wraith as his backup plan has put the entire operation in jeopardy, do you know that? The Wraith is not above killing us and himself just to ensure that *we* don't win. He'll dog our trial till the end, and Sasha Tanner will roll right over our dried bones and snatch the egg."

"I don't think Lincoln cares who kills Carpathian, so long as he's dead."

Marcus chuckled. "Oh, I think he does. No man puts up that amount of money, and then goes to the lengths that he has, to ensure success without desire for victory. Two for the price of one, and whoever returns first gets the gold. We're all pawns in his game."

"Let's ditch this mission, Captain," Hicks said, coming up beside Marcus. "The odds are clearly against us now, what with Tanner and The Wraith on our heels. Let's switch sides. You said it yourself in Kentucky. Let's find Carpathian and offer our services to him. What do we care if he's dead? We serve the highest bidder anyway, right? We always have."

Indeed, they always had, and changing sides was still a possibility. Marcus had not forgotten that. At some point in his life, he reasoned, he'd like to have full function of his knee again, and the doctor was probably the only person in the world to give him that. And like Hicks said, the odds were stacked against them now, despite still outnumbering their competition four to one. Sasha and The Wraith were not common street thugs. They were trained killers with just as big a desire for fame, fortune, and glory as the next man. As much as Marcus himself, in fact. He could not deny that. The Eight had seen a lot of action over the years, had garnered a reputation to last a lifetime. But to kill Burson Carpathian, to be the ones who got inside his impenetrable lair and kill him... Well, that would make them *legends*. Siding with the doctor in the end, while perhaps more practical, would perpetuate the status quo, and where was the glory in that?

"We have time to make that decision, Hicks," Marcus said. "No need to make it today."

"Captain, I—"

Marcus put up his hand and quieted the restless mechanic. "I hear you, but now we need to regroup and get ready for Fort Waco. Let's take a breather, eat a bit of food, perhaps even sleep awhile, then we'll let out again."

"The Union is certainly going to send out a party to find us," Sun said, while getting his arm checked over by Zarelda, "given the way we left Fort Smith."

Marcus nodded. "Yes, but it'll take them awhile to regroup, assuming the whole damn fort didn't burn down."

"Burn down? Now that's a story I want to hear." K-Free grinned with excitement.

Marcus smiled. "And hear it you will, right after I eat something."

"What we gonna do about him, boss?" Jake asked, motioning to Carl with his rifle.

Marcus turned and faced the man. "As I said, your tracking days are over, Carl. But you ain't leaving. No sir. Lincoln has you by the chestnuts. The die is cast. Whether you want to or not, you're in it just like us. And like us, you'll be facing that foreign devil where he stands."

Carl looked around, perhaps searching for an exit. But he wasn't stupid. He was powerful, perhaps one of the most powerful men in the Union, but there was no way he'd escape alive fighting the Wayward Eight.

"Okay," he said, "I'll come with you, but I want an even portion of the take."

Marcus looked around to see if anyone objected to that demand. Only Jake seemed to mind, with clenched teeth and a nervous vein popping out on his forehead. Marcus took that as a good sign.

"Agreed."

Carl put out his gloved hand. "Let's shake on it."

Marcus moved to accept, but saw the swirl of RJ pumping hot and bright through the structure of the glove. He pulled his hand away and with a wry smile, said, "Not on your life, Carl. Not on your miserable life."

*****

The Wraith had ridden half the night, through rain and hail and into a deadly windstorm that blew his Iron Horse off the road. He jumped just before it struck a pine tree and burst into flames. He rolled into a gully, gnashing his teeth against the excruciating pain in his right arm.

A lucky shot. The woman who reminded him of Lucinda Loveless had gotten off one lucky shot. Now, here he lay, bleeding in the middle of a thunderstorm. Thankfully, his shoulder armor had deflected most of the energy of the bullet, and thus it had only grazed his arm and not blown it off; if that had happened, he'd be dead right now, not only from the concussion but from the radiation that would have sickened his blood right good. He was still nauseous, for sure, but already that sensation was subsiding, as he knew it would. He was The Wraith, and by-God, there was no one that could take a bullet like him. *Atomic pistol be damned!*

Where was he? He wasn't sure how far he had traveled. He had slipped past the Union soldiers at the fort and had headed south, laughing and smiling, having left Marcus and his miserable stooges behind. He tried looking around, trying to see if he could recognize anything, any buildings or trees that might give him an idea of where he was. Nothing stood out. It was too dark and he was in too much pain.

He ripped off a piece of his shirt and wrapped it around his arm as a tourniquet to stop the bleeding. It did, but his arm still hurt like hell.

In the light of the burning 'Horse, he crawled through the gully, through mud and water, until he came to rest against a tree trunk lying on the ground. He closed his eyes and felt comforted by the heat coming off the burning vehicle. He slept.

He awoke the next morning to four ugly faces. The men that carried those faces smelled too, as if they'd been on the trail for weeks without bathing. Their clothing was tattered and disheveled, spotted with dirt, mud, and grass stains. Two of the men had beards. And from what he could tell from their arrogant smiles, none of them had very good teeth.

"Who are you, mister?"

The man who asked the question must have been in charge of the miserable group. The Wraith looked into the man's ugly face and blinked. "I'm The Wraith."

They laughed. "What the hell kind of name is that?" another asked.

He ignored the question and looked around some more. They had come in on Blackhoofs. Four of them stood nearby, one with eagle and hawk feathers hanging off its iron neck. That was one good sign at least, The Wraith thought. *Warrior killers.*

"How'd you get like this, mister?" The youngest of the group asked. He was a pretty clean-cut kid, no beard, five or six years younger than the others. Too young to be running with these losers.

"Got into a little dispute at Fort Smith," he said, pushing himself up straight to sit more erect against the log. "The Union doesn't seem to like my politics."

"Looks like it," one said shaking his head in disbelief. "Where you headed?"

On that, The Wraith paused, then he said, "Nowhere special. Just traveling. And if you boys will help me up, loan me that whiskey bottle you got in your pocket there, and a Blackhoof, I'll be much obliged and on my way."

They laughed at him. The one in charge shook his head. "I don't think so, mister." He pulled a pistol and aimed it at The Wraith's face. "You ain't in no shape to be asking us for anything. Now, how's about you hand over those weapons you got? I ain't never seen any like them, and they'd fit my hand just as good as yours I figure."

The others had pulled their pistols too, except for the boy, who held a knife forward in a wobbly hand. Not a single gun among them, however, had RJ. Standard issue pieces: a Schofield Smith & Wesson, a Colt 45, and a Webley Bull Dog. The Wraith raised an approving eyebrow on that last one; he hadn't seen one of those in a while. Wouldn't mind having this one, in fact.

He put up his hands in peace. "Okay, boys, no need for anyone to get hurt. I'll give you the guns. But first, if you'll show me one courtesy, I'd appreciate it." He pointed at the boy. "Son, will you be so kind as to walk over yonder and scrape up a little bit of RJ on the tip of your knife? I seem to have left my blade back at Fort Smith."

The boy hesitated, then moved on a nod from his leader. "Okay, now, hand them over," the man said, cocking his 45.

The Wraith moved his hands slowly to the pistols at his sides. He smiled. "Have you all heard the story about the wolf and the three little pigs? '*Little pig, little pig, let me come in. No, no, not by the hair on my chinny chin chin. Then I'll huff, and I'll puff, and I'll blow your* –'"

He drew his pistols and put rounds in the heads of the leader and another man. Then he pulled both triggers and sent two shots into the chest of the man standing right in front of him. All three were dead before they hit the ground.

"'—*blow yours heads off.*' I always liked that fairy tale."

The boy stood behind the three corpses, holding his knife out, hot, red RJ on its tip. He didn't move a muscle.

The Wraith tucked his pistols away and stood up slowly. He grabbed his shotgun and carefully slung it over his back. He grimaced. The pain in his arm was blinding.

"Thank you," he said, taking the knife from the boy and opening his coat to expose the red, swollen cut from the bullet. He grit his teeth and pushed the RJ into the wound and massaged it in slowly; slow enough to work the searing fluid into the cut thoroughly, but not so strongly as to excite the volatile properties within the red fuel and force it to ignite and blow his arm off. He howled like a wolf, fell to one knee, but kept the knife in place until the RJ had thoroughly cauterized the wound.

When the pain subsided, he stood and handed the knife back to the boy. Then he rummaged around the body of the man who had held the Webley Bull Dog, found the piece and dropped it into his coat pocket. He also pocketed the whiskey bottle he had asked for.

He went to the Blackhoof with the hanging eagle feathers and climbed aboard. He turned it on, and its eyes ignited red with RJ coursing through its frame. He let it trot forward a bit; it was a little wobbly on the left side, but it would have to do.

"Now," said The Wraith, halting the Blackhoof next to the boy who still stood in shock among the three corpses, "I figure the Union will be by directly looking for me. If they do, you tell them that Marcus Wayward did all this, you hear?"

The boy nodded quickly.

"And you further let them know that Marcus is headed to Fort Waco. You tell them this exactly as I have told you, or I'll track you down and kill a fourth pig. Understand?"

"Y—yes, sir. I sure will, sir."

He nodded politely and headed out, leaving the boy and the carnage behind.

He was still in pain, but pleased with himself. If by some chance Marcus and his merry band had escaped Fort Smith, their next best move would be to head to Fort Waco. A place like that would provide support and succor to them as they tried discovering the whereabouts of Carpathian's hideout. A place like Fort Waco was a good place for The Wraith as well, but he wasn't headed there. His destination lay further south, along the Contested Territory - Mexican border, in a pleasant little town called Laredo.

Chapter 11

Fort Waco lay near the town of Waco, in Contested Territory, which was along the Brazos River. In its heyday, it was one of the Union's most prestigious forts in the Contested Territories. The Civil War, plus the unsettled aftermath of the conflict, left it in the hands of a small garrison, which was then hastily overrun by bandits and outlaws of various stripes. Part of the main structure of the fort had burned to the ground, and nobody bothered to rebuild it. Now, like Fort Smith, it served as a shanty town for some of the most inhospitable ruffians in all the country. Unlike Fort Smith, with its strong Union presence, Fort Waco functioned under a kind of tempered chaos, each lawless gang or group practicing its own sense of justice. It was not uncommon to witness duels once every few days. Fights broke out regularly in the three main saloons and brothels lined up along the main road that connected the fort to the town. It was a wild, lawless place. It was perfect for Marcus's plans.

They had arrived two days earlier, after spending half a day in the pine grove south of Fort Smith. No Union troopers had found them, and it didn't appear as if any were in pursuit. So they took their time and gathered themselves along the road, stopping on occasion to interview folks about their knowledge of Doctor Carpathian. Few had any information worthy of the name, and those that did, recommended what they had already planned, which was to ride to Waco and check out the rumor mill among the outlaws therein.

One such outlaw stood in front of him right now, her tasseled blue riding dress hanging down her snakeskin-booted leg which was propped up on a chair nearby. From her mouth hung a cigarette. In her left hand lay a black riding crop. At her hip, she wore a UR-30 Blaster, which she claimed to have lifted from an Enforcer personally. A thick white scar lay across her left cheek, presumably from a bullet just like the disgusting butcher at Fort Smith had claimed. In her balled-up graying hair lay three four-inch long hairpins of pure silver. Rumor suggested that those pins were sharp and encrusted with Strychnine. Marcus didn't doubt it.

"I agreed to this meeting, Captain Wayward," Desiree Ladue said in her broken French-English, taking a long puff from her smoke, "out of respect for you and your infamous Wayward Eight. But I don't recall giving permission for you to bring your entire team. They make me uncomfortable, *n'est-ce pas?* Especially that son of a bitch right there," she said, pointing her cigarette at a man at the back of the room. "Who might you be, *monsieur*?"

"That's Carl Fredrickson," Marcus said. "He's partnered with us on this mission."

Desiree nodded. "*Je vois.* Can't take on the doctor with only eight, eh?" She laughed, which turned into a cough. Desiree finished her smoke and flung it in a spittoon behind her. It sizzled in tobacco juice. "Wise up, Confederate boy. You'll need a lot more than that. I guarantee."

Marcus ignored her last remark. "I apologize for packing this small room so tightly, but in the event that I should fall on this mission, it's important that my people know the information that you have, know it like I do. Memorize it if necessary."

Desiree looked around the room, sizing up everyone with a mild squint. She pulled a toothpick from inside the folds of her dress and placed it in her mouth, rolling it with her tongue until it was lodged comfortably between teeth and gum. "And you trust these people?"

"Yes, ma'am, with my life."

"Really? *Bravo.* I don't trust one lady under my charge."

Her ladies were the infamous Fire and Lace Gang, sometimes five, sometimes six women of notorious reputation and temperament. The gang was comprised of women from all walks of life, from the lowly New Orleans street whore to a senator's daughter. The gang had been in service since before the Civil War, and members had come and gone, some voluntarily, some through death. But Desiree Ladue had survived and had always been their mother. On occasions, she would allow a group of beast sized Mandingo Men to tag along for extra muscle. The ladies did not much like them, but none of them would ever dare challenge Ladue's judgment.

"So what can I do for you, *Capitaine*?" she asked.

"People tell me that you know where Carpathian lives, that you have been there, that you have seen what lies past Payson with your own eyes. We want to know where it is."

Desiree huffed. "Do you now? Well, *Capitaine*, that information don't come cheap."

"Sierra," Marcus said, stepping aside to allow her to move up and place three large stacks of bills on the table. She also produced a bag of coins from her belt and laid it against the stack.

"One thousand-fifty," Marcus said, "and some assorted coins."

Desiree took her leg off the chair and sat down. She eyed the stack carefully. "Not bad, but I have a particular fondness for the Warrior Nation, and every good Indian knows that the magic number is *quatre*... four."

Marcus sighed, nodded to Sierra. She drew another stack from her satchel and placed it on the table. Desiree took it and placed it on top of the others. She eyed it like it was a precious jewel. She nodded. "Very good. We have balance." She put out her hand and clicked her fingers. "Give me paper and something to write with."

Hicks came up and produced both. She took them and began scribbling a map. "Now, I have never seen his hideout up close, *comprendre*, but I do know its basic whereabouts."

"I was told that you had seen it," Marcus said, "up close."

Desiree shook her head and drew borders. "No, that ain't true. When me and my ladies worked further west, we used to go into Carpathian's territory. One night, our camp was ambushed by that son of a bitch and his sickening, scabrous monsters. They took two of my *filles*. We chased them as far as we could, but he runs patrols around his perimeter, *n'est-ce pas*, and they scout out pretty far. We lost two more trying to fight our way through. I had to retreat before we all died. But..." She finished the map and laid it out for everyone to see. She pointed to an 'x' she had drawn on the paper. "This is where we are, Fort Waco. This is the border between the Contested Territories and Carpathian Industries land. We got pouched here." She drew another 'x' then drew a long line into

Carpathian's area and ended it with a large circle. She then backtracked about halfway and drew another '*x*'. "This is as far as we got. The patrol struck us here. But I guarantee, this road goes all the way to his complex."

"How you know dat?" Zarelda asked, coming up and looking carefully at the map.

"Desiree Ladue is no *idiote,*" she said, poking the side of her head with her index finger. She took a cigarette from her silver case, lit it, and blew a large ring of fresh smoke into the stale air of the room. "It is the only road that goes that deep into the Tonto Forest, *n'est-ce pas?* You keep going down that road, I guarantee you will find him. But the trick is getting past his guards. You cannot do that with just nine people. It is impossible."

"You don't know how good we are, lady," Jake said, snickering a little under his breath. "The boss man himself could do it without us. We're just along to keep him alive."

Others chuckled at that. Marcus put up his hand. "Thank you, Jake, for your confidence, but don't understate all y'alls contribution to the team. Everyone is important." He turned his attention back to the map. "And you are certain of this, Desiree? The road you speak of can be picked up here, and taken in this direction all the way into his backyard?"

Desiree nodded, drew the cigarette from her mouth. "*Oui.* Desiree Ladue never lies. The road, of course, may be worn in places, overgrown, as those things are wont to happen. But I see you got two from the Warrior Nation." She motioned to Sun and River. "If they are worth anything, they'll keep you on the straight path. Or better yet, take me and my ladies with you. Fifteen riding strong could easily get past those guards. What do you say? I have a score of my own to settle with that foreign *diable.*"

Marcus grabbed the map, folded it carefully, and tucked it into his coat pocket. "Thanks for the offer, Miss Ladue, but that won't be necessary. Our agreement was cash for information. Nothing more. We are more than capable of finding the place ourselves."

"Finding it, *oui*, but getting inside is another matter. You will fail, *monsieur*. I guarantee it."

"Thank you, no," Marcus said forcefully. "Our business is now concluded, Miss Ladue. You may go."

As she grabbed up the money and stashed it away in various pockets and creases in her dress, Desiree kept her eyes peeled on K-Free's face. She finished her cigarette, dropped it into the spittoon and said, "What's your name, *donzelle*?"

"Kimberly Free."

"Well, Kimberly, when you grow tired of this arrogant *garcon*, you come see me, okay? We need a bright young thing like you in the gang."

She winked, and Kimberly nodded politely, but said nothing. Marcus stepped back to let Desiree leave the room. She took the offer. "Good luck, Captain Wayward. Good luck to you all. Try not to get yourselves killed, *n'est-ce pas*?"

She was gone. Sierra waved smoke out of her face. The rest faded back into the room and took chairs. Marcus sat at the table, took the map back out, and unfolded it. "Assuming that she is telling the truth, I think we have our route forward."

"Was it wise, Marcus," Carl asked, leaning over the table, putting himself in Marcus's view, "to refuse her offer to come with us? That's another six bodies, six guns. We'll need all the help we can get."

"Yes, and then she'd demand part of the take too, wouldn't she?" Marcus pointed out. "Enough to cover her and her ladies' troubles. We don't know anything about her, Carl. Nothing, save that she's an outlaw with a violent reputation. And people on the streets here say she's particularly aggressive against men. Would she take my orders? She may be good at what she does, but she's too rugged. She calls me an arrogant boy? What the hell is she? She's a captain herself, and there won't be two captains in this venture. I learned the hard way a long time ago. Two captains in one unit is a recipe for failure. There will be only one captain in the Eight, and as long as I'm alive, that'll be me." He looked around the room. "Any objections?"

Nobody expressed them, even if they agreed with Carl. Some probably did, but so what? He could not allow Carl Frederickson, himself accustomed to being in charge, to force a change in his authority. Marcus didn't want to be stubborn for stubborn's sake, but under the circumstances, he had to assert his control on the group.

"Good," he said, leaning over the map. "Now crowd around and let's plan our next move."

*****

The Red Maple Saloon was the roughest, rowdiest beer hall in Fort Waco. Everyone who found their way to the fort eventually stepped inside. Every outlaw and gunman this side of the Mississippi had heard about it and its tenacious Canadian owner, Teras Cassidy. Cassidy had won it from its previous owner in a game of five-card stud, and the ensuing brawl that solidified the deal was still talked about in awe around town. Since then, no one had ever seen a night without Mr. Cassidy standing behind the bar, ladling out spirits and talking up a storm. Some wondered if he ever retired long enough to sleep.

"I'll sleep when I'm dead," he said to Hicks as he poured him a shot of tangleleg. "Besides, if I had decided to take a break just now, I might have missed yours and the lady's fine company."

Zarelda didn't like sitting at the bar. She didn't wish to give anyone the notion that she partook in alcohol, but this Cassidy fellow had some interesting information about Carpathian and what they might find when they got there.

"You'll find death, that's what you'll find," he said, pouring a whiskey for Carl Fredrickson who had just arrived. "Before I bought this place, I was running southwest with a few goldpanners come down from Canada. We decided to take the scenic route, and thus we found ourselves traveling south and right along the Mexican and Contested border. The idea was, if no place served us in America, we'd hop the line and go all the way to Mexico City. Well, one night we were sitting around our campfire, see, and we started hearing this groaning, moaning, this fearful sound of pick-axes and shovels. We thought perhaps we had stumbled onto outlaws or something, digging up treasure. We go and took a look, and there they were, the strangest, most disgusting creatures you ever saw, grey gangly flesh glowing red with RJ, digging up bodies in a Catholic graveyard. They dug up about six, laid them out all pretty in a row. And then this man comes along and puts a belt onto each of them with a bandolier crossing their boney chests. Then he lit them up with RJ, and every one of them came back to life, just like that, and walked upright. One of my buddies puked right then and there, the other fainted. After they collected themselves, we hightailed it out of there, and never looked back. We parted company soon thereafter and I came here, and I'm never going that far west again.

"If you find this European fellow, all you'll find is death. Death walking again, death animated, and they say there is no stopping the dead. You'd be smart to turn around and go back home."

Zarelda sat and listened to the story with fascination. She'd heard stories like this about Carpathian's activities before, but never from an eyewitness, and never with such certainty. It was true, then: RJ-1027 was being used to reanimate the dead. It sounded almost like voodoo, like the stories she had heard as a girl from the Queen Mother. Her mama and grandmamma were not voodoo priestesses, but they had taught her to respect the divination and the resurrection of the dead. Cassidy's story confirmed what she had always suspected: RJ had medicinal value, for not only did it animate empty flesh, it kept it alive, without rot, for long periods of time. Carpathian was creating an undead army. She was certain of it now, and the thought of getting into his laboratory, learning everything she could about RJ... The idea excited her. She wanted to leave tonight, to continue their journey and get it over with. She had to know more.

Carl downed his shot and wiped his mouth. "What did you want to see me about, Hicks?"

Hicks grabbed the bottle that Cassidy had placed in front of them. "Not here. Let's go in the back."

Zarelda gave Cassidy a few dollar bills and followed her husband to the back of the noisy saloon. A nagging, sinking feeling came over her. *I shouldn't be here*, she thought. *We shouldn't be discussing this, not with a stranger*. And that was what Carl Fredrickson was in essence. What did they know about him, other than that he was good at killing? How could Hicks trust him? There was something wrong with her husband. She didn't know what it was, but he had changed. Ever since their first conversation in those fields west of the Mississippi River a few weeks back, ever since she had seen those birds. His dissatisfaction of this mission had grown, and now he sought out additional allies to bolster his plan. *I shouldn't be here*, she thought again as they found chairs and a table in a dark corner.

"I asked you here, Carl," Hicks said, "because I think you and I are kindred spirits. Given the level of technology in your weapons, especially your glove, I think you'll appreciate what I have to say."

"Is this about what you were saying to Marcus before in that forest outside Fort Smith?" Carl asked.

Hicks nodded to Zarelda. "Z and I have discussed this already, and we are of the same mind. This mission is doomed to fail. Marcus – God love him – isn't making the right decisions here. Refusing to accept Ladue's offer to come along is the last in a long list of mistakes. I think you'd agree to that."

Carl nodded. "That would not have been my decision, no."

"Exactly, and what's next? Follow that map all the way into the Tonto Forest and up to Carpathian's doorstep? Then what? Knock on the door? How do we get in? How do we coordinate our attack once we're inside?"

"You can't expect Marcus to have dis all figured out now, Hicks," Zarelda said. "We have to get dare first, and see what it's all about."

Hicks shook his head. "I'm not saying that he should have it all planned out in detail, but he should have some notion as to how we will carry out the attack once we get there. He hasn't discussed that at all, and do you know why? Because he knows in his own heart that it's a suicide mission. He's just too damned stubborn to admit it."

"What are you proposing?" Carl asked.

"Z and I have agreed that if Marcus gets us there, we're going to seek out Carpathian and make an appeal to him personally, throw our support behind him, so that we may learn from him, gain technology as well, and Zarelda will finally learn everything she wants to know about RJ. We want your support.

We think you have the mind and curiosity necessary to understand what he proposes to do for the future. A man like you would impress him."

Hicks was pouring it on thick. Carl gave himself another shot of tangleleg and knocked it back quickly. He blew a big sigh through his puffed out lips. "That's a tall proposition, but I have a duty to Lincoln."

"Which will fail if you follow Marcus's plan. If he fails, you fail, and I suspect good ol' Abe hasn't paid you in full for your services either, has he? The mission will fail, and you may well be dead at the end."

"Hicks, love," Zarelda said, taking her husband's hand in her own, and rubbing it like he enjoyed. "Let's calm down, okay? Tain't no reason to get so excited right now. Like Marcus said, we got plenty of time to decide to switch if it comes to dat."

"Marcus won't switch, Z, and you know it. He's got his pride all in it now, what with Tanner and that son of a bitch Robert Gunter on our trail. It's a race to the finish, and he won't allow himself to be beaten."

"But you're talking about breaking up da Eight, Hicks," Zarelda said, concern growing on her face. "Dat's what it means if we do what you ask. Are you prepared to do dat?"

Hicks looked at her sternly. She could see hurt and disappointment in his eyes. "I thought you were on my side, Z. I thought you had agreed to this plan."

"I did, love, I did. I want to know da medical value of RJ, now more den ever, based on what dat bartender yonder said. But why make such a stern commitment now? Let's wait and see what happens. We have plenty of time to decide."

Hicks's frustration with her was clear. He pulled his hand away, looked at Carl. "What do you say? Are you with me?"

It did not go unnoticed by Zarelda that Hicks had left her out of the question. Was *Carl* with Hicks... She resented the slight, but let it go. Like she had said, there was plenty of time to see how things worked out. She had plenty of time to beat some sense into her husband's solid head, whether he liked it or not. The desire to learn all she could about the medicinal values of RJ was strong, but was it strong enough to put the Eight in jeopardy? Maybe, but not yet.

Carl sat back and considered the question. "It's an interesting offer, and I think I agree with it in principle. But I'd like to think about it some more, if you don't mind. I was hired by Lincoln to follow you and to ensure that you did your job, but I have violated that duty somewhat and so things are running on the hoof right now. In truth, I should have walked away and not gotten involved at all. But it's too late for that. I've agreed to help Marcus find Carpathian and put him in the bone yard, yet the chances of that are slim, I know, especially when the man is too bull-headed to accept help when it's offered. So maybe the best thing to do is to understand the doctor and not kill him. I think Lincoln's and the Union's desire to see the man dead is noble; they are looking out for the people and for their own self-interests. Carpathian is an enemy of the state, and therefore, he should be treated as such. But is he *my* enemy? On that, Mr. Kincade, I agree with you wholeheartedly. At some point on this trail, we may have to look out for our own self-interests. But I think I agree with Zarelda right now. We don't have to make that decision today; I'm not prepared to do so, but I would like to discuss it again at some point, hear more of what you have to say. Okay?"

She could see that Hicks was unhappy about Carl's response, but he wasn't one to explode, especially with an audience. He wasn't Jake. He didn't wear his emotions on his sleeve, but he was boiling inside. Hicks took a deep breath, sighed and said, "If you say so, but don't think about it too long, Carl. We may not have time once we're inside the forest to make speedy plans."

They were about to get up and leave when four Union soldiers, hefting blaster rifles, walked in. The sight of the men shocked everyone, including the bartender who stood there with a mug of beer in his right hand. It was pretty obvious, even to people like Zarelda who had not been in the fort very often, that Union soldiers were unheard of in these parts, and they took their lives in their own hands by even crossing the city border. At least two dozen guns were probably trained on them from beneath tables at that moment. Zarelda kept her seat but moved in such a way as to give herself better access to her rifle.

"Dey here for us," she whispered, leaning into the table. She pulled her hair over her face to keep from being noticed.

"Not necessarily," Hicks said.

"Da way Marcus said he left Fort Smith, killing da colonel and all, it's got to be. Why else would dey risk coming in here?"

"How did they find us so fast?" Carl said, turning his face away from the soldiers.

"I don't know," Zarelda said, "but ain't no way we getting to dat door without dem shooting. And I don't see no other way out."

"There is a way out," Carl said. "I could try to teleport us to the other side of the wall with my glove, but I can only teleport one at a time. They might start shooting before I get us all out."

"I ain't being teleported nowhere," Zarelda said, keeping an eye on the blue-bellies as they talked to Cassidy at the bar. Would the man rat them out? They hadn't told him specifically who they were, but since they were the freshest faces in the joint, it wouldn't be hard for him to put it together and start pointing a finger. "We don't have much time. We have to make a decision now."

"Well," Hicks said, "if you won't be teleported, Z, then the only way out is through the front, and that means killing."

She nodded. "I'm ready."

The bartender did rat them out, pointing to the corner where they sat.

"Be still," Carl said, pulling his rail pistol and holding it beneath the table. "Fire on my mark."

"Who died and left you boss?" Hicks said.

"Shh! Both of you. Here dey come."

The Union soldiers left the bar and cautiously started over to their table. They wore the traditional blue uniforms but with some additional heavy armor on the legs and arms. One of them with a slightly darker coat with stripes on his shoulder. Clearly he was in charge, a captain or sergeant; Zarelda wasn't too knowledgeable of rank insignia. It hardly mattered in her mind. A blue-belly was a blue-belly, plain and simple. As long as they bled, they could die.

They pretended not to notice the four men approaching. Carl took another drink, followed by Hicks who just downed the bottle in one swig. Zarelda sat there, looking the other way. When the men stopped, she looked up and said, "Howdy, gentlemen. What can I do for you?"

The officer lifted his rifle and pointed it toward her. "Bartender tells me you all just came into town. Is that true?"

"Yes, sir," Hicks said, in his best, most proper Boston accent. "We just arrived, thought we would have a drink before heading out again."

"We're looking for a man by the name of Marcus Wayward. Do you know him?"

They paused for a moment, as if searching for an answer. "No," Carl said, "can't say as I do. What you want him for?"

"Murder of an officer of the Union army," the man said, "and three soldiers. Plus he killed three men outside the fort. Shot them point blank in cold blood."

Zarelda turned her head and gave Hicks a look. Marcus killed men outside the fort? Where did they get that notion?

"We also know that he rides with a group of mercenaries called the Wayward Eight. You wouldn't know anything about that, would you?"

Zarelda shook her head. "No, sir, we don't know nothing about any Marcus Wayward. We just passing through and—"

"Get up, darkie! Get up!"

Zarelda moved to stand, but Hicks didn't give her a chance. "Nobody calls my wife that," he said, pushing her back into the chair, turning, and throwing the bottle into the officer's face. He followed it up quickly with a pistol shot into the man's chest, blowing him back and into a table, upturning cards and beer mugs. The soldiers behind him fired, but Carl was already moving, taking the nearest soldier with his portal glove and tossing him across the room and into the mechanical piano. Both man and instrument collapsed in a pile of shattered wood, broken keys, and wire.

Zarelda fell to the floor, hiding her head from the blaster fire that passed above and smashed the chairs and table behind her. Where was Hicks? She couldn't tell because everyone in the saloon was now firing. She could barely hear herself think above the roar of guns, but she pulled her repeater rifle and began firing at legs and feet and anything else that did not resemble her husband's or Carl's legs. Body after body fell as her fire ripped through muscle and bone. She finally managed the courage to lift herself up on her knees and hide behind an overturned table. The entire room was in chaos.

Outlaw versus outlaw. Men standing mere feet away from each other firing pistols and punching faces, choking necks, hitting each other over the heads with bottles. And below it all, those that had been wounded or were dead, lay everywhere. Hicks himself was in a fist fight with some ruffian in a black shirt, while the last standing Union soldier was trying to keep himself alive against Carl's heavy shots. Carl couldn't get a good angle on the man; he was pinned behind the remains of the piano and the body of a dead barmaid. The Union soldier was keeping up a good counter fire, but couldn't finish Carl off, nor could he make it to the door. He was stuck; it was just a matter of who fired the last shot.

Zarelda didn't waste time about it. She stood up, despite the danger, and put a round into the man's head. He fell over the barmaid, and just as quickly as it had begun, the fight was over.

All four Union soldiers were dead, including the officer. At least a dozen other souls lay lifeless on the floor. Those that had survived now found it prudent to high tail it out and save themselves, lest the shooting began again. Now only Carl, Hicks, and Zarelda stood amongst the bloody corpses and broken furniture strewn across the saloon floor.

Marcus, Jake, and Sierra entered the bar, weapons ready. "What the hell's going on here?" Marcus asked.

Zarelda went to Hicks who sat on the floor, nursing a broken lip and black eye. "We was attacked by blue-bellies, Captain," she said, kneeling down to get a good look at Hicks's face. "Four of dem."

"What were they here for?"

"You," Carl said, powering down his glove and holstering his pistol. "They wanted you for murder of Union soldiers and for killing three men outside Fort Smith."

Marcus raised an eyebrow. "Outside? I never killed anyone outside."

"Well, for some reason, they think you did," Carl said. "You were lucky we were here."

Marcus looked over the dead on the saloon floor. "What a mess! Can't we go anywhere without leaving bodies behind?"

"Not on this mission," Jake said, stepping over one of the Union soldiers and leaning into Marcus, whispering and pointing to the dead soldiers. "These men left their Iron Horses outside, boss. What do you say we take a couple, replace the ones we lost?"

Marcus considered. "Okay, you and Sierra go pick two and we'll meet you back at camp."

Jake and Sierra left quickly, and Marcus stepped over to Zarelda and Hicks. "How are you?" he asked Hicks.

"I'm fine, Captain," Hicks said, accepting a hand up. "I'll live."

"What were you three doing here anyway?"

Zarelda's heart leapt into her throat. *What do we say?* "No reason, Captain. Just having a drink, gettin' better acquainted."

She wasn't sure if he accepted that answer, but he didn't press the matter. "Well, get Hicks back to camp and clean him up. We'll head out first thing in the morning. Try to get some sleep, so you're fresh tomorrow." He turned to the bar. "Bartender, we're sorry to have—"

But there was no one to hear him. No one alive, anyway. Behind the bar, propped up between beer taps, stood Teras Cassidy's body, its head blown clean off. Where the head had gone, Zarelda couldn't say. But the man's corpse held a beer mug, half full, in his right hand. He held it out as if he were serving someone. Marcus shrugged, leaned over the bar, and grabbed it. He took a long drink, then set the mug on the bar. "Thanks, kindly Mister Bartender."

"This name was Cassidy, and it serves him right," Zarelda said as she helped Hicks to the door. "He ratted us out. He said he'd sleep when he was dead, and dere he is. Good night to him."

She put her shoulder into holding Hicks up, and together they walked out of the Red Maple Saloon.

Chapter 12

Sasha Tanner stood in front of Desiree Ladue. His late informant had recommended against seeking her out, and he wished now that he had listened. There wasn't a woman in all the world Sasha couldn't charm and ultimately tame to his needs. But Desiree was taller than he imagined, meaner than people said, surly, argumentative, and quite frankly, unattractive, in his eyes. She would be a tough nut to crack, and honestly, he didn't even want to try.

He girded his revulsion and asked a question. "They say you know where Doctor Carpathian lives. You've seen the place?"

Desiree said nothing, removed her cigarette and puffed smoke into the air. She sniffled and wriggled her nose, took a long drink from a whiskey bottle, and tossed it behind her to the floor. She burped, cleared her throat, and said, "I want to make it clear to you, *Monsieur* Tanner, that this information is no longer available for money. I cannot be bought like your fellow *mercenaire Capitane* Wayward believed. Money means nothing to me right now, *n'est-ce pas*? You must agree to give me what I want first before I tell you anything."

Sasha nodded. "And what is that?"

"Me and my ladies come along for the ride. This is non-negotiable, and if you agree and then try to back out of the deal, then you will die. *Comprendre*?"

Sasha smiled, chuckled at the audacity of the threat. "You honestly think you can kill me – Sasha Tanner?"

Desiree smiled back, the white scar on her face bending like a snake ready to strike. "It would be easy to kill one man. My *filles* would take you down before you reached the edge of town."

"Did you make the same threat to Marcus Wayward?"

She shook her head. "*Non*, for there were eight of them, you see? *Neuf*, in fact. There was a strange man with a gold, red glowing glove riding with them as well. My *filles* are good, but taking down nine would have been... difficult.

Besides, he had *filles* of his own. I have no desire to see women bleed."

"How long ago did they leave?"

"The Eight?" Desiree searched for the answer on the saloon ceiling. "A couple days. They made a big mess of it on retreat. Killed a bartender and four Union soldiers who were *stupide* enough to come looking for them. They have a good lead on you, Tanner."

She was trying to rub it in, to apply pressure to force him to accept her deal. And the truth was that he had no other choice. Marcus had escaped Fort Smith, and apparently in violent fashion. If the rumors spreading through the Contested Territories were true, he had cut off the head of a Union colonel. That was a hangable offense, no matter what the reason. After all this was over, the Eight would be dogged to the ends of the earth, and probably never be able to step foot in Union territory again. But that was after this mission. Right now, they had a good head start. Sasha couldn't afford further delays. He could not afford to traipse around the Contested Territory looking for information. He needed it now.

He sighed and said, "Very well. We have a deal."

That put Desiree in a good mood. She tapped out her cigarette on the table, lit another, and adjusted the silver pins in her hair. "I like you, *Monsieur* Tanner. You seem like a reasonable man; there are so few in the world. I know *exactly* where Carpathian lives. I did not tell Marcus and his Eight the exact location; he was too arrogant for such information. But I will tell you." She leaned over the table. Sasha could smell the whiskey on her breath. "And then, we will go and kill that *fils de pute*."

Sasha didn't know whether she meant Carpathian or Marcus, but both would be just fine with him. And if Jake Mattia lay dead at the end of it all too... Well, Sasha would not mind one bit. That would be all right with him.

*****

The Wraith did not like waiting; despised it, in fact. But he was in no position to cause a stir, to pull a gun and demand immediate attention. It was a rare occasion that he put himself in a situation like this, with no avenue of retreat, no way to make himself the boss of the scene. He had even given up his weapons to the thugs guarding the hallway outside the hot, dry hovel that he stood in now. He felt naked without his shotgun, vulnerable. And the old, graying major of the Mexican "Golden Army" that stood nearby with his back turned to him, neither cared nor expressed fear of being in The Wraith's presence. That, more than anything, annoyed him the most.

"Why do you fidget, Robert?" Antonio Mariano-Morales asked as he looked at a painting depicting the Battle of Red River Canyon. "You are with an old friend here. In fact, I am the reason you live at all."

That was a rather arrogant and indelicate way of saying it, The Wraith conceded, but the essence of the statement was true.

At the very battle that the old man was looking at on the wall, The Wraith's father had been a cavalry soldier under Captain Robinson. The American troopers, as they moved through the narrow Red River Canyon of the southwest were attacked by a combined force of Mexican insurgents and Warrior Nation allies. The Wraith's father had been tossed from the horse, and his leg was broken in three places. He lay bleeding to death in the river, when Antonio, then a low level insurgent non-commissioned officer, took pity on the young Julius Gunter, pulled him from the cold water, and nursed him back to stability, placing a tourniquet and a splint on his leg. He even stayed with him all night until the American forces were able to regroup and reenter the canyon. Antonio pulled out by then and was never seen again during the war. After the war, Julius Gunter went looking for his 'savior' and found that he had become a captain in the Golden Army, and then later a major. Their friendship grew from there. So it was quite literally true that if Major Antonio Mariano-Morales had not pulled his father from that river, The Wraith would not be alive today.

"My family has paid you back in spades for whatever kindness you have shown us," The Wraith said. "*I* have paid you back more than once. How many bodies have I left in my wake which your gold has paid for? I've lost count."

Antonio turned, and The Wraith got a good look at the man's clothing. Unlike the more savage and rough Mexican line soldier, with his canvas and hard leather vests and leggings, his thick, calloused hands and cactus-like face, the officers of the Golden Army looked more like old conquistadors, with their bright, colorful tunics and ruffled filigree and lace. Since Antonio was, in effect, in 'hostile territory' here in Laredo, he did not wear his finest field uniform, which would include golden armor. Nevertheless, his red, puffy shirt, and the short-crested morion helm that lay nearby on an old desk, made it quite clear that he held a significant place in the Mexican officer corps.

Antonio put out his hands and shrugged. "I did not call you here to discuss new business, Robert. You invited me. Why?"

Stop calling me Robert. "I need a favor."

Antonio nodded. "And that is...?"

"I need ten of your meanest, nastiest soldiers that aren't afraid of dangerous work, aren't afraid to die, aren't afraid to take a bullet for me if need be."

"Hmm! That is a hefty request, my friend."

"I've earned the right to make it."

"And what will you give me, Robert? I cannot just simply *give* you ten of my best men without payment. What is in it for me? And perhaps more importantly, what is in it for Mexico?"

The Wraith sighed deeply. "First, stop calling me Robert. Only my mother has that right, and she's dead. Second, what I will give you is Doctor Carpathian."

The major's face lit right up at the sound of that name. He took a few steps forward. "What do you mean?"

"I mean, I'm going after him, and with the help of your men, I'm going to remove his head and deliver it to my patron. You may have the rest."

Antonio shook his head. "I do not understand what 'rest' means. You must speak more plainly. Your father was never so cryptic."

"My father lived out his days as a lowly swineherd who drank himself to oblivion. I seriously doubt he had over ten words in his vocabulary. What I meant, is that once I am finished killing Carpathian by removing his head from his shoulders, I will give you his complex. Or rather, with the help of your men, I will hold it until you can bring at least a regiment of your Golden Army to secure it in full for Mexico." The Wraith leaned into Antonio until their faces were mere inches away from each other. "Would you like that, Major? Would you like to have Doctor Burson Carpathian's entire store of modern technology, all the weapons and RJ-1027 that the Golden Army can carry? Would that be an acceptable payment for ten men?"

He could tell that the offer had great appeal to the major. His dark eyes lit up as if they had seen an angel, his face flush with excitement. Then his expression turned serious, sullen. "Impossible. You cannot get into his complex even with twenty men. I have never been there, but they say it is an impenetrable fortress."

The Wraith shook his head. "You forget who you are speaking to, Major. I'm The Wraith, remember? I'm good at what I do. The best, in fact, if you want my cold, leveled opinion about it. But you are looking at this all wrong. You are thinking that I'm willing to throw myself at his walls like some blunt tool. That is not how I plan on getting inside his complex. Not this time." He paused, then asked, "You told me years ago, did you not, that you were once a land surveyor for an American mining company?"

"I was, long before the war."

"And did you not say to me once that you spent some time in the Southwest surveying for copper mines?"

Antonio nodded his head.

"Well, I have it on good intelligence, and I will not tell you from whom, that some of those old copper mines went so far as into the Tonto Forest. All I need is for you to map out where you conducted your surveys, where those mines were located, and your men and I will do the rest. We'll find the shaft that goes underneath Carpathian's lair. We'll strike from under his belly, and he'll still be eating breakfast before he realizes that his head has rolled beneath the table."

Antonio ran his hands through his graying hair. "It's been so long ago. I do not think I can remember where they are."

"My father told me that you were the smartest man that he had ever known. You have a good memory, Major. It's legendary. Surely you can search your mind for the details I need so that you can retake the entire Contested Territory and Carpathian's land for your glorious Golden Army. Surely your memory is good enough for all of that."

Antonio considered. He paced the room, looked at the painting again. Sighed more than once. Finally, he said, "Very well. But you will have to return to Mexico with me in order to get these men. I can't give you my mainline soldiers, Wraith; they would never work for a *gringo* like you anyway, and they are being held in reserve for something... else. But I do know men that would serve your purposes well."

The Wraith shook his head. "I don't want a bunch of pot-bellied dirt farmers that—"

"Do not disrespect farmers, my good friend. These farmers, I assure you, will be more than capable of doing what you ask. Trust me on this. My superiors will want to hear this as well, and I can assure you, Wraith, regardless of my relationship with you or with your father, that it will be *your* head on a pike if you betray us."

The Wraith nodded. "All I want is to deliver that bastard's head to my patron, take my money, and disappear into a nice comfortable life. Perhaps to Europe, or Canada. I have no interest in how all this plays out politically or militarily. I serve myself and my patron   Antonio   nodded.   He motioned to the door. "Then let's get going, my friend. We have a long way to travel."

The Wraith stepped out into the hot Laredo sun. He followed Antonio to the Blackhoofs that would take them deep into Mexico. And there, he would get his men and sign their contracts. He'd sign a million contracts if they asked him to, for The Wraith learned long ago that contracts were like dust. He'd signed scores in his lifetime, and most of them he had broken. Once he had his men and they were a hundred miles away from the glaring eyes of their masters, they were his, and he would use them however he wished. He served his patrons, yes, but Robert "The Wraith" Gunter always served himself first.

*****

Marcus could have kicked himself for following the advice of the farmer that they had come across. "Go yonder," the old man had said, pointing a little further south of their current position. "Not as rocky thata way, not as much mesquite neither." The old man had an odd, unsettled look in his eye, similar to the one the boy had shown at Fort Smith. He had been right about the rocks and bushes, but he didn't bother to warn them about the sandstorm.

It came out of nowhere, and right behind them. It was a near thousand foot screamer. The winds kicked up and blew their Iron Horses forward with their incessant force. It was all any of them could do to stay in the saddle. They were speeding as fast as they could across the open, dry and, but Marcus could feel the sand at his back. If he squinted, he could still see everyone. That was good, for too many times he thought that the sand would overtake them and they'd have to rough it out while piles upon piles of soot and dust covered them head to toe. But it was odd: the storm never seemed to overtake them, at least not in the manner that he expected. Nevertheless, they had to find a place to stop and to wait it out. They could not sustain this pace for long; their Iron Horses would start giving out. Iron Horses were not breathing creatures, but even machines had to rest. The sand stabbing itself into every crevice of the chassis would eventually suffocate these powerful beasts.

"We have to stop! Now!" Hicks yelled to Marcus as he sped along beside him. "These things can't take much more of this."

"I know! But we can't stop here. We'll be buried al've."

"If we don't stop, we'll be buried alive anyway," Hicks yelled back. "We can't outrun this!"

Marcus was about to shout something else back when he spotted it, a small clutch of buildings on the horizon. In front of them, the weather was beautiful, near dusk, a clear sky with a hint of blood cloud. There they stood, severa' small buildings, too small for a town, but perhaps an abandoned settlement, or an old mining village, or a ruined fort. It did not matter. That's where they needed to go.

"Over there!" he said, pointing through the mad dust whipping around him.

Marcus accelerated and everyone followed.

They grew closer to the buildings, and now he saw what it was. An abandoned mine, several buildings, mostly in ruins with a shaft and various pieces of equipment strewn around it. Maybe an old copper or silver mine. Two of the buildings were large and likely could hold them and their Iron Horses while the storm blew past. Marcus shifted his 'Horse toward the largest building and laid on the pedal.

They reached the complex, but the doors to the building that he wanted them to enter were closed. *Damn!* He stopped his 'Horse quickly and jumped off, fighting his way through the blinding dust, a bandana pushed up over his mouth and nose. His eyes were protected by his goggles, his duster protected his body. Even so, he could feel the sand, like tiny needles pounding at his back, his neck. Everyone else tried to climb off their Iron Horses, but he waved them down. "Stay put!" He screamed over the roar of the wind. "I'll get the doors!"

He reached the doors and, just his luck, they were chained. He pulled his sword carefully, and with one swipe, cut through the iron loops and into the door itself. He pulled the blade free and kicked them open. He then waved everyone inside. One after another, they came through riding their Iron Horses and disappearing into the darkness of the long building. But when K-Free tried to pull in, Marcus lost his grip on one of the doors, and it slammed into the front of her Iron Horse, pushing the cow-catcher into the ground and knocking her off. Marcus tried to grab her, but the strength of the wind was too great. Her fingers slipped through his hand, and she disappeared into the storm.

"Kim!" He said, trying to reach for her through the blinding sand. He tried walking back into it, toward her last location.

"I got her!"

Carl walked through the sand and up to the door, holding K-Free with his gloved hand. She looked small in the monstrous glove, but she was alive. Marcus stepped aside to let them pass. Jake came up and took control of her errant Iron Horse to pull it inside. Marcus considered going back out there and retrieving his own vehicle, but Carl stopped him. "Don't even try it, friend. It's too dangerous. Ours will have to wait till the morning."

He didn't like the idea of his Iron Horse being left out there in the sand, but he stepped back to let Carl and Jake close the doors and bolt them shut from the inside.

"Thanks for catching K-Free," he said to Carl once the doors were closed and only a whistle of wind through the door crack could be heard. He offered his hand.

Carl took it, and immediately Marcus felt a darkness; a deep, brooding feeling of distress and discomfort, as if he were shaking the hand of the devil. He was, he now realized, shaking Carl's gloved hand, something that he promised never to do. And doing so didn't propel him through a portal, or toss him across the dark building, but it left him weak and wanting, dull and annoyed. He pulled his hand back quickly, tried to pretend nothing was wrong. Carl gave him a curious look, but let it pass. "No problem, Marcus. As a member of this venture, it's my duty to help when others can't."

What did he mean by that? Marcus wondered. *Is he suggesting that I wasn't capable or willing to risk myself to save K-Free?* He tried responding, but Carl had already moved away.

Someone lit a fire, and they collected themselves around it, putting out bed rolls, getting settled, checking their Iron Horses, weapons, and equipment. The wind outside had not let up, and despite the dry hot weather, it was cool inside. Bitter, musky air flowed up from a mine shaft that lay at the far end of the building. A rusty, broken rail line led out of the hole and through the center of the building.

"No one goes into that mine, understood?" Marcus said, fixing his place near the fire. "No unauthorized adventuring from any of you. That includes you, Carl. We're here for the night. We'll leave in the morning, in one piece."

No one argued, too tired, too uncomfortable to even consider entering the mine. What good would it do anyway? The thing was certainly abandoned, probably dangerous, and if nothing else, there were certainly bats. Marcus hated bats. They carried disease, and he did not need anyone coming down with any sickness in the midst of a mission. Marcus laid out his bedroll on the far side of the fire.

They had pushed hard after leaving Fort Waco, to make up for lost time at Fort Smith and to keep the Union from sending out armed parties in chase. Marcus regretted having to kill so many Union soldiers on this mission already, and regardless of what Lincoln had promised in the contract, these fresh killings would remain on their record. New bounties would be inked, and the Wayward Eight would be, once again, enemies of the state. It was a role they had played for a long time, and they would endure it again, assuming they survived this mission, and that was a big 'if'. Marcus looked at everyone around the fire. Still intact and in relatively good shape. Even River had bounced back marvelously from her wounds from before the scalper attack; Jake from his scuffle at Fort Smith; and Sun from his arm wound. As long as they kept things tight and focused, they should be fine.

Hicks sat down next to him. He held Lincoln's box in his hands. "Listen to this, Captain," he said, turning a few gears and positioning the box so that everyone could hear.

It was a conversation between two people, faint, but the voices audible enough. At least to Marcus.

"Is that Pinkerton?" Jake asked, muscling in to get a good listen.

Marcus nodded. "Sure sounds like him. The other guy I don't recognize. Do you?"

"Shhh!" Sierra said, waving her hands. "They're talking about someone!"

Everyone fell silent, leaned in, and listened. The unrecognizable man's voice came through loud and clear. *"See, Pinkerton, I told you."* His voice was agitated, his breath raspy. *"Loveless is a turncoat; she up and disappeared."*

Pinkerton clearly didn't like the accusation. *"Damnit, Wade, this is not suitable conversation for these newfangled things. Shut your mouth!"*

The rest of their conversation wavered in and out as the sand storm outside was clearly interfering with the signal. Hicks turned off the machine and chuckled beneath his breath. "This contraption is so new, they don't seem to understand that we can hear everything they're saying."

"Wait a minute," K-Free said, coming up and pulling the box from Hicks's hands. "If we can hear them, can't they hear us?"

Hicks pulled the box away from her. "That's why I've been keeping it buried beneath quilts."

"You've known about this?" Marcus asked.

Hicks shook his head. "I don't know for sure, Captain. I'm just guessing."

"You should have told me your suspicion, Hicks. They might have caught our conversation about a lot of things. And since we don't know for sure who is at the other end of that thing at any given time, we may be putting our mission in jeopardy. We just heard Pinkerton speaking to someone named Wade. Does this mean that the Union can hear everything we say? Hell, the Union is probably using this to track our movements now. God Almighty, Hicks, you should have told me."

"I doubt that they know where we are, Marcus," Hicks said, trying to waylay fears. "I don't think the Union has that kind of technology. That's the kind of science only Carpathian could concoct."

"Nevertheless, I'm in charge, and I expect to be consulted on these matters."

Hicks looked deflated, clearly embarrassed at such a public admonishment. "I'm sorry, Captain. Shall I destroy it?"

"No, dammit! Just keep it tucked away, and don't bring it out until we finish our mission. And I want to make it clear to everyone. No more talking within earshot of that thing. We need to speak about the mission, we do it far away from Hicks's Iron Horse. And don't you speak around it either, Hicks. As far as we're concerned, it's dead to us until we reach Payson."

"I say we smash it," Sierra said, trying to grab it away from Hicks.

Marcus intervened. "And I say no! It's part of the contract, and we're keeping it until I say otherwise. Now, everyone just shut up and get some sleep."

Marcus stood and stalked away from the fire.

Why am I so unsettled? He wondered to himself. Certainly the raging storm outside didn't help matters, nor had the incident at Fort Smith or the dust-up with Union troopers at Fort Waco. The weather was making his knee hurt. His ear rang. The arthritis in his left hand was giving him fits. He was hungry, tired, and by God, he needed a bath. None of these things were forthcoming it seemed. Perhaps if he returned to the fire, he'd find a few moments of peace. That's all he needed: five minutes of peace.

Someone was on his left side. They had said something, but the ringing in his ear blocked the words. He turned and there Carl stood, smiling a smug, pompous little smile.

Marcus backed off a couple steps. "What do you want, Carl?"

"You seem tense, unsettled. Perhaps I can lend a helping hand."

"What do you mean?"

"Perhaps it's time for a second captain."

Marcus turned on Carl. He wanted to strike out, to put the man down. "Are you challenging my authority, sir? Are you trying to take away my people?"

Carl shook his head. "No, sir. Just offering to lighten your burden. Give me some control over the operation. Let me handle the box. I'll keep it safe, hidden. I can be your personal assistant during this endeavor. You give me the orders, I'll pass them out."

"I thought I made it clear to you back in Waco that there would only be *one* commander on this mission, Carl. The service you offer already belongs to Jake and Sierra. I don't need another," Marcus said, whispering so that no one else could hear their conversation. The storm outside was benefitting something.

"Jake doesn't seem all that enthusiastic about what we're doing."

"He's a passionate man. Sometimes, it gets the best of him. He'll be fine. He's loyal."

"And Hicks? Not telling you what he suspects of the box?"

"It was a mistake, but just that. He'll be fine. I've known these people a goodly portion of my life, Carl. They're family. When it matters, they'll deliver. They always have. I trust every single one of them with my life."

Carl stood there a moment, his expression blank. Then he backed off and gave a short nod. "Very well, Captain. As you wish. But the offer stands. Anything I can do to help. I've given my word to Lincoln to make sure you see this through, and that's what I'm going to do."

Marcus said nothing as Carl walked back to the fire.

He turned again and stood there, trying to get control of his emotions, anger clutching his chest. He took deep breaths, rubbed his aching hand, and listened to sand pelt the barn.

*****

He slept fitfully, tossing and turning on the thin bedroll that lay near the dying fire. His dreams were scattered, unsettled, flipping from one confused image to another. He dreamed of a wall, then a house, a wall again, then fighting the Union, getting struck in the back by RJ fire, The Wraith, Sasha Tanner, his blade slicing through the throat of a Union officer, a man with mechanical legs and a bright red eye. He awoke many times to see the embers in the fire burning low and considered more than once getting up and stoking the flames, but everyone else around him was sleeping so soundly that he did not dare stir and wake them. They had earned their well-deserved rest. *Let them sleep*, he thought, then rolled over and tried again to find what Shakespeare might call 'the sleep in Elysium'. Perhaps not quite that deep or soundly, but something deeper than what he had experienced so far this violent night. The storm outside had dissipated; the wind still blew, but it was calmer, adding less stress to the weak boards of the building they were in. He should be able to sleep well, but he couldn't. Then, just as he was about to fall into a comfortable rest, another dream came to him, and this one held a knife to his throat. The blade was sharp and cold.

"I know who you are," the voice said. It was a woman's voice, quiet, soft, her breath warm on his ear, its scent of cinnamon and fruit almost inviting. "And I know where you are going, who you seek."

"Who are you?" he asked.

She was quiet for a moment, and then she said, "Walks Looking."

"This is a dream."

"I have followed you from Fort Waco, watching you from a distance, making sure you stay on the correct path. I cannot follow you all the way to his gates, Marcus Wayward, for my destiny lies elsewhere. But you will find it, and you will kill the foreign devil. I have seen it in my dreams."

"It's been a difficult trail," he confessed. "River almost dying, me being taken at Fort Smith. Bodies left in our wake. The Union is after us. It is not going well."

"You must stay strong, Marcus Wayward. For yourself and for your people."

"They doubt this mission. All of them in some way or another. They want to ignore the contract, switch sides."

"You mustn't," she hissed that, more forcefully than perhaps she wanted. She calmed back down. "Your fate lies with Carpathian's death. You must see it through. But I have not come to give you strength; you have that already. I have come to you with a warning. One among you is a deceiver, a liar. He poses a great threat to the success of your mission."

"Who?" He wanted to say Jake's name, but could not bring himself to speak it.

"I cannot see his face. The vision is not clear. But I know this: beware the man with the red hand. He will betray you."

Her voice drifted away. Marcus tried getting it back. He opened his eyes, and there a man stood, in the shadows of the weak fire. Carl, his gloved hand extended out, glowing bright red with RJ. His face was devilish in the orange flame, comical and twisted like a clown's.

Beware the man with the red hand.

Marcus rolled to his left just as Carl released a powerful blast of energy that scorched the floor where Marcus used to lay.

Now he was fully awake and coming to his feet. But before he could respond to Carl's attack, Jake slammed into the man's side and took him down. They rolled across the floor, quickly through the flames and to the other side. The rest of the Eight were rousing, grabbing weapons, following the combatants as Jake tried punching Carl in the face, and Carl held off his assailant's attack with the glove.

Marcus pulled his pistol, jumped the fire, and landed on Carl's chest. He pushed the barrel of his gun into the man's throat. Carl stopped thrashing immediately.

"Wait wait wait!" he said, trying to catch his breath and trying not to move to allow the barrel to sink further into his skin. "You don't understand. This is a mistake."

"What you doing firing on the boss, son?" Jake said, grabbing Carl's hair and pushing his head into the floor. "Are you stupid?"

"I wasn't firing at him! I was firing at the woman that was holding a knife to his throat."

"What are you talking about?" Jake asked.

"There was a woman right there next to him. She held a knife on him. She was a member of the Warrior Nation, I think. Dark hair. She had a bandana wrapped around her head, over her eyes, as if she were blind. That's who I was firing at. Not Marcus."

Jake looked up at Marcus. "Is that true, boss? Was there a woman with a knife at your throat?"

Marcus pulled back, holstered his pistol, shook his head, and tried catching his breath. "No, Jake. There was no one there. I was just sleeping. Sleeping… and dreaming."

Chapter 13

Sun made sure that Carl's bindings were tight. He double-checked them, pulled the cord until Carl winced. They were set, and the big man would not be able to remove them or wiggle out of them. They'd hold him to the post until the skin on his bones fell away if necessary.

"You're making a big mistake, Marcus," Carl said, looking up into the sunlight. The sandstorm had died out, and the morning had come in hot and clear. Perfect weather to make good time across the arid, sparse land of the west. "I tell you, there was a woman holding a knife to your throat. She was *real*."

Sun knew the woman Carl spoke about. He feared her, though he would never admit that to anyone, especially River. Not because Walks Looking could beat him in hand-to-hand or in shooting, but because she refused to abandon the Warrior Nation, preferring to try to change things from within. As much as he had tried, she refused to listen to his arguments, and one day, perhaps she would prevail and change everything. On the surface, that sounded wonderful, but in practice, what did that mean for himself and others like him who did not believe at all in the spirit world? Would Walks Looking really be all that different than her father, any more different than Geronimo? If her philosophy were to prevail, would that not simply replace one tyranny for another? The key to change was total and absolute rejection of all Warrior Nation policy. Only then could there be true freedom from old, oppressive ideals.

But surely she had not been here last night. As strong and as capable as she was, even she wouldn't come so far south and force her way through a blinding sandstorm just to give Marcus advice, and confusing advice at that. So that meant Carl had tried to kill their captain. Everyone in the Eight agreed: that was unacceptable behavior.

All except maybe Hicks. He seemed particularly aggravated at the decision to leave Carl behind. "This is nonsense, Marcus," Hicks said, as they gathered up Carl's weapons, his powerful glove, its backpack RJ supply, and the commanding firepower of the rail pistol. He then tied them to the back of K-Free's Iron Horse. "We need him. We need the extra body. We need all the help we can get."

"We don't need Carl Fredrickson, Hicks." Marcus shrugged off Hicks's concern. "He's just a man, and one who just tried to kill me. His weapons will suffice."

"I have no idea how to use them," Hicks said. "And I won't be able to figure it out in time."

"He's right," Carl said, trying to pull his way free, but Sun's knots held firm. "You might be able to fire the pistol, but the glove is another matter. It takes skill and knowledge that you don't have. If used incorrectly, it could explode, killing instantly the man or woman wearing it. Don't be a fool, Marcus. I'm the only one that can use it, and you need it to beat Carpathian. Think carefully about what you are doing."

Sun could not tell from Carl's expression whether the big man was bluffing or not. Was the glove all that hard to use? Could it simply be put on and activated? He did not know, and he was not about to suggest the attempt, lest Carl was correct. Marcus ignored the warning and knelt next to Carl to check Sun's knots. "I've thought about it ever since you tried frying me into bacon. Ever since you tried talking me into giving you control of my people, I've thought about it."

"That's a lie. I wasn't trying to take control. I was offering to help."

"Well, no matter. I can't afford to travel with someone I don't trust. The stakes are too high, Carl, the risk too great."

"But he's going to die here, Marcus," Hicks said, "if we leave him like this."

Marcus shook his head. "He's a strong, capable man. He's proven that often. He'll figure out a way to break free, and by the time he does, we'll be long gone."

No, he won't, Sun thought but did not say aloud. *My knots cannot be broken. He will die.*

"Better him than us," Jake countered, drawing his rifle and pointing its scorched muzzle toward Carl's Iron Horse. "What we gonna do about his ride? If he does break free, he might come looking for us."

"Torch it," Marcus said.

That put a spring in Jake's step. "Gladly," he said, walking toward the vehicle. He opened up with his rifle and a stream of burning RJ ignited against the 'Horse's iron side. A second later, it was engulfed in flames.

Both Carl's and Marcus's Iron Horses had endured the sandstorm all night. It took Hicks and K-Free two full hours to get enough soot and sand out of Marcus's that it would even start. When Hicks tried cleaning Carl's, Marcus waved him off. That's when Hicks got mad at the notion that they were going to leave Carl behind. Why Hicks was so unstrung about it, Sun could not say, but it upset Zarelda as well. The mood among everyone was sour. This was a brutal, unforgiving decision that Marcus had made, but what other choice did he have? No one seemed to like the decision, except maybe Jake, and that worried Sun the most, given how Jake had behaved during the entire trip. There was too much joy in Jake's eyes as he burned Carl's vehicle to ash.

He went over to River and tried to help her up from her bedroll. Shortly thereafter, Marcus walked over. "What's the matter with her?"

She responded to Sun's touch and stood. He guided her to her Iron Horse and put her comfortably in the seat. She responded slowly, mechanically, but she did respond; that was a good sign. "She's afraid of your dream, Marcus. What you saw. What the lady told you."

"I didn't see her face, Sun," Marcus said, securing his own bedroll to the back of his vehicle. "I only heard her voice. It was just a dream. That's all. Nothing to worry about now. The matter has concluded."

Sun said nothing to that, but kept helping River prepare to leave. It would take hours before she recovered from all this, days perhaps. And the thought of leaving Carl strung up to die, the person who had saved her from certain death from those scalpers, would not help her condition. She loved Marcus and would never want to see him killed or even threatened in such a manner as Carl had threatened him, but to leave Carl here like this, with no food or water... This was not something River wanted to see. But Marcus was the boss, and he had led them through much worse in the past.

"Let's load up and go," Marcus shouted as he gunned the engine of his Iron Horse. "We've got a lot of daylight ahead of us. I want to see the Carpathian Industries border no later than tomorrow."

Jake stepped away from Carl's burning Iron Horse and climbed on his own. Everyone else did the same. Hicks tried once more to change Marcus's mind, but it did not work. Sun made sure his sister was secure and ready to go, and then climbed on his own ride. The roar of the 'Horses was almost deafening as the sound echoed back into the building. Marcus took the lead, followed by Jake and Sierra, then everyone else.

Sun and River took the rear, and as their column of Iron Horses left the ruined mine behind, Sun closed his ears to the stream of expletives coming from Carl Fredrickson's mouth.

*****

The Wraith stopped his Blackhoof beside the charred remains of the Iron Horse. It smelled freshly cooked, a pool of blackened RJ cradling its warped skids. A thin line of foul black smoke came off its ruined seat. He could easily feel residual heat from its broiled carcass. It had burned strong and hot for perhaps two, three days. No normal fire would have lasted that long. Only an RJ fire would burn in that manner, with that much intensity. Nearby lay an abandoned mine shaft and building, its large double doors swung open wide. In front of it lay a shirtless man, tied to a post, his head drooped over, his hair a ratty mess. He twitched gently, delirious in the hot sun. His skin was baked red.

The Wraith climbed down from his Blackhoof and walked cautiously toward the man. He motioned for his Mexican farmers to hold tight, to stay put and wait. He drew his shotgun and pointed it at the man as he walked closer. The man did not respond, nor did he even acknowledge that someone was drawing near, so weak and defeated in his confinement. The Wraith rolled the cylinder until a thermite slug fell into place.

He kicked one of the man's boots. "Wake up," he said, kicking it again. "Who are you?"

The man lolled his head up momentarily. He tried opening his eyes, tried speaking, but only a groan escaped.

"Carl Frederickson," The Wraith said, pushing the man's head up with the muzzle of his shotgun, "is that you?"

Carl nodded, coughed. "What—what're you doing here, Robert?"

Doesn't anyone listen? "That's The Wraith to you, you mean son of a bitch. I'm still sore at you for jumping my score up north. That was uncalled for."

"I—I was just doing my job."

The Wraith nodded. "And when you saved that Warrior girl from the scalpers, were you doing your job then too?" He pressed his shotgun into Carl's chest.

Carl coughed and tried to nod. "Yes."

"You cost me a lot of time and grief, Carl. If she had died, it might have forced Marcus off the trail. They might have stopped altogether, but now look what's happened. They string you up like this?"

Carl nodded. "Yes." He wriggled his arms. "Untie me, please. And water... I need water."

The Wraith cupped his mouth. "Bring me a canteen." One of his men trotted forward and lowered one down to him. He took it, popped the cork and poured it over Carl's head. He arched his face up to accept the liquid, letting part of it fall into his mouth.

"Don't be a greedy pig," The Wraith said, "you know how it is out here. You drink too much, you'll cramp up and die."

He pulled the canteen away, drew a knife he had acquired from one of his men, and cut the bindings. Carl fell over and wriggled in the dirt. It took him a moment to recover, but in time, he sat up, rubbed his bloody wrists and reached for the canteen. "More."

The Wraith let him have it. "Now, what did you do to the Eight to put yourself in such a hard place?"

Carl let the water drain out of his mouth and run down his chin and neck. He wiped muddy filth from his face. "I offered to help Marcus lead his team."

The Wraith huffed. "You know better than that, boy. That arrogant bastard ain't going to give up his authority. I'm surprised he let you live at all."

"Well, he won't have long to think about it, I swear. I'm gonna find him, get my weapons back, and strangle him in his sleep."

The Wraith nodded. "Yes, I've had that dream every night since Fort Smith. But that's not our plan. We're going south, southwest."

Carl slowly stood, pressing his back against the post for support. "I'm going right after him."

The Wraith waved a thumb at the black ruins of the Iron Horse. "You ain't going anywhere on that. And you won't be able to catch up on foot. So, you'll ride with us, or you'll stay here and die. Your choice."

He could see that Carl didn't like the offer. In truth, The Wraith didn't like it either. He had no desire to ride with this Union sawbelly, but Carl's weapons, if he could get them back, could be the difference between victory and defeat. If this man could kill five scalpers and a wolfman alone, it was hard to imagine what he could do against Carpathian.

"Okay," Carl said, testing out his legs, walking a few steps. "Then let's get at it. Daylight's wasting."

"You'll need a ride," The Wraith said, rubbing the stubble on his chin as if he were in deep contemplation. Then he looked up at the Mexican soldier who had given his canteen. "Pedro? No, that's not it. Jose? Oh, right, Alberto. Would you please be so kind as to get down and give Mr. Fredrickson your horse?"

"*Que?*"

"I said, get off your horse and... Oh, hell!" He raised his shotgun and put the thermite round into the man's head. The shot tore Alberto from his perch, and he hit the ground hard, twisted and broken. "Why do I bother trying to be polite?" Carl grabbed the reins of the horse to keep it from running from the shot. "You didn't have to kill him. We could have doubled up."

"He was smelly and argumentative anyway. Besides, now you have a coat, and you'll need it where we're going. And grab his musket as well. It's a worthless piece, but it'll do for now."

Carl did as he was told, pulled the coat off the dead man and tried it on. It was tight, but it was better than nothing. He found the musket which had scattered from the shot and slung it over his shoulder. The Wraith held the reins while Carl climbed on the horse. "I haven't ridden one of these in a long time."

"Yes, they are a burden, but what can be done? Just find a place with my men and let's go."

Carl took the reins and followed The Wraith back to his Blackhoof. "I'm just one of your line soldiers, eh? Is that it?"

The Wraith climbed onto his Blackhoof, turned it on, and set it toward the beaten path leading south. "That's right, Carl," he said, letting another thermite round drop into the chamber. "Unlike Captain Wayward, there should be no doubt as to who's the boss on this trail."

*****

Sasha Tanner climbed off his Iron Horse and nudged the hand of the Mexican soldier with his right boot. Scores of black scorpions covering him from head to toe scattered. Nearby lay the remains of a burnt vehicle and multiple hoof marks denoting a large riding party. Over the years, he'd been able to tell which marks were from real horses and which were from mechanical ones. Most of these hoof marks were real; only one set was metal, and all of them headed south.

"Someone was here not long ago," he said to Desiree as she slid off her Iron Horse and inspected the Mexican corpse herself. She stepped over the body, crushed a couple scorpions under her high heel, knelt down, and looked at the gory hole in the man's head. The rest of her ladies climbed off their rides as well and began knocking the dust off their clothing.

Desiree nodded. "*Oui*, and this one got a bad headache."

"Looks like Marcus and his merry band are killing again."

Desiree shook her head. "*Non*, this wasn't Marcus. It was a thermite round that did this, and there ain't too many men in the country that fires them."

Sasha had his suspicion. "Who, then?"

She looked like she knew the answer, but was reluctant to speak. Or angry about it. It was hard to read Desiree's expressions; the scar hid so much. "The Wraith."

He nodded, but he was hoping that name would not come up. "He was in Fort Smith apparently, when the Eight arrived. Marcus said as much, but I didn't want to believe him. Dammit all! I have no desire to get in a scrap with that monster."

"You know him, Sasha?" Desiree asked.

"I've worked with him before. He's a cold-hearted bastard for sure. I don't like the idea of another killer on this trail, especially one like him. We've got enough to worry about with the Eight."

"Looks like it's going to be a race to the finish, *n'est-ce pas*?"

"And one we need to win." Sasha stood and looked south. "But you don't think he joined up with Marcus, do you?"

"No. Robert Gunter is a killer, a *prédateur*. He would not condescend to do such a thing."

"Well, these hoof marks lead south, and I know for a fact that the Eight were riding Iron Horses, and if they are following your map, then they would not have gone south. They would have gone in that direction," he said, pointing westward. "So, The Wraith has turned south and is riding with someone else. I'd guess Mexicans or desperados, given that most of the hoof marks are real. But why would he not follow Marcus? Why turn south?"

Desiree spit. "I don't know, *monsieur*. But I tell you this. If we meet up with that *connard*, I'm going to kill him."
Sasha turned and looked Desiree straight in the eye. "Why? What did he do to you?"

Desiree stabbed a scorpion with her knife. She held the blade up to show the beast writhing on the sharp tip. "It's not what he did to me," she said. "It's what he did to my sister."

Chapter 14

Marcus and Sierra stood looking down the long, nearly hidden path that led into the Tonto Forest. Finally, they were here, right on the edge. But how much further would they have to go, and what would they encounter once they entered that pine thicket? There was only one way to answer those questions.

Sierra pointed. "If we go in there, there's no turning back."

She was right. They had gotten this far, with obstacles to spare. Now, here they were, and Marcus was both elated and nervous. He could lose some of them, or even all of them, wherever that road led to, or he could come out the winner. He did not think it a 50-50 proposition, as Sun might say in his highly educated manner; the odds were definitely not in their favor. *But we're the Wayward Eight, the finest mercenaries around,* he said to himself as he studied the ground, studied the winding creek that lay to their right, the harsh arid land that lay before them, the thick clumps of pine trees that rose up into the blue sky like shards of green and brown mountain. The Tonto Forest was both beautiful and terrifying, a mix of pine forests and dangerous, rocky canyons. No wonder Carpathian had picked it for his lair.

"We might not be able to get very far on our Iron Horses," Marcus said. "This road may be the only entry point level enough and wide enough to support them, and I doubt seriously we'd be welcomed guests if we simply knock."

"We're gonna knock all right," Jake said, standing nearby, holding his knife. "We're gonna knock that bastard's head right off."

Marcus smiled. Jake could be a right bastard himself sometimes, but Marcus was thankful for his fighting spirit. They needed that right now; they needed someone willing and able to go in there, by himself if need be, to slay that monster. Marcus looked around at everyone as they went about their business. Hicks and K-Free were checking the vehicles before they headed further down the road. Zarelda was checking weapons once more. Jake had been fiddling with Carl Fredrickson's glove, but had given up in frustration. River was running her blades over a whetstone, and Sun was hunting pheasant. Sierra stood beside him, talking tactics that he was half listening to. Everyone seemed enthused and ready for action, but he wondered how true that really was.

"How much further does Ladue's map take us?" Sierra asked.

"This is it," Marcus said. "This is where she claims they were attacked."

"Do you trust her?"

"No. I suspect she was holding back, probably to force us to take her with us. But she got us this far, and I don't think any further scribblings on paper on her part would have made all that much difference. Carpathian's hideout lies in there, up that road. We just have to get far enough down it to find Payson."

"We could follow the creek," Sierra said, pointing to the winding water nearby.

Marcus nodded. "I thought about that, but we don't know if it branches or not. It could take us quite a distance out of the way, and our Iron Horses would not be very reliable along the bank anyway. No, we'll start first thing in the morning, go in nice and slow, stopping often to take stock, survey the field. My time in the war gave me pretty good instincts when it comes to topography. I've never fought in such rugged terrain before, but we'll be all right."

"Do you propose we go right up to the gate, if there is one?" Jake asked, only half-joking.

"No, I have a plan for that. Once we get close, Sun and River will do the rest."

They turned and looked at River, who had put her bedroll out beneath a dead pine. She had been very quiet and sullen since they had left the mine. Perhaps she had affection toward Carl due to his protecting her in the past. Of course, she was having difficulty articulating her feelings about leaving him behind, but that was necessary. If there was anyone in the group who understood the power of dreams, surely it was River. The Indian girl in his dream had told him who was a danger, and he had acted quickly to eliminate that threat. It was a tough decision, but a necessary one.

"DAMNIT!" Hicks shouted from beneath his own 'Horse. Marcus ran to him, followed by the others.

"What's the matter?"

Hicks pulled himself out from underneath the Iron Horse, holding his right wrist. The grimace on his face was clear. "I cut myself."

"Let's see," Zarelda said, coming up quickly and kneeling beside her husband.

Hicks raised his hand as if he were trying to blot out the sun, fingers flayed out for everyone to see clearly. A long gash lay across his palm and deep red blood flowed from it. His entire hand was red.

A sinking feeling hit Marcus's chest as he looked at that red hand and remembered the dream.

Beware the man with the red hand.

*****

Sun followed the pheasant into a patch of sage brush. It was a fat, juicy-looking thing, and his stomach growled. They had lived on small scraps of beef jerky and hard tack since leaving Fort Waco. Marcus had insisted that they keep moving, pushing forward, making up for lost time, thus not giving them enough time to hunt or to fish. But now they were camped alongside a river with no plans of moving until first light, which gave him time to do what he enjoyed. He had been educated in the north, taught how to properly use a spoon, knife, and fork. But he could not deny what he was. He was Warrior Nation born, and he enjoyed from time to time the simpler, nobler pursuits of his people. He liked to hunt. He didn't do it as often as he wished, and thus these times were precious. He liked to hunt on his own more than anything, to feel that connection with the earth. There was no great spirit, no spirit animals; he knew this. But that didn't mean one could not appreciate the gifts given by the land.

The bird he pursued was big and colorful, with a bright patch of red around its eye, white spots of feathers along its back, a long tail that bobbed gently behind it as it scratched the soil looking for insects and worms. It was aware of its environment, popping its head up once in a while to look for threats. But Sun was a good tracker, certainly the best in the

Eight, besides River of course. The bird had no idea it was being stalked.

He couldn't kill it with his blaster. That would more or less incinerate it, leaving only scant few feathers behind as evidence that a bird actually existed. He had to kill it the old fashioned way, the traditional way, with a rock; the way a woman might do it. Get up close and hit it hard, knock it out, then wring its neck. He'd done it before, and this one was so fat that it could hardly be missed.

He waited behind the sage until the pheasant stepped out of cover. Slowly, quietly, he rose up on his knees and let the rock go. It hit the bird square in the neck. It flopped across the ground, flapping its wings, trying to gain flight; but its neck was broken most certainly, and it could not get away. Sun dashed from the brush, grabbed the bird quickly and wrung its neck. He was pleased. They would eat well tonight.

He placed his hand on the ground to push himself up, but a soft leather boot came down on it, locking it in place. He stopped and looked up at the figure silhouetted against the setting sun.

"Walks Looking!"

He dropped the bird and tried drawing his blaster, but she kicked his hand away from his holster and pushed him into the ground. Her knees were against his chest, her blade at his throat.

"Don't move, Sun Totem," she said, her mouth close to his face, "and I may let you live."

Sun kept perfectly still, eyed the blade at his neck. "It is true then. Carl was right. You were there, at the mine, with your knife against Marcus's throat."

She nodded.

"Why did you not reveal yourself then? Why did you disappear and leave us to wonder the truth of it?"

"The man with the red hand tried to kill me. I pulled away just before he fired. I came there to warn Marcus of that threat, and he responded correctly. There was no further need for me to stay. Now my dreams of a man with a red hand no longer exist. The threat has been removed. My duty was done."

Sun was not convinced. "How can you know what red is? You have never seen it."

Walk Looking shook her head. "I do not know, but I know that in my dream, his hand was red, and I understood it as such."

"Are you certain of this? Dreams can deceive."

She nodded. "I am. I see no further threat from him."

"But do you see other threats?"

Walks Looking's face changed as if she were searching for an answer. He could not see her eyes, for they were covered with cloth. Her mouth twitched; she wetted her lips with her tongue. "There are always threats with everything we do, Sun. Dreams cannot possibly reveal them all. I saw a red hand; I do not see it anymore. I trust my dreams."

"Then why bother to show yourself now, if your task is finished?" Sun found the courage to move away from her knife and stand. Walks Looking allowed him to do so. She tucked away her blade. "Why aggravate my hunt?"

"I wish to speak to you privately, about River."

"What about her?"

"I want her to come with me. To join my cause."

Sun shook his head. "She would be lost without me."

"She is lost *because* of you. You do not believe in the Great Spirit, nor in the animal spirits. I cannot connect with my own, not because I do not believe, but because something is keeping me from doing so. I have seen the edges of this unseen force, and I know that it keeps me from finding my spirit. Someday I will learn the truth of it and beat it. River is the same. She could connect if she could chant the songs necessary to call upon her spirit, if she had a tongue to give voice to those words. But she could learn how in others ways, and break away from that force that keeps her from shifting. But you fill her with lies, telling her that there are no spirits, that it is all a trick by the elders to control us. I do not like the control the chiefs have over the people any more than you do, but a person must be allowed to find his or her own way. You keep her from the truth, and she suffers because of it."

"And how could she find that truth with you?" Sun asked, growing bolder, moving toward Walks Looking to stare her in the face. "You would turn her into a disciple to follow you around from one fruitless battle to the next like some puppy dog, and she would die out there on the prairie, alone, broken, and where would her so-called spirit animal be then? A snake can die just as easily in war as a human being, easier even, because it has no hands to wield a blade, or no fingers to pull a trigger. A snake can be trampled, skinned, eaten, and as long as I draw breath, my sister will never shift, nor will she ever believe that it is possible."

They stood there, glaring at each other, for a long time. He wondered if she was really looking at him. Could she actually see his stare? She could certainly feel his breath on her skin, feel his heat from the rage he felt inside. He so badly wanted to pull his knife and draw it across her throat. For her to come to him and accuse him of not protecting his sister... There was no one who was more devoted to Flowing River, no one who loved her more, than he did.

He pulled back, rested his shoulders. "I have nothing more to say on the matter."

"I have said my piece, and you will either listen or not. It is a standing offer, however. If you change your mind, she is always welcome with me. But now you must turn your attention to this affair with Carpathian. You and River have an important part to play in it yet, and Marcus Wayward will need your strength before it is all over. Are you prepared, my brother?"

"We are always prepared," Sun said. "We will lay down our lives for Marcus if we must."

"It may come to that," she said, her voice cold, serious. "When you enter that forest, you will—"

Gunfire rang out at the camp, loud, constant, as if a spray of bullets was being released. Then more and more. Several guns fired. Sun recognized them all.

"There is trouble," he said, pulling his pistol.

Walks Looking pulled her blades again. "It could be a scouting party from Payson. Let's go."

Together they ran toward the camp.

*****

It was a Warrior Nation scouting party, seven men on foot, carrying blasters and knives, and Jake could even see one carrying a bow. They were painted head to toe in black and grey and red paint, and they howled as they attacked.

As he took up a defensive position behind his Iron Horse, Jake thought to himself that it could not be the Warrior Nation, because they didn't use RJ weapons. Sun Totem used them, he conceded, but then, Sun wasn't really part of the Nation, other than being born into it. Who were these men, then? And why were they attacking? It didn't make any sense, but Jake scarcely had time to think about it.

A blaster round struck his Iron Horse and put a deep gash in its frame. Luckily, it did not hit any vital parts, so Jake rose up and fired two fists of Grandfather pistols, tracking one warrior that moved along an outcropping of rock, dodging not only his own fire, but K-Free's as well. These warriors were good, he had to admit. They had clearly done this kind of attack before.

"Get away from the vehicles," Marcus yelled over the barrage of gunfire. He himself was pinned down near River's position, both of them holding the line behind the dead pine against an aggressive attack from a man whose face was painted pure, deep grey with white stripes down his cheeks. He held two blasters, and some kind of rifle was strapped to his back.

Jake scolded himself for being so foolish; he had jumped behind his Iron Horse out of instinct, but after hearing Marcus, he recognized his folly. They all needed to find other cover away from their Iron Horses; they couldn't afford having them shot up just before they entered the Tonto Forest.

He waited until the gunfire subsided slightly and then ran. He dodged a blaster shot that exploded across the ground at his feet. He rolled, came up behind a patch of sage and rock, and fired. One of the warriors went down, a gaping hole in his chest. The rest of their attackers shifted position, trying to fill the gap left by the dead warrior.

Sierra was flat on her face, not due to being wounded, but the gunfire leveled against her was so strong that she didn't dare rise up. Hicks and Zarelda were still holding a position behind their 'Horses. K-Free had crawled her way over to where River and Marcus were positioned. The grey faced one and two of his compatriots were pressing the assault against those three. The pine they used as cover was burning like a torch from blaster fire.

That left Sun Totem, and where was he? Had he run from the engagement? No, wait, he was hunting. But shouldn't he be back by now? Without him, they were trying to fight off an attack without their full strength and without a full understanding of the land they were trying to defend. Sun should be here, helping.

Gunfire whizzed past his head, fired in the direction toward the attacking warriors. Jake looked up and saw Sun moving calmly and patiently toward his position, his legs obscured by sage as he walked. He fired round after round, pinning the warriors in front of them. Sun's aggressive stance emboldened Jake, and he tucked his pistols away and drew his rifle. He leaned up carefully to shield himself with dead sage. These bushes would not protect him if the warriors in front of him decided to fire, but perhaps they wouldn't see him move. That was the only hope he had. He raised his rifle, letting the muzzle heat. A stream of smoke emanated from the tip. He let it cook, waited, waited, and then fired.

Rounds of molten fire hailed from his rifle and struck the position where two warriors were hiding. Their screams echoed through the air. They rose up, their backs on fire. Jake fired again, putting more rounds into one of the scouts, ending his thrashing and screams. The other was on fire, but didn't seem to care. He collected himself bravely and fired into Jake's position. It was all Jake could do to protect himself from the blaster rounds as they came through the sage brush and burned it away. Jake huddled like a little baby, cupping his arms across his head to keep from being burned alive. The arm that had been wounded by Sasha Tanner at Fort Smith was now hurting again, being singed by the fire spreading through the sage. Jake tried pushing himself away from the flames, but his boots could not find purchase on the rocky ground. He decided to risk being hit square and rise again, hopefully putting another volley into the enemy such that they would fall back enough to regroup and find better cover. But hands reached through the conflagration and pulled him away.

He closed his eyes and fired as he was being dragged backward. He was screaming too, firing and screaming, hoping that if his shooting could not quell the enemy, perhaps his rage would. He fired and fired until he was safely pulled behind thick rock.

"Thank you, Sun, I—"

But it wasn't Sun who had pulled him to safety. It was a woman, a Warrior Nation woman, her hair black, her skin dark from the sun, her clothing light and soft leather. She wore a bandana around her eyes.

"Jake," Sun said, coming up and finding cover behind them, "this is Walks Looking. Walks Looking… Jake Mattia."

"I know who he is," Walks Looking said, releasing Jake's collar. "You are a brave man, Jake Mattia. You would make a good member of the Warrior Nation."

"Shouldn't you be on the other side," he said, immediately regretting it, "fighting against us?"

Walks Looking managed a smile, despite having to keep her head down from the barrage of blaster fire that was cooking the boulder in front of them. "They are not true people of the Nation, Jake. They are Grey Face's men, allies of Doctor Carpathian. They are what the Nation chiefs would have called *Indeh*, the dead."

"They are animations?" Jake asked.

"Not yet, but they will be soon. They are on a blood path, and they must all be killed. We cannot let one survive, or he will alert Carpathian of your presence."

"How'd they get blasters this far west?"

"Grey Face's range is wider than Carpathian's normal scouts. He rides his own trail. He has killed many lawmen and Union soldiers. He's a scavenger."

Jake nodded. "Okay, then how do we kill them? Their blaster fire is so thick, we can't move proper."

Walks Looking dared stick her head out from cover, looked around as if she could really see. Her head jerked back and forth as if she were following the sounds of gunfire. Then she said, "Follow me."

The duo followed her, crouching low. Jake knew what she was doing immediately. She wanted to go around behind them, shoot them from the back. Jake wanted to shout out to Marcus, K-Free, and River who were still holding their own, to tell them their plan, but knew that would foul it all up. The sage all around them burned, which did provide smoke cover, but these Grey Face men, as Walks Looking called them, seemed to have a sixth sense when it came to spotting targets. Sierra, he noticed, had managed to find protection behind a tiny hillock and had dug out a place for her to lay and fire. Hicks and Zarelda had moved back, leaving their Iron Horses behind, but finding a small patch of thick sage that hadn't been struck yet by blaster fire. The situation seemed, to Jake at least, to be at a standstill. He knew Marcus wouldn't tolerate that for long. He just hoped that the boss would sit tight long enough for them to get into position before he tried an aggressive counterattack.

They went to the left, a large circle around an outcropping of rock along a small ledge. They were almost out of effective blaster range, and thus getting around their attackers from here would not be an issue, assuming Grey Face didn't have reserve men lying in wait. He did not, at least not where Walks Looking took them. She brought them up and around the left flank of the attackers, far below their position, where the sage brush was thin but where small pines and other brush were prevalent and living off the precious water of the creek. She paused. Jake and Sun came up behind her.

"Sun Totem," she said whispering, motioning him forward, "you go up there, about thirty steps, and then crawl up the ledge. Then fire upon them hard. Jake Mattia, you go thirty steps that way, and do the same."

"Where are you going?" Jake asked.

She pulled her blades. They glowed hot blue. "Up the middle."

He did as he was told, though he didn't like taking orders from this woman. Not because she was a woman, but because she was the one who Carl had sworn was in the building at the abandoned mine, and apparently it was now true. Why hadn't she shown herself there and cleared up the matter right away? Why stay secret? He held no love for Carl Fredrickson, that was true, but given the strength and determination of this first scouting unit encountered on the edge of the Tonto Forest, it would have been best to keep Carl in their ranks. She had a lot of nerve coming here now and trying to help.

Nevertheless, he followed her instructions and moved out, counted out the paces she stated, then worked his way up the ledge, watching Sun through the corner of his eye, matching his steps up the ledge. When they had gone far enough for Walks Looking's satisfaction, she motioned them to stop. Then she moved, faster and more gracefully than any warrior he had ever seen. It was as if she were made of water sliding around rock and soil, born to the ground that she covered. She bounded up the ledge, each step perfectly placed, giving her perfect strength as she reached the top and let her blades speak for her.

She did not give a sign to start shooting, but Sun opened fire and Jake put fire round after round into the back of the warrior in front of him. The man didn't go down immediately, but instead managed to keep his feet against the savage attack, turn and throw one final shot toward Jake. Jake had to duck to keep from getting hit, and again, the sage around him burned. But with this immediate threat eliminated, he stood up straight and moved toward Walks Looking.

She was in a brawl with two warriors. Each time they tried to raise their guns to fire, she knocked the barrels away with a swift slash of her blades. They threw their pistols down and drew knives, hoping that that would give them a better chance. It didn't. One stuck out toward her face. She ducked, came up beneath him and drove her knife into his gut. She twisted it as she picked the man off the ground and slammed him behind her, letting his back crack against the hard ground. Her other assailant tried to kick her in the chest, but Sun came up and put him down with a targeted shot into the throat.

The only one left now was Grey Face, and he was standing his ground still against Marcus, K-Free, and River, who had finally come out from behind cover. Grey Face was wedged between two rocks and able to find protection each time the three of them tried to shoot him. Walks Looking ran over to him, shouted something Jake could not understand, and forced the painted warrior out from his cover. He attacked her, using his rifle as a club, thrusting and swinging it each time she tried stabbing him. Grey Face was a good fighter, every bit as strong – and perhaps even stronger – than Walks

Looking. He moved just as fast too, dodging her attack, then counterattacking. She was not having as easy a time with it as she had with the other two. But this time, the enemy was badly outnumbered.

K-Free managed to find an opening and fired her blaster. Grey Face's knee gave out with a splash of blood and bone. He fell, but still held against Walks Looking's assault. Sierra limped into view. She was favoring her right ankle, the heel on her right boot broken and dangling on the side. She supported herself as best she could and fired radiated bullets into Grey Face's back. Finally, he stopped moving, hovered there on his knees, a blank expression on his painted face. Through blinding pain, he held up his arm and shouted a warrior's cry that Jake had heard other Indians give when they knew they were about to die. Then Marcus came up and ended it with a slash across the man's face, literally taking the paint and flesh clean off with one powerful swipe.

Grey Face fell dead.

Jake breathed a sigh of relief and helped Sierra sit down. Her ankle had twisted when her boot heel had broken. Everyone else was okay, minor cuts and abrasions, save for River who had taken this time to go into one of her fits. She lay twitching beneath the burning pine. Jake shook his head. *We should have left her in Kentucky.*

"Go around and check bodies," Marcus said, sheathing his sword. "Make sure they are all dead, but be careful about contamination. And gather up blasters. They'll come in handy."

Jake sat and watched as Walks Looking came up and stood before Marcus. "You're the one in my dreams," he said.

"Yes."

"Where you there that night?"

She nodded.

"Then why didn't you stay and reveal yourself? I made the decision to leave Carl Frederickson behind. You cost us a good man."

"No, as I said to Sun, you did the right thing. And now I must go again, for my destiny lies elsewhere. Your destiny lies deep in that forest. It is a glorious mission that you are on,

Marcus Wayward, and it is your responsibility to see it through." She offered her hand to Marcus. It was the first time Jake had ever seen a member of the Nation extend a hand to a white man. Marcus took it grudgingly, but shook it firm.

Then she was gone, as quickly as she had arrived, bounding through the sage and pine trees.

Jake paused a moment longer to catch his breath, then did as Marcus ordered. He put a final round into the back of one of the warriors that still twitched. He was about to pick up the man's blaster when a glint of metal caught his eye. Jake leaned the man over and beneath him, affixed to a golden chain, lay an amulet of silver, ornately wrought with symbols Jake did not understand, but were beautiful to his eyes nonetheless. He yanked it away from the dead man's neck and held it gently in his hand. He looked deep into the ornate pattern and suddenly his head began to ache, very strong this time, and he doubled over and waited on his knees until the pain subsided.

"Are you okay?" K-Free asked as she started over to him.

He waved her off. "Yeah, I'm fine, Kimberly. No problem."

When she moved away, he stood, still looking into the amulet. An image came to him, an action that he was instructed to take. One that he should have taken a long time ago. The image made it clear to him that it wasn't River who was the problem. No. It was her brother all along, and he must make sure that Sun didn't harm Marcus or anyone else in the group. Something had to be done about Sun.

Jake pulled his knife and looked around. Sun was helping River recover from her seizure. Hicks and Zarelda were checking over their Iron Horses. Everyone else was preoccupied with other duties and cleaning up after the fight. He was alone and no one was paying attention to him.
Perfect.

Jake, his head aching, a voice whispering instructions, walked calmly over to Sun's Iron Horse.

Chapter 15

The Wraith finally let his men pause for rest, some food, and some water. He had been running them hard to make up for lost time. One of the horses came up lame and had to be put down; they ate well that night. Its rider had to double up with another for the remainder of the journey. The rest of the horses were skin and bones, but so what? It wouldn't matter once they found the opening to the mine that Antonio had indicated on his map. After picking up Carl at the abandoned mine, they headed south and found a trail The Wraith was quite familiar with. He had never traveled so far into Carpathian's territory before, but they were close. So close that he could almost smell the copper. The only problem was they had to travel further into the Tonto Forest than he had hoped. It was a larger patch of wood than he first thought. Antonio hadn't bothered to provide him with that important bit of information.

They lay along a ridge line, looking down into a small river valley where the forest began. The Wraith used an old telescope to survey the wood's edge. "I don't see any scouts or any danger; at least not yet."

"Can't know, though, what lies in the forest," Carl said, trying to reach for the scope. The Wraith reluctantly gave it over. "And I'm not sure it's wise to take our horses in there. Too much noise, too much risk of getting caught."

"We can go the rest of the way on foot, but that'll delay us even further. No, I think we take the horses in, but we move by night, all night, until we find the shaft. And kill anything that gets in our way, and I mean kill it, dead, so that it can't go back and squeal to Carpathian."

Carl looked through the scope, followed the line of pine trees all the way west until they disappeared into mountain. He closed the scope and handed it back. "That's another thing I want to talk to you about, Rob—, sorry, *Wraith*. This plan you have of getting in through mine tunnels. Is that really wise? I mean, those shafts are old, and Lord knows how safe they are. We could get lost in there, buried alive maybe. It's too risky a move."

"Yes it is, but that's why I brought the Mexicans along with me."

Carl shook his head. "I don't follow."

"You really think I brought these boys along to fight?" The Wraith scoffed. "Their puny little blackpowder sticks ain't gonna hurt a soul. No, I brought them along to search the mines for me, to dig if necessary. We sit back and let them roam the tunnels, let them find the way. Then we go in when the route is found and clearly marked. If they get lost, or buried alive in the search, who cares?"

"So this contract you have with Antonio to hold Carpathian's town for the Golden Army is bunk."

"Not worth wiping my ass with it. You really think we could hold an entire Enlightened army at bay with just ten soldiers? Antonio isn't as smart as my father said he was. Truth is, he really doesn't understand Carpathian and what he is doing here in this forest, doesn't understand the strength and power that foreign devil is holding. So long as you and I get in there and kill that son of a bitch, the rest is meaningless. We get our money, and I won't ever have to treat with Antonio or Mexico or with America for that matter again. After all this, I'm gone, and there ain't a country or army in the world that'll stop me."

They pushed back from the ledge and stood, dusted themselves off, and returned to the horses. The Mexican soldiers were resting in a small patch of wood, their horses grazing on a few choice tufts of grass. The Wraith slipped his scope into the satchel on his Blackhoof, then broke out his canteen. He drank greedily, letting the water slip out his mouth and down his chin. He wiped his mouth clean and said loudly, "Okay, boys, we'll stay here until the sun drops. Then we'll go in nice and slow, *entiende*, and move by night." He winked at Carl, smiled a little, and then put away his canteen. "Then we'll see how good you all are at being canaries."

*****

On Marcus's order, Sun and River had traveled five miles further into the Tonto Forest alone, leaving their Iron

Horses behind and covered in pine needles, dried bark, and dirt, then going on foot. Hicks wanted time to figure out a way to limit the RJ footprint that any vehicle running on the fuel had, thus reducing the range at which creatures – like the ones controlled by Carpathian – could sniff out intruders. If they were reanimated by the strength of RJ, Hicks argued, then certainly its smell could attract them from long distances. It made sense; even humans could smell the fuel as it burned through vehicle engines or through the use of weapons. But they did not have time for such scientific research, Marcus argued. The Wraith and Sasha were still out there. So Sun and River went in on their own to scout for Payson.

They had not found it yet.

Sun was frustrated. The entire team had pushed over twenty miles into the forest, moving slow and steady, traveling off-road wherever they could, and under strict orders by Marcus not to speak loudly, or to fire weapons, or expend ammunition. Even at night, their fires were to be kept small, if they tried starting one at all. Some nights, they slept without a fire, and it grew cold. But they had gotten far into the forest, and with no major problems, save one small scout team of two dour looking men, with a few augmented attachments to their arms and face. They were easy to kill. The discovery of that team was encouraging: it meant they were in the right area of the forest. But they were twenty miles in, and still no town.

Should we turn around and go back? Sun asked himself this many times over the course of the afternoon. He was worried that moving too far ahead of the rest would prove deadly. They were close to Payson, they had to be, and yet, they had found nothing. *You are one careful man, Carpathian.*

Sun tapped River on the shoulder and signed his request. *Let us move up to that embankment along the road and take a look around. We will see better up there.*

River agreed, and they moved quietly, keeping to shadows that were forming from the sun setting westward. A light breeze blew from the south. Sun sniffed the air. Nothing.

They reached the ledge and took a look. For miles in every direction, nothing but pine forest, a smattering here and there of rock outcropping, beautiful but seemingly empty of any speck of civilization.

Let us move around the bend and see what is on the other side of this hill.

He let River take the lead. She seemed to want to do so, moving past him and taking up a position a few feet from him. She didn't seem to mind the fact that her buckskin boots were worn and threadbare, the toes on her left foot exposed. She ran the risk of cutting her feet on the sharp stones, but she walked confidently along the rocky ledge, hopping over dead pine logs and thick underbrush. For a moment, he lost sight of her, but then she came back into view, then out again, in, out, until they were well past the bend in the road and staring into a different part of the forest. When he finally caught up with her, she was standing near tip-toe on a large rock, peering down into a valley that stretched in front of them for miles. The canopy of the valley was again covered in pine trees, and Sun didn't know what his sister was looking at, but she seemed to be smiling. She began to hop, as if stepping on hot coals. He'd seen her do this tiny dance before, when anticipation of something was too great for her to contain. She was excited, and he didn't know why.

He went to her, tried craning his neck to see what she was looking at. Nothing gave way through the thick pines. "What do you see?" he hissed quietly, breaking his own rule of no speaking. "Is it Payson?"

She was about to sign her answer when the rock beneath her dancing gave way.

River fell down the embankment toward the road. Sun raced after her, forcing himself not to yell out or to grow too desperate. Those things could kill a man in strange territory. He followed her by letting his legs slip down the rocky soil, kicking up dust and pebbles as they fell. River was obscured by dust which the boulder kicked up strongly as it slid down the bank behind her. He violated another rule and prayed, knowing it would likely do no good, but this was his sister, his only family, being pushed down a steep bank by rocks with no thought or consideration on what would be crushed at the end of its slide. He let himself slip down the embankment, not caring about anything but getting down there quickly to save his sister.

But she was okay, bruised a bit perhaps, some cuts on her arms and shoulder, but otherwise fine. The rock had missed her head by margins. Sun refused to accept his prayer as the reason for that, now that she was safe and at the bottom. He helped her up, but she didn't even bother to brush herself off. Through the kicked-up dust around them, she pulled away from his grasp and began walking down the road. Then she began to run, fast, with no regard for what lay along the road, nor in front of her. "River!" he said aloud again. "Wait!"

She was in a full run, and at that speed she was difficult to catch. She had always been the fastest runner, even as a child. What she lacked in speech, she more than made up for in physical ability. Sun did not know if there was any correlation to that; certainly, his teachers had told him that when someone loses one sense, the others compensate, but they had never said there was a connection between speech and running. River ran fast, and he found it difficult to follow.

She turned a corner and fell out of his sight. He picked up the pace, turned the corner as well, and found her there, at the end of the line of trees, still as a post, looking into a valley that opened up below them where the road led into a mass of stark red and brown brick buildings. Sun moved up to her side and looked where she was pointing.

Payson sprawled below, at the mouth of a canyon that stretched as far into the horizon as they could see. The town itself was dirty, unkempt, row upon row of disheveled buildings. They did not lay in ruin, but their sides were barren, just thick red and brown brick and sturdy untreated pine and oak board with no discernible personality, no life. It almost seemed dead, the entire cold expanse of it laid out like a funeral march. Somewhere down there, however, life must exist, for tiny lines of black, red, and white smoke rose up through the morass, small sounds of the hustle and bustle of a town teeming with people. Sun could not see anyone from this distance.

Behind the town lay the canyon, and there was a steady stream of red smoke pouring out of it. Sun turned his head up and smelled the air. Nothing, save for a faint scent of the smoke from the town. The red smoke in the canyon was being blown to the west, away from them. Clever, Sun thought, of Carpathian putting his industry in the canyon, where the natural flow of air would drive the stench of his abominations westward, away from most threats that would be coming from the east. It was difficult to find a town if you couldn't smell it, especially with so thick a forest all around you; all forests teamed with their own aromas. Sun squinted to try to pick out details inside the canyon, but it was too far away with too much obscurity from the roiling red smoke. He didn't want to linger any longer.

Let us go, he signed, and turned back up the road. He stopped dead cold.

Six men stood behind them.

They seemed real, their faces covered with bristles of black and grey hair, their clothing simple brown and tan affair, but reasonably tidy. One wore a grey duster, three wore Stetson hats. One carried a cigar which he put in his mouth. They all had pistols, three carried rifles. Their weapons glowed with RJ.

"Who are you?" said the man with the grey duster. He leveled his rifle at Sun's chest. "We don't allow no Injins here."

"We are…" Sun hesitated, searched for the proper words. "We are lost. What is this town?"

"That ain't none of your business, boy," said the man, cocking his rifle. "You a fancy talking Injin, ain't ya?"

Sun ignored the question and nodded. "I see. Well, then we will not bother you any further. We will be going."

Sun moved as if he and River would simply step to the side and pass them. The men closed ranks to deny passage. "Don't move, or you and your Injin bitch will die. Now, turn over your weapons and put out your hands."

Sun did nothing at first, but then moved slowly as if he were reaching for his belt to remove his blaster. Then, before the man in front of him could see or react, Sun drew his blaster and put a round into the man's chest, killing him instantly. The man behind him was sprayed with flesh and blood as the man's back exploded by the force of the round.

The speed of the shot shocked the other men, and they instinctively dropped to the ground as if pinned by gunfire.

River stabbed another man in the back and ripped her blade out his shoulder, cutting through his lung and ending his life.

Then they ran, taking the opportunity to flee in the chaos. They leapt over the men as they huddled on the ground and ran back up the road, full speed. Sun tucked his gun away; it was too heavy to run with in hand, and he wasn't interested in killing any more. They weren't supposed to kill anything; Marcus's orders. They also weren't supposed to be seen, but things happen, ground loosens and boulders give way. Their cover was blown. The best thing to do was to kill them all, but to fire weapons like Union blasters so close to Payson… Well, they couldn't afford to arouse the whole town of their presence.

So they ran, about a quarter mile down the road, the remaining scouts in pursuit fired a barrage of RJ weapons that forced them to get off the road and re-climb the embankment. River was better at it than he; she took the lead, bounding from one downed trunk to the next, propelling herself up through the foliage like a deer. Sun kept up but had to stop from time to time to hide from gunfire, which quickly made short order of the trunks and even the small boulders. Sun was constantly covered in shattered bark, tree pulp, sap, and rock shards. But he reached the top and found good ground.

He caught up with River, and they ran straight to their Iron Horses. The men following had fallen back and Sun hoped they were stalled in trying to get up the embankment. He did not stop to find out, as they ran further through the pine thicket and then bound back down the embankment and took to the road again. Sun began noticing landmarks: a tree hit by lightning that cracked and now leaned over the road; an odd-shaped piece of rock with lines of granite; the dead remains of a hornet's nest cracked open and hanging from a limb. Their vehicles were near.

The scouts had not given up their pursuit. Sun heard them speaking to one another, their voices echoing down the road, barking orders to spread out and keep searching. They were persistent. They had to be. What was the penalty for allowing someone not invited to Payson to escape, Sun wondered? Their lives, probably. Or perhaps their souls. Carpathian took both. Perhaps death would be better for them.

He'd like to give it to them, but they had to get away. Orders were orders.

They found their Iron Horses, pushed off the pine cover and climbed on. They gunned the engines. Sun heard gunfire behind him, then bullets blaring past his head. "Go!" he barked to River, pulling the 'Horse out of the small clearing and into the road. "Go!"

They sped up quickly, and it seemed as if they were going to get away. Then there was a loud pop beneath his vehicle, and it suddenly jerked to the left. Sun tried keeping it on the road. It jerked again, and then another loud pop. Then the left skid dropped off, striking the ground and bouncing back up into the chassis, pushing the Iron Horse off the road. Sun tried keeping his balance, but without the skid to keep wind shear down, he couldn't control it. It slammed through small trees and bushes, and Sun jumped off just before his Iron Horse struck a tree and exploded.

Fire engulfed the vehicle and the tree that it had hit broke in half. Sun tried rolling out of the way, but the jump had knocked him dizzy. His eyes were unfocused, his movements slow. He tried getting away, but the tree fell right on him, pinning his legs beneath its weight.

He screamed and tried pulling free, but he was too weak, too disoriented. River was at his side quickly, jumping off her Iron Horse, trying to push the tree away.

"It's no use," he said to her, lying back, trying to catch his breath. He pulled his ion pistol from the small holster on his belt and handed it to River, remembering what he had been ordered to do in that Kentucky barn. "Go, and give this to Marcus."

River shook her head, grabbed his arm instead and tried again to pull him free. RJ bullets from the scouts struck the trees around them, igniting the dry bark.

"No!" Sun said, ripping his arm from her grasp. "No more. Take the pistol, and go. You must save yourself. You must take this to Marcus. It's the only way to save the mission."

He could see the fear in her eyes, the desperation as the scouts drew closer. She wanted to sign her refusal, but he grabbed her hand and forced the pistol into it. "Go… NOW!"

She pulled away, leapt over the trunk and disappeared through the trees.

He kept his head up until he heard her Iron Horse emerge and slip away from the scouts' range.

He laid back, his legs in excruciating pain. But he smiled, knowing that he had done the right thing. *It does not matter if I die*, he thought. *What matters is that River survives. What matters is the mission.*

One of the scouts stepped over his head, paused, and stared down at his face. Sun closed his eyes and felt the hard butt of the man's rifle strike his temple.

Chapter 16

"It's River!"

Zarelda shouted to Marcus from the tree. She was standing guard, watching the approach from the direction that Sun and River had gone. Sun was nowhere to be seen down the trail, and Zarelda's heart sank. She jumped down and pulled her rifle from her back. Something was wrong. Something was very wrong.

River didn't even let her Iron Horse stop before she bounded off of it and came toward Sierra and K-Free who grabbed her before she fell face-first into the hard ground. She was crying, sobbing really, her tiny moans sounding tortured and pitiful. Hicks had to run after the 'Horse to stop it, but with Jake's help, they managed to catch it before it slid down an embankment and crashed.

Zarelda came up to River to try to give aide, but Marcus pushed past her. "What happened?" He asked, stopping Sierra and K-Free from taking River to her bed roll. "Where's Sun?"

They sat her carefully on the ground, and she began to convulse, mad twitchings and fiddling with her fingers as if she were keying a musical instrument. "She's trying to sign," Sierra said.

"Can you understand her?"

Sierra shook her head. "I know a few of her signs, but not many."

"I know dem," Zarelda said, pushing past Marcus and falling down beside River. "Come on, child," she said, cooing gently to try to soothe the girl. She rubbed her head and continued to speak softly. "Tell Zarelda now what happened."

It was a long minute before River calmed enough to sign. When she did, her hands were moving faster than Zarelda wanted, but she didn't try to stop her. She let her say everything River wanted before she spoke. "Dey found Payson. It's about six miles up yonder." She pointed down the road that disappeared in the thick pine. "It lies in a valley, in front of a canyon. Behind it is where Carpathian lives."

"What happened to Sun?" Marcus tried to school his patience, but he was obviously annoyed.

Zarelda swallowed, not wanting to say the words. "He was captured."

"Captured? By whom?" Sierra asked.

She let River repeat that information to ensure that she had heard it right. "Six of Carpathian's scouts. Dey killed two, den made a run for it, but Sun's Iron Horse hit a tree, exploded all to pieces."

"How the hell did that happen?" Marcus asked, agitation and surprise in his voice.

River signed, Zarelda translated. "She says one o' his skids gave out, popped right off, and he lost control. She tried to pick him up, but he was trapped under a tree. He ordered her to leave him. She didn't want to, no sir, but he gave her dis…"

River reached into her boot and drew out Sun's pistol and handed it to Marcus with a shaking hand. Marcus took it, looked at it for a long time, and then slipped it under his belt at the small of his back.

"What's that, Captain?" Hicks asked.

Marcus turned and glared deep into Hicks's eyes. "Don't worry about what that is, Hicks. You need to explain to me why Sun's skids came off."

Hicks backed off, surprise on his face. "Wasn't my fault. That was K-Free's job."

"No, it wasn't," K-Free said, jumping to her feet to defend herself. "I was in charge of weapons."

"I don't care who was responsible." Marcus fumed as he forced the anger from strangling his words. "Aren't you our chief mechanic, Hicks? Isn't it your responsibility to ensure the safety of the equipment?"

Zarelda could see anger growing in Hicks's eyes. "Now wait a damn minute. I'm not taking the blame on this. I can't help it if we're moving through rough terrain. These Iron Horses can't take this kind of travel, Captain. These things happen. It isn't my responsibility."

"Then what is your responsibility? What's your responsibility to this group?"

Zarelda moved to stand up, seeing that her husband was gripping his hands into fists. If she didn't intervene, there'd be a fight for certain. But as she tried to move between them, Hicks turned and stomped off.

"Stop fighting, both of you!" Sierra said, her voice raw with anger. "We gotta save Sun. Focus!"

Marcus returned to River, knelt down. He grabbed her face and made her stare into his eyes. "Did they hurt him?"

She shook her head and signed. "She don't know for sure," Zarelda said. "Dey were firing weapons, and she had to get away, or she'd a' been killed too."

"We got to get him back, Marcus," Sierra said. "Before they do something."

Out of the corner of her eye, Zarelda saw Jake, hovering on the edge of the conversation, his head low, his eyes diverted. He seemed nervous, even for Jake. He shuffled his boots through the gravel, kicking up dust. He'd shoot a glance toward River, and then look away again. He was sweating, more so than usual. *What's da matter wit him?*

"Can you show us where Sun was taken?" Marcus asked.

River nodded.

"Okay, then. You and me and Jake will go back, scout out the place again. I want to see Payson with my own eyes, check the lay of the land. We'll go in about an hour, okay? We'll get your brother back, and in one piece. I promise."

His assurance calmed River down a little, and she was able to stand on her own. "You go get ready, and Jake?" Marcus turned. "We go loaded for bear."

Jake nodded and went to his Iron Horse. Zarelda waited until everyone had drifted away, then she followed.

"Jake?" She said, quietly so as not to raise attention from anyone else.

Jake turned to acknowledge her presence, but said nothing. He kept checking his weapons.

"What's da matter with you, eh? You aren't yourself dees days, and haven't been for a while."

"What the hell do you care about what I've been like?"

"You are part of dis mission, no? Part of da Eight? It's my job to care about everyone, including you. It's your job too."

"I'm carrying my own weight around here."

She walked up to him, put her hand on his shoulder. That was a risky move, she knew. Jake was known to snap, fly off the handle when he was angry. And clearly he was angry. But there was something more there; Zarelda could sense it. There was fear.

"You been against dis mission from da get-go. You shot Sasha's informant. Why, I don't know. And you have advocated against even having River and Sun be part of it. How's come?"

Jake turned on her, his eyes red, his face hot and wet with sweat. "Are you accusing me of something?"

"No, I—"

But then she saw it, in his eyes, the truth. *He sabotaged Sun's vehicle.* She didn't know how she knew, but it was plain as day on his face, in the beads of sweat running down his rough cheeks. He'd done it.

She fell back in fear. "You, you—"

"Jake!" Marcus yelled across the camp. Jake responded by picking up his rifle, holstering his pistols. He stared Zarelda down. "If you got something to say, why don't you say it to Marcus himself? Otherwise, leave me alone. I got a job to do."

He walked off, and Zarelda stood there a moment, catching her breath. *Maybe I'm wrong.* Now she wasn't sure of what she had seen. Perhaps it was the hot sun, or the warm wind blowing from the south. Surely she was mistaken. Jake was a grumpy, unruly man, yes, but he would never purposely try to hurt any of them. Would he?

She found Hicks tinkering with his own Iron Horse. "Lover," she said, "we need to talk to Marcus. I'm worried 'bout Jake."

Hicks didn't pull himself up from beneath his vehicle. He stayed there, banging away on the skid. "I'm not going to say another word to that son of a bitch. He accuses me of sabotage. Who the hell does he think he is?"

"He didn't accuse you of nothing." She said, sitting down beside him.

"Oh, so you're taking his side now, is that it?"

It was Zarelda's turn to get angry. "Watch your mouth, Hicks. There ain't no cause for dat. I'm your wife, not your punching bag."

Hicks came out and threw his wrench aside. "Damnit, woman. I'm tired of this. I'm tired of arguing the point. I've had it with him. I don't deserve the accusation, and I sure as hell don't need to be working for him anymore. If he thinks he can put K-Free in charge, so be it. Let's see how far he can get. I'm telling you straight right now. I'm changing sides as soon as I get a chance. As soon as we get in. With or without you."

Zarelda pulled back. Her heart sank. "You'd abandon me, lover? After all dis time?"

She could sense his anger, but his face told a different story. He had spoken out of turn. It wasn't unusual. Hicks was a pretty mild-mannered man, but when he got angry, his mouth would spout off words before his mind realized what he was saying. He could feel regret, but like Jake, he was too damned stubborn to apologize.

He went back under his Iron Horse. "Just leave me alone, will you? I've got a *job* to do."

Zarelda huffed. That was the same thing Jake had just said to her: *I got a job to do...* How odd. She stood and stalked off. *Men!* She had the notion to whip out her atomic pistol and blast both of their heads off. They deserved it. She huffed again, not knowing what to do. Should she confide in Marcus her suspicions about Jake? Should she say something to him about Hicks? A thousand questions swam through her mind. If she was wrong about Jake, then accusing him to the boss could be treason. Then again, Marcus had accused Carl, and he had been wrong about that, and they couldn't afford to lose any more good hands. Telling Marcus about her husband *was* treason. But didn't she have a greater responsibility to the team? The mission? The Eight? Right now, she had no answers to these questions.

She wandered away from the camp, not too far but far enough to lose the conversation that others were having about the night mission that Marcus, River, and Jake were about to conduct. Her heart sank. Would Jake try something against River? A knife in the back? A quick hand to push her off a ledge? A rock to the head? *Maybe I should follow them, volunteer to tag along, to keep an eye on him.* No. She shook that concern off quickly. Marcus would keep his eye on River; he would never let anything happen to her. *And I must stay here in camp... and keep an eye on my own husband.*

*****

"Looks like trouble," Sasha Tanner said as he eyed the commotion in the Wayward Eight camp through his telescope.

He and Desiree's ladies were safely hidden about a mile away, on a ridgeline, looking down at Marcus and his people. They had picked up the Eight's trail quickly after leaving the abandoned mine, and had done well to keep hidden. Sasha had to give Ladue credit: she knew how to stay low and out of sight, a testament to her longevity as an outlaw. No one had spotted them, not even Sun Totem and Flowing River who were, without doubt, Marcus's best trackers. It had been almost too easy, and when the Eight had been attacked by those Indians several miles back, Sasha had prayed that that would spell the end of Marcus and his annoying team. Such was not the case, but there was trouble again, in camp. Sun Totem and Flowing River had gone alone into the Tonto Forest, yet only one had come back.

Desiree snatched the telescope out of Sasha's hand and peered through it. The woman annoyed him so much he could barely stand it, but he had kept his mouth shut, quickly realizing that despite her horrible disposition, she and her bevy of lady killers were an asset.

"Only the Indian girl has returned," she said in her broken English. "I wonder if her *frère* was killed or captured. She is moving about erratically, waving her arms. I can't make anything of it, *n'est-ce pas?*"

"Killed or captured, it does not matter," Sasha said. "Either way, it is to our benefit. I think it's time to go down there and put an end to the Wayward Eight."

Desiree put the telescope down and looked at Sasha with a curious eye. "Are you mad, *monsieur*? They still are seven strong, and they carry some of the most powerful weapons I've ever seen. You did not see what they did to the Red Maple Saloon, *mon amie*, how many bodies they left shattered. *Non, non, non...* That is not our *stratégie*. If my *filles* are killed now, then no Doctor Carpathian later."

"Look, we wait till it's dark, sneak into camp, and start shooting. We can take them, and I have a score to settle."

"Then you go down there on your own, *monsieur*, and I and my *filles* will say our fare-thee-wells now." Desiree climbed up from lying on the ridgeline and dusted herself off. She straightened her hair pins and actually tried to look sincere, calm. She even broached a smile. "I understand where you are coming from, *mon amie*. I have felt that kind of rage myself more than once. But we do not have *infini* supply of ammunition. We have only a few remaining RJ cells to supply our weapons. We must conserve what we have for the attack on Carpathian."

Sasha got up, took the telescope from her and tucked it away. "How do you propose we get there, hmm? Marcus will not allow us to join him."

"They have found Payson," Desiree said, "I'm certain of it. Only River came back. They found it, and her *frère* got into trouble. Marcus will move soon to either avenge or to save Sun Totem. And when he does, we follow him right into town."

"We need to get there first. Otherwise, we risk having to shoot our way past them anyway."

Desiree shook her head, frustration growing on her scarred face. "*Non.* It does not matter who rides into Payson first. Once we are inside, there are other ways to get to Carpathian that Marcus does not know."

"Wait. I thought you said that you did not set foot into the canyon. How do you know where to find Carpathian?"

"I didn't say I know how to find him," she said, pulling a new cigarette from her silver case and stuffing it between red lips. "I said I know how to get through Payson. I have, what do you call it, a *mémoire photographique*? My *filles* and I got into that town; we did not stay long, unfortunately, but I know the lay of its streets." She lit her cigarette and drew long and thorough from it. She puffed out a large cloud of white smoke. "Trust me on this, *monsieur*. Trust a woman for once."

He wanted to, but it made little sense not to attack the Eight when they were down a member. It was a risk, no doubt, but if they succeeded, then they would be in possession of those powerful weapons she spoke about. Trying to ride into Payson on Marcus's coattails seemed like an even greater risk, one fraught with all manner of uncertainty. She did have a point about ammunition, though. They did not have an infinite supply, and if the Eight had more and could hold out longer in a fight, then attacking them could deplete that supply and leave them with no choice but to retreat. Sasha did not have to rely on ammunition. His blades were his weapons. Once he got inside Payson and found the doctor, he planned on ditching these women anyway, but getting inside... He had to admit, her plan of patience was the proper course. He hated admitting that.

"Very well," he said, making sure his words had the proper derision in their tone to make it clear to Desiree that he wasn't happy. "We'll play it your way. And I hope you are right, because if you're wrong, there'll be a devil to pay."

Chapter 17

He awoke chained to a post, much like the one he had tied Carl to at the mineshaft. Only this one was metal, an iron rod, and like a piece of rail track, hard and cold. He struggled, but his arms were too tightly bound behind him. They had him, and there was nothing he could do about it right now.

Strange-looking creatures stood around him, perhaps four or five. He could not tell for sure; the strike to his head by the rifle butt had knocked the hell out of him. His eyes were, at best, fuzzy. He had a headache too, so the weird figures shifted in and out of his view. But they *were* creatures, not men. Perhaps once they had been men. Now, they held the shape of men, but their arms were weapons, their legs were a mixture of steel pistons and augmented muscle boosters. Their faces were sallow and sunken; their teeth dark and rotting. They stood around him as if he were food, a strip of bacon or venison, ready to pounce when given the word. He tried pulling back, but he was held too tightly to the post. The room they were in was circular and somewhere deep in the earth. The air was musty, but he could feel a light breeze flowing from even further down. Perhaps the beasts hovering around him did not notice it; perhaps their thick, leathery skin was immune to subtle touch, their sickly, pungent odor a barrier to fresh air. But he felt a breeze, and he made a mental note to remember it. Wherever there was breeze, lay a chance to escape.

A man stepped through a doorway to Sun's left, followed by another and some wicked thing, larger than a bear and could barely fit into the room. Sun closed his eyes to the abomination; it was too terrifying to imagine.

"Do not be afraid of JP and his pet," the man who had come in first said. He had a distinct European accent. "They won't harm you, I promise. They are here to observe."

Sun opened his eyes again. The beast was massive, and if it stood upright on its metal legs, it could easily reach seven feet. Now, it crouched alongside its master like a child, its arms nothing more than cylindrical hammers, metal maces that could pulverize rock to dust with one strike. A light thread of RJ coursed through tubes that led from its back into its hammer fists. Its right eye was covered with an ocular enhancer that also glowed red. Its head was haloed with a bear trap that hung around its neck like a string of pearls. It stunk of rotting sweat and dung.

Sun's guards stepped back, and the European fellow knelt beside him, his steel-powered legs hissing as he crouched. The man wore elegant clothing, an eye piece much like the beast wore, but it was braided in gold and shone brightly in the sparse light of the room. The man smiled through a nicely groomed mustache and beard. He seemed pleasant. Sun doubted that assessment.

"I'm Doctor Burson Carpathian," the man said, keeping the smile burned into his face. "And you are...?"

"Not a person that should give you concern, Dr. Carpathian," Sun said through a small cough. Apparently they had punched him a few times in his stomach and ribs for good measure while he had been unconscious. His sides hurt; it was difficult to speak many words without feeling the need to cough.

Carpathian raised his brow. "Ah, an articulate member of the Warrior Nation. A rare man indeed. Your accent sounds almost east coast, however. Union, perhaps?"

Sun wiggled his toes inside his boot. His legs felt a lot better from when the tree hit them. They didn't feel broken or otherwise damaged. His right knee hurt a little when he tried moving it, however, and someone had strapped a metal brace on it. "There are a lot of intelligent people of the Nation. Perhaps you would know that if you talked to them instead of capturing and killing them, or turning them into devil creatures.'

"So you know who I am and what I do," Carpathian said, seemingly impressed. "All the more reason why your presence here in my home should give me pause."

Carpathian looked up to a goon nearby and nodded. The animation drew back its fist and drove it across Sun's face, knocking him to the left and spraying blood. Sun refused to cringe or shirk from the blow. He spit red goo, righted himself again, and stared calmly into Carpathian's face.

"I'm sorry my assistant had to do that," the doctor said, "but it's important that you understand the trouble that you are in. Now, perhaps you care to tell me who you are, why you were in Payson uninvited, who was the Indian girl you were with, and why were you riding Union Iron Horses."

"Oh, I do not know *massa*," Sun said with a southern accent as if he were a darkie field hand, "dat's four questions in a row, I do not knows if my Injin intellect can…"

Crack!

He got another shot across the face from a guard, and this one felt like it jarred a tooth loose. The ape-like beast slammed its fists against the ground, clearly overjoyed with the violence occurring before it. Its master stood coolly nearby, his staff glowing with red-hot RJ. Sun imagined that both wanted to take a crack at his face as well. The notion didn't appeal.

"My name is Winter Moon," he said, lying, "and the girl was just some squaw I picked up. We were traveling south to Mexico. We just came upon the town. That is all. We were just passing through."

"And the vehicles you happen to be riding?"

"We got them off a couple Union soldiers we killed near Fort Smith."

Big mistake! Sun knew it the minute he said it, but couldn't take it back once it was out there.

"Now why would two warriors heading to Mexico turn west and come all the way out to my beloved Carpathian territory?" Carpathian shook his head derisively and *tsked* as if Sun had said something naughty. "You almost had me there, Mr. Whoever-You-Are, but I've lived a long, hard life. There aren't many who can fool me with tall tales of adventure." He stood and yelled through the door, "Mr. Edison! A moment, if you please!"

A very nicely-dressed man with short, well-kept brown hair stepped through the door. He was alone, but his presence was stately, prominent. Even the man who controlled the beast seemed to defer to him. He walked over to Carpathian. They greeted each other warmly, and the doctor put his hand on this 'Edison's' back.

"Thomas, I'd like you to personally gather a scout team and head out to find the squaw that this young man speaks about, and anyone else who might be with her. I suspect that whoever he's been riding with will not have gotten far. Such a bright, intelligent young man as this is an asset not readily thrown away. No, they're still around, and you will find them. Then you will kill them."

"It'll be my pleasure, Burson," the inventor said, smiling and looking down on Sun. He had a mean, evil little grin on his smooth, round face. Sun had heard of Thomas Edison, chief scientist and Carpathian's so-called right-hand man. Looking at him now, however, Sun didn't approve. No matter his education or his skills as an inventor, Edison did not impress; not Sun Totem anyway.

"And find out where Grey Face and his little minions are," Carpathian said as Edison left the room. "I haven't heard from him in over a week."

Sun smiled inwardly at that. *Chalk one up for the good guys*, Sun thought as Carpathian turned to the beast's handler. "JP, please escort this man to a cell. I think our best course of action with him is to prepare him for enlightenment, wouldn't you say?"

JP nodded, tugging on the chain around his beast's neck. "Bring a little joy to him in his final hours? I like it. Perhaps a new arm or leg would do nicely. Perhaps fit him with that rail gun Edison has been working on, though his bones might be too thin for that."

Carpathian nodded. "And how about a new jaw? He's got a soft one now. We'll fix him with teeth that can cut through metal."

They both laughed at that. Sun spit blood in Carpathian's direction and flung his leg out, trying to kick the doctor. "You will not fit me with anything, you evil son of a bitch! Your days are numbered, *Burson* Carpathian. Your days are numbered."

The doctor said nothing to that, turned and headed out the door. "Cut him loose and take him below."

His bindings were cut, and Sun jumped up and tried to make for the door. The beast moved after him and, more eloquently than Sun imagined it could, barred his exit. Sun ran into the hammer fists and fell down. The beast opened its terrible mouth and screamed into Sun's face, showering it with spittle and gore. Sun nearly passed out from the stench.

"Don't be a fool, Injin," JP said, coming up and laying his red glowing staff against Sun's chest. "My creation would take it as a personal insult if you were to run from him, and he isn't kind to his toys. He used to be a Russian circus performer, did you know? He played with bears, but they were very unkind and ripped his arms off. Doctor Carpathian took pity on the lad and gave him new life, new arms, and a rail gun for good measure. I'd be delicate in my movements if I were you, lest he grow annoyed."

Before Sun could move, the beast snapped out with its teeth and grabbed Sun's coat and carried him like a lion cub. Sun tried to break free, but its jaws were too powerful. They bounded down a flight of stairs off the room they were in. The way was dark, dank, and smelled of rotting flesh. All Sun could do was scream his dissatisfaction.

"You are dead, Carpathian! You hear me? You are dead!"

*****

The Wraith picked his teeth with the small rib bone of a Gila monster and watched as its meat crisped over the hot spit. He didn't care for the meat itself; he had always found it chewy and unpalatable, but the men had not been successful in hunting for anything else, and Carl Fredrickson had a larger appetite than he'd hoped. The man had literally eaten them out of house and home. So they ate what they could find and endured. *This will all be over soon enough*, The Wraith thought as he picked a tooth and found shade behind a rock pile and tried to ignore Carl's desire to talk.

"We need to discuss what we're going to do once we get inside," Carl said, pitching one of the Gila's freshly picked leg bones behind him. He licked grease from his fingers.

The Wraith shrugged. "It's pretty simple, really. Find Carpathian, kill him, then leave with his head."

Carl sighed. "Nothing is ever as simple as that. Besides, we need to have a plan on how to control your men once we're inside. They don't have weapons worth a damn, and I suspect they'll be more interested in looting than finding the prize."

"They're doing *right now* what they've been brought here to do."

The Mexicans were in a mineshaft and had been so since sunup. They had found two, in fact, but running in opposite directions; one east, one west. The one west had dried up early, with only about a mile of passageway. The one east was a full tunnel, but it had a lot of bats in it, and the men were afraid to go in initially. The Wraith put an end to that nonsense right quick, brandishing his shotgun and threatening to let the Gila monster they had caught that morning bite the ones who were afraid. Gila poison was rarely lethal, but the victim got terribly ill from a bite for a long, long while. That, coupled with the promise of being tied up and baked naked in the hot desert sun, the men quickly found their courage. They had been going in and out all day in cycled shifts, looking for the passage that would lead them underneath Carpathian's lair. They had found nothing yet, but The Wraith was hopeful.

"Once we get inside," The Wraith said, "then it's our responsibility to kill, not theirs. I don't care if they die in the first minute; we're the ones who have to find the prize, as you call him, and do the deed."

Carl shook his head. "You should have just left me on the post. You don't have a clue what to do. Better to die on the post than to die at the hands of Carpathian."

"See, that's the problem with you Union types. You've always got to have a *plan*. Lincoln has a plan, doesn't he, and yet, here we are, two people who were never supposed to meet, let alone join up. How's his *plan* going?" He looked at Carl and waited for an answer. Carl said nothing and instead, turned away and folded his arms in frustration. "Look, you are more than welcome to take that Blackhoof yonder and get. No need for you to hang around any further. Verbal contract annulled. But if you ever want to see your weapons again, I suggest you relax and let things play out the way they will."

Carl huffed. "My weapons are the only things that'll give us a chance."

The Wraith chuckled. "You put too much stock in Tesla's concoctions, son." He leaned over the fire and pulled another strip of meat from the skinny lizard carcass. "Good old-fashioned bullets and knives are the only way to kill."

"Deride all you wish, Wraith, but you don't seem to understand the power of my glove. Do you know how many of those scalpers I killed? Five, sir, five. And one shape-shifter wolf. Have you ever killed a shape-shifter, let along *fought* one? Trust me, it's difficult, no matter how powerful you are. River killed one scalper, and it took her three times longer than me to do just that. I killed five in less than a minute and two UR-30s at Fort Smith. And do you know how I did all that? With that glove you so quickly dismiss. Not only does it allow me to move the enemy around and put them where I want, but it also gives me ten times the punching power of a normal person. Do you know what happens to a face when it's struck with that much force? It's gone, Wraith, gone. So wield all the knives you want, throw as many thermite slugs into the enemy as you wish. When the time comes, you'll see what I can do, and you'll be singing Tesla's praises."

"Carpathian has a skilled inventor of his own," The Wraith said. "Thomas Edison."

"Edison is a cookie cutter compared to Tesla."

"Well, then we have nothing to worry about, do we? Your eccentric inventor is better than his."

Carl shook his head. "You're hopeless."

The Wraith chuckled again. "I tell you what. When we get inside, I'll let you find Edison, and you can rip his head clean off, and deliver it personally to Tesla. How's that for a plan?"

Carl did not respond. The Wraith finished the strip of Gila meat and laid back, relaxing. A few minutes later, one of his men emerged from the mine.

"Did you find anything?" The Wraith asked.

The man knelt by the fire, demurely shook his head. "No, *señor*. Not yet. But we will."

The Wraith wanted to punch the man, to get him moving faster, to work harder. But he didn't. Instead, he motioned to the fire. "Take the lizard, and give it to the men."

The man nodded happily. "*Gracias, Señor. Gracias.*"

The man took the lizard off the spit and returned to the mine. "See, Carl, I have a plan," The Wraith said. "I plan on keeping my men fed and healthy… at least until we get inside."

Carl shook his head again and turned away. "You're hopeless."

*****

The sun had almost set, and Jake, Marcus, and River knelt in pine brush near the edge of Payson, staring down at a town coming to life. It seemed as if the darkness closing in gave reason for its occupants to come out and move around. That's the way it felt to Jake, given River's initial description of the town being near barren in the light of day. Windows filled with RJ-burning lanterns lay everywhere. The place had an eerie, though not wholly unpleasant, aura about it. If they were not here for the purpose of killing Carpathian, Jake might like to run down there, find a saloon, and throw a few back, find a girl, and... Well, the matter at hand was what he needed to concentrate on.

And he tried to concentrate. He had found it so difficult to do so, especially the closer they drew to Payson. And why had he done it? Why had he sabotaged Sun's skids? It was a treasonous act, and he didn't even remember doing it, but it had happened. River had shown them where the charred remains of the Iron Horse lay, and there was no denying what had happened. They found the twisted skids a hundred feet back from where Sun had crashed.

My fault... All my fault.

But what to do about it? Confess? Perhaps that was the best thing to do; come clean to Marcus, get it out there, and let things happen as they would. But no. To do that would mean to confess his weakness. Confessing weakness was not in Jake's nature, and what good would it do anyway? Marcus might up and cancel the mission, and everything they had done up to this point would have been meaningless. No. Confession was not an option. What then? What could he do to make this up to his people, to the Eight? What could he do to make it up to River? He had put her brother in jeopardy. Hell, Sun might already be dead. What could he do to make things right again?

I'll kill Carpathian myself.

They spoke in whispers. "I recommend we wait till first light, boss," Jake said, "then go in. I'll lead the attack."

Marcus nodded. "That flies in the face of conventional wisdom, but under the circumstances, it may be our best move. I don't know if you'll lead the attack, though. I haven't decided that yet. I'm not sure how we're going in. Looks like a maze of roads and alleys in there, and I don't guess they have a backdoor that we can easily go through that'll put us in that canyon without having to race through town. But I think you're right. A morning attack would be best. What do you say, River?"

She hadn't signed one word or uttered one grunt since they had left camp. She was worried for her brother, despondent, her spirit animal wanting to show, but incapable of doing so. Jake wondered why she had so much trouble with her spirit animal, when many others, like the wolf beast, could command the power at will. If you asked Sun, he'd say that spirit animals were a lie, perpetrated on the Nation by its chiefs as a way to control their population through the ingestion of RJ as the catalyst that caused shifting. Maybe he was right, but Jake wasn't so sure. How could the shape-shifter attacking River back east be accounted for? How could hundreds of eyewitness accounts of warriors shifting into likenesses of different animals be true? Again, Sun would say it was RJ usage. Sun was smart, east coast educated, but was he right about this?

Perhaps there was another reason why River couldn't connect with her spirit animal. Perhaps it was the same unseen force that was giving Jake ideas to kill informants and sabotage Iron Horses. If they could make him do things against his will, against people that he had worked with and trusted for years, why couldn't it also keep River from shifting? Perhaps the only person qualified to answer these questions was Zarelda, with her innate connection with the spirits through her knowledge of voodoo. *She knows*, Jake said to himself as River tried collecting herself to answer Marcus. *Zarelda knows I damaged Sun's vehicle. If she says something to Marcus… Perhaps I should kill her.*

Jake shook the notion from his mind and fought against a headache.

River nodded her agreement.

"Okay, so that's the general plan," Marcus said. "We attack by light. But when and how exactly do we get through the town without expending ammunition that we cannot afford to expend? I think it's inevitable that we'll have to shoot our way through, but if there was some way to create a diversion, a way to shock them such that they don't respond until we're far into the town, perhaps on his doorstep beforehand."

Jake looked through Marcus's telescope and squinted against the lack of light. "Not only that, boss, but it looks like he's got some kind of barricade at the mouth of the canyon. How we gonna get past that?"

Marcus shrugged. "We're gonna have to blast our way through. We've got the firepower for it. We just need to hit a vulnerable spot, and—"

River leaned over and clutched Marcus's arm so tight he winced. "What's the matter, River?" he asked. She pointed to her right, over by a smaller path that led from the town. Jake looked.

A long line of men streamed out, some carrying RJ lanterns and other lit devices. Calling them men was generous. It was difficult to parse out details in the shadows cast by their light, but they seemed more machine than men. A least a dozen, fully kitted out with weapons and gross augmentations, headed toward the pine forest, with one man in particular taking the lead. From the large phonographic speakers on the man's back, Jake recognized him immediately.

"Edison."

Marcus nodded. "Indeed. Well, the doctor is sending out his dog to fetch us, eh? And by night too. How clever."

"We better get back to camp, warn them."

"We will," Marcus said, and Jake could see an idea tumbling about behind the boss's eyes.

Marcus got this way when a plan came together in his mind. "What are you thinking, boss?"

"I'm thinking that our prayers have been answered."

Jake shook his head. "I don't see it."

"Come," Marcus said, pushing them both back through where they came. "Let's get to the others and then I'll tell my plan. And let's get ready for Edison's approach. I think that once he meets us in the flesh, he'll gladly give us the key to Carpathian's door. Either that, or his own life."

Chapter 18

It was difficult to see with clouds continuously floating past the moon, but Marcus was fine with that. It would be difficult to fire true in such intermittent light, but they had an advantage: they were lying in wait for Edison and his devilish creatures to move through the gap below their position. Once they were in place, Hell itself would unleash.

He had sent Jake, K-Free, and Zarelda to the other side of the gap with strict orders not to fire until they heard his hand cannon first. He could not see them from his hiding place, but they were there, waiting just like he and Sierra, Hicks, and River. River had been given one of the Union blasters. She hated using it, at first refusing, but under the circumstances, it was the most practical thing for her to use. She would not be able to get up close and personal until the enemy had scattered, and perhaps there would not even be such an opportunity. Marcus had never fought against Enlightened constructs before; this was new territory. He found himself more excited about it than he wanted to admit.

"They're here," Sierra whispered into his ear. Marcus pulled back. She was closer to him than she ought to be. He waved her off.

"Over there," he said, directing her where to go. "Behind that dry log. And remember: don't shoot Edison. Take out his support first."

Sierra nodded and slithered into position. River was at the far end of their triangle, the idea being that, with the aid of the others, they would hit the scouts in the front, middle, and rear. That was the plan, anyway.

Marcus took a deep breath and pulled his hand cannon, cocked it, and waited. The line of constructs below moved into position, led by Edison and, seemingly, a personal human assistant. He and Edison made small talk, or what sounded like small talk to Marcus. More like useless babbling. They laughed. That angered Marcus the most. What was funny about any of this, he wondered. *Are they that confident? That arrogant? Well, not for long.* He rose up on his knees, aimed at the assistant, and fired.

The man fell dead at Edison's feet, his face a deep, bloody cavern.

Jake and the others fired as well, followed by Sierra, Hicks, and finally River. A massive volley of atomic and blaster fire swarmed into the gap and lit up the night, smashing into Edison's constructs, throwing their broken bodies against the rocks and pine that lined the gap. The initial shock of the ambush took them totally by surprise, but it did not take them all out. About half were still standing or alive enough to return fire, and the ridgeline on both sides of the gap began to smolder with returned RJ and blaster fire. Marcus had to dive onto his belly to keep from getting hit. Sierra jumped out from behind her log which was blasted away by one concentrated shot of RJ-fire. The log literally blew into the sky like a firecracker.

Marcus grabbed her arm and pulled her to his hiding place. "Son of a bitch," Sierra said, reaching for reloads on a bandoleer draped over her shoulder. "He's got grenades."

And more than one, it seemed, for one after the other, positions along the ridgeline began to sound with up-thrown dirt and rock, one strike, then another, and another. Sierra managed to crawl back up on her knees and fire again, taking out one construct as her atomic rounds flayed and burned its chest. Marcus rose up as well, hitting another in the shoulder. The impact of the shot turned it right around, but it kept on shooting, seemingly not caring where it fired, so long as it peppered the ridgeline with bullets. Marcus could hear Edison barking orders, and the constructs responded quickly. Some took cover, while others just fired up the line, without caring if they got struck or not. Marcus watched as Zarelda ripped one construct to shreds with shots from her repeater. He smiled. Things were looking good. It was time to move.

"Down!" he shouted, loud enough so that those on the other side of the gap could hear.

Marcus crawled down the ridge about ten feet, finding another boulder to hide behind. He was followed by Sierra, Hicks, and River, who crawled as well to their designated locations. It had all been planned ahead of time. The idea was, as Edison's scouts took casualties, the Eight would tighten the noose again and again, slowly making their way down the ridge, to deprive the enemy of retreat. It was a risk getting closer, but absolutely necessary to ensure that not a single construct got free. No one could escape alive, except Edison, and he had to be captured.

So far, the other seven had followed his orders and had not taken a shot at Edison. This, unfortunately, gave the man free reign to fire and throw grenades. It also gave him time to set up the device on his back.

Marcus took a shot toward Edison, trying to ricochet a bullet off the metal of a dead construct near his feet, in the hopes of distracting the inventor. But it didn't have the effect he wanted. Edison, as calm as walking in a park, turned his phonic blasters toward the ridgelines, one left and the other right, and let it blast.

Immediately, Marcus grabbed his head and felt his left ear give out as wave after wave of blaring sound rushed over his hiding place. This was not a weapon that could be avoided, not out here in the open. Even with the boulder and fallen trees, the powerful sound waves pumping out of Edison's phonic blaster pinned them all. Sierra screamed at the intensity of the attack, and Marcus tried putting his head up to see what was happening to the others. The waves were so intense that even his eyes hurt. Rocks, wood, and dirt blasted across their faces as the sound waves pushed everything in their path at the group.

Who it didn't seem to effect were the few remaining constructs who were trying to retreat their way out of the gap, continuing to lay fire upon the ridgeline. Seeing them move, Marcus suddenly knew the weakness of Edison's weapon. It was powerful, but its strongest waves emanated more forcefully in the direction the blasters were facing. In the dark, it was possible for Edison to miscalculate where to turn the blasters for best effect. Marcus saw an opportunity.

"You keep an eye on those constructs, you hear?!" he said to Sierra, trying to speak over the painful sound waves. "You try to kill anything that you can! Don't let any of them escape!"

"What are you going to do?" she asked, cupping her ears against the horrific sound, while trying to understand what Marcus was saying.

"Knock the hell out of Edison!"

He climbed to his feet, the left side of his face numb, his ear ringing painfully. It was hard to see Edison through the darkness, but the small amount of moonlight offered by the night sky made it clear where the inventor's hands were. Marcus jumped, skid down the embankment, and into the gap where shattered bodies of constructs lay. Burning RJ was everywhere, and he worked through it, careful not to get any on his boots. It lit his path somewhat, but the shadows it cast made it near impossible to get a good view of this target. Then the clouds opened, and the moon shone through, perfectly silhouetting Edison against a tree. Marcus stopped and hit the ground, hiding behind two bodies. The arm of one of the bodies was still animated, as it tried to lift a pistol and fire. Marcus grabbed the hand tightly, wrenched the pistol away, and broke the wrist. He then pulled his own pistol and aimed it carefully at Edison.

Edison tried to shift his phonic blasters again, both now toward Jake's side of the gap. Marcus watched as the RJ pumping through the tubes of the phonic blaster reached a fever pitch. He watched the tubes glow red. He waited, waited, raised his pistol, cocked the hammer... then fired. The shot tore through the deadly space between them and struck Edison in the hand. The man screamed, and the sound waves died.

Marcus pounced, followed by River who had watched the shot from her hiding place. She pulled her knife; Marcus pulled his. Together they struck Edison and took him down to the ground. Despite being nearly five foot ten, he went down hard and fast, shocked at the suddenness of the body blow. His phonic blaster separated from his shoulders. Marcus pulled it away and tossed it aside to keep it from being damaged. Edison struggled to free himself, but when he felt River's blade against his throat, he stilled. He tried calling out to his remaining constructs, but stopped immediately as Jake and Zarelda finished them off as soon as he opened his mouth.

"I'd be *very* still if I were you, Mr. Edison," Marcus said, pushing his knee into the inventor's sternum. "This here is

Flowing River, sister to Sun Totem, the man you and your boss are holding. Or perhaps you've already killed him? Either way, I'd stay still. She's like to give you a red necklace if you don't."

"Who the hell are you people?" Edison asked, winded and clearly in pain. Marcus checked the man's hand. It was bleeding profusely.

"I'm Marcus Wayward, and this, Mr. Edison, is your lucky day."

"Lucky? What do you—"

Marcus raised back his fist and drove it into Edison's jaw.

*****

It had taken awhile to stop the bleeding, but Zarelda had done so with the aid of K-Free and Sierra. Edison dropped in and out of consciousness during the ordeal, more from Marcus's punch to his face than from any blood loss, although the loss *was* substantial. The bullet had gone clear through, breaking bone, tearing muscle, and rendering his hand inoperable. Edison couldn't move it at all, and his pain was high. She could see it in the man's eyes, though he tried to hide it. He was strong, but in a mild shock from the assault. He probably never imagined in all his days that something like this would happen to him while under Carpathian's employment. Now, he sat upright against Zarelda's Iron Horse, his legs and body bound tightly to the skids, his weapons taken away and placed well out of reach. Everyone gathered around, watching as Zarelda put the finishing stitches into the wound.

"It's your lucky day," Marcus said, as he knelt down beside Edison, "because I didn't kill you."

"You should have," Edison said, sitting upright, trying to show no sign of weakness or fatigue. "For if you think I'll help you free your native, you're sorely mistaken."

"He's alive then?" Marcus said.

It seemed to Zarelda that Edison had made a mistake speaking. His jaw clenched as he realized the error, but he didn't skip a beat. He answered defiantly.

"Not for long, once the good doctor gets a hold of him. He won't be himself ever again. He'll be Enlightened, and he'll serve us."

Edison smiled sheepishly at that, and even glanced at River, who stood nearby, a strange, yet hostile, look on her face. Zarelda knew that River wanted to stab the inventor, wanted to exact revenge on the capture of her brother, and Edison was doing everything he could to be obnoxious, to push, to agitate.

"Now look here, *Thomas*," Marcus said in his most insulting tone. "You are alive because I'm allowing you to be so, but anytime I feel like it, I can let River have a go at your throat, or worse, and don't think I won't, if I think you aren't cooperating with us."

"What the hell do you want from me?"

"You help us get inside and free our man, and we'll let your boss live."

Zarelda paused. She looked at Marcus. Was he serious? He had stated from the beginning that they could change sides if things got ugly, but were they at that point yet? And was the capture of Sun reason enough to switch? Sometimes it was hard to divine the captain's intentions from his expressions. Her voodoo training had given her a good sense of facial movements, but Marcus had one of the best poker faces she had ever seen.

Edison laughed. "Are you insane? You can't kill Burson Carpathian. He's got an army of dedicated soldiers at his beck and call. Everyone in Payson, real or animated, will defend him to the end. And that's the beginning. Once you get past the town, you have the canyon to treat with. What you will find there, Mr. Wayward, I guarantee will break you of this silly mission you have undertaken. You don't have the strength to carry it out."

"Look around you," Marcus said, waving his hand at everyone gathered as if he were introducing them on stage. "Do you think we're amateurs, Mr. Edison? Do you think we're untrained killers? Some of us have been killing our entire lives. We just finished destroying your little scouting party in a matter of minutes; their bones and flesh ripped apart like they'd been hit by a blast from the sun. Your doctor is not the only one capable of creating powerful weapons." He leaned in close, smiled. "We have enough firepower to kill everyone in Payson... and then some. Do not lecture me about power, *Mr. Edison*. We have it, and you don't."

"He knows you're coming," Edison said, trying to push forward to force Marcus to pull back. "Your native man talked. He told us everything as pokers hot with RJ were pressed into his back." Edison giggled. "He squealed like a beast, begged for mercy, and they're waiting for you to make your move."

River moved to put her blade against Edison's throat. Marcus stopped her, held her tight, waved over Sierra and Hicks to get her and pull her away. They did, and he continued with the inventor. He took a deep breath and smiled. "Do you think we are the only ones gunning for your boss, big guy? There are others right now as we speak, who are planning their attack as well, who are out here somewhere among these pines and rocks. Do you know that?"

That seemed to take the bravado out of Edison. He stilled, his face sour and serious. "You lie."

Marcus shook his head. "No, it's true. Scores more are making their way here right now. We've seen them. You may be able to fight us off, but what about others, wave after wave coming in, adding pressures that you cannot handle? Face it, Edison. You are in no position to threaten or to proclaim. Your life is in my hands. Now, be a good boy and work with us. Help us get our man out safe and sound, and we'll turn round and ride away."

Edison looked as if he were thinking about the offer. Then his expression turned hateful, defiant. "You want me to help you? Is that it? Well, go hang yourself is what I say. I'd rather die than help a sorry bunch of bastards like you."

He reached over and started pulling the stitches out of his wounded hand. It started bleeding again, worse than before. Sierra grabbed Edison's arm and pulled it back and held her pistol to his head. Zarelda grabbed his wounded hand once more and held tight, pressing a cloth into the bleeding hole.

"Don't worry about him, boss," Jake said as he stood near Edison's weapons. "We don't need his help. We got this."

He hefted the phonic blaster. Marcus walked over to Jake and took the weapon from his hands. The device was big and bulky, with tubes running from its RJ source into another box where the ends of the sound blasters were connected. The entire contraption was fixed to a person's back with three belts. It looked heavy to Zarelda. Marcus pivoted the speakers, testing out their flexibility, looking them over. "What do you mean?"

"I mean, we can use this to force our way past that barrier. You saw what it did to the boulders and dead trees along the ridgeline; tore 'em to shreds. We can do the same."

Edison huffed. "You'll never figure it out. It's not a toy, you simpleton; it's a complicated piece of machinery that the likes of you couldn't use in a million years."

Marcus turned to Edison. "How does it work?"

Edison turned his face like an angry child. "Not telling."

Marcus walked over and laid the weapon at the inventor's feet. "I'm not gonna ask you again. How's it work?"

Edison spit on the ground. "Kiss my ass."

Marcus balled up his fist and knocked Edison out again.

"You should just let me shoot him," Sierra said.

Marcus nodded. "I'd like to, but we may need him as a hostage. I don't believe him when he says Sun squawked, but Carpathian does know that someone is out here. He would not have sent Edison out otherwise. He may be planning for something. It might get real ugly once we get in there, and we'll see if the good doctor cares about his right-hand man enough to save him."

"Captain," Zarelda said, taking a break from re-stitching Edison's hand. "Did you mean it when you said we'd free Sun and den go?"

Marcus waved it off. "Of course not. We haven't come this far to cut tail and run. We're going in. We're going to find Sun, free him, and I'm going to personally wring the doctor's neck with my own hands."

"So." K-Free popped her knuckles excitedly. "When do we go?"

Marcus picked up the phonic blaster and looked at it carefully. "Just as soon as we figure this thing out."

"I'll do it," Jake said, raising his hand as if he were back in school.

Marcus nodded and handed it over. "Okay, you and K-Free go test it. Take all night if you have to."

Jake nodded, a broad smile on his face. He then turned to Zarelda and said, "See, Z. I'm loyal."

Zarelda ignored the statement, but it was not lost on Marcus. He shot a surprising look at Jake as he walked away, then turned to Zarelda. He waited until everyone drifted away to prepare for the attack, then he said, "What did Jake mean by 'loyal'?"

Zarelda shrugged. "I don't know, Captain. He crazy. Been dat way all along this trail. Ask *him* what he meant."

"I'm asking you, Z." Marcus knelt down in front of her, making a point to lean in and whisper. Zarelda kept working on Edison's hand. "Do you know something about Jake I should know?"

What should I say? Should she tell him her suspicions about Jake sabotaging Sun's Iron Horse? *And what if I'm wrong?* She looked straight into his eyes and lied. "I don't know nothing, Captain. As far as I know, he just fine. Crazy you know, like he gets, but otherwise, he okay."

The sentiment was partially true, at least. The fact that Jake had offered to learn the use of Edison's phonic blaster was a good sign. If he wasn't loyal or dedicated to the mission, why would he offer? So perhaps her concerns were unfounded after all.

Marcus dropped it, but still pressed her with questions. "Okay, then what about your husband?"

Zarelda raised an eyebrow. "What about him?"

"Is he okay?"

Zarelda nodded. "Of course he is. Why wouldn't he be?"

"He hasn't spoken to me in a while. Why?"

She shrugged. "Perhaps because you done accused him of sabotaging Sun's skids."

"I did no such thing. We're about to engage in a major battle, Z, and I need everyone sharp and on their toes. We can't have any mistakes. I was just stressing the point that he needed to be more careful. We cannot afford missteps."

She motioned with her head back toward hers and Hicks's camp. "You go tell him dat, Captain."

Marcus grabbed her hand and held it tight. He looked deep into her eyes. Zarelda did the same with his. "Are you sure everything is okay with him?"

"He's fine, Marcus. Hicks is dedicated to dis mission just like me, just like everyone. He won't let you down."

Just saying it made her skin crawl, but she held her expression tight and did not take her eyes off Marcus's face until he blinked. He tapped her hand three times. "Very well. If you say it, that's good enough for me." Marcus stood and motioned to Edison who was still knocked out cold. "Patch him up as best you can and tie his hands down to keep him from trying something like that again. He's an arrogant son of a bitch, but we need him alive."

Zarelda let out her breath as she watched Marcus walk away. She felt sick to her stomach, having to lie like that. Why did she do it? There was no good explanation other than loyalty to her husband. Was that reason enough? She huffed, spit, and went back to stitching.

"I'm not as arrogant as he thinks."

Edison's words surprised her. She fell back, looked up at his face. His eyes were open to slivers, and he forced a smile.

"No talking," Zarelda said, "or I'll stick your eye with dis needle."

"I don't think your boss would like that very much. I'm to be kept alive, isn't that what he said?" Edison cleared his throat and adjusted his seat. "He seems capable, your Captain Wayward, but misguided. He's doomed to fail."

"Shut up!"

"Your husband… Hicks, is that his name? He's the mechanic of your group, yes?"

"What of it?"

"He doubts this mission?"

Zarelda shook her head. "Never. He's loyal and dedicated."

"But if your captain has accused him of sabotage, it must mean the opposite."

"Shut up, I say."

Edison leaned into her and whispered. "I could use a good mechanic at my side. Doctor Carpathian would welcome it. If your Hicks is having doubts about this mission, then tell him to speak to me. I can help him make the right decision once he gets inside Payson."

Zarelda dug her thumb into Edison's wound. The inventor groaned and pulled back, gritted his teeth and slammed his head into the Iron Horse, his eyes rolling back in excruciating pain. "I ain't no turncoat, science man, you'll be wise to remember it. One more word out of you, and like I said, I *will* jab dis here needle into your eye."

Edison shut up, and she finished her stitching. She bandaged his hand tightly with fresh wrappings, and then tied it down so he could not rip anything off. She got up to leave, and he dared speak again. "The offer stands, my lady. Send Hicks to me, and I'll tell him what he needs to know to survive the attack, what you both need to know."

She ignored him and walked away, but his words nagged her thoughts at the back of her mind. Perhaps Hicks was right, she thought. This was a suicide mission. The thought of losing Hicks inside Carpathian's lair was too much to ponder. How could eight people dare to think they were strong enough to go against an entire army of Enlightened? But how could she go against Marcus? *How…*

She found Hicks at their place in camp, cleaning his shotgun. She knelt down beside him. He looked up, smiled. She smiled back, said, "Hicks, my love… Thomas Edison wants to speak to you."

Chapter 19

Jake pointed the phonic blaster toward a pile of rocks that K-Free had assembled for destruction. It was difficult to try to fire the blasted thing in the dark, with only a sliver of moon and the glowing red heat off the contraption itself to light his surroundings, but what could he do? They were going to move against Carpathian soon, and he needed to figure it out. Perhaps Hicks would have been a better choice, being more knowledgeable of machinery than Jake. This sound blaster thing of Edison's was as much a machine as a weapon. Jake strapped it on, and it immediately felt uncomfortable. But of course it would. It had been custom-made for Edison's back, not his.

Jake faced the pile of rocks and pressed the levers on the blaster's handles. A powerful sound coiled out of the blasters and echoed across the dry, rocky land, but only one stone fell from its perch.

"Damn it all!" He said, kicking his hard boot into the ground. "It's more difficult than it looks."

"Maybe I should try it," K-Free suggested.

Jake shook his head. "No, you're shorter than Edison. It's customized to his height, I figure. We're about the same height. It should work."

"It's a matter of projection." She shook her head at Jake's stubbornness. "You gotta get those phonic blasters turned at the right time and lean into it."

She was probably right. Maybe she *would* wield it better, but he doubted she'd be able to handle its bulk and weight for very long. No. Jake had to do it. *He* had to be the one to tear down Carpathian's barricade. He had to show Marcus and even Zarelda that he was loyal to the mission. He had to prove to himself that those terrible thoughts that led to his terrible actions had not overwhelmed him. Jake set himself up for another blast against the rocks and wondered if he had the strength to withstand any further influence. *Yes, I am strong enough.*

He fired again. The air roared with concentrated sound. Two rocks exploded this time, and Jake felt the concussive force of recoil.

K-Free clapped her hands and gave a small hoot. "Good! Much better."

Jake acknowledged the compliment but shook his head. "Still not good enough. That barricade ain't gonna budge on that. Let's go up to a larger set of stones."

"No more around here. Let's move."

They moved further down into the valley, where the trees were thicker but where there were a few larger boulders striped with brighter moonlight. "Good," Jake said, shuffling carefully into place. Walking with the thing was only a slight bit easier than firing. "This'll give me more light to work with. We ain't gonna go in by dark anyway."

K-free studied the rock closely, running her hand over its coarse granite skin to find the right spot. She used her finger to mark an invisible 'x'. "Right here," she said. "Try to focus it right here."

He did, three times, in quick succession. Almost like a tracing round, the first missed the spot, the sound ricocheting off and echoing through the trees. He adjusted, shot again. The rock moved about an inch. Small shards of broken rock and dust sprang into the dark sky on the third shot, and he moved to the right a couple steps to fire again. He was just about to squeeze the levers when a flash of gun metal caught his eye in the shadows along the tree line.

He turned and saw the shape of a face – no, two faces – nestled within the pine needles. Jake turned his body and fired the blaster into the woods, giving it little thought.

Weaker trees at the edge of the line shattered into showers of bark and wood, and the force of the sound through the phonic blasters pounded stronger trees and bent them like twigs in a thunderstorm. Jake fired again and even more trees began to crack and twist. Then he stopped and looked for the strange faces. They were gone.

"Why'd the hell you do that?" K-Free crouched behind the boulder as if she had been the focus of his attack.

"Somebody's watching. Come on."

They worked their way through the pine wood and found a body covered in bark and piled tree limbs. K-Free removed the debris. The uncovered body was a woman's, but broken like the branches around her. Her dress was bloody and near torn off. Her hair a matted mess. Her face unrecognizable.

"My God," K-Free said, covering the bloody face with broken sticks. "Awful."

"There were two of them. The other must have gotten away. Who the hell were they?"

K-Free studied the fabric of the dress. "Ladue's ladies. I recognize the lace."

"Damn! They must have followed us from Fort Waco."

"We gotta tell Marcus the bad news."

"No. Not bad news. Good news."

K-Free shook her head. "I don't follow. How does Ladue following us constitute good—"

Before she could finish, Jake turned toward the boulder and shot the phonic blaster. The weapon cracked like lightning, its sound wave striking the rock hard and shearing off the top like a saber through melon. Jake fired again, and the rest of the boulder cracked in two.

"It's good news, Kim," he said, smiling ear to ear, "cause I know now how to use this damn thing."

*****

Sasha listened intently as the echoes of Edison's blaster roared through the valley below. Then the sound stopped for good as he saw one of the ladies that Ladue had sent ahead to spy come shuffling through the light pine. She was wobbling, stumbling as if she had run into a wall. It was dark, so he couldn't see her full appearance, but he could imagine it.

"What happened, Edith?" Desiree asked as the girl fell to her knees near the campfire. Sasha cold see her clearly now.

Her dress was torn at the shoulder and waist, as if strong hands had tried ripping it off. Her hair was a mess. It didn't appear as if any blood was in it, though Sasha noticed a small red trickle coming from her left ear. Bits of bark and wood also stuck out of her bare arms and calves, and it seemed as if the heels of both boots had been torn clean off. She fell to the ground, gasping for air.

"Edith!" Desiree said, stepping over a burning log and grabbing the girl's chin. She yanked it up roughly and stared into her terrified, shocked eyes. "I asked you a question. *Que s'est-il passé?* Where's Sarah?"

"Dead! DEAD! Torn to pieces by that... that sound machine!"

"Why are you shouting?" Desiree recoiled slightly from the unexpected volume.

"She can't hear well," Sasha said, pointing to her ear. "She's bleeding. They hit them with the blaster."

"Who hit them?" Desiree grabbed Edith's chin again. "Who did this?"

Edith stammered. "Jake... Jake Mattia."

"*Sacrebleu!*" Desiree said, dropping Edith's head and letting the other girls drag her away for aide. "What we going to do now?"

Sasha raised an eyebrow. "What do you mean? It's cut and dry for me. We know now how they're going in, using that damned thing to blow through whatever defenses Carpathian has."

"Do you think it can be *accompli*?"

Sasha shook his head. "I don't know, but they're going to try. Pretty damn ballsy of them, if you ask me, using Edison's equipment; how they got their dirty hands on it is a wonder. I'd admire the attempt if they weren't so annoying."

Desiree spit in the fire. It crackled and sizzled on the wood. "I'm going to *tuer* Jake Mattia for what he did."

"No, you aren't," Sasha said, throwing his arm out and letting his blades sheer through the warm night air, imagining them slicing through Jake's throat. "I'll kill him for both of us."

*****

The Wraith put a thermite slug into the head of the nearest construct. The force of the shot ripped the beast's skull clear off, leaving chunky remains resting on its neck like overripe tomato. Carl stood nearby, fending off the attack of another with a shovel, having ditched his black powder weapon after it had failed to put one of the things down. A shovel proved to be a better weapon, especially the sharp end. He yanked the tip of the shovel out of the creature's head and kicked the corpse away. That ended the brawl. The third in as many days.

The Wraith tossed his shotgun to the ground and roared at the black entrance to the mineshaft. "Find me my access tunnel already!"

His voice echoed down the shaft, and he hoped that those flea-bitten clod-hoppers down there would hear it. It had been four days searching, and three scouting parties had come by. There was nothing else they could do; the constructs had to be attacked so that their camp outside the mine would not be seen. Their ammunition was running low, and the pile of dead scouts and animations was beginning to stink. The Wraith ruffled his nose against the smell. He had considered burying them, but they didn't deserve a proper burial. What they deserved was death, and he and Carl had given it to them each time, while his supposed 'competent' Mexican farmers were toiling in the dark beneath their feet. Probably taking *siestas* is what they were doing, The Wraith figured, in nice, cold damp places underground. *Incompetent cretins…*

He picked up his shotgun and fixed it to his back. "I'm gonna kill someone if they don't hurry up."

"I'm surprised they haven't been buried alive," Carl said. "Truth be told, those mines are highly volatile. If they don't find something soon, we're not going to have any miners left."

"Nor any ammunition." He checked his ammo crate. Plenty of fire and acid rounds; he rarely fired those, preferring instead to preserve them for real killing. He only had a small bandolier of ion rounds. Those were extremely rare, and he wasn't sure exactly how they were used. He'd never fired them. His thermite rounds, however, were dangerously low. He had enough to fill a cylinder twice. That wouldn't last a damn. The Wraith shook his head and looked into the sky. "Lord, kill me now."

The booming sound of RJ weapons echoed through the valley of pines. The Wraith perked up quickly, turned his ear to the sound and listened. More and more sounded.

"That's the Eight," Carl said, "sure as I'm standing here."

"Damn!" The Wraith said, running toward the sound. He stopped and listened again, cupping his ears to hear it better. *Boom! Boom!* "The Eight are on the move."

One of his men came stumbling out of the mineshaft. The Wraith turned and grabbed the man's dirty lapel and smacked him across the face. "Where's my entry tunnel?" He smacked him again. "Where is it? You hear that?" *Boom! Boom!* "That's the Eight making their move. I'm losing to them sons of bitches, and it's because of you."

The man babbled something The Wraith couldn't understand. He raised his hand again to strike the terrified man, but Carl grabbed his arm. "Stop! Let him speak."

He thought about striking out at Carl, but the big man's eyes were vibrant and filled with strength and resolve. It would be easy to strike him, for sure, but not so easy to knock him down. The Wraith growled and pushed the man to the ground. "Very well. Talk!"

"*Señor*," the man said, holding up his hand to block the powerful sunlight. "The shaft... we, we found it. We found the entry point."

The Wraith's mood quickly changed. He picked the man back up and spit words into his face. "Where? Are you sure?"

The man nodded. "Si, *señor*. About five miles that way," he said, pointing abstractly in the general direction of the sounds.

"How do you know?" Carl asked.

"The air, s*eñor*. The air blows from the porous rock above. Clear and cold. And water too, a trickle, but it is there. And it is not the water of a river or creek, you see. It is distilled water, from a cistern or well. It's the place, s*eñor*. We are certain of it. But... you must not go through there. I beg you not to go."

The Wraith raised a curious eye. "Why not?"

"Because, s*eñor*, the way is paved with *los huesos de los muertos,* the bones of the dead. The evil man has thrown his mistakes down there, scores and scores of bodies. Bones and rotting flesh, skulls looking up at you through the foul garbage like death itself. It is Diablo's lair, *señor*. I beg you, do not go."

The Wraith wanted to strike him again. *Not go? This superstitious cretin.* "I've seen more dead bodies than you can count, you miserable worm. Death does not scare me, but it should be afraid of me."

He pushed the man away and drew his shotgun. He rolled the cylinder into place, making sure his acid rounds were ready. "You fetch my ammo crate," he told the man. "And Carl, pack your bag. We're going in, and by God, we'll beat that son of the bitch Marcus at his own game."

*****

Sun dozed in the dank cell, his head against the wall. There was a cot, but it was so flea-bitten, so dirty, that he couldn't hazard the thought of actually lying on it. The thought made his skin crawl, truly and figuratively. So he slept against the cold wall, a light touch of air cycling through its porous materials. The wall was made of old limestone, and it was painful to lay against for long, but Sun did his best.

He heard a voice, shy and tepid, like a boy child. He thought he was dreaming, recalling his own youthful voice, as if he were walking in a dream quest. He thought it funny, but the voice changed to a whimper, and the humor of it was gone. He opened his eyes, stayed perfectly still, and listened.

"Where are you?" he said, loud enough for the question to echo through the cell. "I can hear you, but I cannot see you. Show yourself."

"I am here," the child said.

Sun turned to the wall and placed his hand on the cold rock. "Behind the wall? Are you in a cell too?"

A whimper, then, "Yes."

"Who are you?"

"I am... I do not know who I am anymore, but I used to be called Careless Fox."

"You are one of the People?"

"Yes."

"Why are you here?"

"I was taken from my camp by that foreign devil. One of his steel eagles took me and carried me here. They were trying to take us all, but Walks Looking saved them. All except me."

Walks Looking! She had not mentioned anything about losing young warriors to Carpathian on their last encounter, but then, perhaps she figured the boy dead. Sun leaned over and placed his forehead on the cold stone. "How long have you been here in this terrible place?"

The boy coughed. "I do not know. I cannot tell how many times the sun has risen in this place. A very long time. A lifetime."

"You said that you did not know who you were anymore. What did you mean?"

The boy's sobbing grew louder at the question. Sun regretted asking it, fearful that he had caused the boy pain. But the boy cleared his throat and answered. "I no longer have a left hand. They took it from me and gave me a cold iron one. They also took sight from my right eye and gave me a binocular. That is what they call it. Without my hand and my eye, I am less than who I was. I am humiliated and ashamed."

Sun shook his head as if the boy could see it. "Do not be, young warrior. It is not your fault, and I promise you I will free you from this place. And I will take you back to your people. I will take you back to Walks Looking."

"No," the boy said, clearly despondent and in shock at what had happened to him. "I have shamed them all, and I must die."

"Look," Sun said, standing and pressing close to the wall to make sure the boy heard his words clearly. "You are not going to die, and Carpathian will pay for what he has done. I promise you that. I will free you, and then we will—"

The massive door at the top of the winding staircase that led to the cells opened. Sun could see the sharp spike of lamplight that fell into the hallway as someone heavy took the steps and bounded down, unconcerned about the commotion he, or it, was making. Sun turned to his thick cell door and peered out the small barred window.

There were three men, two guards he had seen before, and another, a big, powerful brute with broad shoulders and a white beard. He had on a thick woolen shirt and tough leggings, as if they were undergarments meant to shield the body from heavy armor that protected vital parts of the man's body; he was certainly built for it.

They stopped in front of Sun's cell, and the big man motioned one of the guards to unlock the door. Sun stepped back and waited. The key popped the lock, and the guard swung the door open, the sound of the creaking black-iron hinges filling the hallway.

The big man motioned Sun forward. "Come," he said, in a higher voice than Sun would have imagined. The man was foreign, no doubt about it. Sun had heard that kind of accent from Eastern European immigrants during school. "It is time for your enlightenment. I am Vladimir Ursul. I am in charge of your reassignment."

Sun shook his head. "I do not wish to be enlightened or to be reassigned. I am smart enough already. I am comfortable in my own skin."

Vlad laughed, strong and confident. "It's not an option, my petulant guest. It has been decided, and do not fear. When it's done, you will personally thank the doctor. Everyone does. The doctor gets what the doctor wants. You will be remade, better and stronger. There is no discussion. Come now, on your own, with your pride. Do not think we will not take you by force."

Sun stepped backward three paces until he was against the back wall. "By force then."

Vlad smiled grimly and stepped back. "Very well. Take him."

The two guards came through the door and straight at him, chains and manacles waving in their hands. Sun waited until they were right on him, then he struck out, driving his fist across the chin of the closest man and kicking the other in the groin. The kicked one fell down. The man hit in the face stumbled back but recovered and tried again. Sun ducked a punch, and then kicked the man in the knee, sending him screaming in pain to the floor.

Vlad sighed deeply and entered the cell. He could barely fit through the narrow door. Sun did not hesitate; he attacked immediately, jumping through the air, feet first, trying to land a shot against Vlad's chest. The man let him strike, but Sun crumpled to the floor. "That will do you no good."

Sun recovered quickly and tried again, punching and striking at Vlad's chest, face, stomach. The man was faster than his bulk suggested. Sun landed punches, but it did little damage. Vlad took a step back, reared back his arm, and drove a hard slap across Sun's face.

Sun flew backward and hit the floor. The other two men, having recovered from their beating, jumped on him immediately and began slapping on the chains. Sun resisted, but the slap had knocked him silly. His eyes were crossed, his face in pain.

"I suggest that you stop fighting," Vlad said, standing over Sun, adjusting his shirt. "Enlightenment comes better without struggle."

"I will never submit to anything you will do to me!"

Vlad smiled. "It matters not. You will submit, or I will—"

A loud explosion sounded somewhere above. The walls shook, and dust fell from the ceiling. It struck again, and this time, the guards and Vlad stopped what they were doing and listened.

"What was that, sir?" One of the guards asked.

Vlad stepped back, looking fearfully at the ceiling. *Boom! Boom!* The walls shook again, more dust fell. The big man shook his head. "I do not know."

"I know what it is," Sun said, pushing himself from the guards and kicking away the chains. "It is Marcus Wayward. He is here to save me, and you are all going to die."

Vlad looked down at Sun, who smiled and winked. "Go on, chain me up and enlighten me. And while you do, your boss will burn."

"Leave him!" Vlad said, turning to the door and moving away.

Sun watched and smiled as they left, knowing that Marcus was out there right now, attacking. Vlad locked the door behind them and they raced up the stairs.

Boom! Boom!

"Do you hear that, Careless Fox?" Sun asked, going to the wall and talking through it. "Do you hear that sound? That is not the Great Spirit coming to save us. No. That is my friend, my family, my sister. The Eight are coming. They are coming, and you and I will ride free once again."

Sun could not contain his joy. He danced, an old dance that his grandfather had taught him. He danced, he sang, and imagined Carpathian's face melting in fire.

Chapter 20

They went in with guns blazing. A cliché, yes, but Marcus could think of no other way. The Wayward Eight was a veritable walking regiment of firepower; stealth was not their creed. With Edison bound to the front of Jake's Iron Horse, they entered Payson, whooping and hollering, firing at windows, lanterns, hanging signs, and doors, using the guns affixed to their 'Horses. Marcus had ordered them not to use their personal sidearms; not yet. They would hold off on that until they reached their destination.

With Jake in the lead and using Edison's phonic blaster, it almost felt as if they were riding through a parade where on-lookers flung confetti, as showers of glass and loose, dry wood flew off buildings as they rushed by. Those citizens, who were out early, shocked by the suddenness of the attack, were either knocked out immediately by sound waves, or were flung through the air to meet their fate through a blast of glass, wood, or shattered brick. Their bones seemed to topple in the wake of the mighty sound. Some tried to fire back, but they refused to attack Jake's Iron Horse, clearly noticing one of their masters strapped to the cow-catcher. *Very good*, Marcus thought, as he pulled up right behind Sierra and K-Free. *Exactly as planned.*

Then others were among them, ladies on Iron Horses, coming on strong behind them, out of nowhere it seemed. Marcus was surprised that he had not noticed them before. Perhaps he had been too focused on the assault, too blindly single-minded. Marcus pulled his Iron Horse up and bumped another. It was Desiree Ladue.

"What the hell are you doing here?!" Marcus screamed over the roar of the attack.

"Same as you," Sasha Tanner said, coming up and bumping Marcus's vehicle. "Now get out of the way, so I can kill Jake!"

"You do that, and the whole operation will fail! He's the only one that can get us through the barrier!" Marcus pointed up the road at the piles upon piles of iron sheets, steel bars, and railway track that had been assembled at the mouth of the canyon like a latticework wall. Only a tiny path, not even wide enough for an Iron Horse, could be seen snaking its way through the layers of protection. "He don't blow that thing, we don't go in. Now, shut the hell up and fall back!"

Sasha gave Marcus an obscene gesture with his right hand. "We're going in, same as you!"

Sasha sped up. Marcus followed, laying heavy on the triggers of his Gatling guns and ripping huge holes into the line of buildings to his right. His gunfire tore through the animated beasts that were now falling into the streets, followed by real human beings, or so Marcus thought they were. It was hard to tell in this accursed town what was real and what was undead. It all kind of blended together.

The rest of the Eight were firing all their remaining ordnance into the waves of opposition. It was a bloodbath, as Marcus expected it to be, but there was no other choice. If he felt any guilt about killing so many – and he probably would later – it was quenched by the realization that not a single one of them would think twice about killing the Eight. All of them now falling into the streets, with picks and shovels, with handguns, rifles, and augmented RJ weapons in place of their arms and legs, knew what their master wanted. They sought blood – and the Eight would give it to them.

The gunfire in response to their assault was growing heavier now as they bound ever closer to the canyon, and Marcus had to shield himself from the errant bullets that sprang off his cow-catcher. The others were doing much the same, with K-Free finding modest protection in the midst of Ladue's girls. Marcus didn't like it, remembering back to Fort Waco when Desiree had made K-Free that offer to join her flock. But those matters would be dealt with later. He was more pleased that Hicks and Zarelda were fighting hard, keeping the pressure on the Payson citizenry, but their ammunition was probably running low; everyone's was.

Together, like a flock of birds, they turned into the final road that led to the entrance to the canyon. The barrier stood about twenty feet high, piles upon piles of brick, stone, steel, and iron. It seemed to Marcus that a breeze could bring it down, but he knew that was an illusion. Only Edison's blaster could do the job.

He sidled up to Jake. "Another hundred yards, and you lay on that trigger. You concentrate that sound on the entrance to the path. You get me?"

Jake saluted. He reached forward and smacked Edison on the back of the head. "Watch this, you sorry sack of pig dung."

Another thirty yards, and Jake unleashed the loudest, most powerful sound wave that Marcus had ever heard. The sound hit the barrier with a cracking *Boom! Boom!*, like a hammer striking rock, dissipating into the dry air like heat shimmer off the desert sand. The ground shook. Jake fired again. *Boom! Boom!* The barrier moved an inch. *Boom! Boom!*

Then it all fell away, from the top first, a few iron bars, a few sheets of steel. Then the entire structure caved, cracking as bolts, rivets, and iron bands began to pop and unleash a river of metal and rock that swarmed down like an avalanche. Marcus had to slow his Iron Horse so as not to run headlong into the debris field. Even the denizens of Payson were shocked at the eruption of the barrier, as many scrambled to find shelter. Marcus laid in on them with the last of his Gatling rounds. Jake struck the barrier once more, clearing a path large enough to accept their vehicles.

Through the dust cloud created by the crashing barrier, the Eight rode. Those that still had ammunition now expended it, clearing the path before them of any Enlightened foolish enough to have tried a direct assault through the toppling barrier. To Marcus, it felt like he was flying through that dust storm they encountered in the Contested Territories, being unable to see where he would come out. Then the air began to clear. He wiped his face and goggles clean, and the canyon opened up before him.

The walls of the canyon were scarred with industry, huge iron factories that pumped black and red soot into the air. Right now, it appeared as if the cooking vats or stoves – or whatever kind of cauldrons Carpathian had in those factories – were running at low capacity. Marcus could see small tendrils of smoke emanating from the towering smokestacks; he could smell their waste even more. It stung his nostrils, and he tried covering his face with a bandana which lay around his neck. It helped some, but the strength of the scent permeated everything. A dead smell, like corpses rotting, but with the distinct scent of RJ, as if everything had been sprinkled with its fragrance from a lady's perfume bottle. It stunk, and the fumes were difficult to absorb.

The canyon opened into a central yard that was criss-crossed with cobbled walkways and dirt paths that ran from one building to another. They were well-worn and covered partially from blowing dust and sand. To the left, far up along the canyon wall, lay a castle. More like the keep of a castle, like those samples Marcus had seen in picture books. It was buried deep into the rock and served as an observation tower, conical-shaped like an old European parapet. Marcus slowed his Iron Horse to a crawl and looked up into the dark glass that shielded the room at the very top of the tower. That's where Carpathian waited. He was certain of it, and all he had to do was get up there and finish the job.

But his more immediate concern was the army of undead lumbering toward their position from the back of the canyon. The yard that was initially quiet and empty, now began to fill with shifting, lumbering Enlightened, all packing weapons, all moving like a slow, steady sweep of death.

Jake pulled up beside Marcus and jumped off his Iron Horse, letting it continue its speedy path toward the undead horde. He collected himself and said, waving, "Goodbye, Thomas. It's been a pleasure."

Jake laughed as Edison, screaming, ran headlong into his undead minions; crushing several below its skids before tilting over and crashing.

Marcus couldn't share Jake's frivolity. "Find cover!" he yelled at the rest of the Eight who had also jumped off their spent vehicles and were now drawing personal weapons. Ladue and her ladies were doing the same. Sasha had already taken cover among the debris line.

Marcus found cover behind a stout pile of twisted rail track. Sierra was nearby. "Aim for the chest. Irradiate those bastards in full. I don't want ammo wasted on head shots."

"You got it!" Sierra said, drawing her atomic pistol and firing true.

He drew his rebel hand cannon, aimed it at the closest undead, and fired. The thing's chest exploded as if it had been stuck by a tiny grenade, splashing the creatures around it with gooey RJ. He fired again, and again, until he had to reload.

He popped his head up to take a look. K-Free was firing strong. She and Jake were holding a position roughly twenty feet away. River, having taken one of the extra Union blasters, was putting rounds into a long stream of animations coming from the east side of the complex. She was doing well, but that wouldn't last. He needed to get over there and give her some relief, as it didn't appear that Ladue or Sasha were all that concerned about helping out any of the Eight, despite the fact that if the Eight fell, so would they. *Selfish bastards!* Marcus grit his teeth, ducked a spread of gunfire, rolled his cannon's cylinder into place, and fired back. Three more went down.

"Hicks!" he called. No reply. "Hicks! Zarelda!"

"Over there," Sierra said, pointing with her gun to a small postern door that led into the canyon wall.

Marcus looked up. "Zarelda! Hicks! Where are you going?"

They did not respond. Zarelda, being led by the hand by Hicks, didn't even bother to turn around and acknowledge the question. As he watched them disappear into the dark entrance, his heart sank as he remembered Walks Looking's warning. *Beware the man with the red hand.*

Anger filled his mind. He gnashed his teeth again and fired a shot at the door that they were entering. It ricocheted off the canyon wall. "Bastards!"

"What do we do now?" Sierra asked, reloading again and then firing into another three animations.

He wanted to rise up. He wanted to go after them. But he couldn't. There were more pressing matters to attend to.

In front of him, as wide and as ferocious as a lion, came one of Carpathian's creations, trundling through the undead mass, pushing them aside like rag dolls. Two small armored heads sat atop its barrel chest, and four powerful arms held equally powerful weapons: a Gatling gun, a flamethrower, a steel drill, and three razor-sharp circular saws whirling at breakneck speed. The monster lurched forward like an ogre; it was the most terrifying thing Marcus had ever seen. He caught his breath, breathed slowly, rose up from his cover, aimed carefully, and fired at its heads.

*****

The Wraith picked his way through heaps of decayed bodies. The Mexican had been right: the way was paved with bones and desiccated muscle and sinew; muddled, rotten clothing; and bits and pieces of metal and iron that comprised attempted and failed weaponized fixtures to flesh. It was a tomb more than a mine, and The Wraith loved it. Not because of the bodies, but because of what it meant. It meant that somewhere ahead, there had to be a shaft or well or some passageway up into Carpathian's complex. The bodies had to have come from somewhere. Someone, or *something,* had brought these failures down to fill the mine. Why they had decided to keep them and not bury them or, better, burn them, could only be speculated. Who knew what devilment roiled in the insane mind of one like the doctor. The Wraith didn't care. All he cared about was finding a way up, and his men weren't digging fast enough.

He'd yelled constantly at them, slapped a couple, even punched one when Carl wasn't looking. That damned old softy wouldn't allow him to beat them like he wanted, like it was necessary to get them to work. If he didn't need Carl so badly, he would not have given a damn and would have shot the man himself. Carl just didn't understand how to motivate men to do one's bidding. That's why a man like Carl Fredrickson was always taking orders and not giving them. Fear was the only true motivating factor. Without fear, nothing could get done.

From where they stood in the shaft, watching the Mexicans dig upward through many feet of porous rock and clay, he could hear the muffled sounds of battle. The Eight were attacking. How was it going? Were they advancing? Had they been stopped? He couldn't tell from the sounds. He was still too far away. But it wasn't good, he was certain of it. Marcus Wayward was in the complex, and attacking, and every minute he waited for these clod-hoppers to dig through meant that it would be much harder for him to find and destroy his target.

"Dig, you sorry vats of pig dung!" He yelled up the shaft. Another pile of dirt fell to the bottom near his feet. The Wraith stepped out of the way. "There's killing to be done!"

Then he heard a crack and a rumble, and quarter-size pieces of granite tumbled down. A collective *hurrah!* echoed down the shaft. "We found it, *señor*," one of them yelled back. "We've hit granite."

"Start picking at it!" He yelled back.

"It's new granite, *señor*. Very solid. It looks like it was once an opening to a well or something. It's been recently put in place, sealed with concrete and bolted to the floor with steel rods."

Apparently, the new constructed seal on the shaft meant that Carpathian was no longer using the mine for his discards. "I don't care if the Devil himself bolted it shut. You get those picks out and start hammering!"

He heard a few feeble smacks, but they quickly stopped. "Too thick, *señor*. It will take hours to get through. We need dynamite!"

"We ain't got no dynamite. We—"

He thought for a moment, then drew his shotgun. He checked his shotgun again to ensure an acid round was in the chamber. "Get your sorry asses out of there. Now!"

The men scrambled down the three ropes that had been grappled up the shaft. When they were all down and had backed off, The Wraith leaned under the tunnel and fired three rounds into the granite. A powerful echo replied, and even Carl covered his ears. Then, there was a strong hissing sound as the acid began to eat into the granite, followed by a billow of green smoke which entered their space. The Mexicans backed off even further. The Wraith stood his ground. It was just smoke, nothing more. It might sting a little if it touched skin, but he could take it. If he could survive being grazed by the radiated bullet of an atomic pistol, a little acid would tickle.

He waited five minutes, and then fired the last two rounds. He waited another five minutes, and then cycled the chamber until thermite slugs fell into place. He emptied the entire cylinder up the shaft. Once the dust, falling rocks, and green smoke subsided, they heard a small pop, then a crack, and then an even louder crack until the entire tunnel collapsed.

The Wraith fell backward, shielding his fall against Carl, who landed flat on the hard ground with a thud. The Wraith closed his eyes and held his breath. A minute passed. He opened his eyes and breathed again. The air was filled with dust, but it was clearing. He sat up, looked into the shaft once again. It had completely collapsed into a pile of granite and concrete. There was a faint light emanating from above.

"Get the ropes!" he said, and his men scrambled to find them among the rubble. They found two and threw the grapples back up the shaft. It took a few throws, but eventually, they found purchase. The Wraith pushed one of his men away so that he could be the first to the top. He slung his shotgun onto his back and pulled himself up the debris pile.

Carl followed, then each of the Mexicans in turn.

The Wraith pulled himself up into a dimly lit, cold room, with pure granite walls. A trickle of water ran down the wall to his right and disappeared down the collapsed shaft. The room had once been a hallway. Now it was nothing but broken and buckled rock.

Along his left were three cell doors. The Wraith stood tall, stretched his back, and flexed his arms. He looked at the cell doors. Dark eyes stared at him through the small barred window in the center door.

He pulled one of his UR-30 blasters and pointed it at the eyes. "Who the hell are you?"

"Sun Totem," said the man on the other side.

Carl came up quick and snatched the blaster from The Wraith's hand. He pointed the barrel right through the window. The occupant fell back.

"You're the son of a bitch that tied me up," Carl said. "I should kill you right now."

"Wait," Sun said. "I was just following orders. That is all."

"Yeah, Carl," The Wraith said, a callous smirk on his face. "Following orders. Sound familiar?"

Carl ignored the mercenary's jibe and kept his focus on Sun. "Yeah, and I'm following my instincts to kill a no good sorry son of —"

The Wraith snatched the gun back with one swift, determined move. "You take my gun again, Carl, and you'll be pushing up daisies. We ain't got time to waste on this sorry Injin. We got to go."

"Free me," Sun said, finding the courage to put his face back up to the window. "Free me, Carl, and I will get your weapons back for you. I know where they are."

That made Carl blink. He paused, stared at Sun for a long time, and then seemed to have a change of heart. His temper waned, and he looked at The Wraith with a softer expression. "I need my weapons, Wraith. With them, we can do a lot of damage."

The Wraith huffed. He had no desire to release this Indian. Hell, he'd hired Medicine Man to find and kill members of the Eight. It made no sense now to help one of them. He was right where he needed to be: behind bars where he couldn't make mischief, couldn't help Marcus win this race. But he couldn't stand here arguing all day either, and despite his desire, he needed Carl. At least long enough to get into the fight.

"Step back," he said, leveling the blaster at the door latch. He fired once, and the massive hole exploded into the door.

Sun came out, naked from the waist up, but intact. Carpathian had not done anything unnatural to him.

"We have to free the boy," Sun said, pointing to his left at the first cell door.

"Now look, damn you," The Wraith said, his face growing red and veins forking on his forehead. "I ain't come here as a liberator. I came here to kill."

"Please. Just one shot."

The Wraith shook his head but aimed at the next door and fired. The entire door blew inward. He didn't wait to see who was inside. "Let's go!"

Carl and the others followed him, up the winding stairs. It was several flights, and the way was dark. But the higher they climbed, the more the sounds of battle filled the air. The fighting was close, very close. Good deal. He'd be able to jump right in immediately.

He came out of the dungeon and into clear air, into a large room that still appeared to be underground. There were no windows and no sunlight from the outside. The Wraith paused and looked for a door. A large shadow crossed his path, and he was immediately swept aside by an ape-like creature with hammers for arms.

The strike knocked the wind out of him and tossed him halfway across the room. He fell into the furniture, and perhaps that was the only thing that kept him from cracking his skull wide open on the floor – the cushions of the chairs softened his fall. He slid across the floor through broken glass and wood, pulled both pistols, and fired at the beast.

The thing was ravenous and it came at him with no concern for its welfare. A bear trap that circled its face snapped and deflected the shots. The Wraith couldn't believe it, and for a moment, paused to reflect on how such a massive creature could move so quickly and respond to gunfire so well. The reason stood behind it, he finally noticed; a tall, thin man carrying a staff of blazing RJ. The man was barking orders at the beast, and the creature was responding quickly, moving left, right, deflecting shots, waving his hammer arms around as if he were clearing a room. The Wraith fired and dodged, fired and dodged, until he had worked his way back to the spiraling staircase.

The others had finally made it to the surface. The man behind the beast shook his staff at two of the closest Mexicans and a long stream of RJ pulsed from the head of the staff and cooked the men where they stood. The rancid smell of burnt flesh made The Wraith's stomach lurch. Luckily, it was empty, and he was able to bite down the nausea and keep fighting. Carl and Sun had no weapons, but they were doing their best to distract the beast's handler, throwing things at him and dodging his staff shots. They then tried picking up loose guns dropped by the dead Mexicans, and poked bayonets at the beast's legs.

The other prisoner whom Sun wanted freed now came up out of the stairwell. A boy, nothing but a young Warrior Nation boy. Thin and frail, weaponless and afraid. The Wraith noticed that the youth had one metal hand, and something circular and iron had been pressed over his eye.

The beast noticed the boy emerging as well and turned the barrel of its long rail gun toward the stairs.

The Wraith shot and hit the rail gun's muzzle square, spinning the beast round like a top. The rail gun fired into the ceiling, the strength and velocity of the round ripping through the building's structure and causing it to shake like an earthquake had struck its foundation. The beast fell on its back. The Wraith fired again at it, but his shot was hindered by a stream of RJ that scorched the floor in front of him, splashing his hand with the hot red fluid. He screamed at the sudden pain shooting up his arm and looked up. The man controlling the beast was near him now, setting up to fire another RJ stream.

"Die, you dog!" the man said as he stuck out his staff and fired again.

The Wraith barely rolled away, feeling the scorching heat of the RJ blast seer the back of his coat. He rolled and fired, causing the handler to duck for cover.

"Over here!" Carl said on the opposite side of the beast. The Wraith looked and found Carl standing at an obscure door behind a tapestry that he had pulled down. Sun Totem was trying to reach the boy and take him toward the door, but the beast was in the way, writhing on the ground trying to right itself from the last few Mexicans who were still alive and stabbing at it with their bayonets. It fired its rail gun wildly again and pounded the ceiling with incredible force.

The ceiling above the beast buckled and collapsed, covering it with rock, concrete, and broken oak beams. The Wraith took his chance, stood quickly, and ran to the boy. He got there before Sun, grabbed him up and took off toward the door being held open by Carl. He handed the boy off to Sun and jumped over one of the beast's flailing hammer arms. One of the Mexicans had been trapped under the collapsed ceiling as well, and his arm stuck out from beneath the debris. He was still alive, but The Wraith ignored it. He had saved enough people today. It was time to kill a few.

He reached the door and they ran out, followed quickly by a final spray of RJ that ignited the tapestry. The Wraith took the steps in twos, bounding upward, his heart beating so hard he thought he'd collapse. A cool breeze met his face as they ascended, and he knew they were going in the right direction. Another six steps and they came out into sunlight, into a central park area where utter chaos reigned.

Scores, perhaps hundreds, of men, women, animations, and other hideous, foul creatures converged on a pile of iron, rock, and steel debris where Marcus and many others held a defensive line. The Wraith paused to watch wave after wave hit the barrier and fall in mighty sprays of blood, RJ, and bone. It was a marvelous battle, and one that he hadn't seen since the Civil War. He felt like weeping.

He holstered his pistols, drew his shotgun and rolled slugs into place.

"Come on, boys," he said. "Let's join the war!"

*****

"Tell me now," Zarelda said, as she followed Hicks down a long stone staircase through a factory of disassembled mechanical body parts, make-shift weapons, half-dried corpses, and pulsing RJ vats. "What did Edison tell you?"

Hicks had been elated since he had spoken with Edison last night. He couldn't wait to get inside the complex, but he had refused to tell her anything. He better now, she thought, or she was going to turn right round and forget this whole venture.

"He told me where all the secrets were hidden," Hicks said, slowing down to turn and look her in the eye. He wore an ear-to-ear smile. "All of them. Blueprints, procedural manuals, diagrams. It's a gold mine of information, Z. All we got to do is get to it, and it's ours."

Zarelda pulled on his hand, stopping him on the steps. "Why? Why he give you all dis?"

Hicks stared at her angrily. "Because we're kindred spirits, Z. He's an inventor; I'm a mechanic. He understands, like I do, the value of technology. He says that he'll help me understand all of it, including how RJ can be used as medicine. I asked him about that on your behalf. He says it can be. You knew it all along, Z."

He pulled her further down the stairs. She let him, but her heart was heavy. She could hear the battle continue outside. She had heard Marcus calling for them through the din, but she had refused to even acknowledge his voice. Why? Fear? Pride? Embarrassment? Lack of loyalty? Perhaps all of those things. But what could she do? Hicks was her husband and he was right: she did want to learn the medicinal purposes of RJ, not only for her own professional gain – she could not deny that – but also to help her people back home, the thousand score poor and destitute that needed medicine to live. If she could learn how to use RJ to save lives, then it would be all worth it in the end.

"Wait," she said. "What's da catch? He ain't giving all dis up for free. What we got to do?"

"You'll see."

The stairs ended in a large room lit with RJ lanterns. Zarelda froze, in awe at the display of mechanical devices and maps, diagrams, blueprints, and various other equipment and weapons strewn all around. Half-Blackhoof, half-skeletal constructs hung down from steel cable from the ceiling, like devilish marionettes at a play. Union blasters with their casings all ripped out and replaced with gears and triggers and RJ pumps, were lying in groups of ten on workbenches. Various pistols and knives, swords, spears, all fitted to amputated hands and arms. And alongside them were fifteen, no, twenty, constructs heavy in chains, fastened tightly to the wall, but their RJ sources had not been attached yet, and so they were still and quiet, like sleeping babies.

"Lawd God," Zarelda said, raising her atomic-repeater in fear that any one of them might pounce. "Dis is da devil's playground."

"No," Hicks said. "This is Edison's personal laboratory."

He was like a kid on Christmas morning. He moved from wall to wall, looking deeply into the measured lines and scribbled notes and mathematical equations that filled the pages. He touched nearly everything, more than he should, more than was prudent, but there was no stopping him. Zarelda should have stopped him; she knew she should have. But she hadn't seen him this excited in a long time. Truth be told, so was she. For a brief moment, she forgot all about the battle raging outside, all about her friends and colleagues in the Eight, all about Marcus and his clear disappointment in her. She followed Hicks deeper into Edison's laboratory and marveled at the wondrous technology on display all around her.

"Come," he said, grabbing her hand again and making for the back of the room.

They reached the far wall, and in it lay a sturdy oak door, reinforced with thick iron bands. Hicks knelt and wiped his hand over the locking mechanism. It was the most elaborate lock Zarelda had ever seen. It was long like a dead bolt, but it had iron wheels with numbers on it. Hicks pulled a scrap of paper from his pocket and began rolling the wheels left to right.

"What ya doing?" she asked.

"Edison gave me a code number to open this door."

"Why? What's behind it?"

"A secret weapon, he said, one that will end this fight and put us in the good graces of Carpathian. We do that, he said, and everything we want will be ours."

Zarelda felt a sinking feeling grip her chest. She shook her head. "I don't know, Hicks. I don't think we should—"

Hicks rolled the last wheel into place, the door clicked, and he pulled it open. "Come on, girl, let's do this now. Let's become famous."

She followed him in. It was dark, but Hicks seemed to know right where a lantern lay. He took it, pushed a button on its side three times, and the RJ inside lit the mantel pure white. The room illuminated, and in the center of it lay a monstrosity like nothing Zarelda had ever seen.

It was a spider. No, it was a half-spider, half-man construct. At least seven feet tall, but its mechanical legs, four in total, were curled up beneath it as if it were sleeping. The creature's chest and shoulders atop the iron torso lay limp like a wilted flower, its eyes closed, its arms dangling at its side. There were no guns affixed to its frame, but there were hard points where weapons could be mounted if desired. Its entire chassis filled the storage room end to end.

Hicks beamed in the lantern light. "This is it."

"Dis thing? What da hell can we do with dis?"

Hicks pulled another piece of paper from his coat pocket and unraveled it. "Edison gave me a code to put into its carriage. And then I'm supposed to control it. He also gave me some commands."

As he opened the storage door, Hicks knelt and shuffled beneath the mighty creature. He popped open a small compartment on the thing's undercarriage and rolled numbers once again into place. First, nothing happened; but then a red glow stirred in its belly. RJ then coursed through tubes to its torso, and it lurched, first forward, then back. It lurched again. Hicks fell back. Then it stood straight up, its torso coming to life, but its chest and face stayed dark and unresponsive.

Hicks stood, clapped two times, and then said, "Awake!"

The eyes on the construct's head opened, glowing red. A whirling noise came out of its mouth. It turned its gaunt face and looked square into Hicks's eyes. Hicks smiled. "Genius," he whispered, and then looked back at the paper.

"45267," he said.

"What da hell was dat for?" Zarelda asked.

"It's a code that's supposed to imprint my voice into its brain. Once it does this, it will—"

One of the spider's legs shot up and impaled itself through Hicks's shoulder. He screamed. "Stop! Stop! Halt!"

Zarelda raised her repeater and tried to fire, but another leg activated and pushed her back through the door. Her shot went wide, peppering the ceiling and causing little damage.

She scrambled to her feet, but the beast smashed through the wall, with Hicks still stuck on its leg. His screams were terrifying, the blood pouring down his chest as he tried pulling himself off the sharp blades of the leg. Zarelda scrambled back and fired, hitting the creature in the chest, but it didn't seem to do any good. It pushed itself through the rubble it had made of the wall and worked itself toward her, dragging Hicks along. Zarelda fired again, but her bullets ricocheted off its iron casing.

Betrayed! Edison had betrayed them. She should have known that this would happen, should have told Marcus the truth from the beginning. About Hicks, about Jake, about everything. Now her husband dangled on the end of a sharp spider arm, and what could she do about it? She tried. She flung herself at her husband, dodging a slashing leg move from the beast. She reached for his shoulders, tried pulling Hicks free, but the construct was too fast, too agile with those mechanical legs. It pulled Hicks away from her and shoved her aside like garbage. She hit a workbench hard, and a pile of gears and pistons fell atop her. The beast stabbed its legs through the pile, trying desperately to impale her as well. But Zarelda was too fast. She shot up through the pile, striking it with several rounds. One of its legs crumpled, but still it stabbed and slashed. She rolled again and found a way out.

"Help me, Z! Help me!"

Hicks's voice was almost too much to bear. Like a little child's, pleading for his mother's help. She tried again, shooting then moving to reach Hicks once more. Even with a damaged leg, it was too fast, too responsive. It slashed at her again, this time catching her flesh and tearing a gash into her right shoulder. She jumped away and tried once more to grab her husband. This time, it cut her left shoulder, more deeply than the other.

Zarelda emptied her rifle into its torso. Half the bullets flew past it harmlessly; the other half ricocheted off the iron as it spun to deflect the shots.

It's over. She knew this. There was nothing more she could do. The construct was too fast, too quick. She felt a tear drop from her eye. She turned and ran to the stairs.

"Don't leave me!" Hicks screamed as the spider thing pinned him to the ground and began scraping his back, cutting away his coveralls and undershirt. "Help me!"

I can't save you. She paused on the stairs and looked back. The beast was stabbing her husband in the arms and legs, piercing his flesh and letting him linger in agony, letting him bleed out on the floor. *I can't save you,* she said again to herself as she raised her rifle and aimed it at her husband's forehead. *But I can give you peace.*

"Goodbye, my love," she said through tears.

She pulled the trigger.

Chapter 21

Marcus ducked as the two-headed animation struck out again with its circular saws. The saws cut through a piece of rail track with a shower of colorful sparks like fireworks. Some hit the nape of his neck, singeing skin and causing him to wince while scrambling for cover. He had already put three shots square into the beast, and yet it kept coming, angry as hell, with RJ-bleeding wounds and all. It didn't seem to feel pain, and Marcus had never known anything to withstand that much firepower and keep coming. Not from his pistol anyway. He'd tried drawing his sword, but the beast seemed to understand the attempt and kept him occupied, kept him moving from cover to cover.

Sierra and the others were engaged in their own pitched battles, with scores upon scores of animated and real citizens of the town filling the air with buckets of lead. The number of bodies streaming through the gap in the barrier that Jake had made seemed endless. But the wild southerner was having fun blowing them back with Edison's phonic blaster, thus keeping their position from being overrun. Marcus could tell, however, that the machine was beginning to weigh heavily on Jake. His back was drooping, his arms falling on occasion to his side. Marcus had tried to go over to help out, but the four-armed monster would not let up. Sierra had tried standing ground with her captain, but Marcus had sent her off to defend River and K-Free from the onslaught of another monster, this one holding back at range and pounding the protective debris with Gatling fire from a hand-held barrel belt-fed from a large wooden crate on its back.

How many of these damned things does Carpathian have? How long could they hold out? And where were Hicks and Zarelda? If they had not deserted them, their position would be much, much better, and they could create a gap in the attack that would allow them to move forward and seek the doctor.

And to that end, where was Carpathian? He had not shown himself yet in the fight, content obviously to sit behind his thick walls and observe, letting his minions do his dirty work for them. Was he observing? Surely he was aware of the fight. There was too much firepower being expended, too much shouting, too much debris and smoke in the air for anyone within miles not to know that a battle was raging. So where was he? The Eight had come here to find him and kill him, and they had fallen into just holding on. Something needed to change fast. They just needed a moment's peace to break from their defensive positions and move forward. Marcus had learned long ago in the war that if a unit was not moving forward, it was moving backward, and wars were not won by armies falling back.

"Sun!" Sierra cried over the rattle of gunfire.

Marcus looked to where she was pointing, and there he was, coming out of a building with The Wraith close behind, and another man that Marcus did not recognize at first, and then it hit him. "Carl. What the hell is that son of a bitch doing here?"

Sun saw Marcus and ran across the yard, impervious to the gunfire pounding all around him. He was like a mindless beast, determined to plow his way through the on-coming animations, stabbing a few as he went with what Marcus assumed was an old bayonet. River then saw her brother and tried pulling herself out from behind her cover, but K-Free held her back. Marcus motioned for her to stay put as he dodged a strike from the creature's whirling drill. The beast was clearly growing anxious with its inability to land a serious blow, and it struck again, and again, until its drill wedged between a steel beam and a large chunk of granite. The blade whirled uselessly, and Marcus took his shot.

He drew his sword and stepped up in front of the beast. It tried knocking him back with its saw. Marcus swung his blade, all popping and snapping with visceral energy, and took off the creature's saw arm with one mighty stroke, sending stump and saw through the air to land harmlessly a few feet away. Its heads roared and it tried to raise its flamethrower. A feeble stream of super-heated RJ burst from its barrel, but Marcus was able to dodge it easily, swing upward, and cut the weapon in half. The RJ within its casing splashed onto the beast's chest and face, burning metal and flesh together. The creature howled but Marcus did not relent. He raised his sword in both hands above his head, aimed the blade at the massive chest, then drove it through the armor and out its back. The beast stopped screaming and moving, stood there jerking and kicking as if had a short-circuit. It turned its heads toward Marcus, stared through him. Marcus smiled, winked, put his boot onto its chest, and pushed it back, letting the blade slide back out. The creature toppled down the rubble, its two tiny heads smashing on the hard yard ground.

Sun jumped over the beast and appeared at Marcus's side. "Nice kill."

Marcus smiled and patted the warrior on his shoulder. "Damn good to see you, old friend."

He was about to say something else when a small boy appeared at his side. In all the commotion, Marcus hadn't noticed him until now.

"This is Careless Fox," Sun introduced. "I freed him. But more importantly right now, do you have it? My pistol?"

Marcus checked the holster at the small of his back. Secure and fully loaded. "Yes, now stow that boy somewhere safe, or he'll be dead, sure as shooting."

"I can fight!" the boy cried.

"I like your spirit, young warrior, but this is no time for little boys with more gumption than brawn. Sun, hide him, then go help your sister."

Sun nodded and pulled the boy away, and now that the four-armed monster was dead, Marcus took a moment to survey the field.

The arrival of The Wraith and his entourage had forced the animations to split their assault. The Wraith looked like he was having the time of his life. He stood there like steel, screaming obscenities at constructs as they moved forward trying to get close, putting slug after slug into their heads and chests. Carl was doing his best with an old musket, but it was clear to Marcus that the man wanted to find his own weapons; he seemed almost naked as he held the matchlock against his shoulder. The thought of handing Carl's weapons back over to him ran a chill down Marcus's spine. Would it be prudent to do so? Would Carl hold a grudge for the way they had left him at the mine? If it had been Marcus that had been left like that, he certainly would have held a grudge and would, without question, seek vengeance. He had made a mistake. It was clear now that the man with the red hand had always been Hicks, but the thought of Zarelda being a part of that deception... that had struck him hard. If the circumstances were not so dire, he would have gone after them and killed them with his own hands. They had betrayed him, but more importantly, they had betrayed the Wayward Eight. Could he find the courage to forgive them someday, if they all got out of this alive? And would Carl forgive him? He didn't need Carl's forgiveness, nor was he inclined to ask for it. Right now what he needed from the man was his powerful weapons. He was the only person present who had used the glove before, and Marcus needed those deadly results here and now.

Marcus climbed out from behind his cover and raced over to K-Free's abandoned Iron Horse. It was surrounded by Payson citizens who were using it for protection while firing at Tanner and the Ladue women who had found cover behind a pile of iron castings. Marcus laid into them, sweeping the air with two short, swift flicks of the wrist. His blade cut three in half immediately, stuck halfway into a fourth. He yanked it out and finished the man off with a strike to the head.

He dove beneath the vehicle and flicked open the storage compartment of the central chassis where Carl's weapons had been safely stored for the assault. Within lay a leather bag. He pulled it out and scrambled back to cover, avoiding shots as they buzzed over his head and erupted against piles of concrete.

He caught his breath and then surveyed the yard once more. Now, all he needed to do was to get across it, find Carl, and return his weapons. From his vantage point, The Wraith was visible, and certainly Carl was over with him somewhere, assuming he hadn't already been shot down. Marcus found Sierra and waved her over. He drew his hand cannon and covered her while she crawled to his position.

"How you doing?" he asked her as she came up beside him.

"We're running out of ammo, Captain. We can't hold on much longer."

He nodded. He hefted the bag. "I got to get these to Carl."

"Carl? Carl Fredrickson? Where the hell is he?"

He pointed to where The Wraith had set up shop. "Over there somewhere. Came in with Robert, I reckon. You cover me while I run these weapons over to him."

Sierra shook her head. "No, you got the better pistol and more rounds. Plus, if your knee gives out in mid-run, we're dead." She took the bag away from him. "You cover me."

Marcus was about to protest, but saw the resolve in her eyes. She wasn't going to argue, and they had no time for it anyway. "Okay. Go."

She ran. He pulled his pistol and downed one, two, three constructs as they turned their attention and rifled arms toward Sierra as she raced past them. She was faster than he imagined, especially for one in a dress with armored accouterments specially modified for field operations; he was sure the hastily repaired heel on her boot didn't help matters either. And she didn't hesitate to point her atomic pistol and lay waste to three Payson citizens, who now lay in the hard dirt with sucking chest wounds that festered with radiation poisoning. Marcus couldn't help but smile. Sierra was good, very good, and not afraid to take risks; it was, after all, why he considered her just as much second-in-command as Jake.

The one animation that troubled him, however, was the creature with the Gatling gun. It had cleverly sat back from the main assault and had full range of the entire yard. It turned its gun toward Sierra and opened fire. Marcus responded by firing three quick rounds toward it. One round ricocheted off its Gatling and forced it to spray bullets into construct reinforcements which had just arrived from deep inside the canyon. This gave Sierra just enough time to reach The Wraith and toss the bag to Carl. She went down into the dirt, sliding into cover, aiming her pistol, and taking two more down with terrible wounds.

It didn't take long for Carl to come out from behind his cover. First, Marcus saw the man's rail pistol take out four Payson citizens in a row, one after the other, the velocity of the round tearing through four separate chests. Then his glove came out, and a large portal opened. He stepped through it and out again ten feet away. He fired more rounds and another line of citizens fell. He did this again, but this time on constructs that he forced into the portal and then to reappear in front of The Wraith, who then promptly blew their heads off with aimed fire slugs.

The sudden force of Carl's attack, plus The Wraith's and Sierra's continued assault, shifted Carpathian's mob to the left, which gave River and K-Free ample targets to shoot. Marcus smiled. Things were looking up. Now all he needed to do was to help out Jake.

He turned just in time to scream, "Jake, look out!" and see Sasha Tanner leap onto the man's back and slash at the phonic blaster with whirling blades.

*****

Jake had but a second to hear Marcus call to him, then try to turn to meet Sasha's attack. He failed, and the European journeyman crashed into his back and ripped apart the phonic blaster. It peeled off Jake's back like a piece of dead skin and hit the ground, snapping in half. The device made one last bleating screech, then died altogether. Jake followed it to the ground, his face and neck scraping along the rough clay and gravel. But Sasha clearly did not anticipate the inertia of the attack, and he went flying through the narrow passageway of the destroyed barrier and collided with a group of citizens. He struck them hard, his blade reaching out to slash some of them in half. Jake managed to gather himself, shrug off the pain in his jaw, draw his Grandfather pistols, and fire. But Sasha was too fast to be struck. Instead, the powerful slugs from his pistols shattered a Payson man where he stood and ended the life of two others.

"I'm going to kill you," Sasha said, rolling through the people and coming up facing Jake. "You have cost me everything, Jake. Time and position. I could have gotten here first. I could have killed Carpathian and been gone before the sunrise. Now, look at it. A bloody mess!"

"This ain't no time to settle scores, Sasha," Jake said, surprised to find himself trying to speak reason. Usually in a situation like this, his adrenaline would kick in, and he'd go after the one that had given offense, but he felt a kind of serenity, as if something or someone was holding him back.

He didn't have a headache, which surprised him, nor were there any voices or thoughts tickling the back of his head. Perhaps it was the loss of the phonic blaster that had settled his mind; having it on and firing it had been most gratifying, as if he were playing some fancy symphony while watching wave after wave of Carpathian's goons melt away at the tremendous sound waves. But it was gone, and Sasha's blades were real.

They sprang from his forearms, reaching out through the deadly space for Jake's throat. Jake put up his arm and took a slice across the wrist. He howled and fought to keep hold of his pistol. He fired, but Sasha was too swift, already running at full speed toward him. Jake fired again, and this time, he found meat.

Sasha back-pedaled as the bullet from Jake's Grandfather pistol struck his shoulder and came out the other end with a splash of blood. The impact nearly rocked him off his feet, but he found support against a shard of granite, shrugged off the shot, and kept coming. Jake fired again, but this time the shot was deflected by one of Sasha's blades. Sasha took Jake to the ground with his healthy shoulder. Jake tried pressing a pistol into Sasha's stomach, but the man was too strong, too fast, even wounded, to allow enough time to aim. The shot went long, and Jake found his face being pressed into the ground, Sasha's hands around his throat.

"Choke!" Sasha screamed. "Choke!"

Jake dropped his pistol and slowly, painfully, pulled his knife. He gripped it hard, turned the blade inward, and began stabbing Sasha in the side. One, two, three deep thrusts, but nothing seemed to subdue the man. There was a wildness in his eyes, a madness that Jake could not fathom. Then Sasha's eyes turned red, much like the eyes of the Pinkerton man at the barn in Kentucky. Jake gasped for air as the fingers around his throat dug deeper and deeper. He kept stabbing the European, but nothing seemed to move him. Jake tried to breathe, but the air would not come, and slowly his chest began to ache, his eyes began to close. *I'm going to die... I'm going to die...*

Then Sasha was torn off of him, as if a tornado had touched down and yanked him from the earth. Jake opened his eye and saw a massive figure standing over him, gripping Sasha by the throat. Jake scrambled away just in time before the creature's large spiked boot struck the ground. It was the creation with the Gatling gun for an arm; it had come out of hiding and had taken position in the rubble. And now it stood there, blocking the rising sun, holding Sasha up like an offering to the gods. Sasha struggled to free himself, tried cutting into the beast's arm, all the way to the bone. The creature opened its steel jaw and growled like an African gorilla, then shoved its gun into Sasha's chest and opened fire.

Sasha shook like a rag doll against the bullets as they ripped through his body. Jake couldn't bear to see what was happening. Sasha was a right son of a bitch, but no one deserved to die this way. The beast kept firing until Sasha's body split in two, the force of the bullets ripping him in half. Jake moved to keep Sasha's discarded legs from hitting him. The creature finally stopped firing, held Sasha's remains like a bouquet of flowers, and then flung them over the barrier.

Jake didn't hesitate. He climbed to his feet, raised both pistols and fired them point blank at the creation. One clicked empty; the other hit the beast's chest plate and ricocheted away. That got its attention. It turned, screamed, and then tried to fire.

Marcus's sword cut through the ammo belt on the Gatling gun, severing its bullet supply. He then swung upward and cut the Gatling's barrel in half. The creature fell over the debris, roared in pain as if it had actually been wounded. It rolled and rolled across shards of granite and steel, whimpering like a lame dog. Jake wanted to fire, but the display was almost comical. He couldn't pull the trigger. Marcus too just stood there, amazed at the beast as it contorted itself in many disgusting, hideous ways to try to get away. When it finally found solid ground, it rolled twice then sprang free and ran through the animated horde.

Bullets again hit the debris around Jake.

"We can't stay here," Marcus said, coming down beside Jake to keep from getting hit. "We've lost this position. Too many coming in from Payson."

"I'm sorry, boss," Jake said, holding his wrist and letting fresh blood drip through his fingers. "I'm hurt bad. Arm may be broke."

Marcus checked it quickly. "Thankfully, no, but damn you're bleeding hard! We've got to move. Can you walk?"

Jake nodded, then Marcus whistled loudly to catch River's attention. She, Sun, and K-Free were holding position about thirty feet away, still throwing rounds into the on-coming construct mob.

Marcus motioned toward The Wraith's position. "We leave here, go toward Carl. We'll reestablish our defense there."

"He ain't gonna like it, boss," Jake said, coughing.

"I don't care what he likes," Marcus said, helping Jake to his feet. "This is a matter of life and death. It's our life I care about. We'll kill him if he tries to stand in our way. Now… Go!"

Together they ran toward Carl's position, firing as they went.

*****

He hadn't had this much fun since the Civil War. Nothing better than putting slugs in on-coming attackers, like he had done at the Battle of Fredericksburg – only then it was with a percussion cap musket. One, two, three fire rounds into three unfortunate constructs. One, two, three into three more, then he watched as their bodies burned. His Mexicans had skedaddled or had all died. He did not know; he did not care. He stood his ground, behind a tall iron crate, turning the cylinder of his shotgun and striking one terrible creature after another. His arms bled, his face was cut and swollen in places, his left eye nearly shut by a shard of rock that had hit him in the initial firefight. Did any of this matter? No. Not to Robert "The Wraith Gunter.

"Die, you monstrous son of a bitch!" he screamed at the exploding head of a construct that had gotten closer than he wanted. "Meet your mother in Hell!"

Reloading, he let two get too close and had to knock them away with the butt of his gun. One drove its chainsaw arm into his thigh. Legging and flesh ripped away. The Wraith gnashed his teeth and took the pain, gouged the animation's eye out with his knife. The other dove at him with open blades.

He ducked, kicked out with his boot, and sent it flying into the iron crate. Its head popped open like a fat tick.

Carl was suddenly at his side.

"It's Marie's Heights all over again," The Wraith said, locking the cylinder into place and firing them up once again. "Shootin' fish in a barrel."

"Let's get out of here," Carl said, training his rail pistol into the undead horde and dropping another line of animations. "We can't keep this up. They're going to overrun us soon enough."

"Where are your balls, Carl?" The Wraith cackled. "You leave them in the mine?"

"I'm exhausted, damn you, and I'm running out of ammo. I didn't come here to kill the whole goddamned Carpathian army. Hell, I didn't plan to come here at all. And look at you. You're bleeding like a stuck pig. How long you gonna hold up with all those wounds?"

"You old softy. When did you start caring so much about me?"

Carl shook his head, used his glove to drive two animations into the iron box. They dissolved into an ugly smear of gory red. "This ain't about you, dammit! It's about preserving our tactical options. Did you learn nothing in the war? We're beat. We can do this all day, and they'll keep coming. And where does that leave us? Dead, with no option to return again someday when the odds are in our favor. Marie's Heights, yes… but there, you knew that the Union had a finite number of men to throw at that wall. We have no idea how many of these things he's got, and that's not counting Payson townsfolk. We're licked, Wraith. Be a man and admit it."

Admit it… hell! Maybe Carl hadn't come all this way to tussle with the Enlightened army, but The Wraith sure as hell had; and there was a big reward waiting at the end of a decapitated mad doctor. All he needed was to break that horde coming at their position, and then he'd make his move to the structure behind them, the one built right into the wall of the canyon, the one that this evil dead mob was protecting.

"You do what you have to do, Carl," The Wraith said, cycling his last remaining fire rounds into place. "I'm gonna kill a foreign devil."

Carl cursed something, but turned and tried to sprint away from their position. The Wraith turned back to the horde, but then heard a loud '*thunk!*' behind him. He fired another slug then turned to see what had happened.

Carl lay on the ground, knocked cold. A woman, badly battered and spattered with mud and blood, stood over him holding an iron pipe and a Union blaster. Though she was disheveled and wobbled on weak legs, he knew her immediately.

"Ladue!"

"So, you recognize my *ressemblé* to my sister, eh?" she asked, keeping the blaster barrel high and tight against his sweaty forehead.

"I don't know why the hell you're here, Desiree, but this is no time for arguments. Back off. I have a job to do."

"Your job is to die for *assassinat ma sœur*."

"You don't know anything about what happened. You weren't there. It was a mercy killing, and that's the truth. I don't have time to discuss it." He threw a glance at the animated mob lurching its way forward, trying to keep his head low and out of the barrage of gunfire hitting their location. "My job is to kill Carpathian. Now, step aside before you get hurt."

As he said it, she fired, but the hammer arm of the massive beast that had assaulted them inside the warehouse came sweeping into view and knocked her through the air, surely breaking ribs and throwing her twenty feet away. She hit a post and fell limp to the ground. The creature ignored Carl, stepped over him and moved toward The Wraith.

The Wraith took a grazing shot from the mob that tore a deep gash into his forehead. But he was alive and he raised his shotgun to fire. The creature's sniveling little handler shot a gout of RJ from his staff that covered the shotgun, forcing him to drop it. The Wraith watched as his favorite weapon burst into flames and crumpled to ash. He drew a UR-30 blaster, but it was easily knocked from his grasp as the hammer swept through the space between them and struck his wrist square. His bones shattered.

It's over! He knew this now, and perhaps Carl had been right. His stubborn pride, his blind fury to complete the mission at all costs, had left him nearly weaponless and with a broken wrist to boot. And now this beast stood over him, blotting out the sun, raising both hammers to end it once and for all. The Wraith tried drawing his last blaster, but couldn't muster the strength to pull the trigger.

Bullets peppered the beast's side, and it fell back, wounded severely, but still able to react to its handler's orders. The Wraith looked up and saw Marcus and his gang moving to take his position. Marcus flew through the air, a shadow against hot sunlight. He drove his sword through one of the hammers, severing it at the beast's elbow. Its handler tried to react, but gunfire from Sierra and Sun Totem forced him to flee into the building that he had come out of. His beast did the same, screaming like a wounded wolverine. They were gone, and in their place were Marcus and the rest, pouring fire into the horde that never seemed to subside.

Hands grabbed the lapels of his coat and pulled him up. "You got ten seconds to gather yourself and get," Marcus said, "or I guarantee you're gonna die. We'll give you cover. Now, go. And take Carl with you."

He had almost forgotten the big lug, lying face down in the dirt, still out cold. Desiree had popped him good. The Wraith could see the gash on the back of the man's head. *He could be dead*, he thought, scrambling to his feet and grabbing his knocked-aside blaster with his damaged hand. It hurt like hell, but he'd be damned to escape this chaos without firepower.

"I'll see you again, Marcus," The Wraith said, holstering his pistols and taking hold of Carl's collar. "And *I* won't be so generous."

Marcus ignored him and turned to the animated horde.

Pulling Carl along, he moved behind Marcus's gang, letting their defense shield his retreat. He moved slowly toward the debris, saw an avenue of departure through the broken barrier that did not contain Payson citizens firing their weapons. He turned toward that place.

He stepped over Desiree Ladue's broken body. He paused. *I should leave her here... no good, useless bi—*.

He sighed and grabbed her boot with his broken hand. The pain was excruciating, but he bore it and pulled her along as well, shaking his head and pledging to make changes in his life when he got out of here… If he got out of here.

"From here on out," he said as his pulled their limp bodies out of the canyon and into safety, "I'm gonna stop caring so much about people."

Chapter 22

Marcus spotted her through the corner of his eye. Zarelda, moving fast from the depths of the building in which she and Hicks had fled. Hicks was not with her.

Some kind of gangly spider thing followed her, but her focus was on their position. She lay on the trigger of her mini-repeater, blowing huge radiated gaps through the mass of Payson citizens which had breached the debris field and had taken control of their old position. Marcus threw a few bullets her way to help clear her path. He sighed, looking at the damage that he had done to help her, and then seeing how quickly the gaps recovered as an endless stream of constructs and citizens poured in.

Zarelda jumped over their defensive position. She slid into place next to Marcus. "Where's Hicks?" He asked curtly. *Where did you both go? Why did you betray us?* Those were the questions he wanted to ask, but held his tongue.

"He's dead!" She shouted, reloading her rifle and getting herself into position to fire. Her face was raw; he now noticed she had been sobbing. "He's dead, you see! Are you happy about dat?"

He didn't know what to say. Was he happy about Hicks's death? No, not at all. Was he happy with their actions that had led to his mechanic's demise? Even less. But there was no time to argue or to bicker about it. The horde was closing in, and he and his people were running out of time.

"Shut up and fire," he said to her. He pointed right down the middle of the mob. "Give me a lane of approach right through there." He assumed that her ammunition supply was greater than all the rest. She might be the only one that could bring to bear the kind of firepower that they needed right now to finish this job. *How ironic*, he thought. *The accomplice to the traitor may be the only one to save us in the end*.

Zarelda rose and fired through the mass. In a shower of flesh, wood, iron springs, and sprockets, the animated army divided like the Red Sea. It was almost divine, Marcus thought, seeing the sheer beauty of the assault. He marveled in it, remembering Robert E Lee's famous line… *It is well that war is so terrible, lest we grow too fond of it*. Those were true words, but in the current situation, there was no other way around the sheer volume of the dead that lay all over the canyon yard. They had to expend all ammunition in this manner, for the location of his next move lay far behind the horde.

The head and face of a large man popped out of the iron door in the canyon wall. Marcus had never seen this man before; he had not been part of the battle. And why he took a look outside wasn't clear. Perhaps he was surveying the carnage; perhaps he was checking the weather. It didn't matter, really, for Marcus knew what lay behind that door, what that man was protecting.

"River!" Marcus called, waving her over.

She came over crouching, her mood and enthusiasm for their assault rekindled by the reappearance of her brother. There was almost joy on her face, a red sheer of excitement, euphoric in its nature. He had seen that look before, when she anticipated having to use her blades in battle. He did not disappoint her.

"I need to get to that door," he said, pointing through the gap that was closing quickly. "I need your help. Can you cut me through?"

She nodded, threw down her blaster, and drew her blades. He patted her shoulder. "Stay close."

Zarelda, Sierra, K-Free, Jake, and Sun turned their guns toward the gap and fired everything they had. Whole lines were devoured as the bullets of fire and radiation slammed into them.

Marcus jumped out of cover. River followed. They shot through the gap, running at full speed, lopping heads, stabbing necks, causing the horde to pulse to the left like a flock of sparrows fleeing the crows. The spider creation had rambled into the crowd and was trying to step delicately, as if it were under inherent orders to protect Carpathian's lesser creatures. But its awkward way of movement inevitably forced its sharp legs to pierce its smaller brethren. Marcus couldn't help but chuckle inside. The good doctor had created too many constructs, too many bodies that were impossible to avoid.

They reached the door. Marcus tried the latch. Solid and immovable, through wrought iron and old oak. He pressed his shoulder into it. Nothing. He pushed again. The same.

"Back," he said to River, pushing her away. He raised his sword and drove it into the door.

A foul smoke rose from the blade as it cut and burnt its way through the lock. He pulled the blade back out, put it back in, carving as he went, until the lock on the door fell inward, severed from the door.

He pushed it in with his boot.

Inside was a foyer of sorts, lit only by RJ casks on the crudely cut walls. Near the back of the room stood the man, inside a smaller room the size of a large closet with double-doors. He smiled maniacally, almost in taunt as Marcus ran toward him. The doors of the closet the man stood in began to close. River tried to race past Marcus. He put up his arm and barred her way. He pushed her aside.

"Sorry, River," he said, putting his shoulder forward and taking large steps. "This is my fight."

Marcus leapt through the doors just before they closed, and slammed into the chest of the waiting man.

*****

The man was solid, like iron, and Marcus bounced off his armored chest plate and nearly fell to the floor. But he caught himself in time to duck a swipe from the man's gauntleted fist which contained a knife. Judging from the liquid dripping from its sharp edge, Marcus wanted none of it. The good news was the closet was too small for such activity. In the man's haste to try and stop this invader, the blade impaled and caught on the wall.

The closet shook and then ascended; that's what it felt like to Marcus. They were moving up, faster than he could imagine a closet moving. *How* was it moving? Another new technology by Carpathian, no doubt. Where they were going was unclear, as there were no windows for him to see through. It didn't matter. It could rise all the way to the moon for all he cared. As long as at the end, he'd find Carpathian.

The man tried pulling the blade out, and Marcus took this time to drive his fist across the man's face, and then followed it up with a swift kick to the back of his leg. The man groaned and fell. Marcus wanted to finish him off with a slice from his sword, but the closet was just too small for an effective swing, nor was he willing to draw his pistol and shoot. Such a high-speed bullet would clear the man's body and go through the wall, and what havoc would that cause? Marcus certainly didn't want this moving closet to fall. If they were going up, it was best to keep going until the closet stopped.

Instead, he punched again and again, until the man's cheek was black and puffy like a rotten plum. The man could not take much more; he fell over to the wobbling floor and tried to speak. Marcus knocked him cold with a short, sharp kick with his boot.

The closet jerked to a halt, and the door opened. Only part of the way, and it opened seemingly between floors, as if their brief but violent exchange had shook the closet so much that it broke down. Marcus turned to the opening door. Subdued light emanated from the top part of the opening, like the flickering of a candle or an RJ source. Marcus tried pushing down on the floor, as if his strength alone could propel the closet to move up enough for him to step off easily. It was too heavy to budge. He sighed, glanced once more at the armored lump on the floor to ensure that he was not going to suddenly awake, then pulled himself up and out through the gap.

The room he pulled himself into was cold and dark, save for a few candles and a dimly-lit RJ lantern. There was smoke in the air from a cigar. At the far end of the room, etched into the rock, lay an unlit fireplace with a crenellated iron mantle. The only other things Marcus could see were shapes of various pieces of furniture: a chair, a table, a desk. Curtains covered a long, curving window that clearly looked cut over the canyon yard. Marcus could hear the sounds of battle below. The fight still raged.

He turned again to the closet suspended between floors. He could now see that there were thick cables and wheels attached to the top of it, and they clearly were holding it from falling. Marcus looked again into the closet; the man still lay there, but he was stirring. Marcus drew his sword and cut the cables in half.

It plummeted, down and down it went, until with a puff of dust, hit the bottom floor and shook the room in which he stood. Marcus looked over the edge of the shaft that had held the closet. He smiled. *One problem solved.*

He heard the flick of a lighter. He drew his pistol, turned, and saw a shadow of a man near the far corner, sitting on a simple wooden chair. The man raised the lighter to his cigar and drew deeply, letting a waft of smoke drift through the dark room.

"Congratulations, whoever you are," a voice said, a voice heavy with a European accent. "You have just sent Vlad Ursul to his death."

"Unlikely," Marcus said, stepping forward to get a better view of the man. "His armor will protect him."

"Perhaps so." The man chuckled and stood, pulling strongly from his cigar, and stepping into better light. Marcus saw his face clearly.

"Carpathian."

The name came out of Marcus's mouth before he realized what he had said. It was obvious. From the descriptions that he had heard, and from the man's deep accent, it could be no other. The doctor was not as tall as he had expected; reality and legend clashing indeed. But he stood steady on metal legs, and his wine-colored vest, golden chain, and black duster had that distinct air of European pretension that he had seen in Sasha Tanner's clothing. Carpathian also had metal hands. His face was scarred but covered neatly in a thick salt-and-pepper mustache and beard that rested below an eye piece that glowed RJ red. Atop his head stood a short black hat. He wore an amiable grin.

"I am Captain Marcus Wayward of the Wayward Eight." Marcus drew his sword and let its energy brighten the room. "And you won't leave this building alive."

The doctor stood still, drew one last puff from his cigar, and then dropped it to his hardwood floor. He stamped it out and smiled again. "There have been many people, some better than you, who have tried to kill me, my good man. They have all failed. What makes you think you are the one to finally succeed?"

It was Marcus's turn to smile. "Because I'm the best."

Carpathian nodded. "Is that so? Well, young man, let's put that to the test, shall we?"

Before he could even flick his sword, Carpathian slammed out with his fist and connected against Marcus's chest, propelling him through the room and into a small table with a vase of yellow flowers. The speed of the attack almost knocked his sword from his hand, but he was holding it with his right hand, the one not broken in the war. He held it tightly and braced against the shattered table. The wind was knocked out of him, but there were no broken ribs. His armored chest plate had protected him from severe damage.

Marcus gasped for air and rolled out of the way as Carpathian came at him again with stomping steel boots. *Slam slam slam!* Over and over Marcus rolled, and again and again Carpathian hammered with his legs, trying to find flesh, bone, anything to crush under the violent attack. Marcus rolled and managed to slide his hand cannon out of its holster. He came to a stop on his back, raised the barrel, and fired.

The shot tore Carpathian from his feet, and propelled him through the air much like his attack on Marcus had just accomplished. But there was no penetration of the bullet; Carpathian had armor beneath that fancy vest. The shot gave Marcus time, however, to rise to his feet and fire again.

Shot after shot found empty space as the doctor, on his steel legs, ducked and dodged faster than anyone Marcus had ever seen. The man was lightning fast, moving from cover to cover, foiling every aim and shot until the furniture in the room lay tattered, broken, rippled with bullet holes. Marcus fired his last shot, cursed, and tossed the gun away.

He raised his sword and went after the doctor, who now stood strong in the center of the room. Marcus leaned in and swung the blade. Carpathian knocked it aside. He swung again, found a little meat, and blood spattered through the air. That moved the European devil a little to the left. He tried pulling a pistol. Marcus cut it in half, but got a little too close in the swing, and another steel fist reached out and grabbed his coat.

With one mighty thrust, Carpathian flung Marcus through the air. The mercenary tried gathering himself, tried bracing for whatever he was going to hit.

He struck the center of the curtained window, and the entire glass structure collapsed outward in a spray of shards that cascaded down the outside wall of the tower. Marcus expected to fall with it, but the curtain caught on the broken glass and held him suspended in the air inside a cocoon of thick velvet, hanging half in and half out of the room. Light from outside flowed inward and Marcus held on for life.

He tried pulling himself up. Carpathian obliged him by grabbing his coat again and flinging him across the room in the other direction. Marcus hit the far wall, square. His sword fell out of his hand. He hit the floor hard, reached for his weapon, but Carpathian grabbed it up before he found the hilt.

Marcus crawled backward until he was leaning against the wall, blinded by the light streaming through the broken window. He shielded his eyes with a trembling hand, the one with the weak wrist. Both hands hurt, his knee ached, his head pounded. Even beneath his armor, his bones screamed in agony against skin that was clearly sore and bloody from so many impacts. *I have failed*, he said to himself, trying to reach out again for his sword. *I have failed.*

Carpathian kicked his arm down and stepped in close, grabbed Marcus's sword himself, and held it forward as if to strike. "Good try, Mr. Wayward. You and your people have gotten further in this deadly affair than anyone else, and have killed more of my charges than I could have imagined. In fact, you've set me back in my plans a goodly while, I'm sad to say. Congratulations. But it's time to bring this nonsense to a close. Time to put an end to your miserable little life."

Marcus coughed and spit ran down his face. He nodded. "You're right. You have won. But there is one more thing I'd like to say beforehand."

"What?"

Marcus reached behind his back and felt the grip of Sun's Ion Pistol. "Nobody touches my sword."

He pulled the pistol and fired into Carpathian's chest. The doctor shook at the impact of the ion round. He dropped the sword, stumbled back, tried getting control of his hands but his metal fingers flopped around like schools of fish on a beach. He tried sitting down, but his legs refused to yield to commands. Then, as suddenly as the wave struck him, his arms, legs, and back locked, and the red glow of his eye piece winked out. He stiffened and fell over like a broken barn slat.

Marcus did not move for a moment, letting the adrenaline in his veins subside and the aches in his bones lessen. Then, he climbed slowly to his feet, stretched his back, and hobbled over to his sword, favoring his weak left knee. He grabbed the sword and then walked over to the doctor. There the man lay, rigid as a corpse, save for his uncovered eye which was alive and darting around the room as if looking for an exit. For the first time since Marcus had faced Carpathian, he saw true fear in those foreign eyes.

He liked it.

He grabbed Carpathian up and dragged him to the broken window. "You're not as clever as you think you are." Marcus hoisted the stiff man over the window sill and held the top half of his body over the edge. "You should never let a stranger into your home without first checking him for hidden weapons."

"What are you going to do with me?" Carpathian asked.

Marcus was surprised that Carpathian could still talk, although the Ion Pistol was specifically meant to disrupt machinery and not flesh. For good measure, Marcus punched the doctor in the face with the hilt of his sword, leaving a blood mark across the man's cheek. He then raised the sword. "I'm gonna remove your head from your shoulders and let your body tumble to the ground. And all of your animations will witness this, and they will know that their king is dead."

It looked as if Carpathian was trying to nod. Instead, he spoke. "Okay, Mr. Wayward. You have me where you want. I'm yours to do as you wish. But before you strike that final blow, I beg you to look around. Look at the battle that rages below. Look at the weapons that your people wield. Look at the lanterns that burn in my home. Look at it all and tell me that it isn't a paradise that I have brought to your America."

"You have brought death and desolation to this country."

"On the contrary. It is a thing of beauty that I have brought to this country. Perhaps you do not see it, but look beyond the surface, Marcus Wayward. Look deep for the truth of it. RJ-1027 has changed the world and for the better. It has made the weak strong, and I can make them stronger. I can make your rebellion stronger. If I should fall today at your blade, what do you think will happen to your people, to your Confederacy?"

"How did you know I was a Southerner?"

"The twang in your voice gives it away," Carpathian said, a wry smile on his thin lips. "Only I stand in the way of the Union and total annihilation of the south. If I fall, the Union and their puppet scientists like Tesla will destroy the people you admire and respect. It has already begun, and you know what I'm talking about, don't you?"

Marcus saw the truth in it, remembering back to their run-in with Tesla in the Midlands. It seemed so obvious now, looking deep into Carpathian's dark red eyes, eyes that had just a moment ago been clear and shallow. Of course, Lincoln wanted the doctor dead. Of course, the Union wanted him dead. Getting rid of him would remove a large barrier from their designs on the south. Getting rid of Carpathian would guarantee the Union's continued control of America. And once the Confederacy fell, then so too would the Warrior Nation. Marcus saw the entire thing play out in Carpathian's blood red eyes.

"You're smart enough not to fear me and my creations, Marcus. The power and energy that I have gifted to the world are the way of the future, and a man like you stands to profit from this more than any other. In truth, my death will spell the end of you and Jake Mattia, Sierra Icarus, Kimberly Free, Sun Totem and Flowing River, and even Zarelda Kincade, the traitor that she is. So, the decision is in your hands. You can take my head off and let my corpse fall, or you can pull me up and hear what the future has to offer the Wayward Eight, or should I say seven?"

Marcus looked out at the battle still going strong in the yard below. It was funny that no one down there was even paying attention to what was happening above them, as if they were oblivious that their messiah was mere feet from death. Marcus looked back into

Carpathian's eyes, and once again, the future rolled through those strong currents of red.

Marcus pulled Carpathian from the window and set him down gently on the floor. He sat down beside him. "Okay, doctor... Speak."

Chapter 23

Marcus walked down the back staircase from Carpathian's living quarters, holding a heavily laden satchel. He felt almost euphoric in the descent, as if suddenly all the pieces of the puzzle, all the pieces of a chess match, had moved into place. It didn't matter anymore what Lincoln or the Union or anyone else wanted. All that mattered was what he wanted, and what it meant for his team as a whole.

He stepped out of the building and into the canyon yard. It was quiet. The fighting had stopped, although the ground was littered with the dead. Scores, perhaps hundreds of bodies, lay everywhere, a testament to the strength and perseverance of his team. But even the bodies did not matter anymore. What mattered was the new mission that he had been assigned.

He found them where he had left them. Even River had made her way back from the building and to her defensive position beside her brother. They were all there exhaustion gripping their faces, concern and confusion clouding their mind. Even the small warrior boy that Sun had freed from the dungeon. He had come out of hiding and was now standing beside River. Marcus stared at his metal hand and eye piece. They looked wonderful.

Jake was the first to talk. His voice wavered. "Hot damn, you're alive."

Marcus stopped in front of them. He smiled. "I am indeed."

"Did you kill him?" K-Free asked. She had received several cuts and bruises from the brawl. They all had, it seemed. But they were alive. All of them, except Hicks, of course, and no harm would come to them again in this place. All of Carpathian's creations and monsters stood silent and still all around, watching the group with cold, blank stares. It was as if someone had turned off the switch and ended the killing.

"He's… not a problem anymore."

"You got his head?" Jake asked.

"No. I have something better."

He dropped the bag and it exploded open. Gold and jewels and piles of money spilled out. Those with enough strength to gasp did so. Sierra knelt beside the bag and ran her hands through the wealth. "This has got to be, well, at least as much as twice what Lincoln offered. Three times, perhaps."

"And all for us," Marcus said.

"So, what are you saying?" Sun asked, moving up to stand over the opened satchel. "Do we work for Carpathian now?"

Marcus nodded. "We're mercenaries, Sun. That's what we do. The highest bidder wins out."

"But all of this," Sierra said, pointing to the bodies all around. "What was all this for?"

"For the bag that lies at your feet, Sierra," Marcus said. "For the fact that Carpathian's army was ordered to stop. For the fact that I will see you all leave here alive."

"Not all of us," Zarelda said, looking as if she would burst into tears again.

Marcus ignored her and instead said, "So we are done here. We have gotten what we came for. It's time to leave and start our next mission."

"What about this?" K-Free held up the vocal reiterator. Marcus took it from her hands. He put it up to his ear. He heard voices. He dropped it. "Sorry, Mr. Lincoln, but you will have to fight your own battles."

Marcus raised his boot and smashed the wooden box into several pieces. "Now let's go."

"Where are we going, boss?" Jake asked.

"I cannot tell you that right now. But once we're out of here, then I can—"

"I ain't going."

They turned to Zarelda, who stood there with her rifle in her hand as if she were going to shoot if anyone drew near. She was shaking, and there was pure fury on her face. She breathed deeply. "Hicks is dead. One of dat bastard's creatures killed him. And I don't care to speak about why he was killed or what he was doing when he was killed. He was a good man, Marcus, no matter what you might say or think of him. He was my husband, you see, and family is more important to me den all of this."

"But we're your family," K-Free said, looking as if she too would shed tears.

Zarelda shook her head. "Not anymore. I will never work for dat foreign devil, as long as I live, you hear? And I will not work for you ever again." She stared at Marcus.

"Then go," Marcus said, pointing toward Payson. "Find your Iron Horse and leave us. No one will stop you."

Everyone was in shock at his words. Their faces showed their dismay and confusion over the abruptness of his acceptance of Zarelda's defiance. K-Free started to speak again. Marcus put up his hand and gave her a stern look.

Zarelda stood for a moment, stared deeply into Marcus's eyes, perhaps surprised herself at the lack of argument. Then she nodded, wiped a final tear from her face, turned and walked away.

They watched her climb on her 'Horse, gun it to life, then slip through the remains of the barrier. Marcus waited until he could no longer hear her engine.

"Load up!" he said, grabbing a discarded Webley Bull Dog from the ground. He nodded in pleasant surprise. He hadn't seen one of these in a long time. He shoved it in his pocket. "Pick up weapons and ammo. All you can carry."

They ran inventory over the area, grabbing blasters and ammunition, RJ weapons, grenades, and knives. They packed everything on their Iron Horses, then mounted. Sun doubled with River; Careless Fox with Sierra.

As they were moving through the barrier and into the streets of Payson, Jake pulled up to Marcus. "Where we riding, boss?"

Marcus turned to Jake and smiled, remembering the mission that he and Carpathian had agreed to. "We're riding to glory, Jake Mattia. We're riding to glory."

THE END

About the Author

For the past 20 years, Robert E Waters has served in the gaming industry, first as a Managing Editor at The Avalon Hill Game Company, and then as a producer, designer, and writer for several computer game studios. He is currently a designer at Breakaway LTD. His first book for Zmok Publishing is, "*The Wayward Eight*".

Robert has been publishing fiction professionally since 2003, with his first sale to *Weird Tales*, "The Assassin's Retirement Party." Since then, he has sold over 25 stories to various online and print magazines and anthologies, including stories to Padwolf Publishing, The Black Library (Games Workshop), Dragon Moon Press, Marietta Publishing, Dark Quest Books, Mundania Press, Nth Degree/Nth Zine, Cloud Imperium Games, and the online magazine *The Grantville Gazette*, which publishes stories set in Baen Book's best-selling alternate history series, *1632/Ring of Fire*. Most recently, Robert has put his editorial skills to task by co-editing the anthology Fantastic Futures 13 (Padwolf Publishing) which features science fiction and fantasy stories about Earth's potential future. From time to time, he also writes short fiction reviews for Tangent Online. He also served for seven years as an assistant editor for Weird Tales.

Robert is currently living in Baltimore, Maryland with his wife Beth, their son Jason, their cat Buzz, and a menagerie of tropical fish who like to play among the ruins of a sunken Spanish Galleon. His website can be found at:

www.roberternestwaters.com.

Zmok Books – Action, Adventure and Imagination

Zmok Books offers science fiction and fantasy books in the classic tradition as well as the new and different takes on the genre.

Winged Hussar Publishing, LLC is the parent company of Zmok Publishing, focused on military history from ancient times to the modern day.

Follow all the latest news on Winged Hussar and Zmok Books at

www.wingedhussarpublishing.com

Look for the other books in this series

For all your fantasy, science fiction or history needs look at the
latest from Winged Hussar Publishing